Paper Wings

by
William Vickers

Bloomington, IN Milton Keynes, UK
authorHOUSE

AuthorHouse™
1663 Liberty Drive, Suite 200
Bloomington, IN 47403
www.authorhouse.com
Phone: 1-800-839-8640

AuthorHouse™ UK Ltd.
500 Avebury Boulevard
Central Milton Keynes, MK9 2BE
www.authorhouse.co.uk
Phone: 08001974150

This book is a work of fiction. People, places, events, and situations
are the product of the author's imagination. Any resemblance to actual
persons, living or dead, or historical events, is purely coincidental.

First published by AuthorHouse 5/23/2006

ISBN: 1-4259-2079-9 (e)
ISBN: 1-4259-2081-0 (sc)
ISBN: 1-4259-2080-2 (dj)

Library of Congress Control Number: 2006902214

Printed in the United States of America
Bloomington, Indiana

This book is printed on acid-free paper.

This book is dedicated to Dan Maycunich for inspiring me to take this journey.

Thanks Dan, for relieving me of my mind pain.

Chapter One

Sympathy for the Devil

Through a blackened hole in the darkness of night two beams of light appeared from a sable supercharged cruiser barely distinguishable from the rain-slick blacktop highway. The vehicle was headed south out of Indianapolis towards a destination that loomed larger than the plume of vapor that followed, down a lonely stretch of highway known as U.S. 31.

Staring through the rain-pelted windshield were the steely eyes of Detective Sonny Rafferty of the Indianapolis Metro Vice Squad. Sonny's adrenaline was rushing through his veins like a puma chasing its prey. All-the-while, his favorite CD was fueling the frenzy by blaring out an old Stone's hit:

Please allow me to introduce myself
I'm a man of wealth and taste
I've been around for a long, long year
Stole many a man's soul and faith
And I was 'round when Jesus Christ
Had his moment of doubt and pain
Made damn sure that Pilot
Washed his hands and sealed his fate
But what's troubling you is the nature of my game

Sonny was sandy-haired, broad-shouldered, six foot tall and 200 pounds of blue twisted steel, honed to a razor's edge. His mind was tortured between good and bad, black and white and the so-called gray area that everyone seems so quick to claim. Sonny's soul was tormented between good and evil, and he had no idea evil was going to rear its ugly head in a way that would forever change his life.

Sitting across the seat from Sonny was his protégé, J. R. Robey, a young black rookie detective, handpicked by Sonny himself.

"Sonny, you better slow down, curve's up ahead!"

Sonny shook his head, snapping out of his trance. "Hey, Junior, give me a 'Sit Rep' on Cassian and an E.T. A. on our girl!" yelled Sonny while turning down the volume and easing off the gas pedal.

"Here's the situation," responded J.R. "Mindy Wright left in a Metro cab at 19:30 hours to meet Cassian at the Starlight Motel. With the way you're driving, we should arrive there well in advance."

"Yeah," said Sonny. "Just another dumb 15 year old pissed off at her parents. Trouble is, she has no idea what she's getting into. Junior, call base and see who our backup is tonight."

J.R. picked up the hand mike, "Metro 1 this is Victor Mike 2, over."

"Victor Mike 2 this is Metro 1," a static charged voice replied.

"Metro 1,The O.I.C. would like to know who our backup is tonight and what their E.T.A. is, over."

"Metro 7 is your backup, and their E.T.A. is 21:30 hours, over."

"Roger that, Victor Mike 2 out."

Sonny's mind stayed fixed on his prey.

"Junior, this guy's record with young girls is as long as my arm. We've got to do this thing right this time and put him away for good."

"I'm all for that," agreed J.R.

"You know," said Sonny reflectively, "my girls are 14 and 16 years old. I don't even dare to picture them in this situation. There's good and bad in all of us, but I believe that there's a darker entity out there. I feel the need to change that tonight."

Sensing Sonny's dark mood, J.R. decided to change the subject. "Hey, Sonny, I have a question that I've wanted to ask you for a while."

"What is it, Junior?"

"Well, why do you call me Junior?'

"Because I like you," said Sonny with a half smile. "Besides that, your Mama told me to call you Junior because it'll keep you humble. I've gotta do what Mama says or she'll start quoting bible verses to me again. You know what that's like."

"Yeah," laughed J.R. "Mama knows her bible."

Lightning flashed and thunder rolled as Sonny pumped up the volume and pressed down on the gas pedal. As the wipers strained to rid the windshield of its deluge of water, he gripped the wheel of the big Crown Vic and guided it into the lights of Centralia. In the background, Mick Jagger screamed;

"Who killed the Kennedy's?'
When after all, it was you and me
Let me please introduce myself
I'm a man of wealth and taste
And I laid traps for troubadours
Who get killed before they reached Bombay
Please to meet you
Hope you guessed my name, oh yeah
But what's confusing you
Is the nature of my game, oh yeah

Sonny noted how hauntingly desolate it looked. Only a few dim streetlights led the way through this Moorish looking hamlet. The streets were empty. The stores had closed early in this rural farm town. The only thing that remotely looked alive in the cold, bleak mist was an oblong neon sign with the words blaring: STARLIGHT MOTEL; a smaller vacancy sign blinked at the bottom. Sonny drove past the sign into "Ray's Garage's" parking lot, adjacent to the motel. He pulled the black sedan between two parked cars and turned off his lights.

"We won't be noticed here," said Sonny, cautiously observing the motel and surrounding area. The run-down motel consisted of a long line of 24 rooms with the office on the left. A vehicle was parked in front of room four and room six. All the other rooms were dark and seemed unoccupied. "We'll stake out here until the girl arrives."

"This place looks like a dump," said Junior.

"Before the Interstate was built, U.S. 31 was the main north/south passage through the state. Back then these roadside inns were pretty nice," said Sonny. "Now they're used as sex stops. I'm gonna walk over and take down the license plate numbers. Gotta call 'em in and see what's up."

"Has the motel office been informed of our raid?" asked J.R.

"No," said Sonny. "Go see if they have another key to that room and tell the manager to stay put."

3

As Sonny meandered down the rain-puddled street in his dust-colored slicker and brown fedora, trying to look inconspicuous, J.R. knocked on the office door. A hefty man of about 65 years came to the door. As he opened the door and spotted the young, black detective, his look of surprise quickly changed to a hard scowl.

"No vacancy!" exclaimed the old man.

"I'm Detective Robey of Metro Vice Squad from the city of Indianapolis," said J.R. sternly. "I have a warrant here to search one of your rooms." J.R. pulled out the warrant along with his detective badge.

"I'm not in any trouble am I?" he said with nervous eyes.

"No, I'm looking for a Harold Cassian. Why don't you check your books and tell me if he is staying in any of your rooms."

"Okay," said the old man grudgingly, "but I run an honest establishment here. I don't get involved in my customers' affairs. Most people come here for a one-night stand or less, and then they leave. I don't ask who they bring or who they leave with."

The portly manager walked behind a counter and thumbed through the pages of the registry and declared, "No Cassian here. There is a man by the name of Bob Strange in room four. He's been there for two days now and is paid up for the week. A small businessman, I believe."

"That's fine," J.R. said. "We are going to have to search the room anyway to verify that he is whom he claims to be."

"I don't want any trouble here. Bad for business you know," said the manager sarcastically.

"We'll do our best," assured J.R. "Do you have another key for that room?"

"The cleaning lady has it, and she won't be back till morning."

"Okay, you stay put until we check things out. There'll be a couple of uniformed police officers arriving here soon and they will fill you in on all the details."

"Stay right here?"

"Yeah, stay right here. Stay off the phone and relax," said J.R.

Sonny had just hung up the microphone when J. R. slipped back into the cruiser.

"Any problems?" quizzed Sonny.

"I think I ran into the owner of the motel, and I don't think he cared for my color. When he first saw me he vehemently declared, "No vacancy!" and tried to slam the door in my face."

"Oh yeah!" laughed Sonny, "typical Midwestern corn-belt bigot. There's a few around this area you know. Did he tell you where to go and how to get there?"

"No;" smiled Junior. "I just whipped out my badge and search warrant, and he fell right into place like a good ol' white boy."

Suddenly, a car pulled into the Starlight parking lot and headed towards the lighted room with the number four above the door. Sonny recognized the white Chevrolet sedan as an Indianapolis Metro cab when it pulled up to the parking curb.

"That must be the Wright girl," said J. R.

"Yeah, Junior, the package has arrived," said Sonny.

A young, rather slim girl with long blonde hair stepped out from the left rear door of the taxi and walked toward the lighted doorway. Sonny carefully observed the nervousness of the young teenage girl with the overly made-up face of an older woman. She was struggling with an over-filled backpack hanging on her left shoulder while her red swollen lips were sucking in smoke from a lit cigarette. The youngster wore an opened denim jacket with a cropped shirt exposing her white middle, and denim pants which was stacked on top of a pair of four-inch pumps.

As the door opened, she walked in. A stocky, thin-haired man sporting a white tank top rushed out to pay the cabbie and just as quickly rushed back in.

Sonny anxiously grabbed the transmitter from the dash. "Metro 7 this is Victor Mike 2, over."

No answer.

"Metro 7 this is Victor Mike 2, come in please!"

"This is Metro 7, over."

"Is that you, Lujak?"

"Lujak here, over."

"Be advised that the girl has arrived and has entered the motel room. What's your E.T.A.? over."

"We are approximately 15 minutes from destination, over."

"Metro 7, come in with lights out and no sirens, over."

"No lights, no horns, roger that, anything further? over."

"This is Victor Mike 2, negative, out."

A jagged arc of electric streaked across the sky followed by a deafening crash of thunder as the heavens opened up with another barrage of water forcing its way to the earth. Sonny started the engine. "We're going to move in for a closer look. I can't see a damn thing through this rain!" He pulled up next to the car in front of the lighted room knowing that he would not be noticed, thanks to Mother Nature.

The two detectives could see Mindy's silhouette from the light against the window shade of the modest out-dated motel room. It looked like she was arguing with someone not in view. Then all of a sudden, a male silhouette appeared and backhanded her in the face; once, twice, three, no—four times! She then disappeared from view.

"What the hell! That's not supposed to happen!" exclaimed J.R.

"Check your weapon, Junior, we're going in!"

"Our backup's not here yet!"

"Can't wait for them, that girl's in trouble!" said Sonny, grabbing the mike. "Metro 7, this is Victor Mike 2."

"Metro here."

"The situation has deteriorated. Must go in now, can't wait! Come in with lights and whistles ASAP, over."

"We're doing our best. It's raining like hell here! Be careful, Sonny!"

"Roger that. Victor Mike 2 out."

Sonny threw the transmitter down while checking the cylinder and chamber on his Smith & Wesson 38 Special. "You ready, Junior?"

"Ready!"

"Let's do it!"

With their weapons drawn, Sonny stood on the left of the door with J.R. on the right, Sonny yelled, "Open up, Police Officers!" One thousand one, one thousand two, no answer; just rustling around heard from inside the room. Sonny gave Junior a nod, and with a swift kick burst through the door.

"Hands up, hands up, I said hands up over your head!" yelled Sonny.

Startled and confused, Harold Cassian threw up his hands while muttering incoherently.

"Up against the wall, frisk him, Junior!"

With J.R. in charge of Cassian, Sonny turned to his left and noticed two girls sitting on a king-sized bed. The girl on the right side of the disheveled bed was Mindy, chattering her innocence while big tears were sliding down her red swollen face. While trying to quiet her down, Sonny noticed a little nymph-like creature sitting naked on the left side of the bed near the corner of the room. She had a pixie face to match her blondish Tinker-bell hair, and had pale boyish breasts .Her eyes were glazed as if in a drug induced stupor. Sonny then made a quick search through the bathroom; nothing in there. As he came out of the bathroom he noticed a door to his right, which led to the room next door. While walking over to check the door, he tripped on a tri-pod leg of a video camera and knocked the whole thing over. Through the confusion from Mindy's babbling, Cassian giving J.R. a hard time with the cuffs, and the discovery of the video camera, it dawned on Sonny that this asshole was making child porn.

"These cuffs are hurting me, they're too tight! Loosen these up you fucking nigger!"

With thunder crashing outside and rage boiling up inside, Sonny's eyes just glared at the pornographer. Then suddenly he snapped!

"Shut the hell up you piece of scum!" He grabbed the man, turned him around, gave him his best right to the jaw and then a left to his eye, sending Cassian crashing through a table and chair. Sonny picked him up, cocked his right arm again, and—

"Sonny, Sonny!" yelled J.R. "Stop, you're gonna kill him! What's the matter with you? This isn't how you taught me to do our job!" Calm down, take it easy. This is Junior speaking to you now. Snap out of it, Sonny!"

Sonny shook his head and then slowly lowered his right hand while staring straight into the pedophile's eyes. He set the table back up, turned Cassian around and slammed his head on the table to get at the handcuffs.

"You're right, Junior, I'm sorry. I don't know what came over me."

Sonny was always noted for living on the edge, even when he was a uniformed cop he would sometimes let his feelings overpower his professional common sense.

"Hand me the keys and I'll loosen the cuffs."

J.R. gave the keys to Sonny.

"Go ahead and read him his rights."

While J.R. was reading Cassian his Miranda rights, Sonny started loosening the cuffs on his wrists. Except for a little whimper, Mindy was quiet now. The pixi in the corner just sat and stared at Sonny.

As the last remnants of a thunderbolt faded away, Sonny looked down at Cassian and asked, "How do those cuffs feel now?" The ruffed up deviate rolled his head over till his eyes met Sonny's. With blood pouring from his lips, he glared at Sonny. Sonny could feel those demon eyes staring right through him, or was he staring past him. Then the evil one smiled that *Lucifer* smile. With a sudden chill down his spine, Sonny jerked his eyes to the left and saw the ever-so-slightly turning of the doorknob on the side door that *he didn't check!*

With utter fear shrouding his soul Sonny screamed, "N-o-o-o-o-o-o-o!" and rolled off the back of Cassian while going for his handgun. At the same time, that door flew open followed by a barrage of lead from a Mac 10, spraying total chaos everywhere. Pandemonium set in! The noise was horrific, drowning out the screams of terror as bullets ripped through flesh, tables, lamps, glass, and tearing window dressings away from the wall, while metallic shell casings scampered across the floor. It was utter *helter skelter!* With his back to the floor next to the bed where Mindy sat, Sonny raised his gun at the darkest shadow in the night filled room, and fired his weapon repeatedly, until the chamber was emptied.

Surely he would meet his death any second now. Only the burning feeling in his shoulder let him know that he was still alive. The gunfire stopped and that dark shadow against the far wall stumbled forward and fell at Sonny's feet. Sonny yanked his feet up and cringed for a few seconds until he noticed no further movement. He then turned over and got to his knees, and using his good arm, struggled to get up.

With the stench of adulterated black powder in his nostrils and a stinging in his shoulder, Sonny stumbled to where his sidekick lay dying. As his ears started retrieving sound again all he could hear was a constant annoying scream from the far corner of the room. Sonny lowered his head to Junior's chest. He could hear the gurgling of his lungs as they searched for air.

"Hang on, Junior," cried Sonny, "I'll call an ambulance!"

He staggered out to the car and fumbled for the mike.

"Officer down! Officer down! Need an ambulance at the Starlight Motel, Centralia! Lujak, where the fuck are you? Where's my fucking backup— Metro 1, get me some goddamn help!" cried Sonny desperately.

As voices scrambled across the net, Sonny dropped the transmitter, and with lost hope, headed back into the infamous room number four.

Sonny pulled a flashlight from the right side of his trench coat and shakily shined it in the direction where Junior lay. With pain searing through his right shoulder, he cradled Junior's head in his good arm, and quietly sobbed, "Junior, I'm sorry. I'm so sorry. How could I have let this happen to you? How could I let you and Mama down like this?"

The self-condemned soldier of society gently lay Junior's head down with the reverence of a well-trained priest, and focused his light on the death face of Harold Cassian, who lay next to Junior. He shoved Cassian's body away from his dead partner. Then, he shined the light toward the bed where Mindy had sat chattering away just a few minutes before. There she was, sitting up against the wall, staring straight at him, expressionless, arms at her side, mouth half open as if ready to speak. She reminded Sonny of a little rag doll that his younger daughter, Sonja, slept with when she was a toddler. Only, Sonja's doll didn't have a . . . small red hole above the right eye! In his disbelief Sonny grabbed Mindy's arm to get her to speak, but like the rag doll she just fell lifeless to the floor.

Stunned, and with the stench of death hanging heavily all around, Sonny felt his sanity slipping away. That was until he heard the stuttering whimper of the little waif cowering in the corner of the room across the far side of the bed. Sonny quickly climbed over the bed and reached out for her. The terrified little girl grabbed his hand. He pulled her to him and held her tightly.

"It's all over. You're going to be all right, darling," assured Sonny. He awkwardly pulled his coat off his wounded body. As the girl clung to him he draped it over her bare shoulders. "You'll be just fine," he whispered.

While softly stroking her head, Sonny could hear the wailing of the sirens resonating outside the room.

Sonny cried shamefully for he knew that he alone must bear the sins of this room. He had fallen into the Abyss.

He knew. He knew that his greatest sin that night was having… sympathy for the devil!

Just as every cop is a criminal
And all the sinners saints
As heads is tails

Just call me Lucifer
Cause I'm in need of some restraint
So if you meet me
Have some courtesy
Have some sympathy and some taste
Use all your well-learned politesse
Please to meet you
Hope you guess my name, um yeah
But what's puzzling you
Is the nature of my game

Chapter Two

Lost Souls

When dusk engulfed the evening, Sonny Rafferty once again, like a child of the "Pied Piper," gravitated down that secluded maze of highway known as U.S. 31. It had become Sonny's own personal "Lost Highway;" the highway to hell. The road led to many little sleepy towns throughout the flat Midwestern corn-belt, but on that stormy night six years ago, led Sonny into the Abyss, the place of the dead, the place of departed spirits. It wasn't supposed to happen that way, but it did.

On the day after the raid at the Starlight Motel, the headline on the front page of the Times read: TRI-STATE CHILD PORNO RING BUSTED; followed by, four dead including Metro Police Officer. The article totally consumed the front page of the morning edition. Sonny was recognized as a hero, as was J.R., while Mindy was seen as a victim of circumstance. Frank Cassian was the gunman that killed J.R., Mindy, and his own brother, Harold.

Frank was the dark shadow that Sonny gunned down while desperately trying to save his own life as well as the others. The Cassian brothers had been operating a child porno ring for over a year covering a three state region of Michigan, Ohio, and Indiana. They were also linked to at least three other missing girls in the tri-state area. The little girl who survived was Cindy Atwood, a runaway urchin from Portland, Oregon, brought to Centralia by Frank Cassian. Cindy was eventually sent back to her parents in Boulder, Colorado, and received several months of psychiatric care.

Mindy Wright's unsavory parents sued the police department and Sonny for negligence, thus leading to the dismissal of Sonny from the department and an undisclosed amount of money paid to the Wrights in a plea agreement with the state.

J.R. was buried at a local cemetery as an honored hero.

Sonny was eulogized in the public eye while being chastised and then fired by the department. That suited him just fine, for he figured that he owed a debt to J. R. and Mindy for his actions leading to their demise. However, this did not relieve him of his guilt, nor did psychotherapy or pleas from Samantha, his wife. Myra, J.R.'s mother, forgave Sonny though she never really blamed him for J.R.'s death. Sonny, to her, was the closest thing to a son that she had left. Not until Sonny slipped back into his introversion from his childhood did he forgive himself.

He then garnered a license to be a private investigator. Nothing too serious, nothing over the edge, just doing something that he was good at.

From within the private confines of his automobile, Sonny's ears swallowed up the soft, rich tones from the mellow-voiced crooner, Gillian Welch. She was a sylph-like creature with a sad sound of Appalachia that filled the air with her sereneness. Sonny was smitten by her honest, unassuming voice, and her beauteous common look. Gillian sang songs from a generation past, songs from Sonny's legacy.

Sonny's favorite song by Gillian was a heartbreak love tune called "Paper Wings". To Sonny, Paper Wings' imagery was an allegory of his disillusionment of God and of his spiritual beliefs that he had adhered to all of his life. Gillian sang to his soul.

Paper Wings all torn and bent, you made me feel that they were heaven sent

Paper Wings not real at all

They took me high enough to really fall

Your paper kisses faded too soon, just like a paper rose even a paper moon

Paper Wings

Paper Wings

Paper Wings

Oh how could I expect to fly with only paper wings

While tailing the unsuspecting sweethearts that motored ahead,

Sonny eased his mind off his beloved Gillian and reverted back to two days ago in his quaint little office that sat atop the flower shop in South Broad Ripple. The voice that first entered his head was that of Myra Robey, J.R.'s mother, whom Sonny hired as his personal secretary.

"Sonny, Mrs. Weiler is here to see you," announced Myra.

"Show her in," said Sonny as he closed the cover to the Hemingway novel and slid it into the desk drawer.

She was a tall, rather nervous woman, Sonny recalled. He saw worry in her eyes and more lines in her face than a 38-year old lady should have. She looked to be a proud woman.

"What can I do for you?" asked Sonny.

"My name is Sarah Weiler and I think my husband is having an affair with another woman."

"I know," Sonny said calmly. "Please have a seat. In your file here you told my secretary that you suspected someone. Who might that be?"

"His secretary," she said coldly.

"His secretary?" said Sonny.

"Yes. Jim, my husband, is the owner and foreman of Weiler Construction on 31st and Vine, in Speedway. His secretary's name is Jeri Rucker."

"How long have you suspected their affair to be going on?"

"For several months he's been coming home late. Sometimes he doesn't get home until early morning," she said, wiping tears away.

"Here, this may help," said Sonny, offering her a tissue from the box atop his desk. "Have you confronted your husband about this, Mrs. Weiler?"

"Yes, several times, and he denied that anything is going on, and then gets angry with me saying that I don't trust him. Sometimes we get into fights over this."

"Does he get physical with you in these fights, Mrs. Weiler?"

"No, but he tears things up and yells at the children. The whole family is upset, you know."

"So you want me to get confirmation of your husband's infidelity, right?"

"What I really want is for my husband to stay home, and for my kids not to be upset, and for things to go back to the way they were before my husband hired that bitch of a secretary!" exclaimed the jilted housewife.

"I can't help you much there,' said Sonny, "but what I will do for you is to tail your husband after he leaves work each night and record any wrongdoing on his part. Would that satisfy you, Mrs. Weiler?"

"Well, I guess so, but I'm not really sure that he's cheating."

"Oh, he's cheating on you all right, and I'll get you the proof," assured Sonny.

"All right then," said Mrs. Weiler, getting up to leave.

"I'm sorry about your situation, and I know this is painful for you, but you are absolutely right. You should know the truth about your husband," said Sonny.

"Who do I pay?"

"Just see Myra on the way out and she'll take care of all of that. Oh, by the way, I'll need a photo of your husband, type of vehicle that he drives, license plate number, and his work schedule."

"I can tell you that he drives a yellow quad-cab 4x4, pickup truck. Weiler Construction Company is stenciled on the sides. I don't remember for sure, but I think the street address is stenciled on too. You can't miss it. It looks like a big yellow school bus. Is there anything else that you need?"

"No, Mrs. Weiler, I think that should cover it. I'll get right on the case tonight."

"Thank you very much, Mr. Rafferty."

"You're most welcome," answered Sonny.

Cases of marital infidelity were easy for Sonny. There was no real criminal, no real crime. Just somebody that slipped across that thin gray line, just a misdemeanor of sorts, good and bad intertwined, and he didn't have to unravel it, just record it.

Sonny awakened from his thoughts to the intrusive chattering of his cell-phone.

"Hello, Sonny?"

"Yeah, it's me; hi Sam, getting off work?"

"Yeah, baby, I'm on my way home right now. Guess what I have sitting between my legs?"

"Uh, the burning bush?" quipped Sonny.

"Besides that," she replied.

"Uh, hell, I don't know, the neighbor boy?"

"Get serious, you big ape," she said playfully.

"You've got me stumped, Sam. If it's not the neighbor boy then I give up. Whatcha got sittin' between those two luscious thighs of yours?"

"A bottle of champagne," she said finally.

"Champagne?"

"Yeah, I finished the last Waverly editorial today, so I thought we could celebrate like we used to in the old days when one of us would close a case."

"Waverly . . . Waverly, oh yes, that's the nursing home debacle that you were covering?"

"Yes, that's right. So what time are you coming home?"

"I don't know yet, Sam. I followed my suspects from Speedway south to Franklin where they stopped at a cozy Italian eatery called Mario's. They are now returning to their vehicle from the restaurant, so we'll probably be returning to Indy soon. As soon as these two lovers part, I'll be coming home."

"Okay, baby, but I don't like celebrating alone, and you know I'm getting kinda horny," said the amorous redhead.

"Well, that sounds mighty invitin', so why don't you start on the champagne when you get home, and see if Mr. Rogers will satisfy you until I get there."

"I don't like Mr. Rogers," pouted Samantha. "He's slow and boring, just like his namesake. Besides, the batteries are dead. I can wait for you."

"Okay," laughed Sonny, "but it might be awhile. It looks like my suspects are heading south on U.S. 31 instead of going back to Speedway."

"31 South!" exclaimed Samantha. "I thought you said they would head back north."

Sonny sensed the anxiety in Samantha's voice. He knew she was thinking about that Centralia debacle from the past. "I did, but I was wrong, I guess. Look, I've got to close this case tonight for my client, Mrs. Weiler. Then I'll come home," he assured her. "Enjoy the champagne, baby."

"Be careful. I love you," said Samantha faintly.

With Samantha on his mind, Sonny reverted to the melancholic sound that was flowing from the voice of his lovely country songbird.

Angels were singing, didn't you hear?

If only I listened close, when they whispered in my ear
Paper Wings
Paper Wings
Paper Wings
Oh, how could I expect to fly with only paper wings,
I tried to fly but found that I had only paper wings

Sonny followed the taillights of the yellow truck into the town of Centralia.

"Just as I thought, they're headed to the Starlight Motel," Sonny said aloud.It seemed quite eerie coming back to where he discovered the harshness of the real world. To the place where just six years ago he came face to face with his own mortality, but time heals the wounds so they say.

The truck exited the highway just past the Starlight Motel sign and pulled up to the front office. As Sonny passed the motor inn he could see the clandestine lovers embracing. He pulled up to the parking lot next door which used to belong to Ray's Garage but was now Peggy Sue's Barbeque. He noticed the small diner was still open, and had a couple of vehicles parked in front of it.

Sonny pulled his car into the parking space closest to the motel. He quickly opened his door and stepped out with his camcorder and slid alongside the shadow of the building. He then slipped behind a dumpster just a few yards away from the motel property. Sonny had a perfect view of the couple so he placed the camera to his eye and started recording the hot lovers. Soon they broke away from each other, and Weiler got out of the truck and entered the office to pay for a room. He soon exited the office and moved his truck next to room number two. Only after Weiler and his girlfriend entered their room did Sonny stop recording.

"That's right," he said to himself, "go on in and have a good time. I'll be here when you get through. Then we'll wrap this thing up. I think I'll go have myself a cup of coffee, so you both take your time," he said, barely audible.

"Can I help you, doll?" asked the eager voice that cut through the air so sharp that it snapped Sonny's eyes from the menu up towards the mascara laden eyes smiling down at him. "My name is Peggy Sue. I'm your waitress for tonight."

"Oh, uh . . . well, I'd like a—"

"Our special is a pork barbeque sandwich plate for three ninety-five. Best in the county, which doesn't say much for this county," joked the loquacious hash slinger.

"No thanks, I'll just have a cup of coffee." Sonny noticed the corner of those smiling eyes starting to turn down so he quickly added, "What kind of pie do you have in that glass showcase over there?"

"We have apple and lemon left, and they're really good!" exclaimed Peggy. "I made them myself."

"Well, I guess I'll have to try a piece then. I'll try the apple."

"One apple pie and one hot black coffee coming right up," she said with a loud smile before dashing away.

Sonny watched Peggy Sue intently as she scurried about the diner preparing his order and cashing out the last customer left, besides him. She's not bad looking, he thought, full figured, about 35 years old, over-died hair but styled quite nicely. She's quite a chatterbox, and smiles with her eyes like Sam does. She seems a little shop-worn though no ring on her finger; must be divorced. One, maybe two kids; must have spent the divorce settlement on this diner. Yeah, that sounds about right, thought Sonny.

"Here you go, Cowboy, wish you would let me fix you a real meal."

"Nah," said Sonny, "this will do just fine. Why don't you sit down for a bit, Peg, you look like you could use a break. I'll buy you a cup of coffee."

"Let me close up first," she replied. Peg turned the sign around in the front door window, then went into the kitchen area and released the cook of her duties. As she emerged from the kitchen she stopped by the coffee machine and poured herself a cup of coffee. She then sat down at Sonny's table.

The cook emerged from the kitchen heading toward the front door.

"Make sure you tuck Karen in for me tonight, honey," said Peg to the cook. "Make sure you set the clock for tomorrow morning."

"Okay, Momma," said the slender teen as she closed the door.

"The cook's your daughter?" asked Sonny.

"Yeah, her name is Kristin. She's my evening cook, and she helps out on weekends. She's 17 and is a junior in high school. She's kinda shy, doesn't have a boyfriend yet. I don't know what I would do without her. Karen's my youngest daughter. She's 10 years old."

"So you just have the two girls?"

"Well, I had a son that would have been 12, but he died from crib-death when he was a baby."

"You mean SIDS?"

"Yeah, that's what the doctors called it."

"I'm sorry."

The now despondent looking waitress took a long sip of coffee, while her eyes seemed to be staring at her past. "I think about him often," she finally said. "I sometimes wonder how he would look and what he would be like today." She suddenly lifted her eyes to meet Sonny's. "Are you married, Cowboy?"

"Call me Sonny."

"Is Sonny your real name?"

"Yes it is. My grandmother gave me that name. You see, after I was born my mother would often lay me in a big oak rocking chair in my grandmother's bedroom while she did chores around the house. My grandmother was bedridden, dying from cancer, and friends would often visit her. The first thing she would tell them when they entered the room was 'Don't sit on Sonny, don't sit on the baby!' No matter how weak she became she would always worry about her grandson. I guess she called me Sonny because I was the first boy born into the family, following four sisters. My grandma died seven weeks after my birth. My mother loved her so very much that out of respect for her she named her last born Sonny."

"That is such a sweet story," said Peg.

Sonny couldn't help but notice Peg staring at the ring on his left hand. She looked up at Sonny again. Her eyes melted into his, and with an unpretentious smile she reluctantly asked, "So, you *are* married, aren't you?"

"Yes," said Sonny, "I've been married for over 20 years now."

"That's my luck," declared the saucy blonde waitress. "You know, men are like parking spaces, the good ones are always taken and the others are handicaps."

Sonny laughed. "So what's your story, Peg? What brought you to a one-horse town like this? I can tell from your accent and demeanor that you aren't from around here."

"It's not a pretty story," said Peg. "My 'old man' left me when I was pregnant with Karen. He always blamed me for the death of our son. When I saw that he wasn't coming back, I divorced his ass."

"So, you used the divorce settlement to start your own business?"

"Hell, no, Cowboy! That no good bastard left the state and I haven't seen nor heard from him since. My parents left me a small inheritance when they were killed in a car accident by a drunk driver, several years ago. I bought a new car, left Arkansas, and then fate guided me here, I guess. They say that the Lord works in mysterious ways, but I say that God sure is a mystery to me."

Sonny grasped Peggy's hands in his and held them tight. "That's really a sad story . . . but you seem so upbeat and happy. How do you do it?"

"Happy, hell yes I'm happy!" exclaimed Peggy. "I got rid of the worse husband a woman could ever have. I have two lovely daughters, my own business, and have the prospects of finding a good man to share my good fortunes with," she said brazenly. "I need another cup of coffee, how about you, Cowboy? Want a refill?"

"Sure."

The spirited waitress bounced up and headed toward the kitchen counter.

Sonny was mesmerized by Peggy's voluptuous derriere, watching it sway back and forth inside the thin white fabric of her uniform as she sashayed through the room. She brought back with her two cups of coffee and a candle. As she bent over to serve the coffee, the buxom blonde's milky breasts caught Sonny's attention. He had known many women in his life, but none swelled him up with overwhelming desire like this woman, except maybe Samantha, his wife, who seemed a million miles away right now.

He knew that it had to be more than lust to make him feel like this. After all, he wasn't just a kid gawking at a "Playboy" centerfold. No, there had to be more, something real. Maybe it was her candor, or maybe it was in her mannerisms. What was this spell that she cast over him? Sonny didn't know, but he felt wanton.

Peg then walked over to the wall next to the door and turned off the lights of the diner. Only a small nightlight appeared from within the kitchen. Looking through the window next to the table where he sat, Sonny could see the pale yellow of a lonely street-light. Peg then eased herself back to their table and pulled out a book of matches from her pocket. She struck a match against the book cover and lit the candle. Sonny gazed at the flame. Through the sulfurous smoke he could see those eyes with their corners turned up while her red lips were pursed to blow out the match. Peggy then sat next to Sonny in quiet solitude. Love and lust had spread their web across their kindred souls.

Sonny turned his face toward Peggy's and gazed intently into the shadow of her eyes. "Your eyes always seem to be smiling. Why is that?"

"Because they like what they see," she said.

"You should not hide them with eye make-up because they represent your natural beauty."

"Why, thank you, you are the perfect gentleman."

"Did you know that your eyes are the window to your soul?"

"I never thought about them that way. Tell me, Sonny; what do you see through that window?" she whispered.

"The question is, Peggy; what does your soul see through that window?" said Sonny.

"I see a handsome face. I like your face, Sonny. I like your nose." She reached up and stroked softly across the bridge with her finger. "It gives you a strong face. Makes you look like a Spartan warrior. A fighter," said Peggy. "It makes me feel safe. I see a man that makes me feel warm inside," she confessed. "I see shelter from a storm. Tell me, Sonny, what do *you* see when you look into my eyes?"

"Well, when I look into your eyes I see a babbling brook flowing over stones, turning into a stream that cascades down a mountainside as a waterfall, and then pouring into a raging river that runs into an ocean, wanting to mix with the rest of the water. That's what I see, Peg. I also see those same waters as a lost sea of despair, wishing desperately that a glimmer of sun would peak through the clouds and dance across its surface."

"What do you think about us, Sonny, you and me?" asked Peg in quiet desperation.

"I don't know what I think, Peg."

"Do you love your wife?"

"Yes, very much so," he said.

"Then, how do you feel?"

"I feel like I'm waist deep in quicksand, but I don't want to climb out. I feel like a boy lost in the dark, but I welcome the loneliness of it."

While searching his eyes with tender passion, and her own lonely heart pounding in rhythms of love, Peggy brushed his face with hers and with a coo in her breathy voice whispered, "What's *your* story, Sonny?"

"To be honest with you, Peg, I'm a private detective from Indianapolis. I've been hired by a woman to spy on her husband and his mistress. I followed the two suspects to that motel next door. She had a suspicion that her husband was cheating on her but she needed proof, and tonight I'm getting her that proof on video."

"That motel next door is no good, Sonny. I tell you it's no good," she said soberly.

"I know. I'm just going to videotape them as they leave, and that'll be all that I need for the case."

"No, you don't understand, Sonny. People around here claim that place is cursed. Let me explain," said Peggy. "When the girls and I left Arkansas we had no destination in mind. I just drove and drove 'till we wandered into this little town. When we arrived here I knew right away that this was where we were going to live. We stayed at the Starlight motel for weeks in room number four. The old man that ran the motel also owned Ray's Garage next door. His name was Ray Jenkins. Behind the garage was a bungalow that went with it. The old man seemed to be a cantankerous sort but he cared for me and my girls; kinda took us in as his own. Ray offered to sell the bungalow and the garage to me for an unbelievable low price. I told him that I didn't need the garage. He told me that I must take the garage too, that he had no use for it anymore. Ray told me that he had two sons that used to run the garage, but they both died so he didn't want anything to do with it anymore. I paid Mr. Jenkins $60,000 dollars for the property and buildings." Peggy stopped for a moment to gather her thoughts.

"Go on," urged Sonny.

"Well, the old man seemed very depressed, you know, real gloomy most of the time that I knew him. I knew that he didn't have any friends. When I opened the diner up and started meeting the townspeople, I found out why."

Beads of sweat started to form on Sonny's forehead, as he knew that he was about to re-live that horrible night all over again.

"Are you all right?" asked Peg.

"Yeah, I'll be okay. Go on with your story."

"I was told that men were taking young girls into room number four to be used in making child pornography. It gives me chills to think that my girls and I lived in that room for over two months. Anyway, one night the police raided that motel and a little girl and a cop were killed during a gun battle in that very room. They said that there was another little girl present, but she was saved by a second cop's heroics."

Sonny couldn't take it anymore. "That's enough!" he strained.

Startled, Peggy jerked away with a confused look on her face.

"I was that other cop," said Sonny.

Peg's confused look quickly turned into a look of horror. In a low quivering voice, she said, "Listen to me, Sonny. Is your last name Rafferty?"

The tortured detective nodded his head, yes.

"Then you must hear the rest of the story," she begged.

"All right then."

"Jenkins became terminally ill last year. I went to see him on his deathbed because, like I said before, he had no other friends. Sometimes he would hallucinate. He pretty much confessed to the same story that I was told except . . . ."

"Except what?" quizzed Sonny.

"Sonny, Ray Jenkins was a third party in that porno ring. He was there that night."

"I don't get it. I was the only one left in that room, me and the little girl. If there was anyone else there, I would've killed the bastard!"

"He was the man at the front desk, Sonny. Frank was in the back room of the office. After the black police officer informed Ray of their raid, Ray and Frank went to room three which had a connecting door to the room with Harold and the girls in it. Only, Ray didn't have a gun so he stayed hidden, but saw everything through the door opening. The most terrifying thing that Jenkins said before he died was, "Rafferty, I will drag you down to hell with me for killing my sons!"

"What do you mean, his sons?" asked Sonny, bewildered by Peg's divulgence.

"Ray Jenkins was the father of the Cassian brothers. Apparently he had hidden behind the alias of Ray Jenkins for years. That's why the police never caught on to him. He has vowed to pay you back, Sonny."

Sonny sat there at the table in disbelief. Finally, he got up and headed toward the door with Peggy right behind him.

"Sonny, please don't go," begged Peggy.

When Sonny reached the door he turned and gazed into her teary eyes, and she in his. Suddenly, he clutched her and she clutched him in a wild embrace. Their lips met with a deep violent passion. She could feel his inflamed desire and he, her sensual cravings. Just two lost souls searching for answers. Then, just as suddenly, fate pulled them away.

"Maybe in another place . . . another time, baby," he said desperately.

"I know," cried Peggy. "I know. Thanks for stopping by, Cowboy."

Sonny then turned and bolted out the door.

Heartbroken, Peggy slowly fell to her knees while clinging to the open door with tears of passion rolling down the glass pane like droplets of warm summer rain. Sonny sped away into the shadow of night leaving the lovers from the yellow truck for another day. For tonight, he again escaped the chasm of lost souls.

Chapter Three

Impala and the Hole in the Wall Gang

The cherry-red Chevy glided with ease through the winding wooded streets in the park-like neighborhood lined with large traditional homes of Colonial and Tudor designs. With the downtown just a few minutes away, Brendonwood provided a near perfect setting for a young couple to raise a family. The shiny red sedan seemed swallowed up by the surrounding shaded landscape as its driver, Samantha Rafferty, maneuvered through the sinuous streets of the upscale neighborhood.

On the front bumper of the car was a vanity plate with the word "Impala" inscribed on it. Impala was not only the model type of the vehicle, but was also the title that Sonny gave Samantha when they first met. He was so enamored by the tall redhead's flaming locks, the quickness of her wit, and her sleek exterior that he named her after that swift reddish antelope that roamed the plains of central Africa.

For Samantha's 35th birthday, Sonny gave her an Irish-Setter pup which had deep red fur, and named her Impala. Then for her 40th birthday he purchased the red Chevy for her.

Sonny loved women. He made no bones about it. He especially loved his wife and his daughters, Sonja and Danielle. Samantha was his queen and he treated her like one. He doted on his two girls even though they were total opposites. Sonja was a meek scholastic type like her mother was at that age. Danielle, on the other hand, was athletic, tomboyish, and took after Sonny with her looks and demeanor.

Samantha Rafferty, called "Sam" by her friends and family, was the daughter of Big John Taylor, the grandiose owner and Editor-n-

Chief of the Indianapolis Times newspaper. Samantha was in charge of investigative projects.

Big John had once envisioned his daughter taking over his throne someday when he retired, but Samantha turned down all his promotions because she felt that her niche was in the investigative arena. She was a reporter at heart, and she had no desire to do the hiring, firing, and over-seeing of the news machine as a whole. As far as Samantha was concerned, she was now at her pinnacle with the newsprint business. Her only other professional goal had been to be a news reporter for the electronic media. At one time, the thought of reporting the news live on television absolutely thrilled her.

Over the years, Samantha had been offered jobs by the local stations and once by a major affiliate, but out of piety for her father and family, she never left the Times. Besides, television reporting was a young woman's game now. Still considered attractive, but now in her 40's, time had passed her by.

Dusk had consumed the community by the time the red Chevy arrived in front of Sonny and Samantha's two-story colonial styled home.

As the leggy redhead exited the car she could see the image of Mary Parks, her housekeeper, standing in the front door. Mary, Myra Robey's sister, was a plump, African American woman of about 60 years. Mary was not as pretty as her younger sister for she had lost an eye somewhere in the deep bowels of East St. Louis, and now sported a shiny black patch where her left eye once resided. Nevertheless, she was more astute at meeting male friends and more outgoing than Myra. Mary was a woman of her own mind. Her philosophy was that no job was too demeaning, but not having one was.

Samantha tipsily approached the front door, while clutching a bottle of champagne in one hand and her purse in the other. Mary came out of the door to meet her.

"Where have you been, Ms Samantha?" she asked with a scowl. "I've been troubled sick that you might've been in a car wreck or somethin'."

"Oh, Mary, you worry too much," said Samantha..

"Worry too much! Worry too much! That's all I do is worry, what with both girls gone, and Mr. Sonny and you not home at this late hour! Why didn't you call?"

"I'm sorry," said Samantha. "I worked late, and afterwards stopped with some friends at Deiter's Nasch for some cocktails."

"I can see that," said Mary.

"I already talked to Sonny. He's going to be home late tonight. Besides, you don't answer the phone anyway," joked Samantha, trying to calm her mother-some housemaid.

That quieted Mary some. Samantha was right. She wasn't good at answering the telephone like Myra was at Sonny's office. She always feared that she might mess up, or forget an important message if she answered the phone, with her lack of education and all. Besides, they had an answering machine anyway, she reasoned. Samantha always checked it soon after she arrived home every evening.

"How's my other kids?" asked Samantha.

"Impala's been walked. She's been good, don't make no noise, don't make no fuss, but that Rufus and Napoleon been chasing that cat around the house all day. They're just like a couple of youngsters, them two boys always makin' a ruckus. If they was real kids I would've had a keen switch on their behinds today," complained Mary.

"Mary, would you be a dear and get a bag of groceries out of the car for me? I've got to piss real bad," begged Samantha.

"Okay, ma'am. You go on in and relax."

Samantha tried slipping through the front door quietly, but her frolicsome canine crew was waiting for her. Impala, with a nudge from her cold wet nose, Rufus, the little Chihuahua doing back-flips, and Napoleon, the long-eared, stubby legged Dachshund, were all barking in sheer delight at seeing their loving master. "Okay you guys, I love you too, but I'm in a hurry, so settle down," she commanded with little results.

Samantha pulled down her silk briefs just low enough to make a quick seat on the commode, and at her sudden gush of relief looked up. There they were, all in a row, just sitting there staring at their lady master. "No, no way guys," she said. "Rufus, Napoleon, outta here!" Napoleon dejectedly turned and walked out with Rufus playfully running past him in search of that arrogant silky-haired black feline, "Captain Midnight", for a round of mischievousness.

"Not you, girl," said Samantha to Impala, as the reddish brown Setter got up to leave. "You're one of us." Impala turned around and walked back to her master and lay her head on Samantha's knee, all-the-while staring into her eyes. "Oh, by the way, girl, do you happen to like Champagne?" Impala answered with a whine of devotion while her sad brown eyes stayed fixed on her masters, not knowing or caring that Samantha was joking with her.

Samantha leafed through the mail that was lying on the counter as Mary was putting the groceries away.

"Need a ride home, Mary?"

"No, ma'am, I have a friend picking me up tonight."

"Oh yeah, who's picking you up?"

"Earle Rose," said Mary quietly. Mary eyed Samantha to see her response.

"Earle Rose... a man? You've got a boyfriend?" teased Samantha.

"No, ma'am, No, he's just a nice man that lives in our apartment complex."

"He sounds interesting. You must tell me more about him."

"Well, he takes me to the grocery store so I won't have to ride the bus, and he's a church-goin' man—and he don't drink no more either."

"Well, I'm glad for you, Mary. I'm happy that you've found a boyfriend. Maybe you can find one for Myra."

"I didn't say nothin' about no boyfriend, Ms Samantha. I'm too old for that nonsense, and Myra can do for herself. She already has a man that takes her to church."

"That's good," smiled Samantha. "So what time is Earle picking you up?"

"He should be here anytime now."

"I'll have to meet him sometime," she said, hitting the replay on her answering machine.

"I think you would like him. He's pretty good to us, and he adores our little Shauna," said Mary.

Beep . . . "Samantha, this is your Mother. Call me sometimes. I haven't heard from you this week."

Beep . . . "Sonny, Mrs. Weiler called and said that her husband hasn't come home tonight. She said that she tried to reach you on your cell phone, but you didn't answer," said Myra dutifully.

Beep . . . "Hey, Sam, this is Gina Pirelli. Remember me? I just got back from Iran. Call me. We've got to get together soon. Bye."

"Wow, Gina's back!" exclaimed Samantha.

Mary looked at her with a puzzled look.

"Oh, she's a T.V. reporter friend of mine whom I met in Washington D.C. a few years ago. She's been overseas for half a year now. We've got some catching up to do."

Mary smiled at Samantha's vivaciousness. She liked seeing Samantha and Sonny happy because they showed the exuberance of children. She and Myra both considered them as their own.

The recorder cranked out another call from some telemarketer. Then, beep . . . "Is this Rafferty? Hey, Rafferty, you're going down," exclaimed the malevolent voice. "Do you hear me? If I'm going to hell, you're going with me!" Click.

Mary and Samantha looked at each other in astonishment.

"That's just a crank call," assured Samantha.

"What do you mean, honey?" asked Mary with worriment. "That man meant harm to you or Sonny."

"No, no, we get those calls every once in awhile. We used to get them more often when Sonny was with the force. Give it no thought, Mary."

"I don't like that, no ma'am, not one bit. That call is a bad omen. I can feel it. I fear that somethin' bad is gonna happen," said Mary, her eye widening.

Knock-Knock-Knock! . . . Knock-Knock-Knock!

Samantha and Mary both jumped with fright. Mary ran over to the front window and looked out.

"It's just Earle," she exclaimed, opening the door to let in her friend. As Mary fussed with Earle, Samantha thought about Sonny heading down south on highway 31 and possibly returning to Centralia.

"Don't you know how to ring a doorbell, Earle? You nearly scared the begeezus out of us!" scolded Mary.

"I'm sorry, Mary," apologized Earle. He then looked toward Samantha with his head bowed. "I'm really sorry, ma'am, I didn't mean to scare y'all none."

Samantha smiled to ease the tension. "I hear that you and Mary are an item?"

"Ma'am?" he said.

"Mary seems quite taken by you,"

"Well, she seems a fine woman to me, ma'am," said Earle sheepishly. "I enjoy her company."

"Well, are you gonna drive me home or are you gonna make me walk?" snapped Mary.

"No, ma'am, I'm ready, and the truck's runnin'," Earle said hastily.

Mary turned to Samantha. "Are you gonna to be all right?"

"Oh yes, dear, I'm going to have some champagne, take a nice warm bath, and wait for Sonny to come home. He should be here soon."

"Okay then. Goodnight, ma'am," she said.

"Goodnight, Mary. Nice meeting you, Earle."

"Same here, ma'am; goodbye," said Earle.

"Bye."

Samantha locked the door, then turned and walked up the curved stairway to her bedroom to change into her evening attire.

Her bedroom was filled with Victorian styled furniture. The natural beauty of the solid oak and quarter-cut oak veneers enhanced the design of the delightful reproductions. The chestnut brown finish of the fine nostalgic pieces cast a golden hue against Samantha's pale skin as she removed her work garments.

A uniqueness that Samantha had was her love of garter belts and hosiery. She didn't like the confinement of pantyhose. As she released the last garter strap, she slipped her thumb inside the stocking top and slid the gossamer fabric down the contour of her long shapely leg. She then folded the material meticulously and placed it into the small box from which it came, and placed the box with many others alike in the top drawer in her lingerie chest. Samantha then slipped off her black elastic belt of garters and softly placed it into the second drawer from whence it came.

Samantha was quite in vogue for an Indianapolis working girl. She was no stranger to the distinctive apparel shops that lined Broad Ripple Avenue.

She had quite an array of lingerie, mostly due to Sonny. Sonny knew how and what to buy for his frau. She was every man's dream to buy for, at Christmas, anniversaries, and birthdays. She was tall and slim, like a model of sorts, and the stores were always stocked with her sizes.

Sonny selected a perfume for her on their second Christmas together. He confided in an Estee Lauder representative at a Lowenstein's Department Store, which was sheik at that time. Being that she was a redhead, and full of spunk, Sonny bought for her Estee Lauder's

"Cinnabar" which, when combined with Samantha's body oils, produced a redolence of spice and sweetness that was unrelenting to Sonny's sense of smell. Sonny found the cologne distinctive, that it didn't linger in the air. He could not smell the spicy essence until he was within just inches of Samantha's softness. The allure was overwhelming and drew Sonny into the enchanted forest of the femme fatale. Samantha had found "Cinnabar" in her stocking every year since. Here came Santa Claus.

Samantha's perky little breasts bounced freely as she unsnapped the back of her lace brassiere. The light pink protrusions centered on the round mounds seemed to reach out to their newfound freedom. She slid the matching low-cut briefs down past her slender thighs dropping them to her feet. She then stepped out with her left foot, and then with her right, grabbed the panty with her toes and sent the silky undergarment flying into the clothes hamper about ten feet away. It was a perfect shot, as usual. She perfected this shot through many a hurried changings in her break-speed style of life.

Samantha could feel the coolness of the room rushing up her legs into her groin, like a ray of sun shooting up from the earth's horizon during dawn's early light. The uninhibited news journalist enjoyed her nakedness. She loved being free of social and psychological restraints on one's behavior. This was her escape from her work environment where she felt restrained, controlled, and bridled. She even had a secretly concealed spot in the backyard where she would often sunbathe topless.

Samantha stretched her arms upward, releasing tension from the upper torso, then bent forward at a 90 degree angle, dropping her arms to the floor, causing a stretching of her lower back. She then dressed herself in a pair of azure pantaloons with matching top, and donned a darker, blue komono of Japanese design. Then she gathered her work garments and hung them neatly on a rack inside the closet in a section designated for the cleaners.

Samantha glided down the stairwell, followed closely by Impala, as she headed toward the kitchen to put her canine crew to bed for the evening, and to partake in some libations and her evening relaxation ritual.

They were called "The Hole in the Wall Gang," headed by the red Irish-Setter, "Impala," who was the most genteel of the group. Then there was the short-legged, "Napolean," and the ill-named, short-tempered Chihuahua called "Rufus." Captain Midnight, the black furry feline, was also part of the gang. They got their name from a hole that Sonny made for them in the back wall of the garage that led to a 12'x 24' kennel in the backyard. Plus, they were known bandits, or at least one of them was. One time, Sonja and Danielle had a week-long fight over missing underwear, one claiming the other one was stealing hers and not returning them. It was all Samantha could do to keep peace between them. Then one day, while Sonny was cleaning the kennel, he happened across three pairs of panties, one slightly abused bra, Sam's garter belt, a lipstick, and three of his socks. That settled the dispute between the girls. From then on when something came up missing they knew where to look.

Napoleon and Rufus were relegated to their hole-in-the-wall home for the evening, as Captain Midnight retired to an upstairs bedroom.

Impala lay at Samantha's feet and watched the cork pop out of the bottle, spewing sparkling wine over the sides. Samantha poured the libation slowly into a long-stemmed crystal goblet and watched the bubbles suddenly rise up the slim-fluted sides towards the top to form a frothy head. She then took a sip to experience the fruitful and tingly flavor of the effervescent wine. With a firm approval from her taste buds, she downed the rest of the drink; then filled another and did the same, and then another, but this time for sipping purposes only. Now she was feeling relaxed, but did not want to get drunk before Sonny returned home.

She took her drink into the den, and in the darkness sat cross-legged on her Japanese tatami in a yoga position. She rested her hands on her knees with palms up, forefingers against thumbs, and eyes closed, releasing tension that she had accumulated throughout the day.

After her period of relaxation, Samantha thought it time to check on the events of the day. She squinted her eyes to give the sensitive rods and cones of her retina time to adjust to the brightness from the 32 inch screen that consumed the darkened room. The voice that emitted from the box seemed to be that of Jessica Marlow, the news anchor for WYNG, Indianapolis. Samantha listened attentively to her as she spouted the news of the day.

"Tonight we have with us, returning from her laborious assignment to the war-torn Middle East, Gina Pirelli, our foreign news correspondent," said the anchorwoman. "Gina, glad you're back."

"Thank you, Jessica. It really feels great being back on American soil," answered the attractive, black-haired reporter.

"Tell me, Gina, what was it like being in the gulf region for the last half year?"

"It was quite grueling at times considering the bad weather and lack of facilities. The local people were actually very nice to us though."

"What do you think the outlook will be for Iran?"

"It looks auspiciously good," claimed Gina. "The Iranians themselves are pushing out the old regime and establishing a new one with more liberalities. They don't want what happened to Iraq and Afghanistan to happen to them. Their younger generations wanted change all along. There's a lot of demagoguery and posturing by different factions over there right now. It will be interesting to see in the end who their political leaders will be."

"Again, it's good to have you back, Gina. We look forward to watching your upcoming reports and specials on your experiences in the Mid-East."

"Like I said previously, it's good to be back, Jessica. Thank you."

As Jessica stared back into the center camera, she ended with, "This is Jessica Marlow on WYNG with the news that you can use. We'll be right back in two minutes with the local news, after a word from our sponsors."

Samantha turned down the volume as a vociferous commercial consumed the screen. "So the prodigal son returns," she said to Impala, as if she understood. The redhead poured herself another drink in celebrating her girlfriend's arrival while waiting for the news to return.

"Hello everyone, I'm Jessica Marlow, back with the local news. Waverly Incorporated is in the news today, again denying reports from the Indianapolis Times of fraud and self-dealing in connection with a string of nursing homes scattered throughout the state, which are owned by the parent company."

Samantha was suddenly gathered in with great interest as the spectacled brunette continued with her report.

"During the past several weeks, the Times has produced a series of stinging reports accusing Waverly owned nursing homes of patient neglect, leading to possible deaths due to understaffing in these facilities. In the last report by Samantha Rafferty, she explained about self-dealing. Ms. Rafferty said that self-dealing involves at least if not more than one of three things: exporting profits from a local nursing home to a corporate parent, divvying up some of the parent's costs among its local homes, or the local homes' purchase of goods and services from themselves. The executives of Waverly claim that there is a legitimate place for these transactions. Ms. Rafferty says that such deals among nursing home insiders raise the question of whether these arrangements are designed to siphon money from a home, thus depriving patients of benefits while gathering in inflated government reimbursements. Rafferty said that proof of these accusations shall be forthcoming, and may lead to indictments of several nursing home operators in Indiana from the Waverly group. Ms. Rafferty also pointed out that in the past, self-dealing has figured prominently in the Enron Corporation debacle and other corporate scandals."

"We will now take you to Waverly's headquarters in St. Louis, Missouri, where we have our own news reporter, Lori Jung along with John Losch, Waverly Enterprise's C.E.O. who repudiates this story."

"Mr. Losch, would you please tell us why the American Health Care Association has brought these charges against you?" asked the diminutive journalist.

"I'd like to make one thing perfectly clear. Waverly Incorporated has not been formally charged with any crime. These are accusations coming from the Indianapolis Times which we feel are unfounded. It's true that we've had some homes in Indiana that were negligent and under-staffed, but we are in the process of rectifying these problems. All nursing home owners have problems like these from time to time because of the shortage of healthcare workers. We are doing the best we can to solve those problems. As for the last accusations from the Times, it's totally false," claimed Losch.

"Keep lying, Losch," said Samantha aloud to the television. "We just printed the proof tonight, and you'll read it in the morning edition of our paper," she said confidently.

Losch continued, "The Indianapolis Times has been hounding our company for three months now, and as I stated previously, we have fixed or are in the process of fixing the problems. These last accusations are just preposterous."

"Thank you for your perspective, Mr. Losch. Now, back to you, Jessica," said Lori.

Samantha was undaunted by Losch's comments. She saw him as

just another white-haired, dark suited C.E.O. bastard caught up in his own smugness. As Jessica continued with her reporting, Samantha poured herself another drink. She thought of calling Gina to talk about getting together for lunch or such when John Taylor suddenly appeared on the television screen. Samantha stared in surprise at the powerful image on the screen.

"Why is Daddy talking to Jessica when this nursing home project belongs to me?" she wondered. "Daddy would never go over my head," thought Samantha.

"So, Mr. Taylor; is it true about the latest crime that you have accused Waverly of?" asked Jessica.

"Well, let's just say that the projects that we were focusing on were addressed by Mr. Losch and his associates," answered Taylor.

"So, are you saying that the latest accusations of possible fraud didn't originate from your paper?"

"No, I didn't say that."

"So then, are you saying that maybe your investigative staff was shall we say . . . over-exuberant in their reporting?" quizzed the reporter.

"Could be," he answered.

"Well, isn't it true that your own daughter, Samantha Rafferty, is the head of this investigation, and is the editor of these Waverly reports?"

"Yes, but."

"So, you're saying that she's been accusing Waverly of crimes that she may have no proof of," drilled Jessica.

"No, I didn't say that!" boomed the voice of Big John. "Sometimes Samantha over-extends her boundaries. That's all I'm saying. Besides, seventeen out of twenty Waverly nursing homes in this state have been found negligible to their patients to some degree, and in defiance of state codes. The state has stepped in and the homes are now complying with their orders."

"Were any homes shut down?"

"Yes, one, Ginger Hills Extended Care Facility in Chapel Hill was closed for two weeks, and then re-opened by the State Board of Health after the proper changes were made."

"So, do you think there will be any indictments handed down from the prosecutor's office?"

"No, I don't think so. Also, I would like to say that I believe Samantha and her staff did a fine job of protecting the elderly in our great state," he said with swagger.

"Thanks, Mr. Taylor, for straightening things out for us."

"My pleasure," replied Big John.

"Daddy, you son-of-a-bitch, why are you doing this to me!" screamed Samantha at the television. "Wait till tomorrow when my last report hits the streets. We have proof of fraud, and we have names!"

Confused, Samantha decided to wait until tomorrow to confront Big John about interfering in her work. Even though he was the boss, he gave his daughter free rein, and she planned on testing him on that.

"Hello, Gina?"

"Is that you, Sam?"

"Yes it is," exclaimed Samantha, giggling like a schoolgirl.

"Oh, Sam, I've missed you so much," Gina giggled back.

"And I've missed you. Are you home for good?"

"Yes, I'll be here for awhile."

"I saw you on television tonight. How was it over there, really?"

"Oh, my God, how did I look?" squealed her vainglorious girlfriend. "I had just gotten off the plane when we made that interview!"

"I thought it was live, you looked great, girl," said Samantha.

"Oh, Sam, I met the nicest guy over there. A French journalist would you believe. Do you know what it's like to make love in the sand with a French journalist?"

"No, what's it like?" asked Sam excitedly.

"Don't try it!"

They both laughed foolishly.

"Hey, Sam, how's Sonny been doing?"

"Oh, he's been okay. He's in his own little world most of the time, but he comes out every once in a while to see me."

"Is he home with you now?"

"Not right now. He's on a job tonight, trying to track down some kind of an adulterous affair. Danny's moved out, and Sonja is up at Ball State settling in with a girlfriend off campus."

"So you pretty much have an empty nest."

"Yeah, I guess you could say that."

"Girl, you've got to get a life. Look, when I'm through with this gig I'm going to put in for D.C. again. That's where the action is. You remember the fun you had when you were out there before. You should go back there with me, Sam."

"Oh, let's don't go there, Gina."

"Come on, Sam, you fell in love there, remember?"

"That was just happenstance. Hey, when are we going to get together so you can tell me about your adventures in the mysterious Middle East?" asked Samantha, changing the subject.

"I'm busy for the next few days, but I've got to visit a gym soon. What say I call you when I'm free, and we can do the gym and lunch scene like we used to?"

"That sounds great, Gina."

"Okay then. I've got to run girl. I'm going dancing with an old friend tonight, if you know what I mean!"

"Okay," smiled Samantha. "Make it soon."

Samantha reluctantly set the phone down. It gave her a vicarious thrill hearing Gina Pirelli tell of her adventures. She was quite envious of her girlfriend, for Gina had the career that she had always coveted; that of a television news correspondent.

Samantha turned off the television and slumped down into the deep cushions of the davenport. She mused in the quietude of the darkened den. Though her senses were clouded with drink, memories began to slowly appear. Memories; like pictures on display, revolving around and around in her head; pictures of the beltway boys, the wining, the dining, the Capitol building, and Georgetown pubs. Samantha smiled at the thought-sight of Gina, with all her promiscuities, and of her own cherished memories of the young rich senator from Indiana by whom she was seduced. Warmth filled her loins as she envisaged their lovemaking on his leer jet while flying from Washington D.C. to New York. He entered into her innermost chambers infringing upon hallowed ground that once belonged to only one man, Sonny Rafferty. It didn't stop there. Samantha found, that in Troy, she developed a thirst for love, lust and power. It was a thirst that even though she repeatedly tried, she could not quell. Suddenly, guilt flooded her soul, and her thought-memories quickly dispersed.

Samantha abruptly sat upright, startled by a loud crashing sound coming from the far corner of the house which caused Impala to bark nervously. Already emotionally tense, Samantha tried to hush her friend while goose bumps rose up on her neck. She could only think of two things. The frightening phone call that she received earlier that evening, and where the hell did Sonny put that gun? Not wanting to turn the lights on for fear of exposing her location, Samantha desperately rummaged through her secretary and discovered a penlight. With help from the miniature flashlight she found the key to Sonny's desk. Through the darkness she scurried over to where the desk was. Then suddenly, she heard a dog's sharp, injured cry. "That sounds like Rufus," she whispered in quiet desperation. Impala barked abruptly again. As Samantha hurriedly opened the middle desk drawer she heard Rufus's injured cry for help end with one final yelp. "They've killed Rufus!" she declared. With her heart racing she reached in and pulled out the gun. There it was; Sonny's Smith and Wesson 38 special. It had never been fired since that night in Centralia. Samantha checked the cylinder. It contained six bullets. She made her way into the kitchen. The disturbance had died down, but she thought she heard voices in the garage. The side door of the garage led into the kitchen pantry. She set her eyes upon that door. She was thinking of calling 911 when the talking suddenly stopped. The sound of heavy footsteps approached the pantry door. Samantha broke out in a cold sweat as panic set in. She leaned against the corner of the refrigerator to steady her quivering body. She raised the weapon with both hands and trained the barrel toward the center of the pantry door just like Sonny had shown her many a time. Hyperventilation took over her lungs, keeping pace with a pounding heart that seemed ready to burst through her chest. Then all of a sudden, that malevolent voice resonated in her head; "Is this Rafferty? Hey Rafferty! You're going down, do you hear me? You're going down!"

The footsteps were now at the door, and Samantha watched as the doorknob slowly turned. Her trembling hand released the safety, and she pulled back the hammer, but she started feeling so . . . dizzy . . . so faint . . . so weak.

Chapter Four

Oh Danny Girl

The creaky pantry door opened ever-so-slowly. An eerie dark image appeared from behind the door and leered at the lady in waiting. The shadowy figure held its arms open as it stepped heavily towards the petrified woman.

Samantha muscled up a "Stop or I'll shoot", but nothing emitted from her larynx, for her throat and tongue were too desiccated from the extreme air exchange caused by her terror. In her weakened state the pallid skinned redhead vacillated from left to right, and right to left with the 38 special, trying to squeeze the trigger which seemed to her to be a monumental task. She finally fired the weapon and missed high right, and the odious looking creature lurched forward and swatted the gun out of her hand. He then back-handed the panic-stricken girl which sent her flying into the kitchen table, and then again, sending her crashing onto the terrazzo floor. Impala attacked the intruder, but she too was sent flying through the darkness, landing with a whispered thud. Dazed, Samantha tried crawling towards the den, but two large hands suddenly grasped her ankles. She kicked furiously, scraping her legs against the hardened concrete and marble flooring. Through her wild kicking Samantha managed to free herself, leaving her silk pantaloons behind in the hands of the dreaded intruder. As she got up to run she was pounced upon again. This time the malicious viper flipped her on her back, ripped open her komono and her silk shirt; split her legs apart, and entered her private passage. Samantha tried to scream, but her parched throat betrayed her. He was big, real big! She could feel the tender fabric of her flesh being torn away. His girth felt like a tree trunk ramming her insides.

Then, through her excruciating pain she saw his hooded face, just a few inches from hers. It was a hideous face, evil, and satanic. The lecherous reprobate spoke glossolalia in a lowbred voice while a malodorous discharge drooled from his mouth onto Samantha's face and neck. Just when she thought she was going to pass out from her pain and his stench, she heard a familiar growl, as Impala attacked the invader's hindquarters. Samantha saw an opening. While he was flailing at the dog with one arm, she knocked his support arm off her chest, which made the evil stranger lose his balance and fall to the side. She slid out from underneath his huge mass and low-crawled on her elbows toward the front door of the house, hoping to escape the dark intruder.

When Samantha finally reached the door she grabbed the knob and shakily pulled herself up. She could not hear Impala anymore; or the intruder. What happened to Impala, she wondered. She would so hate to lose her close friend. Samantha unbolted the front door, and the fresh night air welcomed her along with the light from the street lamps. I must hurry to our neighbors to call the police, she thought as she stepped out the door. But she felt something was wrong. She couldn't breathe! There was a garrote around her neck that was getting tighter and tighter! She was dragged back inside the house while desperately gasping for air. She was shoved to the floor with a knee planted heavily into her back while the cord around her neck yanked back her head. Was this how it was going to end, by a garroting, without seeing her kids and her beloved Sonny, again? Life was becoming dim. Samantha wanted to utter one final prayer before the lack of oxygen robbed her of her last thoughts: "God, bless my family oh heavenly father." And then . . . total darkness…total silence. . . .

I can hear a muffled voice. Can't quite make it out, sounds familiar though; might be an angel, dreamed Samantha.

"Mother, wake up!" said Danielle, while staring down at the figure lying peacefully on the polished terrazzo floor. With her consciousness slowly returning, and her cheeks aglow with a rosy blush, Samantha opened her eyes.

"What are you doing here, Danny?" she asked bewilderingly.

"I came to collect my softball equipment from the garage to use in a tournament at Terre Haute tomorrow. When I came inside and turned on the lights I found you passed out on the kitchen floor with Impala licking your face."

Samantha struggled to get to her feet. Danielle gave her a hand at getting up.

"I found Daddy's gun lying on the floor next to you. You weren't going to shoot me were you, Mother?"

"No, I wasn't going to shoot you," Samantha snapped back. "You know, you could have come to the front door first, like normal people would. I thought someone was breaking in. Look at me, I'm still shaking," she said, holding out her hands. "I feel exhausted, kinda strange, like I was violated or something."

"Let's sit you down at the table and I'll make us some hot tea," suggested Danielle, feeling a little unsteady herself.

Danielle set a kettle of water on the stove and ignited the gas into a flame underneath, and then sat down with her mother.

"If you would have been in the living room, or upstairs, you would have seen me pull into the driveway," said Danielle.

"I was in the den."

"That explains why you didn't see me or hear me drive up. I'm curious, Mother, why did you leave your car outside tonight?"

"I was going to take Mary home, as usual, but she had someone else to pick her up."

"Oh yeah, whom may I ask?"

"Oh, Mary has a boyfriend now."

"You're joking! Who is he?"

"Earle Rose is his name. He has an apartment close to Mary and Myra's. He seems like a nice fellow."

"No kiddin', that old one-eyed Aunt Jemima got herself a man! All right Mary! That goes to show you that there is hope for everyone," joked Danielle.

Samantha smiled. "Don't be calling her Aunt Jemima, Danny. People might think badly of you.

"Come on, Samantha, get out that box of pancake mix and put a patch over Aunt Jemima's eye and tell me that's not our Mary," challenged Danielle.

"Okay, okay, your right," said Samantha. "Now tell me what went on in my garage earlier tonight."

"When I pulled up to the garage, I saw that boy from next door milling around inside with the lights off."

"Do you mean, Jimmy Hansen?"

"Yeah, Jimmy. He said that Rufus and Napoleon were out running around, and he knew that they were usually kept in the house or in the kennel, so he collected them and brought them back to the garage for you. Jimmy claimed that he couldn't find the light switch, and stepped on Rufus's foot while searching for it. Rufus was howling when I came in. I don't think he was hurt that bad, but you know Rufus; he's like a little kid, seeks attention. When the little nipper saw me he quit crying. He gave another little yelp when I picked him up by the nape of his neck. He's okay now. I also dropped the equipment bag when I pulled it off the top shelf, so that might have scared you too."

Both Danielle and Samantha popped up from their chairs as the whistle blew on the teakettle. Samantha poured the hot liquid as Danielle retrieved a box of various teas from the pantry shelf.

"What's your poison?" asked Danielle.

"Give me the green tea, the one with caffeine. I'm going to try to stay up for your dad tonight."

"You don't have to work tomorrow?"

"No, but I've got to call your grandpa. We have some discrepancies on one of my news articles that we might have to address sometime tomorrow. I don't know how those dogs got loose. I made sure the door was latched."

"It was wide open, Mother. Those dogs are smart. They've learned how to unlatch the door. I guess you need a doorknob with a lockset in it."

"Yes, I'll have Sonny fix that. In the meantime, I'll just hang a padlock on it. That should keep the little buggers in. Oh, by the way, did you thank Jimmy for bringing the dogs in?"

"Hell no, I told him to get his ass home, or I would tell you that he was peeping in your windows. He ran like hell," smiled Danielle.

"No, you didn't!"

"Yes, I did."

"Little Jimmy Hansen? He wouldn't do that. I know his mother well."

"You may know his mother, but you don't know little Jimmy

Hansen," she mocked. "Do you remember our clandestine spot in the backyard where we used to sunbathe topless?"

"Yeah, I do . . . Oh, my God! You don't mean. . . ."

"Yes, he used to watch us," said Danielle.

"How could he? That spot was perfectly hidden."

"Yes, except for the big oak in the Hansen's backyard,"

"That oak's pretty far away, Danny."

"Not if you have binoculars."

"How long had this been going on?"

"About four times, before I stopped him."

"How did you do that?"

"The first time that I saw him watching, I did nothing. Actually, it was quite titillating knowing that a young boy was staring at my nakedness, thinking that he was getting away with something. The second time he was up there I put my hand inside my bikini bottom acting like I was pleasuring myself. That didn't work, so the next time I went butt-naked, but I still couldn't shake that little pervert from that tree. Do you remember last summer when Jimmy was walking around on crutches with that broken leg?"

"Yes, I remember," said Samantha, curiosity abounding. "I heard that he had an accident on his scooter."

"Yeah, right; anyway, I needed a secret weapon. So, I remembered a discussion between you and your friends about Mr. Rogers," said Danielle, looking at Samantha for her reaction.

"Mr. Rogers? How did you find out about Mr. Rogers?" chided Samantha.

"Sonja and I both used to eavesdrop when you had your friends over to the house in the evenings. You thought we were in bed asleep, but we would lie on the floor atop the stairs to hear what adults talk about."

"What other secrets did you find out about me?" said Samantha.

"Well, I found out that Daddy's favorite playthings are something called a burning bush and a fur pocket. From the way I heard it they belong to you. Oh yes, you and Sonny like to sleep naked together."

Embarrassed, the red-faced mother waved her hands in retreat and exclaimed, "That's it, no more, if you tell me any more I may have to kill you!"

"Don't get mad at me," laughed Danielle. "We are both grown women now. Anyway, let me finish my story. So I snuck into your room and found Mr. Rogers, took him outside, and put on a show for Jimmy Hansen. So Jimmy, having only two hands, one for holding onto the tree, and the other holding the binoculars, had to let one of them go so he could play. Guess which one he let go?"

They both laughed heartily.

"Very amusing story, next time, clue me in on things at the beginning. After all we are both grown women," joked Samantha.

"Very well," said Danielle. "So, Mother, why were you so frightened tonight?"

"Let's see, where do I start? I was quite stressed out from the events of the day. I was expecting Sonny home tonight to help me celebrate closing a case that I had worked hard and long on, a case that Dad seems to want to sabotage. Sonny's chasing some lovers, way south of town near the Centralia area. Then I got this threatening phone call from some crazed male, probably from someone whose toes I've stepped on. At least I think it was directed at me."

"What did he say?" asked Danielle curiously.

"It's not really what he said as much as how he said it. It was quite a scary voice. He directed his anger at Rafferty. I don't think Sonny has made any enemies lately. He's been pretty docile since he's been in business for himself. He screens his clients to filter out cases that might involve violence. So I just assumed that this individual was directing his anger at me. All of that, along with all that commotion in the garage had me spooked. So I got Sonny's gun and was preparing to protect myself. I guess I must have just passed out. Then it seemed like someone grabbed me from behind, and was choking me with a wire or cord or something. My next memory was that of looking up into your face."

"Wow! That's pretty heavy, Mother. How much have you had to drink tonight?"

"I had some champagne with my staff at Deiter's Nasch after work today, and about half a bottle since I've been home. It's not what you think, Danny, I'm of sound mind. I wasn't drunk. I'm not an alcoholic just yet. A couple of more nights like this might put me there though."

"You must have hallucinated about that choking incident," said Danielle. "That seems quite melodramatic."

"Anyway, I'm quite all right now. I guess you're anxious to get home so you can rest up for your big tournament tomorrow."

"Yeah, I guess so," said Danielle quietly.

"Well, I'm going upstairs, draw a bath and soak awhile as I wait for Sonny's return. Is Matthew going to Terre Haute with you?"

"Yes, Mother, Matt's taking me."

"By the way, how have you and Matt been getting along after three months of wedded bliss?" Samantha asked, glancing at Danielle for her reaction.

Studying her thoughts for a moment, Danielle answered with a whine, "Mom . . . Mom, I've got a question for you, but I don't really know how to ask it."

"Well, girl, after the startling revelations that you've shown me tonight, there's no question that you could ask that would shock me or that we can't find an answer to," said Samantha.

"Mom, when you and Sonny were first married, did he, you know, want to 'do it' all the time?"

"Do you mean sex?"

"Yeah, and I mean *all* the time," said Danielle.

"When we were first married we both liked having sex, and quite often, I must add. There was no discrepancy there, but we soon learned of many activities that we enjoyed together. No, that wasn't a problem with us," said Samantha. "Hell, you and Matt were having sex long before you were married; you both shacked together for over a year."

"That's right, Mother, but he was nice to me then. We would go out and do things. We had a social life back then. After I put that ring on his finger, he's been like a rabbit on a date, and he tries to slide that thing in anywhere he can make it fit."

Samantha thought for a second. "Do you remember back when you were about 13, and had just grown breasts?"

"Yeah," said Danielle, slightly confused

"You had trouble with some young derelicts in school trying to fondle you. You came to me and I sent you to your dad. What advice did Sonny give to you?"

"He told me to kick their asses," said Danielle, remembering the event.

"So what did you do?"

"I kicked their asses, but this is an adult situation now. I can't kick his ass, he's a grown man!"

"Well, let's tell Sonny, he'll kick his ass," said Samantha, half meaning it.

"No, Mother, Dad taught me to be independent. I can't expect him to fight my battles for me,"

"You're right," said Samantha, "besides, he'd kill him. No father wants any boy screwing his daughter, doesn't matter if their married or not."

That cracked a smile on her daughter's face.

"Look, Danny, Sonny and I have never really had any major problems with anything, let alone, sex. As a matter-of-fact, I wish he would pay more attention to me. He's changed since Centralia, though he's still a good husband and father. I guess I shouldn't complain. You know, the girls on my staff have often discussed their marital affairs, and I can tell you what they do when their husbands get out of line."

"What's that, Mother? I'm grasping for anything. I'm tired of feeling like a piece of raw meat."

"Close up shop!" said Samantha abruptly.

"Close up shop?"

"Yeah, cut him off. No more nooky."

"Gee, Mom, that's a little extreme, don't you think?"

"Extreme hell, make him treat you like a lady. Tell him if he doesn't, he can grow that mushroom in somebody else's backyard."

"I don't know," hedged Danielle, "he might leave me."

"Let him," snapped Samantha. "If he leaves, you don't want him anyway. Look, you know Merle, the black lady from my staff at work, right?"

"Yes."

"Her husband was that way, you know, over-sexed and all that. When they were first married she used that method on him. Merle says that it's foolproof because men think physical, instinctively, as where women reason more. In other words, we're smarter than men."

"Isn't Merle's husband, that big lineman on the Colts' football team?"

"Yes, Darryl Bullock, all 315 pounds of him, but Merle's the boss in that family."

"Okay, I'll try it," said Danielle. "Thanks for your advice, Mom."

"You know, until tonight you hadn't called me Mom since you were about five years old. Why is that?"

"I don't know, I guess because Sonja's not here, plus I miss living at home. Sonja's your little girl. She's the one that calls you Mommy, Mommy this Mommy that."

"You wouldn't happen to be a bit jealous of your little sister would you?"

"Maybe I am a little. She was always your favorite."

"And you were always Sonny's favorite," said Samantha. "There's a reason for that."

"I'd like to hear it," said Danielle.

"When you were born, I was still going to college. Sonny spent more time with you than I did. Two years later, Sonja arrived. She was a rather sickly baby, needed a lot of attention. By the time we got Sonja straightened out you had already grown well attached to your father, and he to you. You became sort of a tomboy and gravitated towards sports. You were very much an extrovert, very expressive, outgoing. Your dad doted on you and you him. Sonja, on the other hand, was more introspective, more private, and even peevish at times. She clung to her mother. Yeah, she's whiney and is a bit spoiled, but we love both of you the same," explained Samantha.

"I always felt that you didn't like me much, because I was a bastard child," said Danielle, bluntly.

"What? Who told you that?"

"Come on, Mom; do the math. You were three months pregnant when you married Daddy. You didn't want me. I just interfered with your college plans and your career. I was an unwanted pregnancy."

"There's nothing further from the truth," said Samantha.

"Are you trying to tell me that I was a planned pregnancy?"

"No, you weren't planned but . . . why don't you let me tell you the whole story about how Sonny and Samantha's worlds collided."

Chapter Five

Highpockets

Danielle was on tenterhooks as the revelation of her origin was about to be revealed to her by the lady in blue that glided up the long stairwell. Yes, the lady in blue, the frightened woman that she found passed out on the kitchen floor; a real person after all. Not just the woman that was married to her father or just the person she called Mother. Not just someone that she gave her unrequited love to, but maybe, just maybe, the nurturer that reciprocated her love back.

Danielle was giddy, almost whimsical, as she slid her hand along the balustrade while following her mother up to her bedroom. It was not often that she or her sister was invited into Sonny and Samantha's chamber. With few exceptions, their room was used mostly for refuge from a late-night thunderstorm or a bad dream. To the girls, it felt like such a safe haven, a place where nothing could harm them.

This euphoria that Danielle felt was a semblance of the feeling she had as a child when she and Sonja were kept in the house on rainy days, and their mother would allow them to play in the garret. She remembered the joy she felt as her mother would lower the hidden staircase to the attic that held a lifetime of memories that belonged to Sonny and Samantha, but now was shared with her and sis.

She remembered how Samantha and Sonny caught them dressed up in an unusual array of clothing that, at that time, was recorded by camera and now stashed in a picture album somewhere in the house.

Sonja had Samantha's tie-dyed "Grateful Dead" shirt on, and wore

47

a pair of four-inch clogs that belonged to her mother when she was a teenager. Danielle's attire consisted of a catcher's mask and Sonny's old jock strap pulled up over her jeans, and she was pounding a catcher's mitt with her fist, yelling, "hey batta," "hey batta," "hey batta," when they were suddenly surprised by their parents.

The thought of that day put a big smile on Danielle's face because she remembered her embarrassment when she found out what an athletic supporter was used for. To this day, as hard as she searched, she could never find where they stashed those pictures.

"Why don't you call Matt and tell him that you are going to be a little late, while I start my bathwater," suggested Samantha.

"Okay, Mother," Danielle replied.

Their bathroom was a large L-shaped room just off the bedroom. The main section of the room entertained a double sink, commode, and shower, while the rear of the room contained a porcelain-topped vanity with a tri-view mirror and bench, and a grand antique tub that was built for two, and very often used that way. A marble shelf ran along the far side of the tub, and held as many as 20 candles of various shapes and sizes. Above the shelf, incased in the wall, was a CD player containing only the sounds of "Enya," or the blues of "Clapton," depending upon whom was in charge of that particular evening, Sonny or Samantha.

Samantha opened the chromed faucets of the tub into a steamy flow, and began lighting the many candles while Danielle conversed on the phone with her husband.

While on the phone, Danielle couldn't help but notice the amber hue that enhanced the room, and the smell of spices that lazily hung about. Then, there was the large nude portrait hanging above the king size mansion bed next to where she was talking. It was a beautiful painting of the backside of a woman lying on a fainting couch of sorts. She had a blue cloth draped over the top of her legs where she lay, as if asleep. Danielle also noticed her having beautiful auburn hair resembling her mothers. She and Sonja always thought it so beautiful a painting.

Samantha dispersed several spices and oils into the bubbly bath as warm steam fogged the room. She slid easily out of her silk garments and looked at herself in a full-length mirror. While surveying her body she noticed a little roundness in her, otherwise, taut belly. Must be the champagne, she thought. She noticed that her breasts still pointed straight out. At one point in time they tilted upwards somewhat, which she thought was a little odd. That, and her high-rise ass, as Sonny used to describe it, was the reason he had given her the nickname of "Highpockets" when they first courted. He still called her by that name every now and then.

Out of the corner of her eye, Samantha caught Danielle staring at her. "Oh, I didn't hear you get off the phone with Matt," she said, a bit embarrassed. "Is he okay with you staying awhile longer?"

"Yes, he's okay with it, Mother, and he said not to worry, that he would drive me tomorrow. Besides, Terre Haute is only about two hours away. That's enough about Matt and me, I want to hear about Sonny and Samantha," said Danielle.

"Let me sit down and take my make-up off first."

Danielle stood behind her mom. They both studied each other in the mirror.

"May I brush your hair, Mother? I've always wanted to."

"Why, yes my dear, I'd love that."

"Mom, that painting hanging above your bed, is that you in that picture?"

"Why yes it is," said Samantha proudly. "Sonny had that made for me many years ago."

"But you had to pose for it. Weren't you embarrassed at all?"

"Heaven's no, girl. The man that painted that portrait was quite the gentleman, and a very fine painter I might add. His name is Jaques Tuqua LeBlanc. He's French, and lives in south Indianapolis. He has his studio close to Sonny's office. Sonny and I still run into him and his bohemian girlfriend at parties every so often."

"It's beautiful," said Danielle.

"And very tastefully done," added Samantha.

"I wish I was beautiful like you, Mom."

"You are beautiful, dear."

"Not like you. My thighs are too big, and so are my boobs."

"Pshaw! I know a lot of girls that wish they had breasts like yours."

"Not softball players."

"No, not softball players maybe, but after this summer your softball playing will be over, won't it?"

"I guess so," she reluctantly replied.

49

"Well, be happy with what you have, my dear. Besides, after your sports playing days are over your legs will trim down. At least they're muscle, and not fat."

"Yeah, I guess you're right, but I'll never be a model."

"Do you want to be?"

"No, not really," said Danielle.

"Then don't worry about it, and don't let Sonny hear you talking like that. He thinks the sun rises and sets on you."

"Really, Mother?" she asked.

"He really does. Sonny is devoted to both his daughters, but you're special to him."

Samantha eased her slender body into the steamy warmth of the bathtub. Danielle took her place on the plush vanity bench. She watched her mother's eyes smile as she began telling the love story of Sonny and Samantha:

"Of all the young stallions out there, your dad was the one that captured my heart. I knew that he was much different than the other men that I had met. It was in the spring of 1978 . . . . "

As she continued the story with Danielle, Samantha's subconscious mind dug deep into her archives and produced, for herself, the original version, as it once happened:

It was a dreary four-hour drive from the heart of Indianapolis to the northern most region of the state. The cherry-red Mustang motored its way through the evening's drizzled mist with ease. Behind the wheel of the sporty mechanical beast was Samantha Taylor, the vivacious daughter of Big John Taylor, owner of the Indianapolis Times newspaper. Samantha was on her first assignment for the Times, and for her Journalism Today course at Valparaiso University.

The black pavement made a sharp left curve heading toward Mt. Baldy, but Samantha guided her Mustang straight ahead, exiting onto "Dunes Highway." Then suddenly, there it was in the gloaming, the great white albatross to society; the state penitentiary. Its immense whitewashed walls seemed monolithic, and stretched for a distance of several city blocks. Towers with gun placements rose out of the top and were placed at regular intervals, with bright amber lights looming above, fighting off the shadows of night. Along the prison's periphery ran a 12' high chain-linked fence with several strands of barbed wire strung along the top. It was an ominous sight, but the young reporter wasn't going to let that deter her from her journalistic duties.

Samantha inadvertently pulled into the wrong parking space, but it was a nice spot against a curb close to the front gate, which she deemed quite lucky.

The tall, slim college student was bent over, retrieving her purse and notepad from the back seat of the Ford coupe when the blue-uniformed corrections officer walked up. With her well-rounded designer jean derriere wriggling, as if waving at the free air, a strong masculine voice suddenly rang out.

"Ma'am, I must inform you that this is a no parking area."

Samantha suddenly turned around and hit her head on the door molding, subsequently dropping her possessions onto the pavement below, scattering her personal items in every direction. "Shit!" exclaimed the saucy redhead. "Couldn't you be a little more discreet?" she scolded while trying to reclaim her belongings.

"I'm sorry, ma'am, let me help you with your things," said the officer.

As he reached down to assist, he noticed that her silky white shirt had loosely fallen away from her chest, exposing a pair of young, un-haltered breasts, pink tips and all. This exhibition of risqué innocence took the breath away from the awestruck young officer.

She looked up and their eyes met; hers green and luxuriant, his deep blue and curious.

"Hi, I'm Sergeant Sonny Rafferty, Michigan City Department of Corrections," he announced.

"I'm Samantha Taylor of the Indianapolis Times," she said in a more subdued tone.

Their eyes suddenly broke from their transfixed state and both went back to the task at hand, with the sergeant subsequently lying prostrate on the ground retrieving a contrary lipstick from under the Mustang.

"What does it feel like to murder someone?" asked Samantha defiantly. She knew that she had stunned him with the question but she wanted results. He did look quite handsome, standing there brushing off his uniform, looking astonished by the redhead's candor.

The officer didn't answer right away, partially because of the frankness of her question, and partly so that he could absorb some of her beauty. He was quite fixated with her piercing green eyes and her bright red locks cascading down onto her shoulders in a bouncy fashion.

"Well, the cat got your tongue, officer?"

"Please call me Sonny."

"Okay, Sonny, how does it feel to be a murderer?"

"You don't murder animals, you kill them," he answered.

"Oh, that's a bourgeois answer," rebounded Samantha.

"But it's true. The murderers are inside those walls, not standing here in front of you. Besides, I'm just a subordinate."

"So you're just the gatekeeper?" taunted Samantha.

"That's right. At least that's my assignment for today. That and keeping the protesters calm during their candlelight vigil tonight. Most of these people are too dogmatic to talk with, so we just leave them alone as long as they don't become violent."

"So you think just because someone has a difference of opinion that they aren't worth listening to."

"No, I didn't say that. Remember, I'm just the gatekeeper. What do I know? Besides, they'll get their, kum-by-yas in tonight, I assure you."

"That's lame, Sonny, that's really lame," said Samantha.

"You've got moxie, Highpockets, I like that," smiled Sonny. "Do you mind me calling you Highpockets?"

"Now, why on earth would you want to call me Highpockets?" asked the curious collegian.

"I'm not trying to be fresh, but I love the way that little pocket on your blouse rides high up on your left breast, and I've noticed your long legs and high firm ass that causes the pockets on your designer jeans to sit high up. All of that turns me on," he said boldly.

"That is really sexist. You are quite the Neanderthal."

"I take pride in that."

"So tell me, Sonny, how did you acquire this job?"

"Well, I wrestled with boredom and boredom won."

"You're such a wag," declared Samantha. "What I mean is what kind of man takes on a job of this nature? You know, as a correctional officer."

"Well, you have to be able to kill for money and die for love," quipped Sonny.

"Oh, that's real brave."

"Kismet is the reason."

"What?"

"Kismet, it must be my kismet to become a correctional officer. It's my destiny foretold to me by the Fates, I guess."

"What do you mean by Fates?"

"In Greek and Roman mythology the Fates are three goddesses who control human destiny and life."

"So you don't believe in God?" questioned Samantha.

"Oh yes, very much so."

"You can't believe in both Greek mythology and the Christian God from whom the Bible speaks."

"Who says I can't?"

"Now you're getting pretentious."

"Actually, I was brought up in a little Pentecostal church over on Chicago Street about 10 blocks from here."

"Do you mean that you were a—?"

"That's right, a holy roller," he pre-empted.

"I wasn't going to say that."

"Don't worry, Highpockets, I'm not a proselytizer. Besides, I don't attend there anymore."

"Why not?"

"Well, I got the holy part down just fine, but I couldn't get a handle on the rolling part, so I quit going."

"Sonny Rafferty, God's going to get you for talking like that!"

"Don't worry. God has a sense of humor. What kind of church do you go to?"

"I'm a Presbyterian."

"Isn't that kind of like being a refined Baptist?"

"No, it's not!"

"Just thought I would ask," said Sonny.

"You are becoming quite incorrigible, you know that."

"I can't help it. I have this malady," feigned Sonny.

"Oh yeah, I'm curious, what kind of malady is it?"

"It's called curvature of the mind."

Samantha looked at Sonny and broke out in laughter, as did he. Sonny took notice at how Samantha laughed at him with her eyes.

"How old are you, Highpockets? You look a little young to be a reporter at a prison roast. You look more like a journalist for some *haute couture* publication."

"High fashion has yet to take hold in the Midwest, though we do support the idea, even if it's not high on the feminists' want-list. We feminist tend to think less visceral nowadays and are more pragmatic. So therefore, we as women journalists are trying to figure out why our country must be so barbaric to each other as in this execution. By the way, I am also a 19 year-old third year college student at Valparaiso University."

"I thought so. By your guise I saw you as a rich college chick trying to get a feminist angle on the American lifetime practice of dealing with the criminal feature of our society. But I pictured you more as a "Vasser-Queen."

"What's wrong with Valparaiso?" chided Samantha. "I could have gone to Vasser. I was accepted, you know, but I decided to keep my roots planted here so that I could help my father with his newspaper in Indianapolis."

"I understand now," chortled Sonny. "You're a daddy's girl."

"You know, you could show a little more decorum," snapped Samantha.

"Do you mean that I'm not treating you like a lady? I thought you to be a reporter."

"You must take a perverse delight in disagreeing with me."

"I'm sorry. It's just that I've never enjoyed listening to all that bleeding-heart liberal guff."

"I have a right to opine," stated Samantha, feeling a bit slighted. "You don't expect me to abstain from asking any questions at all do you?"

"Hey, you've got some good points there, Highpockets. Why don't we get together after the execution and discuss them?"

"Don't patronize me, Sonny Rafferty!"

"I wonder what makes you so irascible. It must be that flaming red hair and your tenacious attitude. Are you of Irish descent by any means?"

"Go to hell!"

"Bingo!" Sonny laughed teasingly while the angered journalist sneered at him. "Okay, Okay, why don't you re-park your car in the correct parking lot, and then I'll personally escort you to the conference room that we have set up for the news people."

"I think I'm going to interview the protesters first, you know, get some insight on that bleeding-heart liberal guff," said Samantha sarcastically. "I can find my own way to the conference room, thank you."

"All right, but I probably won't be here when you get back, but there will be a uniformed officer at the gate. Just show him your media pass and he will let you in. I must go prepare for the execution," hinted Sonny.

"Wait a minute," said Samantha. "I don't get it. I thought you said that you were the gatekeeper?"

"Who, me? No way. I'm a sergeant, you know. I'm in charge of all the other officers working the grounds tonight. They're not exactly gatekeepers either. We're here to make sure the protesting stays orderly, and to escort people with the proper credentials onto the prison grounds."

Sonny checked his watch. "In about half an hour I've got to go on up to X-row to prepare Zeke Gibbons for his execution."

"Go on!" Samantha burst out while shoving Sonny's chest causing him to fall back on his heels.

"What?"

"You're kidding me, right?"

"No, really, that's my job."

"You son-of-a-bitch, you had me going!" exclaimed the exuberant newswoman while shoving his chest once more. "I bet you're the executioner, right?"

"No! No, I'm not the executioner," replied Sonny. "I just cuff-up the prisoner and walk him to his impending doom. I don't even strap him into the chair. Two other officers do that."

"But you are part of the execution crew, right?"

"In actuality, I'm just working on X-row temporarily," admitted the young sergeant.

"What exactly is your job here, Mr. Rafferty, if indeed that is your name? What kind of imposter are you?"

"Oh, I'm not an imposter. Technically, I work on the emergency squad. On the "E" squad we do cell extractions and search for contraband, and check for any signs of inmate dissension. I'm working X-row now because I'm barred from the prison's general population."

"Why is that?"

"I've got a bounty on my head."

"Wait, I don't understand," said the puzzled reporter.

"Recently I discovered 25 bags of reefer hidden in a cell, ready for distribution. The would-be recipients didn't care for that. Neither did the dealer. They all belonged to the Disciples gang. I also found a cache of shanks and a zip-gun in the rec. yard that apparently belonged to the Aryan Nation. Those skinheads are still pissed about that. Then I stumbled across a lead pipe barely sticking out of the ground, and found it filled with black tar heroine. The Latin Kings frowned on that, so they all put a bounty on my head of $10,000 to have me killed."

"I don't get it. Where do these people get this stuff?"

"They get most of the contraband from the guards themselves. Very little comes in by way of visitors. We make sure of that. They make their own weapons from various items that are used in the prison compound."

Samantha was becoming awed by the sergeant, and he sensed it.

"I've got many more stories that I could tell you about, Samantha. Only, I don't have the time, so why don't we meet at the Polka Dot pub on Chicago Street, at say, about one o'clock? It could only benefit your reporting."

The cunning redhead foxily shifted her smiling eyes to the side and peered up at Sonny. "Say, Sergeant, if you get me into the execution room I'll meet you at the Polka Dot tonight."

"Oh, I can't do that," said Sonny. "That room will be filled with relatives of Gibbons and the victims, along with a clergyman and a few chosen reporters."

"It might behoove you to consider my offer because after I redact my report and call it into the Times, it would make for an opportune time for us to get to know each other a little better, if you know what I mean," she said through her sly smile. "I'll be back."

Samantha coolly climbed into her mustang and drove to the parking lot where the protesters were gathered.

While Samantha conducted her interviews she couldn't help but look over her shoulder at the young officer pacing back and forth, pondering her offer. She liked his cleverness. She must have interested him, for he had kept up with her in their verbal warfare, and defended himself well against her offensive tirade when she first arrived. But you can't outfox a fox, she thought confidently. She fed him the hook, line and sinker with her stoic banter, and then reeled him in with her submissive behavior. Should I let him off the hook or should I fry him in the pan and eat him, joked Samantha to herself. Meeting Sonny at that little pub down the street would put me in a precarious situation, she thought. Kinda like sleeping with the enemy. But he seemed so damn handsome and sweet, and I suspect under that gruff exterior, maybe a little innocent.

When the young reporter appeared at the front gate, Sonny opened it, and in grand style, doffed his cap and took a sweeping bow.

"Well, my ladyship of Vasser, may I have the privilege of meeting with you again?"

"I shan't have the time," she feigned.

"But come now, your ladyship. You are the Vasser Queen, and I, of a princely nature, seek your company."

"Let's not quibble, gatekeeper. I must be on my way."

"Aw, come on!" begged Sonny, "you have lambasted me, ridiculed me, and pretty much have eviscerated me from the seeds of my family. I am weakened by your beauty. Can't you see? You're like a queen bee. I can't compete. You win this round, give me another chance."

"Why should I? If I am the queen bee then I can have anyone I want," she said with a false arrogance.

"Yes, but I can get you an interview with the man that's next on the execution list," he said shrewdly.

"Who may that be?" she asked with interest.

"Van Rochelle, the college campus serial killer. He would be a great interview on the subject of the death penalty."

"And when would this interview take place?"

"In a couple of days," he smiled.

"How are you going to pull this off?"

"A friend owes me a favor, plus it'll cost me a little money."

"Does everything in this place have a price tag on it?"

"Pretty much so; it's not much different than the outside world."

"So, what's in this for you?"

"I'll have a chance to see you again," he muttered.

"Well, I'm flattered, I think. All right then, Sergeant, I'll meet you at one o'clock at the Polka Dot on Chicago St."

Sonny shook his head in wonderment as the pretty redhead disappeared into the compound, all-the-while smiling to himself loudly. All I had to do was to beg and make an ass out of myself, he mused . . . She's worth it.

Chapter Six

The Polka Dot

The Polka Dot was a little tavern, a basement pub to be exact. It was Sonny's favorite place to unwind. Retiring to the pub was so much more relaxing than the prison scene. Sonny knew that only too well. When he started at the prison after serving two years in Vietnam, he spent many a night making life adjustments while sitting at the end of the bar with Ol' Pete and a bottle of beer.

"Hey, Pete, what's happening?"

"Hey, Sonny Boy, how ya doing?" said the squat bartender.

"I'm just fine, Pete, and you?"

"I'm working my ass off. We had a big crowd tonight, with the protesters and all. But it's good for business."

"Yeah, I suspect so."

"What'll ya have, Sonny, the same as usual?"

"You got it, Pete, a Blatz and a glass; a clean glass."

Pete was a short fellow but stocky, with Popeye arms and a shaved head. Pete liked to amuse his customers with his impersonations of Popeye, and of Curly of the Three Stooges. Sonny liked Pete a lot because Pete always picked him up when his spirits were low.

Pete slid the opened bottle and empty glass towards Sonny. "So you gave ol' Sparky a workout tonight eh?"

"Yeah, we fried Gibbons tonight."

"I say good riddance to bad rubbish. You know, these people came in here tonight blubbering about the inhumanity of it all. If only they could've seen how the victims had died. Heck, Gibbons had been on death row for twelve years. His victims are all but forgotten. If you ask me, that jerk lived twelve years too long."

"I agree, Pete, but hey, he finally got his just rewards in the end. Besides, he was good for business tonight."

"Yeah, but all of his friends here drink mostly wine. Hell, I ran out three hours ago. Had to send Greta to Al's Thrifty-Mart to get some more."

"Ah yeah, the horrors of doing business," said Sonny in a tease.

"It's a rough life, kid, but somebody's got to hang their big belly behind this bar. It may as well be mine."

"Hey, Pete, I'm meeting a girl here tonight. Do you think she and I could hang around after you close?"

"Sure, kid, no problem; just lock up when you leave. So, Sonny boy's got a girl eh? Where did you meet her?"

"She's a newspaper reporter from Indianapolis."

"Oh geez, another limp-wristed liberal dame," grumbled Pete.

Sonny snickered at his barroom buddy, as he viewed Pete's philosophical tirades as quite comical.

"What's she look, like?"

"She's real tall, about five-ten, slim—real slim, with long, radiant hair that seemed to have a red glaze to it when the sun shone upon it."

"So, you say that you met her today?"

"Yeah, just a few hours ago," he sighed.

"I hate to break this to you, Sonny boy, but the sun ain't shined at all today."

"Oh well, it seemed like it did, anyway."

"Tell me, kid, what kind of a rack did she have? I like a woman with a nice rack."

"I didn't notice, Pete. I was impressed with her beautiful hair and with those piercing green eyes of hers. They seemed to stare right through me."

"Oh God, she's got you!" exclaimed Pete.

"What do you mean she's got me?"

"You're heart struck, boy. She's pulled on your heartstrings."

"So, what does all that mean, Pete?"

"I mean that you're in love with her, kid, I can see that glaze over your eyes," kidded Pete. "And with a limp-wristed liberal dame at that," he added while shaking his head.

"Oh, it's not like that at all, Pete. I've got her eating out of my hand already," assured Sonny.

"Oh yeah, I bet she doesn't wear any panties."

"I wouldn't know, Pete, I've only known her for a few hours," said Sonny, slightly embarrassed.

"What I mean, Sonny boy, is that it sounds like whomever ends up with her will find that she wears the pants in the family which means the guy is going to wear the panties, if you get my drift," said Pete.

"That won't happen to me," assured the young officer.

"I've got to go, kid. My fans are calling me from the other end of the bar."

With the last vestiges of Willie Nelson's "Nightlife" leaving the jukebox, and a half dozen empty Blatz bottles staring at him, the forlorn sergeant began to think that his young collegian beauty had stood him up.

Suddenly, Sonny felt warm air grace the back of his neck, which resonated into a whisper, "Of all the juke joints in all the towns in this mixed-up world, I happen upon the one that finds you in it." Her redolence was even stronger than the blue, stale cigarette smoke that hung in the air.

"Highpockets!" exclaimed Sonny as he jumped up from the stool to give her a hug. "I thought you weren't coming!"

"I was wondering myself. I had a couple of unplanned interviews and a personal tour from your captain."

"So, what do you think of our facility?"

"I think I need a drink, that's what I think."

"Hey, Pete; here she is," boasted Sonny of his prize.

"Boy, you are a tall drink of water aren't you? And easy on the eyes too, I might add," said Pete.

"Well, thank you, Pete, that's very nice of you," said Samantha.

"I should thank *you* for showing up, because this guy's been sittin' in this corner pining all night over you."

"Hey, Pete, the lady wants a drink," said Sonny loudly.

"Oh yes, forgive me for my manners, Miss, for women of your stature rarely grace these premises. What can I get for you, my dear?"

"I'll have a beer like Sonny has."

Pete looked at Sonny and Sonny at him. Pete shrugged his shoulders while Sonny nodded his head with an I-told-you-so look.

"One Blatz for the lady," declared Pete.

"Yeah, and make sure you bring her a clean glass," chided Sonny.

"Clean glass, clean glass, can you believe this guy?" said Pete, talking directly to Samantha. "One time, mind you; one time in three years he gets a glass of beer with a cockroach floating in it and he won't let me live it down. I keep telling him there ain't no cockroaches in here, that it must have fallen off his shoulder!"

Samantha laughed heartily as a smiling Sonny Rafferty accepted his chastisement in good humor.

While retrieving the beers, the loquacious barkeep added, "But youth must be served, so I put up with this lunk. He does leave me a tip at the end of the day, which is more than I can say for most of these bums in here," he said in a resonating voice which garnered mild protests from the small collection of lethargic club regulars that were still there.

Sonny led Samantha to a little table in a darkened corner of the room.

"I would like to apologize for the condition of this place tonight. It's usually a lot cleaner, and the people a bit more lively, but it's closing time, and the place was packed with customers today that came for the execution."

"Don't apologize," said Samantha. "I like it here. This place has ambience."

"Ambience, oh, you mean that hazy blue smoke that's burning your eyes, and that drunk with his head lying on the table next to us snoring to the tune of "Brahm's Lullaby?"

"No, silly, you know what I mean. It's kinda cozy," she said while resting her head on his shoulder. "Especially after a day like I've had today."

"You, how about me?" said Sonny.

"Aw come on, I wasn't that rough on you today was I, Sergeant?"

"I will say this. Your guile and pertinacity make you the epitome of a news reporter," he replied.

"Why thank you, I'll consider that as a compliment."

"Can I have my balls and my spine back now?"

They both laughed heartily. As they laughed Sonny placed his hand on hers. He trained his eyes to her eyes as their laughter moderated into a soft silence. "I'd like to say that you are so breathtakingly beautiful .

. . I mean that sincerely," said Sonny.

He lowered his face toward hers. Their noses touched. She could feel his warm breath against her soft lips. Then suddenly, she turned her face from his.

"Have you been looking down my blouse again, Sergeant?" kidded the redhead.

"What? . . . How did you know about that?" blushed the sergeant.

"Oh it's a trait in most men and a ploy by most women, especially when there's something they want from the man."

"Why, you little vixen!" said Sonny.

"Pretty clever aren't I," she snickered.

"Yes you are. I will say that. You can add embarrassment to the long list of items that you have shackled me with this evening."

As Samantha and Sonny prattled on about the day's events, the Polka Dot patrons slowly departed and went their own separate ways into the night.

"Last call!" shouted Pete as he was cleaning up the bar. "Do you kids want another drink?"

"Sure, Pete, two more of the same," shouted back Sonny, a little less vociferous than his barkeeper friend.

"Why, soitenly, nyuck-nyuck-nyuck-nyuck!"

"Pete, you are in rare form tonight," said the young sergeant.

Samantha smiled in awe of Pete's mimicking of the outlandish Stooge. "He's pretty good, Sonny."

"He's goofy if you ask me."

Pete delivered the beers and then proceeded to remove Charlie, his inebriated friend, from the table next to where Sonny and Samantha sat.

"Do you need some help with him?" offered Sonny.

"Nah, I'm just going to walk Charlie home. He lives just two blocks down the street. I can use the fresh air and exercise," he joked. "Make sure you turn all the inside lights off when you lock up, Sonny boy."

"Okay, and leave the outside light on, right?"

"Yeah, you know the procedure, kid."

As Pete trudged by Samantha with Charlie dangling by his side he looked straight at her, and in his best gravel voice added, "Nice meeting you Miss Oleeve Oil, yuk-yuk-yuk-yuk-yuk."

Samantha nodded obligingly, and smiled to the point of laughter as the two "amigos" lumbered up the stairs and out the front door together. She turned to Sonny and declared, "I like your friend. He really is fun."

"I think he's nuts," quipped Sonny.

"He might be a little nuts but he is so exhilarating. You have to admit that."

"Yeah, he's quite a fella," agreed Sonny. "Do you want to know what he said when I first told him about you?"

"Yeah, what was his response?"

"He said 'tell me kid, what kind of a rack does she have? I like a woman with a nice rack."

"Do you mean?" (Samantha pointed toward her chest innocently).

"That's right," quipped Sonny.

"So, what did you tell him?"

"I told him that I didn't notice your chest because I was so enamored with your eyes, and your hair and face."

"Bullshit!" teased Samantha while hammering his ribs with her elbow.

"No bullshit," declared Sonny, wincing from the playful but pointed blows of her bent arm. "I really told him that."

"Come on, you guys are all alike. When you notice a girl, the first things you look at are her boobs."

"That's not true. I am a man of discretion when it comes to the women that I meet. Anyway, the first thing that I noticed about you was that high-rise ass of yours waving at me from that red Mustang."

Samantha mused for a moment, leaving Sonny bogged down in his own quagmire. "Okay, now let me get this straight. You think that I'm beautiful but . . . my tits are too small, right?" she said with a smirk.

"No, no, that's not what I meant at all," said Sonny defensively. "I think that you are aesthetically perfect."

"Oh, okay, that answer will suffice for now, Officer," she said smugly.

Sonny let out a sigh of relief.

"Sonny, did you notice that Pete never carded me? Why is that, I wonder?"

"Because of me, probably," he replied.

"Oh yeah, you've got connections with him like you have over at the prison, eh?' she said tongue-in-cheek.

"No, it's not that." This goes back a few years," he said somberly.

Samantha sensed the gaiety in Sonny turning to melancholy. She eased her red locks gently into the hard chest of the young sergeant. "Can ya tell me about it, Sonny?" she whispered with her soft eyes begging his.

Sonny slowly swallowed the last of his malt beverage and caressed the soft locks of the lady lying up against his chest. "I was in my first tour of duty in Vietnam—"

"Vietnam?" quizzed the stunned reporter, snapping her head up.

"No, I am not a baby killer," said Sonny in quiet defense. Actually, I was in the Military Police. I didn't get into any combat situations until the end of the war when we were trying to get everyone to hell out of the country."

"I know you are not a killer," Samantha whispered while softly placing her head back into Sonny's warm chest.

"Anyway," continued Sonny, "I was called back home because my mother had died. I was devastated. The one person that really loved me, believed in me, no matter what I did, was gone. Oh, those words that I wish I'd said. They haunt me to this day."

"She sounds like she was a wonderful lady." said Samantha, feeling his sorrow.

"We buried my mother, then, while searching for answers that couldn't be found, I happened upon this little pub. It was a quaint little place, almost hidden except for the neon sign hanging outside. I went inside and sat down at the bar and ordered a beer. I sucked that beer down as fast as I could. At that point in time I didn't care if I lived or died. I just wanted to ease my pain. So I ordered another. This time, the little surly bartender watched me with an evil eye. I sucked that beer down. The barkeep then came up to me and asked, 'What's your name, kid?' I had a nameplate on the dress uniform that I was wearing, but I guess he wanted to know my first name too. So I told him, 'Sonny Rafferty, Sir.' And he said, 'Well, Sonny boy, how old are you?' I got into his face and said 'I'm 19 goddamn it! What are you going to do about it, send me to Nam?' I usually don't use the Lord's name in vain, but I figured he had let me down too."

"So what happened next?" asked Samantha.

"He got right back into my face with a look of rage. Suddenly, I could see tears well up in his eyes. He calmly said, 'No son, I just want to have a drink with you.' Pete drank beer with me the rest of the night. I woke up the next morning on his couch in his apartment above the tavern. And boy, I could smell the bacon and eggs frying, and the aroma of fresh brewed coffee. Ol' Pete's wife was a good cook. She accepted me just as Pete did. After a hearty breakfast, Pete drove me down to the bus depot and sent me packin' back to Vietnam. I signed up for a second tour because I stupidly thought I could make a difference over there, since I had failed my mother back here. It wasn't until later on that I found out why Pete didn't throw me out on my ear that night. Why he took to me the way he did."

"Why was that?" asked Samantha, her curiosity stoked.

"His son was a fighter pilot and had been shot down over Hanoi in 1967. He was an M.I.A. then, and still is to this day. But Pete keeps smiling, keeps joking, as if his son is going to walk through that door any day now."

"Do you mean they never found his son's remains?"

"Nope," said Sonny.

"So what happened to the rest of your family?"

"By the time I returned from my second tour, Dad had sold the house to the National Lakeshore and skipped on back to Tennessee, and eventually remarried. My sisters had already married and went their separate ways."

"Do you ever see your dad anymore?"

"Oh yes, we visit each other every so often. He's doing fine. But, Pete, he was there for me. He believed in me, a young punk who didn't give a shit about life, when his very own son was lying somewhere in the jungles of Vietnam, and he not knowing whether his boy was dead or alive."

Sad tears slid down Samantha's cheeks. Both she and Sonny sat there several minutes staring into space, feeling each other's warmth, interconnecting their love with one another.

With both hands, Samantha wiped the tears from her eyes. "Look what you did now you big ape. You made me cry."

"You look pretty when you cry."

"But I'm sad when I cry."

"Then you're pretty when you're sad. Besides, don't cry over me, or

Pete. The way I look at it is that a little hardship goes a long way towards a good friendship."

"You seem to have all the right answers, you smooth talker you. It's getting late, and I've got classes in the morning. I need to go, big guy."

"Say, what day do you want me to set up your interview with Rochelle?"

"Oh, don't bother. Everything's been taken care of."

"How's that?" asked Sonny.

"Captain Stover set me up for Sunday. He said that Sunday would be best since it's visitation day anyway."

"How did you pull that off?" asked the perturbed young sergeant. "The Captain doesn't do anything for nothing."

"He was quite a gentleman about it too. He offered to take me to lunch afterwards, and of course I accepted."

"He's 38 years old, you know!"

"I know," answered Samantha nonchalantly.

"He has a steady girlfriend, you know."

"So?"

"So he's had two kids by her."

"He must be a healthy male then," she teased.

"Okay, have it your way."

"I plan on it."

"I will say one thing about you, Highpockets. You are a lesson in futility. You are a deviant, you know that don't you?" he said while turning off the lights.

"You are a deviant, you know that don't you?" mocked the animated reporter while following the young officer through the pub.

Sonny tried to muster up some disgust on his face, but as he turned and stared into those glittering green eyes of the redheaded prankster, his disgust melted into a mild look of frustration at best. "You know, Samantha—"

"My friends call me Sam," she said in a breathy tone.

"You know, Sam, in spite of all your shenanigans you still drive me crazy."

"Who, me?" she shrugged innocently.

"Yeah you; you're kicky. You've got panache, and I like that. I must be crazy, but let's make it you and me, kid. How about it; another date?

I'll take you somewhere special."

"I don't know. I'm pretty busy with the newspaper, and school and all. My career comes before playing with boys."

"That's okay," agreed Sonny, "just include me in there somewhere."

"Are you going to walk me back to my car?"

"I could, but mine is parked here behind the Polka Dot. I can drive you."

Samantha's mischievous eyes stole Sonny's stare, and with her sly smile she uttered softly, "Close your eyes, Sonny. Close your eyes. Keep your hands at your sides," she added.

Sonny did as she said. He then felt her warm breath on his face. Then the two fleshy folds of her lips softly grazed his, and then gently pressed against them. It was all he could do to keep his arms at his sides. It then seemed that she slumped down some, but Sonny followed, for her luscious lips had been tantalizing him all evening.

Then suddenly, she broke contact. He opened his eyes.

"Here," she snapped while shoving a pair of three inch clogs into his hands. While the unsuspecting officer held tight to the shoes, it became apparent that Samantha was up to her chicanery once again as she snatched the officer's cap from his head and scurried down the street barefoot, laughing playfully.

"You stole my cap you little imp!" cried Sonny, scampering after her. After sprinting about three blocks, and with his lungs desperately gasping for air, Sonny thought, how in the world does that girl run so fast? Here he was, out of uniform, with a woman's shoe in each hand, running like a madman down the streets of Michigan City at 3:30 in the morning; chasing an antelope of sorts, for there is no woman that could possibly run that fast. What would the captain think? As he chased the fleet-footed reporter he noticed that she passed up a side gate that led to the parking lot. That's a break for me, he thought. He opened the gate and the red Mustang suddenly appeared in his sights. As he closed in on the Mustang, Samantha hurdled the fence and they both collided against the red sports car.

"I beat you!" declared the heavily panting redhead.

"The hell you did," said Sonny breathlessly. The frolicsome couple romped and bantered about like a couple of school chums until Samantha finally collapsed against Sonny's chest from sheer exhaustion.

"I could have beaten ya if you hadn't tricked me and gotten that head-start," said Sonny, perspiration dripping from off his nose.

"Not on your best day," came back the muffled reply. "I was a track star in high school."

"I can tell. Do you know what you look like when you run?"

Samantha looked up, "I can't wait to find out. What do I look like?"

"You remind me of an Impala."

"A car?" she said with a slanted look.

"No, silly, an Impala is an antelope that's fast as the wind and bounds through the plains with such grace and ease, and it is endowed with beautiful red fur that glistens in the sun, like your hair glistens in the night's light. It reminds me of you, only it has horns, but doesn't really use them like you do yours," he joked.

Samantha smiled lovingly into Sonny's blue eyes, for she was through bantering with her young counterpart. Sonny was the first person to boast of her gracefulness. He had been flirting with her all day and had now finally won over the young collegian's heart. "Darling, you've held my heart captive since my eyes first met yours," she said. She put her arms around his neck and pulled herself up to his face and kissed him hard. She could smell his sweat, a musky smell of wilderness that brought on an overwhelming desire to taste his sex. With her face flushed, she feverishly licked his skin; his neck, his ears and his face. She kissed him again, deep, a soul kiss, and simultaneously drew her legs up around him while he braced against her car. The softness between Samantha's thighs ground hard against his groin.

She had never realized this lascivious nature in herself until now. The heat of passion consumed her violently from within while her mouth ravenously searched deeply into Sonny's, as if trying to touch his soul.

With a free hand Samantha slipped the buttons open on her silk blouse to allow Sonny free access to roam his hands incessantly over once forbidden territory that now ached for his touch. Sonny caressed her hardened jewels and softly squeezed the swelled mounds that supported them.

Suddenly, her crescendo of lust culminated into a climax that emitted a surge of warmth from within the soft folds of her womanhood. With a loud shriek, she folded up into Sonny's arms.

Samantha slowly but shakily came to her senses. "I can't do this, Sonny. Let me go. Let me go! Not here, not now," said the vexed young journalist

"Okay," Sonny said. "I'm sorry, Sam, I just thought—"

"You just thought what? That I was easy," she said angrily.

"No, that's not it at all, Sam," Sonny pleaded. "You were just showing your feelings for me like I have for you."

"It can't be this way, Sonny. I've got my career to think about, and the newspaper. I have people depending on me. I can't ruin all of that over some whim that I have."

Sonny grabbed her arms, "You listen to me! I've waited too long for you to come along. Don't run away from your feelings, Sam. Don't abandon me, please! Just think it over, will you?"

Perplexed, Samantha turned away and slowly climbed into her car. "I've got some thinking to do", she mumbled. "So long Sonny." Sonny watched the red Mustang disappear into the night.

He shook his head in disbelief while picking Samantha's shoes up off the pavement, wondering about how many men in this crazy world were head-over heels in love with a girl that runs barefoot through the city streets and drives a hot red Mustang the same way. Though he didn't feel like it, he had to smile at that thought.

As Samantha headed back to her dorm in Valparaiso she pondered about the consequences of her actions that evening. Why did I leave so abruptly? Will Sonny want to see me again? He doesn't even have my phone number. Is my career so important that my life must be devoid of love? Suddenly, loneliness grabbed at her throat. She sobbed, for she had broken her own heart, and maybe his.

Meanwhile, Sonny walked slowly back towards his car, trying to absorb the happenings of that evening. One thing that he knew for sure, he must see her again. For she, in his eyes, was the end of the rainbow.

As Sonny neared the Polka Dot a lit cigarette appeared through the opening of the blinds in a room atop the pub. The eyes of Pete Sawatski spotted the blue uniform of the young officer approaching.

"Mother, Mother, wake up, Danny's come home!" he said excitedly.

"No, dear, that's not Danny, that's probably Sonny Boy again," said Martha.

"But Mother, he has his dress blue uniform on," he pleaded.

"Sonny wears dress blues too, dear. Come to bed now. Danny will come home soon, dear. Come get some rest."

Pete crawled into bed and buried his tears into his pillow as Martha softly stroked his smooth round head.

Chapter Seven

Van Rochelle

She walked stately into the room with an air of confidence about her, along with a professional suavity. But as the steel door clang shut, the cold, concrete blocks of gray solitude chilled the spirit of the young journalist.

Van Rochelle's dark, piercing eyes searched the young female figure just as an eagle would scour the landscape so as to discover, seize, and capture its delicate prey, and then frighten it into submission before devouring it. He had done this on many occasions, at least seven times previous, according to court documents. Only this time, his prey would escape her impending doom, but not before experiencing the mental rape by the crazed genius's psyche that would leave her forever feeling violated.

"Hello, I'm Samantha Taylor from the Indianapolis Times newspaper, and I'm here to interview you on the subject of the death penalty if. . . if that's okay with you?" she said nervously while glancing back over her shoulder to make sure the guard's face was showing through the small window of the steel door.

"It's all irrelevant," he said smugly.

"It's, it's what? I don't understand?"

"Oh, I'm sorry, I apologize. I'm Van Rochelle and I'm innocent," he said with a touch of sarcasm.

"Innocent of what?" she asked.

"I'm Innocent of the heinous crimes that I've been incarcerated for. And by the way, don't be afraid to look at me, my dear, for I won't harm you. I would greet you properly as a true gentleman would greet a young lady of your stature, but these barbarous bullies have me shackled as if I was going to fly away to heaven . . . or hell. I apologize for their rude behavior for I would so like to softly greet your lovely hand with a kiss."

Feeling less inhibited, Samantha relaxed with a trusting smile. Van Rochelle was innocent looking enough. Smallish in size, he was a momma's boy with boyish good looks and a child-like face, and had long, wavy to curly hair. Samantha was drawn in by his soft brown eyes that ached for a woman's attention, a vast change of demeanor from a few minutes earlier. He didn't quite fit the mold of a serial killer's profile.

"So come, my nymph-like creature, come sit by my table. Let's chat," he said jauntily.

Samantha sat across the boy-like serial killer with her back toward the door. "So, Mr. Rochelle, what do you consider irrelevant about my question?"

Rochelle was fixated by Samantha's dark emerald eyes and puffy red lips."You know, Samantha, you have already charmed me with your beauty. I think you might feel sensually attracted to me, also."

"I think not," she abruptly replied."

And you seem so young and chastely," he added while ignoring her reply. "You must be the Vernal Equinox."

"No, but I appreciate your concern," she said lightheartedly.

"If you were a ship you would be deemed seaworthy to the highest degree. And with your flaming tresses and soft full lips, I picture you as a siren from the depths of the sea whose mellifluent singing lures unsuspecting sailors to their deaths."

"I feel flattered, Mr. Rochelle, but I must move forward with my questioning."

"Call me Van. Rochelle is just too French."

"Okay, Van. Now can we go on?"

Rochelle sat back and clasped his hands together.

"Yes, my lovely, carry on."

"So, Van, why do you consider your views on the death penalty irrelevant?"

"It doesn't matter what I think about the death penalty. They're going to murder me anyway."

"But you were found guilty by a jury of your peers."

"What did that jury really know about me and what did they know about the alleged victims, except that they weren't alive?"

"Are you trying to tell me that you didn't murder those women?" asked Samantha.

"That's right, Sam. May I call you Sam?"

"Only my friends call me Sam."

"Well, Samantha, I certainly hope by interview's end I will have earned your respect *and* your friendship."

"We'll see," said Samantha, cautiously.

"Actually, I believe that five of those girls died by accident."

"By accident?"

"Yes, we engaged in some 'rough sex'."

"What's rough sex?" she asked curiously.

"It's when a couple is so 'in sync' when making love to one another that they cross over their sexual boundaries mixing pleasure and pain. It takes you to new heights in lovemaking. It's like a sexual euphoria, if you will."

"What about the other two girls?"

"They seemed to have a death wish," he said shiftily.

"Why should I believe you?" asked Samantha, curious for his reaction.

"Maybe you shouldn't. We are all illusionists, you know. Trying to be something that we are not, and hiding what we are," he answered tersely. "Didn't anyone ever teach you that there is just a thin gray line between right and wrong, lust and love, genius and crazy; and yes, pain and pleasure? Did you know that good causes evil and evil good? Think about it, Sam. Anytime you clean up a mess in one place you create another elsewhere. It's a continuing cycle of life. There is no utopia, Samantha, no perfect society, nor perfect minds, for that matter. Not here, not on earth. We don't reach our Shangri-La until after we die. You can read about it. It's in the Bible."

"I read the Bible," whispered Samantha in quiet defense.

The provocative sociopath continued with his vexing riddles, "Are we nothing more than lost souls marking time, waiting for death, waiting for our next life? I just may have helped those women reach their goals, their peaks. Eternal life, isn't that it? Isn't that what we all crave?" asked the cunning Frenchman. "It is appointed for man once to die. We are not of this world, and I don't think that we can get out of this world alive. Do you my lovely?"

"I guess not," answered the bedeviled reporter.

"I've got the answers, but look at me. They label me as an iconoclast. I've been disenfranchised from society."

Rochelle's web of deceit was attractive to the young journalist. He had her curiosity stoked. Her mind was now becoming a bit muddled by the inauspicious prisoner's quaint views on life and death. But she was determined to stay the course though her interests were inadvertently taking a turn towards the life of the serial killer instead of the death penalty.

"Tell me, Van, why did these girls gravitate toward you?"

"I'll tell you, my dear. I'm a Gentry, as was my mother and my father. I am a suave sophisticate, and I inherited my mother's good physical features, and consequently became a ladies man. I excelled scholastically, and pretty much became a career college student. All of my lovelies were nearly a decade younger than I at the time. I guess they saw me as a professor type, a mentor of sorts, especially in the art of sensual lovemaking. But do you know what really attracted these lovelies to me?"

Samantha shook her head negatively as her prying eyes begged the answer.

"I'm good at keeping secrets."

With a look of mild surprise she asked, "Keeping secrets?"

"Keeping secrets is one of my most valuable assets. My mother taught me how to keep a secret, and she taught me how to love women. I became a disciple of my mother. My father, he was loud and boisterous, and I didn't like that. My mother, on the other hand, was soft and nurturing. I was pampered by my mother. My father hated me for that, I believe. Yeah, keeping secrets is why those young lovelies confided in me. Do you keep secrets, Sam?"

"Why yes, I guess . . . sometimes."

"Do you know that I have a secret about you?"

"Now, how would you know anything about me? You just met me."

"Oh, I know all about you, Samantha Taylor."

"Tell me more."

"Can you keep a secret?" teased the sinister killer.

"Tell me more," she yearned.

"Well, here goes. You are Samantha Lee Ann Taylor, whose daddy is Big John Taylor, the owner of an Indianapolis newspaper. You came here to see us last Monday night to get the 'skinny' on the Gibbons execution. You ran into a Sonny Rafferty with whom you spent the early morning at the Polka Dot."

"That Sonny Rafferty!" exclaimed the young reporter.

"Don't blame Sonny, he's my friend. He comes to me for all his advice on romance. Besides, I believe that he may be in love with you. Why should you be miffed at Sonny? You dumped him and are going out with the captain today."

Samantha started to speak, but Rochelle shushed her as he raised his finger to his lips.

"Don't ask how I know. It's a secret," he whispered loudly. "Look, Samantha, I know secrets about you that Sonny doesn't even know about; things that you don't even know about yourself. I'll tell you what. If you confide in me I'll confide in you. Is that a deal?"

"That's a deal," agreed Samantha with interest.

"You're going to have to scoot back from the table, my dear."

Samantha hesitated.

"I must see you, all of you. You must trust me, my darling," said Rochelle with excitement in his eyes.

Samantha nervously checked over her shoulder for the guard's face, as if seeking his approval.

"You needn't look for the guard. He's worshiping the large girth that's hanging over his belt. He goes by the name of Jumbo McCain. I detest that fat indolent slob. Don't you just hate people like that, Sam?"

Samantha didn't answer, but through her trepidation she eased the chair back from the table as to Rochelle's request. Van scrutinized the unsuspecting reporter from her crimson top to her long silky legs. With a look as if in a quandary, Rochelle rested his chin in his hand.

"What is it?" asked Samantha with a nervous laugh. She felt uncomfortable being put on display like that, as if being placed on a pedestal.

"You are not of voting age yet, are you?" asked Rochelle smugly.

"I don't know what that has to do with anything."

"Oh, you don't do you? You ask permission to talk with me about the death penalty because I'm a professional criminal, yet you're not much more than a schoolgirl. You're just a rookie."

"I have qualifications!" she bristled.

"You may think that you have the qualifications, but where's your experience?"

"I have none," she said, turning her eyes away.

"Look, I'm not trying to chastise you, my lovely, but I may expose some things about you that may make you feel uncomfortable with yourself. You seem very much oppressed about something. I think I know what it might be. That's my main secret that I have about you, and I believe that I can help."

Samantha felt bemused by Rochelle's riddles, but was drawn in by his cool confidence. "Do you wish to expound upon that or are you going to keep me guessing?"

Rochelle smiled cunningly. "I woke up this morning feeling good, knowing that I was to be interviewed by a journalist. I've been interviewed many times since I've been here, and I relish every minute of it, Sam. I seize upon these moments to tell my story. I know that I will still be executed, but at least I will get my story out. So today, into my life walks this fresh, young, intrinsic beauty of serendipitous nature, and I'm supposed to expose my soul to her? Why, you still have your mother's milk dripping from your chin, and I can see that you have just recently sprouted your own breasts. You have on a pin-striped business suit that you think will make you look older, and except for the short skirt, makes you look a little foolish looking. A young woman like you could lose her soul in a house of reprobates such as this."

Blood rushed freely into Samantha's already flushed cheeks as Rochelle entered her fragile zone. Her defenses suddenly broke down, and tears welled in her eyes.

"You may be on a mission for your father's newspaper, or even for a school project, and you may become a great journalist someday, I don't know, but I do know that's not your real quest in life, Samantha."

The air hung thick with Rochelle's dramatics and Samantha was stifled by it as the insolent murderer captured her mind.

"You're suppressing your desires, Samantha. You must expose your sensuality."

"I can't," she admitted remorsefully. "I don't know how."

"Let me help you," said Rochelle. "Look, you're a tall girl. I bet you were kinda gangly looking in high school, and with your red hair, probably not very popular. Am I right?"

"I had friends."

"Girlfriends, but not boyfriends, right?"

She shook her head as she thought back. "Right"

"You probably thought of yourself as an ugly duckling."

Tears slid down Samantha's florid cheeks.

"You've had a frustrated sex life up till now, haven't you, Samantha?"

No answer.

"Look, I'm a much traveled man on the rigors of life. I've been there. Tell me your worst sexual experience that you've had with a guy. Be honest with me now."

"I . . . I can't . . . Why must you ask this of me?"

"Because I can help you, Samantha; I can take your young soul out of bondage and help you become the person you want to be. Tell me, Samantha . . . of your worst sexual experience."

"It . . . It was when I jerked off Johnny Newman in a movie theatre so that he would take me to the senior prom." she sadly admitted.

"It was even worse than that, wasn't it?"

Samantha didn't answer.

"Did he take you?"

"Yes, but he soon left the prom to go with his friends. I had to call my parents to bring me home."

"And the next day they all made fun of you, didn't they?"

"Yes . . . I just wanted to fit in, that's all."

"That was cruel. Was there any other experiences that stick out in your mind?"

"No, just the usual groping and teasing," she replied.

"If it helps you, Sam, I'm no respecter of men either. They are a cruel animal at times. You must forgive the iniquities of the human race and only tell your secrets to your lovers. Now, I'm not going to ask if you're a virgin or not because it doesn't matter. I believe that if you are fresh in mind that you are fresh in body. I can help you, Samantha, but you must do exactly as I say. We haven't much time before 'fat boy' comes to retrieve you."

"Okay, Mr. Rochelle," she said submissively, "I'm ready."

"First of all, take that scarf, ascot, or whatever it is from around your neck. It's choking you. A woman's neck is one of her greatest pleasure points. Expose it."

Samantha tossed her neck scarf aside.

"Now, unbutton your suit coat and your blouse. The key word here is exposure. Exposing your sensual pleasure points will free you of your oppression."

Samantha looked back nervously at the door's small window.

"Don't worry," chided Rochelle, your back's to the door, he can't see what you're doing."

As Samantha quickly unbuttoned, Rochelle noticed the wild look in her eager eyes. She pulled open her blouse exposing her ripe, yearning breasts to the lecherous rapist; a most unlikely candidate one would have thought before this incursion.

"Very nice, my dear, your breasts are flawless. You are a young Aphrodite. You have your legs crossed in a most conservative way. That's not good. Uncross your legs."

Samantha did as he asked.

"Now, open them wide."

She now hesitated.

"Fear not, my lovely coquette. In spite of what they say, I do not bring young girls to their demise, I enlighten them. I liberate them. Let me liberate you, Samantha."

With a crazed look in her eyes the young reporter spread her legs wide, laying open a vastness that funneled back to her crevice that lay hidden behind a taut strip of thin azure silk stretching from atop her Venus mound.

"Perfect, my dear, I've noticed that you prefer silk stockings and garters over the generic panty-hose. Why is that, may I ask?" said the enamored Frenchman.

The heat of passion coursed through the redhead's veins. "Too confining," was her breathy reply.

"I call it style, my dear. You have style and grace, and are most statuesque. You are definitely high brow, top shelf."

"Do you want me to take them off?" she asked in quiet desperation.

"No, of course not, they add contrast to your unblemished ivory skin."

"I mean, do you want me to take my panties off?" she feverishly begged

"No, my dear, this is your quest, not mine. But as my eyes devour your beauty, my imagination runs wild seeking your sensual pleasure points, now barely hidden under your silk blouse, and behind the taut diaphanous covering that holds an un-cultivated field of silky red sprouts."

Samantha emitted a hissing sound as bazaar love steamed freely from between her thighs. She reached inside her blouse to tweak the pinkish protrusions that lay hungrily beneath the silky material.

"No, you mustn't, my dear."

"Why not?" she begged.

"No stimulation for gratification. Think of me as the lover of your dreams. Think of me as . . . Sonny Rafferty."

Samantha slowly squeezed her thighs together, closing her gap, and moaned softly while quietly capturing the tender rush of love.

"You see, my lovely, I have redeemed you of your past injustices."

Van's soporific voice had tranquilized the heavy lidded young redhead into a trance-like sexual slumber. Rochelle reveled in his triumph, in his conquest of the cub reporter, just as he did with the other young lovelies, only in a slightly different way. This time, he let his victim live. But his euphoria was short-lived with Jumbo McCain staring through the door window. Suddenly, the steel door unlatched, and the big oafish guard barged in.

"Well, if it isn't Porky Pig," Rochelle vociferated, hoping to startle Samantha out of her stupor. Samantha came to, and noticing the situation, bent over as to gather her belongings while buttoning her clothing.

"Do I smell Twinkie Breath? Are you eating on the job again?"

"Shut-up," shouted McCain. "I've come to get the lady. It's time for you to go, Miss," he said to Samantha.

Samantha stood up and faced the guard, her face still flushed but her dignity intact. She slowly followed the unsuspecting Jumbo to the door. As the portly correctional officer held open the door, Samantha, still mesmerized by her experience, turned to face Van. She opened her mouth to speak but Van interrupted.

"Remember, darling, it's about what you conceal, not what you reveal. It's about . . . I've got a secret."

Half satisfied, with her finger to her mouth in thought, she looked back into Van's soft brown eyes and asked, "How did you get caught?"

"I got tired of winning. Can you believe that?" he answered in his own astonishment.

"Van . . . if it was different, and we weren't in this place, would you have—"

"Killed you?" he said bluntly.

Samantha nodded, yes.

"No, my lovely, you were better than the rest."

Feeling somewhat relieved and pacified with Rochelle Samantha walked through the door only to be called back one more time by her platonic lover. She stuck her head back into the cold gray cell for one last remembrance of Rochelle. The demented killer stared at her, coldly, and raised her scarf up to his devious smile and uttered, "**We have a secret.**"

Chapter Eight

Tremont Inn

Samantha's body convulsed as she wretched violently trying to rid herself of the vile memories perpetrated on her by the lecherous, Van Rochelle, but bringing forth only the green bile that her liver produced. Her mind writhed in agony. She felt closed in as if a miasma was forming all around her.

Rochelle was right. She was too young and inexperienced to compete with someone of his nature. In a small sense she felt liberated by the treacherous sociopath. In a larger sense she felt violated by him. She wasn't Daddy's little girl anymore. Van saw to that. He gave her a mind explosion.

For years she had longed to mature physically from the gangly ugly duckling that she was, and when she reached maturity, was raped by the mind of a serial killer. What frightened her most was that she enjoyed it. She felt nothing like it before except when she was with Sonny. Sonny, she mused, he seems so far in the past now. If only I would have stuck with him.

Samantha splashed cold tap water on her face. It felt refreshing, revitalizing her some, but did not relieve her of her transgression. Why did I have to be so hoity-toity with Sonny, she thought. He was so nice and handsome, plus he introduced me to pleasures that I never before experienced.

The young reporter looked in the mirror. She didn't like what she saw. The face that stared back at her looked older, more shop-worn than the one she remembered.

"You idiot, you stupid bitch!" she rebuked. "If there was a slut farm you'd be the lead pig!"

Samantha splashed more cold water on her face before heading out the door of the visitor's washroom. She slipped out the door with her head down, hoping not to run into Captain Stover. All she wanted was to retreat back to her safety net, her dormitory at Valparaiso University, and not to emerge for a long, long time.

Oomph! The impact was jarring, causing her to drop her briefcase and purse. Just a horrible ending to a totally wretched morning, thought the young collegian as she looked up— into those deep blue eyes that she had longed for.

"Oh, Sonny!" she cried out.

"We've got to quit meeting like this," he said with a broad smile.

Samantha didn't answer at first, but instead, wrapped her arms around his neck and began smothering him with kisses. "Sonny, you must take me away from here. Take me far, far away from this place," she tearfully begged.

"Okay," said Sonny, noticing the urgency in her voice. "I'll pick up your things."

The big Olds roared down the highway with grace and ease. It was old but it was gold to the young sergeant, especially with the precious cargo that it was carrying.

Sonny was fascinated by Samantha's buoyancy as she chattered incessantly in animated jubilation at her gallant stallion for rescuing her from the depths of the dank prison. He savored the exuberant sounds of the blithe, red-haired chatterbox.

"Where are you taking me, big guy?" she asked.

"Where do you want to go?"

"Anywhere with you," she replied, her eyes glistening with appreciation.

"Are you hungry?"

"I could eat. Actually, I'm famished," she openly admitted.

"How would you like to go on a picnic?"

"That sounds great, Sonny, where at?"

"I know of this park in the woods"

"Wow! What a coincidence. First you come by just when Captain Stover was called home on an emergency, and now you're taking me on a picnic. How convenient. I feel like the prized pig," she jested. "You're a sly one, Sonny Rafferty, yes you are. You had this all planned out, didn't you?"

"Maybe I did, so what? All's fair in love and war."

"So what, you say! He's your boss. He could fire you."

"He won't fire me. Besides, he's got a steady girl and a couple of kids."

"Sonny, what interests you? What are your hobbies?" asked Samantha inquisitively.

Sonny thought for a moment. "I guess hanging out with Pete, seeing who can tell the biggest lies. And I like working out at the gym, you know, pumping iron and all that guy stuff."

"You have no girlfriend right now?"

"Nope, but I'm looking mighty hard," he said with a hearty smile.

"Well, look no further. I'll be your girl, you big lunk, if that's all right with you. Well, is it?"

"You'll have to give me a minute to think about it."

"Give you a minute! What do you mean, give me a minute, mister?"

"Well, you look like you're pretty high maintenance to me."

"You're damn right I'm high maintenance. It takes a lot to keep a woman like me happy. Are you up to the task, Sergeant?"

"In your case, I feel it incumbent upon me to accept your offer. That, and an apology for the shabby treatment that you have bestowed upon me in our brief beginnings," said Sonny.

"Apologize!" exclaimed Samantha, jumping up in the seat on her haunches.

"Okay, Okay! Maybe apologize is too strong a word. We can discuss that at a later date."

"Yes, at a much later date," quipped the redhead. With that, she wrapped her arms around Sonny's neck and smothered him with short kisses.

"Whoa, girl!" said Sonny nervously, while passing several deer along the parkway. "Didn't your daddy teach you anything about seat belts?"

"Daddy's not here now."

"It's just that I don't want to run over the park deer."

"What deer? I don't see any deer, and besides, I'm not driving," whispered Samantha while sliding her fingers inside Sonny's shirt to tease his chest.

The brown-eyed doe and her fawn stared in wonderment at the big motor machine meandering down the parkway in zigzag fashion with the two humans inside engaging in lustful banter.

"Here we are, Highpockets, Tremont."

"Tremont, what's a Tremont?" asked Samantha, rising up from Sonny's shoulder.

"The village of Tremont is where I live. I grew up about a mile back up the road from here. Yeah, Tremont boasts of three taverns, a train station, and the infamous Tremont Inn."

Sonny parked his Oldsmobile in front of the Inn, just off the highway.

"Why are we stopping?" asked his befuddled passenger.

"This is where I stay," boasted Sonny.

"Here?" asked Samantha, examining the old dilapidated building.

"Yeah, you don't like it?"

"Oh yeah, yeah I like it. It's just that it's . . . old. You know what I mean?"

"Sure it's old. That's what I like about it, Highpockets. It's got character. The original owner of this hotel used to be an old Indian Chieftain called Big White Cloud. He was a snake oil salesman by trade. He sold a product called, 'The Elixir Of Life.'"

"I thought you said he was a chief. Didn't he have any chiefing duties to do?"

"I guess that must've been in his earlier days."

"What happened to the Old Chief?"

"He died about 20 years ago. One of his ex-wives shot him. Clarence and Verna Greeley are the owners now. You've got to meet them, Highpockets. They're a hoot."

"Yeah, I bet they are," she replied

Clarence Greeley was an angular man, spindly and stiff at best. He was looking over a pair of black-rimmed bifocals when Sonny and Samantha approached him at his familiar spot behind the hotel desk. Samantha was a bit taken aback by Clarence's evil-eyeing of her, but Sonny greeted him with a smile.

"Look, Sonny, I told you that if you were going to bring women of ill-repute in here to do the dirty deed with that you must bring them at night, or else come through the back door."

"Clarence, you've got this all wrong. This here is Samantha Taylor, my girlfriend. She's a college student at Valparaiso University," explained Sonny.

Clarence turned his attention to Samantha. He observed her for a bit, like a robin observing an earthworm right before snatching it from its hole. "Look, Miss, if you plan on doing the dirty deed with this fine young man it will cost you five dollars for an hour."

Sonny gave up on the cantankerous old character and looked to Samantha and chuckled, "He gets a little confused at times."

Samantha smiled uneasily.

"Hey, Clarence, where's Verna, in the kitchen?" asked Sonny.

"Yes."

"Could you tell her that Sonny's here to pick up his picnic basket?"

Clarence furrowed his brow at the young tenant and answered, "I'm not talking to that fussbudget."

"What?" answered Sonny, surprised by the old coot's reply.

"I'm not talking to that old fussbudget. She burnt my toast."

"I did not burn your toast," replied the distinctive voice of Verna Greeley from within the kitchen walls.

"Yes, she did," countered Clarence, "she burnt my toast this morning, so I'm not talking to her."

Verna came out of the kitchen still shouting, "I did not burn your toast you old goat! You said that you wanted it brown so I made it brown. Oh hi, Sonny. Hello, Miss."

Sonny smiled amusingly at the odd couple, while Samantha greeted Verna with a nod.

Clarence yelled at Verna, "Succubus!" and then quickly turned his back to her.

Verna yelled back, "Incubus!"

He reiterated, "Succubus!"

"Incubus!" she yelled again.

"Succubus!" he said again.

"Hold it right there guys," demanded Sonny, hoping to diffuse the quarrelsome couple. "A couple of pieces of toast aren't worth fighting over. Besides, Verna, I'm here for the picnic basket that you prepared for Samantha and me. By the way, this is Samantha. Samantha, Verna, the best cook in the house."

Verna nodded her head in acknowledgment of Sonny's girlfriend, but the round little lady had a timid look to her. "Sonny, I've got something to tell ya."

"What is it, chicken not done yet? That's okay, Verna, we can wait for it."

"That's just it, Sonny. The chicken's been done. I fed it to the other tenants."

"Oh no, Verna, you didn't!"

"They were so hungry, and I couldn't let them go without a Sunday dinner. I might have some Spam left. Let me make you both a Spam sandwich."

"No thanks, Verna, that's not exactly what I had in mind."

"I'm sorry," she said with a pout.

"Oh, don't worry about it. I've got some stuff up in my fridge that I can throw together," he assured her. Sonny turned to Samantha. "I'm sorry, Highpockets. Verna's really a good woman, but kinda simple. Her ship ain't quite reached shore yet."

"Oh, I understand," said the redhead.

"I so wanted this afternoon to be special for you."

"Oh, it is, it's been quite an attraction, so far," said Samantha.

"Oh, it gets better," said Sonny. "Wait until you meet some of the others."

"Sonny," said Verna calmly. "Behind you," she nodded.

Sonny and Samantha both turned around. Samantha gasped at what she saw.

On the last step of a stairway coming from the upstairs stood a pitifully gaunt-looking young woman in all her nakedness. She owned a head of golden curls, but they were a tangled mess. What were once young buoyant breasts had now lost their elasticity and sagged noticeably. She had a jaded look about her that showed her to be much older than she was.

From the background Samantha could hear the words, "Oh Genevieve," spring out, as they stared helplessly at the woman. She gazed at Sonny in anticipation of what he was going to do.

Sonny studied Genevieve's sad eyes, and then walked up to her. "What's the matter, darling?" he asked softly.

The timid girl patted her left thigh methodically as if to music from within her head. She then raised the first two fingers of her right hand to her mouth, and in rapid fashion moved them back and forth as if gesturing for a cigarette.

"Are you out of cigarettes, baby?" he asked.

She nodded once, then, turned her head as tears slid down her cheeks. Her blue eyes begged Sonny. She tried to talk but only stuttered. Sonny shushed the young addict, then took her in his arms and pulled her to him. A scene too often repeated. "Verna, you got any smokes around here?" asked Sonny.

"No, Sonny. You know that me and Clarence quit smoking years ago."

"How about Suggs, or Strutts; are they here?"

"Oh yes, most all of the tenants are here. They're at the dining table eating your chic—uh, eating dinner."

"Well, see if you can scrounge up one cigarette from amongst them, will ya?"

"Sure, Sonny," she said, and scurried off to the dining room.

"What's the matter with her?" asked Samantha, about the emaciated blonde.

"From the glazed look in her eyes she's high on coke, or Quaaludes, or something," said Sonny. He grabbed a hand full of curls and tugged her head back. "Yeah, she's got white residue up her nose. She's taken coke today," he said disgustedly. "Goddamn it, Genevieve, why do you keep doing this to yourself? What the hell's wrong with you?" he scolded.

The blonde just stared at him with those sad eyes. In angst of Verna's return, and feeling uncomfortable with Samantha being there watching the ordeal, Sonny snapped at Clarence, "Hey, Clarence, how come you took your cigarette machine out anyway? Don't you know that you've got a house full of smokers here?"

Looking dumbfounded, Clarence finally answered, "Martin Suggs and Howard Strutts kept breaking into the damn thing. I couldn't stop them. The vendor was the one who finally removed it, not I. He couldn't make any money from it, he said."

Verna finally returned with a sour look on her face. "They're all a bunch of asses, Sonny."

"Not one of them would give you a cigarette?"

"No," grimaced the round little woman. "Martin Suggs thinks he's Elvis again, and told me that Elvis doesn't smoke. Howard Strutts just made weird faces at me. Little Sheba flipped me off, and Baby Zeus just sat there and laughed at her. Mrs. Whatley offered me her snuff-box. Sir Charles says that he smokes only a pipe, and Little Buddy Graham took a walk down the tracks. Cherry Pie's not here either. Suggs said she went out to get laid. I wish that I'd never served them your chicken, Sonny. They don't deserve anything to eat."

"That's alright, Verna. Forget about it. I'll just run across the road to Carl's tavern and buy a pack."

"Sonny; today is Sunday. The taverns are closed on Sundays."

"I know, but Carl will let me in anyway."

"I doubt that Carl is there, Sonny."

"Why do you say that, Verna?"

"Because Carl's a Baptist, you know; one of them all day Baptists. Heck, their preachers are so long-winded that Carl and Jesse sometimes don't make it home until mid-afternoon."

"But Carl owns a tavern for chrissakes!" exclaimed Sonny.

"Yes, I know, but he must be one of them drinking Baptists."

"I didn't know that there was such a thing."

"Well", said Verna, vexed by her own previous answer, "I reckon there is now."

"I'll just drive over to Sewel's gas station on Waverly Road then," said Sonny.

"Yeah, they ought to be open. I don't think they're Baptists," said Verna.

Sonny couldn't help but snicker at the simple-mindedness of Verna. He turned to Samantha, "Will you please do me one big favor and watch Genevieve? She's a little skittish right now and she needs somebody sane to be with her. It's a little crazy around here, as you can see."

"Yeah, I know what you mean," agreed Samantha. "But what about this guy?" she said, pointing to Clarence.

"Clarence? Oh, he's a big wuss. He talks mean but he's docile as a kitten. Say, Verna, can you keep a tight rein on the old man while I'm gone? Samantha's a bit leery of him."

"No problem, Sonny. If he gets out of line I'll bust him one right in the chops!"

"You and who's army?" snapped the old man.

"Me, and my frying pan you old loon!"

Clarence mumbled and walked away knowing that this time he was no match for a sparring with his wife.

Sonny gave his new girlfriend a quick kiss as he tried to untangle himself from Genevieve. She clung to him like a frightened kitten but he managed to break lose and headed out the door.

Samantha felt sympathy for Genevieve and took her hand. "Come, let's you and I go up to your room and get you dressed," she said to the girl.

The hollowed-eyed girl shook her head no and sat down in the stairway. "M-m-must w-w-wait for S-S-S-Sonny," she said shakily.

"But you're shivering, dear. Come with me at least into the parlor where you can feel the sun coming in," coaxed the redhead.

"She's not going to budge from that spot."

Samantha looked towards the parlor from where the astute sounding voice came. "Why do you say that?" she asked curiously.

"The mind intimidators have stolen her sanity."

"What?" said Samantha, confused, holding her hand over her eyes trying to make out the image emerging toward her from the sun-filled parlor. He seemed to be a very handsome man, middle-aged with a thin mustache and his hair slicked back in Ronald Coleman fashion, and he sounded a bit British.

"The drug dealers, my dear; I'm afraid nothing can help her now. She's too far gone, poor little Genevieve. She was such a pretty young lady too. For three years now we have tried to save her. Lord knows Sonny has, but her drug demons won out. She once had an innocence about her that Sonny and I both adored. But she is just a wasted form now," he sighed, "poor little waif."

"And who might you be?" asked the inquisitive reporter.

"I must deeply apologize, my dear. I'm Sir Charles Haley," he said with a bow. "I couldn't help but notice the commotion attributed to sweet Genevieve as I was relaxing in the parlor engrossed in the Sunday news, which was of little importance anyway. You may as well leave her be. She's in her own little world. She won't budge from there 'till Sonny returns. She is like a faithful collie in that way."

"But she's cold and shivering."

"Oh, she runs around here naked quite often. Nobody pays much attention anymore."

"How about the Greeleys, don't they object?"

"Aw, the old fellow gets a bit pissed, but not even he has the heart to throw her out. She's our sweet little Genevieve."

"What is the strong attraction between Sonny and her?" asked Samantha in a jealous tone.

"Make no mistake, my dear, you're Sonny's girl. He as much has told me so. Sonny's the only person in this place that I can carry on a normal conversation with. He has told me all about you, and I must say, thus far, you have met my expectations that I had drawn from Sonny's ranting and ravings."

"Thanks, I hope that I live up to my billing," she said facetiously.

"The attraction between Sonny and Genevieve; there isn't much of a story there," lamented Sir Charles, "but there could have been. Since we have each other's attention let us retire back to the parlor, Ms. Taylor. It is most comfortable in there."

"I shouldn't leave Genevieve. I promised Sonny that I would look after her."

"You mustn't worry. She'll be fine. That stairwell has been her perch here for quite sometime now."

"Couldn't we at least put a shawl or something around her shoulders?"

"She won't accept it. She won't accept anything unless it's a cigarette. Unfortunately, she is hopelessly hooked on that filthy habit also," sighed the Englishman.

As Samantha entered the parlor, the pleasant aroma of cherry-blend filled the air as smoke from Sir Charles's briar pipe billowed in the oblique shafts of sunlight passing through the windows.

"Oh, tobacco, the American native's greatest gift to the white man, and the deadliest too," declared Sir Charles. "Tobacco is just like a woman. Looks rich, smells and tastes great, and then in the end, will kill you or make you wish you were dead. Sorry ma'am, I apologize for bringing the female gender into my boastful lamentations."

"Don't apologize. I love your play on words. You seem very knowledgeable in semantics."

"Oh yes, my dear; I am or was, shall I say, a journalist as you are practicing to be. Actually I'm a writer. I write murder mystery novels. I faired quite well in that genre. That is, until about 10 years ago."

"Why, what happened?" asked Samantha.

"My wife was brutally murdered. The cops never found the killer. That was a mystery that I couldn't write an ending to."

"I'm so sorry," said Samantha.

"I haven't been able to put anything together since. While running from life I stumbled across this place. Now I just live off my residuals, and the bottle."

"I think that you should be able to write again," said Samantha candidly.

"No, Ms., I could write back when I participated in life, but now I'm just an observer, and I like it that way. You've met the Greeleys and Genevieve already, so why don't you let me introduce you to the other nuts of Tremont Inn."

"Okay," said Samantha, intrigued by the Englishman writer.

Sir Charles led Samantha through the doorway of the inn's dining room which held a huge dining table with the Inn's residents seated all around. "Over in the far right corner by the walker sits, Mrs. Whatley. She is 82 years old and cognizant of her surroundings, though she doesn't act it at times. She has lived at this hotel for nigh on to 35 years. Mrs. Whatley once was Chief Big White Cloud's mistress back in the 40's and 50's. Do you know about Chief Big White Cloud?"

"Oh yes, Sonny filled me in on the Chief."

"Well, Mrs. Whatley stays here for free. Rumor has it that old White Cloud hid 50,000 dollars in or around the Inn, and the old woman is supposed to know where it's hid. Clarence has been eyeing that old woman for 20 years now, and she hasn't led him to the money yet."

"Very interesting," said Samantha, a bit skeptical.

"The fellow with the long sideburns that's staring at you is Martin Suggs. He thinks Elvis is still alive. He claims that he saw him up in Kalamazoo recently."

"And I did too you son-of-a-bitch!" yelled Suggs to Haley. "Say, is that Ann Margaret with you? Come here Ann and sit on my lap. We'll talk about old times."

"Pay no attention to him, my young lass."

"It's kinda hard not to," said Samantha nervously.

Sir Charles smiled warmly at Samantha and continued on. "Across from Suggs is Howard Strutts, a clone of James Dean, or so he thinks. The dark-haired brown skin girl is from Trinidad. She is an ex-Carney stripper known as Little Sheba. She won't tell us her real name. She's a wrestler now. She wrestles in South Bend and at the Amphitheatre in Chicago most of the time. The little muscle-bound fellow next to her is Baby Zeus. He met Sheba in a burlesque tent at the LaPorte County Fair several years ago. They've been together ever since. Little Sheba is the most obnoxious woman that I have ever met. She curses like an Aussie sailor. Baby Zeus *was* a sailor and isn't much nicer than Sheba. They are both scurrilous characters. Together they're like two midget wrestlers, especially at night. They are two very noisy bed partners, I must say. Then there is Cherry Pie. She is not here today but is a regular member of our family. She is, let us say, very promiscuous. Her trouble is that some of her boyfriends play kind of rough. That only happens once though, because they then meet the wrath of Sonny Rafferty. Nobody wants to tangle with Sonny. He is as good as they come when it comes to brawling. Anyway, that's our family. I actually loathe these people, but Sonny takes to them like kith and kin. Occasionally you'll hear the creaking of bedsprings from the one-niters, but basically Tremont Inn is a boarding house rather than an Inn. I almost forgot, Little Buddy Graham. He's a black ex-con from Michigan City. Sonny invites him out here on the weekends to perform. He usually travels by way of the South Shore train. He's a mean guitar player and a fine 'blues' singer. You ought to see him and Sonny sit down and sing 'Stormy Monday.' It's quite the sight. If you can understand the happenings at the Tremont Inn, then your intelligence, my dear, has no limit. If you can deal with the shenanigans from these idiots then you are a rare find, a precious stone indeed, because this is the real cuckoo's nest."

Sir Charles walked Samantha back to the lobby to check on Genevieve, and then back into the parlor where he lit up another smoke of cherry-blend. "Now, you are probably wondering about Sonny and Genevieve's connection in all of this."

"The thought has crossed my mind," said Samantha.

"The sign of a good writer is one who captures the audience and holds them at bay until he tells his story before giving the ending away. Won't you agree?"

"And that you have accomplished, Sir Charles," said Samantha.

"Genevieve and I arrived at Tremont Inn at about the same time, several years ago. I was on my downward spiral at that time. Genevieve, on the other hand, was a young hippy from San Francisco that found her way to Tremont Inn by way of a foiled trip to Woodstock. She seemed vibrant and refreshing even though she had done her share of drugs. And the girl had a heart bigger than the bell-bottoms that she wore. She and I had a thing going for awhile. Sure, she was just 18 and I was in my 40's but it didn't seem to matter. That was until her drug habit escalated. That's when Sonny arrived looking for a place to stay. He had just returned from Victnam. His mother had died and his father and sisters had moved on. He was like an orphan. He fell for Genevieve like a ton of bricks. Who wouldn't? But she wouldn't have any of him. No. Drugs were her love, not Sonny. Oh, he tried to save her many times. Hell, we all did, but she just couldn't shake that demon off her back.

Then one day, when she was fresh out of rehab, she said she was going into town to do some shopping to start her new life off right. She didn't return that day, the next day, or the next. After being gone for about two weeks, one night we found her in front of the Inn. She was hurt bad, real bad. We rushed her to the hospital. After some extensive surgery she pulled through, and her wounds finally healed. It's kinda funny. The doctors healed her body but couldn't heal her mind. She was gone. We lost her. She hasn't been right sense. Meanwhile, Sonny did some investigating and found out the names of the men that mutilated Genevieve's body so. Two of the men suddenly turned up missing. No one has heard from them since. The third one was found floating face down in Lake Michigan shortly after Sonny found them out. A lot of cops came snooping and asking questions about Sonny, but he had good alibis. We made sure of that. They killed our precious flower, our dear Genevieve. At least they may as well have. The girl out there on the stairway isn't Genevieve. Genevieve's gone. Some foreign imposter inhabits her body now. We have saved up money to send her to a psych unit in Chicago. The government will pay some. Sonny seems to think it might help her. I think not. But who am I but a broken down machine myself. Sonny is the one with the hope. He still holds some tenderness for her, that's all. God bless him."

"You know, this is quite a story," said Samantha with tears in her eyes. "It's not one that I want to write about, but one that I'd like to participate in."

Suddenly, Samantha heard Sonny's voice in the lobby. She rushed in as he was lighting Genevieve's cigarette. "Oh, darling, I've missed you so," she cried while hugging his neck.

"I told you that I would be back soon," said Sonny. "Did you think I was going to leave you here alone with these people for very long?"

"Oh no, Sonny, it's not that. I just missed you. That's all. Actually, I'm getting kinda used to this place now."

"Well, don't get too used to it because I'm taking Genevieve up to her room and grab some grub from mine, and we are going on our picnic."

"Can I see your room?"

"Oh no, you've seen enough disasters for one day. I'll be right back."

Chapter Nine

Paradise Woods

With love abounding they traipsed down the railroad tracks like two frisky lambs, Sonny with all his tomfoolery, and Samantha's spontaneity to his playful antics.The amorous redhead was in all her splendor as she displayed her dazzling auburn tresses to the warm spring sun while frolicking with her handsome beau.

"Say, Sonny, how far do these tracks go?"

"They run from South Bend to Randolph Street in Chicago. They call this the South Shore Line. It boasts of an electric commuter train that runs several times a day, stopping at various locations along the way, loading and unloading commuters."

"From where does the train get its electricity?"

"Look up. That's an overhead electric cable that the train antenna comes into contact with. It's quite a clever idea that's been around for ages."

"Quite fascinating," said Samantha. "How far do we have to go before we get to the picnic grounds?"

"A bit further, yet."

"How much is a bit?"

"About half a mile, and by the way, it's not really a picnic area. The place that we are going to is where I grew up, but the National Lakeshore tore down the house several years ago. You'll love it, Sam, it's very tranquil."

"After the day that I've had I could use some tranquility," mumbled the redhead.

"Hey, Highpockets, are your feet hurting you yet?" said Sonny, eyeing her bare feet.

"No, my feet are tough, but I have a feeling that you're gonna to have to buy me a new pair of stockings after today."

"Okay, but can I keep the high-heel pumps? They go with the clogs that I have up in my room."

Samantha smiled cleverly at Sonny. "Collecting women's shoes, you must have a foot fetish, eh?"

"No, but I know this girl that keeps giving them to me to carry as if she doesn't want them anymore. At this rate I figure I'll have a whole closet full by summertime. Just, how did you come by such tough feet?" asked Sonny.

"When I ran track in school I would often run the cinders without shoes to toughen my soles for competition."

"You must have been some runner."

"I won my fair share of meets."

"Now you're gloating."

"I am not. I happened to excel at track when I was a kid, that's all."

"You're still a kid," said Sonny boyishly.

"I may be a kid, but I've got you carrying my shoes and jacket."

"I'd carry your school books if you had some. That's the type of boy I am," boasted Sonny.

"By the way, Sonny, what did you excel at when you were in school?"

"I excelled in carrying school books."

"What kind of trophy did you win for that?"

"I won nothing."

"Why nothing?"

"I always came in second."

They both laughed heartily, but Samantha's laughter slowly dissipated into deep thought. Sonny noticed the melancholic look about her. "Is something wrong, Sam?"

"Hey, Sonny, do you really think I look like a kid?"

"Well, uh, sure, but what do you mean, Sam? What's bothering you?"

"I mean this suit that I'm wearing, is it too old for me? Do you think

I look foolish wearing it?"

"No, not at all, Sam. If anything it makes you look business like, you know, professional looking."

"But that's just it. I'm not a professional yet. Hell, I've still got two years of college left."

"I don't understand, Sam. What's eatin' you? It's that tussle you had with Rochelle today, isn't it?"

"I wouldn't call it much of a tussle. I just kind of gave in to him. I don't know what happened."

"He got to you. That's what happened, isn't it?"

"Things were kind of topsy-turvy this morning. It was quite bazaar in there. I guess that I was too presumptuous to begin with. He saw that as a facade, which it was I guess, on my part anyway. He took me into his confidence, then, ridiculed me, and soon I was caught up in his debauchery. Sonny, he's so chameleon-like. It's as if he cast some kind of subliminal spell on me. He snatched secrets from my past that nobody knew about except me. It's as if a light emitted from his soul. He had me doing things, which to me were lewd and lascivious."

"He didn't touch you did he?" asked the concerned Sergeant.

"No, he was shackled, but . . . only with his eyes."

"Rochelle is damnable he is. He deserves his own hell."

"The thing is, Sonny, I felt euphoric through it all. He had me mesmerized until the very end. Then the light that he emitted from his soul suddenly vanished, and a dark, salacious creature took him over. Do you know what it's like to let your soul crawl in bed with evil?"

"Oh yes, I've been there a few times myself. It makes you physically ill."

"Exactly, I was puking my guts up just minutes before you rescued me this morning."

"Look, Sam, I've spent the last four months on X-row, and have at times become attached to Rochelle myself. He reminds me of a fine-tuned V-8 engine with a couple of fouled plugs. Don't worry, Sam, the Furies will take care of him for what he did to you."

"Furies? Are those some of your Greek and Roman Mythology God's again?" asked the amused redhead.

"Oh yeah, they are three terrible female spirits who punish their perpetrators of un-avenged crimes."

"That really puts my mind at ease," she said facetiously.

"Well, if it makes you feel better, I shot Rochelle in the foot once."

"Wait a minute. You shot the guy in the foot once and he still likes you?"

"Yep, you've got to remember that Rochelle is a perfectionist; a genius except for a few glitches, of course. He likes people who put out effort to do things right, and he loathes the slackers. I had been at the correctional center for only about three months when I was pulling guard duty in tower number 10. Rochelle and four of his buddies from X-row tried to escape that night. I saw them trying to hook a rope onto the wall so they could climb to their freedom. I fired a warning shot and that damn Rochelle started firing a zip-gun at me."

"What's a zip-gun?"

"A zip-gun is usually made from a pipe, nail and a rubber band. Rochelle's gun fired shotgun shells. Anyway, I commenced to firing at the escapees. When I shot Rochelle in the foot they gave up. Van asked me later why I didn't just kill him. I told him, 'hell, I tried to but I'm not a very good shot.' He got a kick out of that and we sort of became friends. You know, in a guard-prisoner way."

"How come they made it that far in their escape in the first place?"

"Rochelle bribed officers into bringing in jewelry wire. With the jewelry wire they cut the bottom bars on their cell doors. The guards have a bar ringer that they run across the cells bars, and any change in the sound detects a problem of some type. Rochelle told me that their guards were too fat and lazy to run the bar ringer across the lower bars. That's how they escaped from their cells. Then they stole a door key long enough to emboss it in soap and carved a wooden skeleton key from it. They then cut through a barbed-wire fence and made it to the wall."

"That sounds like a made-for-TV story."

"It really happened, Highpockets. I know because I was there."

Suddenly, a South Shore train horn blared at the unsuspecting couple. Sonny took a quick look behind them. "Grab my arm!" he yelled to Samantha, "we're going to jump down this embankment. Just roll with me!"

They made it off the tracks just as the train zipped by. Samantha looked at Sonny in total shock.

"There's one thing I forgot to tell ya, Highpockets. You can't hear these damn electric trains until they're right on you."

"Oh yeah, thanks for your belated advice," she said shakily.

"I'm sorry. Are you hurt?"

"Just my pride, mostly," she said. "My leg is bleeding a bit. I must have scraped it on some rocks while rolling down the embankment." Sonny pulled off his shirt and began making bandage strips from it. "You don't have to do that, Sonny."

"It's my Sunday-go-to-meetin' shirt. Don't worry, I've got another," he said. Sonny then examined her bloodied leg. "Your cuts look superficial but you do have several of them. We'll get them bandaged up. You'll be alright."

"Let me take my stockings off first, they're ruined anyway."

"Need my help?" volunteered Sonny.

"No, I can manage, myself," she said with a gleam in her eye.

Sonny noticed that except for the cuts and contusions, Samantha's legs were just as silky looking without her stockings as with, only whiter.

"And just think, we could have taken the car," said Samantha while pulling off her hosiery.

"But where else would you find excitement like this?"

"I don't know about you, but I could use some of that tranquility that we were talking about earlier."

"Yeah, we'll go get us some," said Sonny while searching through the weeds. "Right now I've got to find where I slung your shoes."

Shortly after recovering from the train incident Sonny and Samantha arrived at their destination.

"How do you know that this is the place?" asked Samantha. "It looks just like the last mile and a half that we've walked, railroad tracks and woods, woods and railroad tracks. I expect maybe to see an Indian soon, or a bear."

"I know this place like the back of my hand," said Sonny with pride. "Everyone knows what their own back yard looks like."

"Okay, Daniel Boone, I believe you. You're not going to roll me down a hill again are you?"

"No," laughed Sonny. "I'll be gentler with you this time. I promise."

A canopy of leaves covered the wooded property. Only the area where the home once stood was there sparse growth. Little shafts of sunlight found their way through small openings in the foliage created by a breeze that slowly sifted through the branches. Three hundred yards of property was all that separated the South Shore tracks from the Dunes Highway, thus creating Sonny's paradise woods.

Sonny grabbed Samantha's hand and eagerly scurried down the embankment and crossed a homemade bridge atop a drainage ditch and into the woods to where his house once stood.

"So this is where you once lived?"

"Yeah, this is it," said Sonny, as childhood memories churned through his head. "My sister and I used to play amongst that stand of Sassafras trees," he said, pointing toward the slender rough-barked trees in what once was the front yard. "And that big Crabapple tree to your left once produced thousands of little sour apples that we used for battles with neighbor kids from down the road. Over to the right is where Mom used to have her flower garden. Why, you can see some of them still growing now in the wild."

Samantha realized why Sonny wanted to come here. It wasn't just the tranquility of the woods. This was Sonny's solitude. He came here for the memories of days gone past. She could see it in his eyes, hear it in his voice. To Sonny, the house was still standing. Through his eyes the garden had bright red, yellow and purple blooms opening up to the sun. The neighbor kids were there, behind their forts in a major crabapple battle, while his mother watched dotingly from the kitchen window. Samantha sensed that he wanted to come to closure with his past. It must have been a happy childhood, she thought, being that it was so hard to let go. She felt somewhat privileged that he wanted to share his past with her.

"Hey, Highpockets, over here!" yelled Sonny, grabbing Samantha's attention. "Look what I've found."

Samantha walked hurriedly but carefully through a briar-laden thicket to where Sonny was. "How did you get over there?" questioned Samantha while gingerly pulling the prickly briars from her clothing.

"It wasn't through that briar thicket," he answered.

"Smart ass! Why did you leave me back there all alone?"

"You looked as if you were enjoying yourself, daydreaming and all, so I went exploring. Look what I found," he said while pulling an olive colored blanket off a wicker basket.

"My my, what do we have here? A picnic basket, who would have thought, in the middle of the woods? How ironic. Boy, Sergeant, you are the real Robin Hood aren't you?" mocked the sassy redhead.

Sonny grinned. "I'll be Robin Hood if you'll be Maid Marion."

"Wait a minute. Let me figure this out. You did save me today from those prison walls, not that I couldn't have found my own way out, mind you. Then, you proceeded to take me to the funny farm of Tremont acres, yet you did rescue me from a speeding locomotive, only to lose me in the forest."

"But, I did happen upon our dinner," Sonny added.

"You're right. Let's eat. I'm starved. But I'm curious, Sergeant. How does a feast like this suddenly appear in the midst of a jungle?" asked Samantha.

"I must confess. Sir Charles brought it in the Olds. He's been out this way before. He and I used to bring Genevieve here hoping that it would do her good. Look, a note from Sir Charles," said Sonny while opening up the food basket.

"Read it aloud, Sonny. I'm eager to hear what he has to say."

For two zealous lovers

May this afternoon be a festive one

In the serenity of your paradise woods

And may this succulent haute cuisine

Stir the passions in your souls

To be as one

Respectfully yours,

Sir Charles of Lancashire (Tremont Inn)

P.S. Sonny, I could not see a moment like this ruined by being in haste. Your cooler with the beer and cold cuts were just too gauche for a lady of the magnitude of Miss Taylor. The crepes, canapés and grapes shall suit her just fine. By the way, the Pinot Noir is from my private stock. You owe me big time!

Good luck,

Charles

With his spunky Maid Marian dining on the canapés and crepes, Sonny lay next to her, gazing at the thin slices of sun shining through the green forested roof while occasionally receiving a token grape from his newfound sweetheart. Samantha's hair looked almost crimson within the darkness of the woods while her fair skin showed pallor against the shaded backdrop.

The desirous redhead was in her own heaven. It truly is serene here, she thought while sipping the dry red wine. The wooded enclosure seemed to her as an amphitheatre, and the breeze a symphony.

Sonny rose up from his slumber. "Sam, let's you and I make a toast."

"Whom shall we toast to, Robin Hood or Maid Marian?"

"Both," said Sonny, feasting his eyes upon her beauty. "Let's toast to our world's colliding." They both raised their long-stem goblets. "A toast to each other; to who we are, not what we are; to the deep future but let us not forget our shallow past, and may we die young at an old age."

"Here, here," said Samantha.

"Cheers," said Sonny.

"Boy, that Sir Charles knows his wines," said Samantha while licking the last red droplet from her lips.

"Heck, he should, he's been around the world twice," said Sonny. "He's a wine connoisseur all right. I'm not much of a wine taster myself though."

"If you're gonna' hang with me you better learn because I enjoy a fine wine. Wine is a sophisticated beverage. You're not one of those immature beer guzzlers are you, Sergeant?"

"Not really. I'm not much of a drinker anyway. I like to keep a keen sense about me."

"That's good. I know whom I'll call the next time I need a designated driver," she teased. "I say that we now toast Sir Charles for this exquisite dinner and drink."

"I'm with you on that," said Sonny, refilling their glasses. "I raise a toast to Sir Charles, my good friend, and the sanest person at Tremont Inn. Cheers."

With that, their glasses clinked and they downed their fruity beverage.

"Sam, we must toast Dionysus," said Sonny.

"Let me guess; another Greek God, right?"

"Good guess, Sam."

"How many of these gods do you have anyway? We're not going to drink to all of them are we?"

"Why, Highpockets, Dionysus is the god of wine and revelry. We must give him a toast."

"Oh my, yes," said Samantha, raising her glass to Sonny's. "To the god of wine, fruit of the vine, make no mistake, thanks for the grapes." With the clink of their glasses they drank another round of Pinot Noir.

"Do you really believe in all that Greek Mythology stuff?" asked Samantha.

"No, not really," replied Sonny.

"So, you do believe that there's a God?"

"Yes, somewhat; I told you before. Don't you remember?"

"Yes, I remember, but you don't sound too sure of yourself now."

"Well, I haven't seen him part any seas lately. Have you?"

"No, but I believe there is a God because I have faith."

"Look," said Sonny, "I believe in God because I was raised that way. Do I pray to him? Sure I pray. It's just that . . . the answers are a little slow in coming. Besides, it seems wrong to blame God or the devil for our own transgressions. If there is a God, he gave us the power to reason. We make our own judgments, good or bad. Trouble is, most people want to play the middle. You know; that gray area between right and wrong. And they don't want to be responsible for their actions so they blame an outside entity and think that gets them off the hook. Yes, Samantha, I believe in God. I just wish that he believed in me."

"Sonny, how do you do it? How do you go to work at that dreadful prison and then come home to a house full of malcontents?"

"What do you mean, Sam?"

"I mean that you've got so much going for you. You're a young intelligent man. You don't fit the mold for this kind of life. You can do much better."

"Look, Sam, I know what you're trying to say. I also know that there is no panacea for the prison problems that our country faces today. The prison is so devoid of love. There are young boys thrown into the system after sometimes making just one mistake in their lives. They are cast to the wolves and are released back into society as damaged goods. I'm trying to change all of that, trying to do some good. Sure, there are times that I wish I could leave, but that's all I know how to do right now. And about my friends at Tremont Inn, they're not a bad sort. They're just a bit rude and crude. They're harmless, really, Sam. They're just orphans kicked out of society. All they want is to be free. The trouble with some of them is that they want to be free of their social conscience. That's where they run into problems. I try to work within the system, myself."

"Sonny, tell me about those three men that hurt Genevieve? What really happened to them?"

"I see that Sir Haley's been running his mouth again. I'm no murderer if that's what you're thinking."

"I'm sorry, Sonny, I didn't mean to imply that, but what about the cops?"

"The cops, are you kidding? They took one look at that cuckoo's nest and laughed at us, and then sloughed us off. They figured Genevieve as just another whore who deserved her just rewards. Talk about being free of social conscience. Strutts cried like a baby when we found Genevieve. Sir Charles was devastated. Baby Zeus and Suggs wanted to find and kill the perpetrators, but I knew that they were out of their league. So that just left it up to me. I took care of things," he said with an empty stare.

"Can you tell me more?" whispered Samantha.

Sonny poured himself another drink.

Samantha noticed coldness in Sonny's eyes. Up 'till now she had been infatuated with the young sergeant's rugged handsomeness and boyish charm, and astonished by his altruistic ways. But now she sensed a sudden change in his demeanor; a change that she didn't particularly favor, but one that stoked her curiosity. She poured herself another drink while Sonny was absorbed in thought.

Enchanted by the green forest quietude, with her mind swirling from drink, Samantha softly buried her crimson locks into the haven of Sonny's hard, sinewy chest. Sonny had become quite an enigma to her. She did not want to judge him. She wanted to learn his ways, to try to understand his world, no matter her naiveté toward it.

With the deftness of a sculptor she traced his chiseled features with her soft fingers, receiving a tender kiss as they passed over his lips. With a slight tug of his chin she guided his softening blue eyes down toward hers and feasted upon his countenance.

"Tell me your thoughts, Sonny, I want to know everything about you," she whispered. "You're such a mystery train," she cooed.

Torn between the esthetic softness of her body and the inquisitive hardness of his mind, he chose the latter. For as much as he desired her physically, he longed for her trust and assurance even more. Though apprehensive, he seemed ready to expose his soul. He so desired this. Sonny stood up with Samantha clinging to his middle. "Come walk with me."

A little perplexed, Samantha answered, "Sure baby," and grasped his arm tightly. They headed back towards the home-site. As they walked, Sonny talked.

"You know, Sam, one Christmas, when I was a kid, my parents bought for me an air rifle. You know, a BB gun. Oh how I coveted that BB gun as it sat in the store window all summer. Nothing could have pleased me more. I loaded it up with BBs and headed outside to try out my shooting skills at various targets in and around the yard. I started shooting at birds and whatnot, and not having much luck. Then I happened by chance to spot an old bird's nest up in that crabapple tree. I figured it to be abandoned being that it was winter and all, so I thought I would use it as a target. I shot once, and to my surprise a little baby bird fell to the ground. Astonished, I picked it up and was suddenly struck with a sense of guilt that was overwhelming. He was just a fuzzy little thing, big eyes, not yet opened, no feathers; almost transparent looking. I could actually see his heart pounding as he breathed laboriously trying to survive the trauma from his fall. His mother frantically protested as she flew from branch to branch trying to get a closer look. The little bird died in my hand. I cried. For some reason or other I was overwhelmed with grief. I even buried the little fella. I also buried that BB gun in my closet where it would never be fired again by me."

Samantha saw the hurt in Sonny's eyes. She started to speak but resisted. She just laid her head against his shoulder while tears of sadness slithered down her cheeks. A melancholic feeling abounded as they wondered arm-in-arm through his wooded castle.

Sonny continued, "Ten years later I found myself in the jungles of Vietnam at a place called An Loc. We were evacuating civilians from the area and were receiving heavy artillery and mortar fire. The North Vietnamese army was on the move to take back the southern Vietnamese provinces. My job was to board the wounded and civilians onto rescue helicopters that were flying in to extract them from the area. It was total chaos as ordinances were exploding everywhere. Men, women, and children were scurrying around in mortal fear. It was a hopeless situation. The air was a sheet of steel as the choppers came flying in. A young woman ran up to me with what was obvious to me but not to her, a dead child in her arms. She was desperate, yammering at me to save her and her lifeless child. I quickly helped her onto the last space available on an over-crowded 'Huey.' Then suddenly, I was shoved aside by two South Vietnamese army officers. They grabbed her and her daughter, threw them to the ground, and took her seat on the bird. I was so shocked by such a display of cowardice that it compelled me to reach in with one hand and grab that ARV N colonel by his lapels while pulling out my 45-colt with the other and pointing it right into his stupid face. I screamed into his face to get out! He wouldn't budge. I shouted, '*Di-Di-Mau,Di-Di-Mau!*' That arrogant bastard gestured to his gold crest on his uniform lapels while spouting back his own gibberish. In the meantime the Warrant Officer who piloted the Huey was yelling at me to let him go, 'Too much incoming, have to lift off!' he screamed. I lost it. I unloaded one right into the middle of that gook's forehead. I shot him right there on the spot. I yanked his body out and his buddy quickly followed. The Warrant Officer flying the bird stared at me in disbelief. He was so shocked, I guess. Hell, we were all in a panic. He could have turned me in for war crimes, dishonorable discharge and all, but he didn't. I have a vivid memory of wiping the blood out of my eyes and catching a glimpse of a young mother in her sloped hat and black pajamas, clinging to her child from the open door of that Huey helicopter as it ascended into the heavens in a flurry of dust and a hail of bullets, taking them to their newfound freedom. You see, Sam, I never think about capping that ARV N officer, but I often think of that little bird in my hands trying so desperately to survive. You tell me, Sam, am I a killer or a hero? I don't know myself. I just know that there is no in-between. Not for me anyway. What I did was instinctive. People say that we will pay for our sins when we die. How foolish thinking that is. We pay for our sins while we're alive, believe me."

Shivers ran down Samantha's spine as she listened to the tortured soul of her beloved prince. How could she have fallen in love with someone who frightened her so, yet made her feel so secure, so happy inside.

"Life is full of episodes, incidences, and happenings for all of us," continued Sonny. "It's events of phenomenal proportions that take us to task. How we react, no one knows. There is no standard made, never was. Hell, I would have never thought in a million years that I would run into a bunch of people like the ones at Tremont Inn, and actually live among them, but I did. Now they are going to raze the Inn."

"What?"

"The National Lakeshore wants to demolish the hotel."

"How can they do that?" asked Samantha.

"The Indiana Parks Department bought the property several years back just as they did my parent's property. They leased the land back to the Greeleys for a fraction of the price. I guess the lease must have run out and the Greeleys didn't renew it in time, so now the park department wants to add the property to the National Park."

"What are the tenants going to do?"

"Aw, they'll do alright. Mrs. Whatley will probably go to a nursing home, and we're sending Genevieve to a place that will give her the best in psychiatric care. The others can fend for themselves."

"It all seems so sad," said Samantha despondently.

"Nothing stays the same, Highpockets. You know that. I mean, look at *me* now. You've come into my life and my life's in turmoil again," he laughed.

"What about Sir Charles, Sonny, what'll he do?"

"Sir Charles is going to do what Sir Charles wants, independent of what others may think. Why, are you stuck on the guy?"

"Well, he does serve up a mean picnic lunch," joked Samantha.

"Yes he does, I'll give him that, and he thinks that he's a ladies' man."

"And oh, so British; yes, those Brits; so suave and debonair they are."

"Yes, but he's an old man."

"Do you mean old as in age or old as in experience?"

"Hey, wait a minute girl, what about me?"

"Oh, you bloody Americans, you're so vain. Vain but hot, yes, you'll do just fine," she kidded.

Samantha kissed him quickly and then playfully ran away. The sound of laughter once again filled paradise woods as the frolicking young couple chased each other to and fro while celebrating each capturing with breathless kisses and caressings. They, along with the chattering of the chipmunks, the bantering of the squirrels, and the melodious chirping of their winged friends, seemed to enchant their small forest.

Chapter Ten

Mystery Train

With her back lying securely against his chest, Samantha relaxed in Sonny's arms as he rested against the tree. With her eyes closed in a state of rapture, she slowly tossed her head back and forth as Sonny nipped and nibbled artfully on her satiny neck and delicate ears. The young reporter felt Sonny's love growing for her. That impassioned her but Sonny resisted these natural feelings as he did not want to lose her again. So he pulled away to let his passion's wane.

"Say, Highpockets, when you were a kid did you ever play a game called Mysteries and Mansions?"

Samantha turned to him, looking a bit frustrated but still euphoric, even as the strange feelings within her dissipated. "Of course I played Mysteries and Mansions. We used to have a blast playing it at St Regis boarding school," she said.

"Did you throw the board game away too like we did?" asked Sonny.

"Yes, we did. We thought it too childish for us since they gave the answers with the game. It depended on the spin of the wheel and the luck of the draw from the mystery cards or the mansion cards. It was rather an ordinary board game by itself, that is, until we re-invented it."

"Yeah, then it became a cult classic among kids. How did you play the game, Sam?"

"St. Regis was an all-girl's school, and once a week we would play, each of us telling of the biggest mystery in her life. They would vary from, when I got my first period, and or the how and why of it, the mystery of why mommy has so many boyfriends, why brother spends so much time in the bathroom; what did the word 'fuck' mean, and where did it come from? And when we were younger, where did babies come from? You get the picture, right?"

"Yeah, I think so."

"So, the winner of the best mystery would get her room cleaned and chores done by everyone else for a week. Then the next week we would play again. And whoever won the mansion's part got their homework done for them for that week."

"Did you win any?"

"I won a few times, mostly on mansions. At that school we were all well-to-do 'Pollyannas,' you know. And we all wanted the same mansion or good ending to our lives. I won one time for wanting to live in a mansion with Rod Stewart. Everyone loved him at that time. I still do when he sings 'Tonight's the Night.' We had this one girl, Carla Dodson, who had a mystery that we couldn't figure out for seven weeks."

"What was it? It must have been good."

"Now, we were grade-schoolers, mind you. She told us that she once saw her mom make a giant mushroom grow on her daddy's stomach, using only her hands. She claimed that her mom made it from modeling clay. We didn't figure that mystery out until one of the girls went home for a weekend and talked to her older brother. Boy, were we surprised! We all still laugh about that today when we see each other. How about you, Sonny, how did you and your friends play the game?"

"Well, we would sneak out after dark and meet at an old burnt-out restaurant down the road a ways. We started out playing the game with three boys, including myself, and four girls. Our object was to scare the crap out of the girls with the scariest stories that we could come up with. That was for mystery. Our mansion was a utility closet in that old building. That was where the winner would take a member of the opposite sex with them for five minutes of whatever while everyone else sat outside the door and listened or joked and cheered you on. When I would win I would always take Tara Potts in the closet with me. She was a cute little thing. Wouldn't let you do much more than kiss her, but I didn't care. I just liked the taste of her lips. Besides, her boyfriend was a lineman on the football team. Fortunately for me, whatever went on at Mysteries and Mansions never left that old burnt-out building.

Occasionally a girl would win. That Suzie Brocklander would always pick me to take to the mansion. She had an overbite that I swear would rip your bottom lip off when she kissed you, but boy she had some body for an eighth grader, and didn't mind sharing it with you. Funny thing about Suzie though, she wouldn't even talk to me in school because my parent's weren't affluent enough, but boy she sure loved that Mysteries and Mansions."

"You were quite the Romeo," jested Samantha.

"No, I just had good mysteries. Every summer, dad got a two-week vacation from where he worked and would take his family back to Tennessee with him to see Grandma and Grandpa. Well, Grandma was super-religious. I mean, this woman had a black-belt in holy-rolling. One thing about people that claim that they know God so personally is that they know the devil even better. I know because they talk about him more. Don't do this, don't do that. Sonny, the devil's gonna get you for that. Oh no, Sonny, don't do that, you'll go blind. The devil will see to it."

Samantha laughed, "I get the picture."

"Grandma would always tell me the scariest, most heinous stories that I had ever heard. I mean to tell you, they were pure evil. Those stories could raise the hair on the back of the Pope's neck. For me, going to see Grandma was like a Catholic going to a confessional. The more I confessed, the more evil stories I would get for Mysteries and Mansions. I loved Grandma."

"Is she still alive, Sonny?"

"No, she's gone on home to be with the Lord, I think. Anyway, one night I told one mystery that was so scary that I had all four of those girls in that closet with me at the same time—and one guy."

Samantha and Sonny laughed heartily.

"Then suddenly it all ended one night when a girl went home with charcoal ass and her father found out. The next time that we met to play we got busted. We had built ourselves up to seven boys and fourteen girls by then. Yeah, the cops hauled us to jail, called our parents, gave us our lectures and made us the scourge of society at that time. Grandma was right. The devil got me. Oh, we tried some séances and strip poker in that old building when we were older, but it didn't last. Nothing could beat Mysteries and Mansions."

"Hey, Sam, have you any real mysteries in your life? You know;

something that you can't solve?"

"I've led quite a sheltered life compared to you, Sonny, so I'm sure there are some mysterious family secrets that I wasn't told about. Let me think . . . Oh yes, there was one instance with my father back when I was about fourteen and my brother was twelve. I caught my brother, Chance, rummaging through my parent's closet looking for money, sex magazines, rubbers, you name it. My parents spoiled him rotten, and he was quite ornery because of it. I was about to threaten to turn him in when he suddenly discovered this wooden chest about the size of an over-sized shoebox. For some reason or other that chest drew my interest."

"I'm curious, what was in that chest, Sam?"

"To our surprise it was a gun. I thought it was a toy until Chance released the cylinder on it and real bullets fell out. I quickly grabbed the gun from my brother before he got one of us shot."

"A lot of people have guns hidden in their house for security reasons, though I must say it's quite dangerous leaving it in an unlocked box. So what was so strange about that?"

"Oh, the chest was locked but Chance jimmied it open. Up till then I never saw Daddy with a gun or saw one in our home. Daddy could never shoot anyone, even a burglar. He's just a big old pacifist type of guy. Why, I've never as much as heard him raise his voice, except at Chance occasionally, but that's understandable because he can do some pretty stupid things at times."

"Let me ask you this," queried Sonny, "Did that gun have a holster with it?"

"Why, yes it did, I believe. Why do you want to know that?"

"Oh, no reason, just curious; go on with your story."

"What we found next was a mystery that maybe you can help me solve."

"I'll sure give it a try."

"We pulled out an 8x10 picture of Marilyn Monroe from that box. I thought, why would Dad want a picture of an actress that had been dead for years? I mean, she's beautiful and all, but come on now. There are a lot of beautiful actresses still alive."

"So you're telling me that you would not have a problem with it if it were a picture of a live actress such as Raquel Welch?" quizzed Sonny.

"Of course not, heck, she could even be stark naked it wouldn't bother me. But a dead actress, that's a little morbid, don't you think? Besides, I know that it is the inherent trait among men to collect photos of gorgeous women for their own self-interests. Who do you think buys Playboy?"

"You've got a point there, Highpockets."

Samantha continued, "Then we found a couple of telegrams addressed to John Taylor. One said, 'Nice clean job, too bad, pretty girl, checks in the mail,' signed, Bobby. The other one said 'Thanks for the votes we needed the south, checks in the mail,' signed, Joe. Can you decipher that Sonny?"

Sonny thought a minute as the cloud of mystery garnered an air of suspicion around it. "Say, Sam, do you know anything about John F. Kennedy?"

"Of course, he was our first Catholic president and was in office back when I was a baby. He was assassinated in Dallas, Texas; I believe on November 22nd, 1963."

"Boy, you sure know your history, little girl,"

"I should. Daddy has a huge picture of him hanging over our fireplace in the den at home. He was Daddy's favorite. I think it was because he was an Irish Catholic."

"But I thought that you were—"

"Presbyterian?"

"Yeah, Presbyterian," said Sonny.

"Mother and I are, but Daddy is an Irish Catholic, half-Irish but all Catholic. Mother says that it is more socially acceptable to be a protestant in Indianapolis. I never thought about it much. I went to early mass with Daddy and Sunday school with Mother. I figured that God was in both churches. So what do you think, Sonny? Do you think that you can solve the mystery? At first, when we found the gun, Chance thought that Daddy might belong to a mafia, but then we realized that Daddy wasn't Italian. Plus he was just too gentle a soul."

Certain revelations spun in Sonny's head but he wasn't about to disappoint his ladylove with his own speculation. "No mystery here, Sam. Marilyn Monroe is an icon. You'll find her face plastered about anywhere, and she'll probably still be popular 20 years from now. As far as the gun goes, it was probably for protection of the family even though he most likely wouldn't have used it anyway. It probably made your dad feel secure. As far as the telegrams go, it appears to me that he might've been involved in politics in some way. I don't see any real mystery there," lied Sonny.

"You must be right, Sonny. My mother told me the same thing. Of course I didn't tell her about us sneaking into their closet, but I did ask her what Daddy did when I was a baby. She said he was involved politically to get an Irish Catholic elected into office. I wish that you could meet my family, Sonny. You would so like them. Daddy can be a bit snarly at times, but he doesn't bite. Mother likes high society, but she has always been there for Chance and me. And Chance, what can I say, he's my little brother. He's a little crazy at times, but I love him."

"How did your dad get into the newspaper business?"

"He won a small fortune in the stock market I'm told, and he has invested wisely. The Times is his baby though. He started the company a little over two years ago. Of course, his goal is to be the largest newspaper in the mid-west someday. That's the way Daddy thinks."

"You're pretty crazy about your dad aren't you?"

"Can you tell?" asked Samantha, her eyes gleaming.

Sonny laughed slightly. "Oh yes, you're definitely Daddy's little girl alright."

"I'm going to tell you why, Sonny. First of all, Mother is somewhat distant. Oh, she raised us proper, but she's always had her own agenda. She wanted to be a socialite, and now she is. Whatever floats your boat, I say. Daddy was gone from home a lot, but when he returned I was his number one priority. Mother and Daddy sent me to an exclusive all girls' school until my junior year when I begged to go to a public school to mix with the boys and all. Mother objected, but not Daddy. As it turned out, I wasn't quite the prize catch that Daddy made me out to be. I made very few friends even though I was outgoing. I wasn't the prettiest girl around either, another fallacy by my dad. Of course, in his eyes I may have been beautiful. Well, I finally got this boy to take me to the prom, and I'm not going to tell you what I had to do to get him to ask me. It was quite disgusting though. So I got all gussied up, put on an evening gown, corsage and all. Hell, I barely had enough tits to hold that strapless gown up. I remember being self-conscious about it and tugging on it all night, trying to keep my boobies from popping out. As always, Daddy made a big fuss over me. He even hired a photographer friend of his to take pictures of me with my date. I could tell that things weren't going well by the way my date fidgeted around so much during the picture taking. We went to the prom, and as luck would have it, I got dumped there without even a first dance. My date left with his friends and I was stuck there. The girls wouldn't even talk to me. So, upset and totally humiliated, I gathered enough courage to call home. When Daddy drove up, there was his little girl, bawling her eyes out on the steps in front of the school. Big John didn't say a word. He just put his big arms around me, kissed me, and led me to the car. I was too ashamed to look my own father in the face, but I could feel the hurt in his eyes. While driving through town he made one stop at a phone booth. He made two calls, one to tell Mother that we weren't coming home right away. The next thing I remember is getting out of the car and Daddy escorting me into a neon-lit nightclub, called 'Bennie's Bungalow.' As I walked through the door the hatcheck girl asked 'may I take your wrap Miss Taylor?' I handed her my wrap and euphoria started to set in. I could hear a black woman singing with the band as we walked arm in arm through the second door. When she saw us she stopped, as did the band. The M.C. then ran up to the mike and announced 'Ladies and gentlemen, we have with us tonight the queen of the ball, Miss Samantha Taylor, escorted by her father, Big John Taylor. Please put your hands together and make them welcome.' Daddy danced the first dance with me. Then the men just lined up the rest of the evening to dance with me, the ugly duckling whose Daddy turned into a queen for one night. That was three years ago. Now you see why I love my Daddy so much," said Samantha teary-eyed.

"He was right about one thing Sam, you are beautiful. You'd be the queen at any ball."

"Why, thank you, Sonny."

Sonny took Samantha in his arms and softly kissed the tears from her eyes.

"Who had the biggest impact on your life, Sonny? Your mom or your dad?" she quietly asked.

"Probably my mom; she was everything a mother should be, plus. Dad was alright, but he didn't always give sound advice. The person that I really looked up to was my older sister, Maggie Mae. Oh yes, she was a feisty one, she was. She taught me how to stand up for myself."

"Tell me more," urged Samantha, "She sounds fascinating."

"She was a skinny redhead, not beautiful like you, but pretty in her own way. She had light auburn hair and lots of freckles, and a lively temper. We were raised up attending the same church and learned about the same God from our mother. Maggie Mae was religious alright. She was eye for an eye spit in your eye religious. When we first moved here from Tennessee we were considered, 'white trash' by the locals. Even going to school became a grueling task with all the harassment and name-calling. Two of my sisters quit school and went to work at 'Delmonicos' as hash slingers. But not Maggie Mae, nope, she was going to get her education come hell or high water. She even had designs of going to college, but it was tough out there, Sam. I remember hearing my dad tell me on my first day of school that if he ever heard of me getting into a fight in school that he would give me a whippin' when I got home. That was some of Dad's poor advice. But the young naïve trooper that I was, I heeded Dad's advice and got the shit kicked out of me for the first three years of my school life. I hid my cuts, hid my bruises, I even cried in silence. I didn't want to make waves. Then all of that changed in the fall of '63. I remember it well because it was a week after the Kennedy assassination. In those days, grade-school kids and high school kids rode the same bus. I was in the third grade and Maggie Mae was a senior in high school. On this one particular morning I was getting jostled pretty well by a local by the name of Billy Jenkins. I had to sit by Billy on the ride in to school. He and his friends wouldn't let me off at the school bus stop. They just kept shoving me around. I was scared. Maggie came to my rescue when she saw my dilemma. She and Billy got into a shoutin' match. Then he called her a name that I couldn't make out, but I knew that it incensed Maggie because she dug four deep claw marks into Billy's left cheek. Billy popped her one right there; knocked her out. The bus driver finally stopped the damn bus, came back and pulled me off Billy. I wasn't winning but I'll be damned if he was going to treat my big sister like that."

"Oh, my gosh!" gushed Samantha. "Was Maggie alright?"

"Oh yeah, she soon came to."

"So, what happened then?"

"Well, Billy and Maggie were thrown off the bus for a month, and both got three days suspension from school. They didn't do anything more to Billy for hitting Maggie Mae."

"It's a shame that he got away with hitting your sister like that," said Samantha angrily.

"Oh, he didn't. It took me six years before I caught him coming out of a tavern drunk one night."

"You're kidding, how bad?"

"You can go to the carwash in town today and see him if you want. That's where he works. He's the hook-nosed man that walks with a limp because of his plastic knee. And if you look close enough, I swear you can still see four little claw marks on his face. After that incident I wasn't scared anymore."

"That Maggie, she sounds like a girl that I would like to meet. Did she go on to college?"

Sonny turned his eyes down. "No, Sam, she never finished the school year out."

"Why, what happened to her?"

"She was struck and killed by some Jew bastard that passed a line of traffic and ran through the bus's stop sign. He just missed me, only because I ran ahead of my sister while crossing the highway."

"Oh how terrible," gasped Samantha. "That must have been traumatic for you."

"I mostly remember the screeching of the tires, and turning around and seeing the scattered papers floating through the air, and my sister tossed about like a rag doll by that big-finned Cadillac. And what was worse was seeing my poor mother running down our driveway, and the look of horror on her face when she saw her spunky little redhead lying dead on the black asphalt. One thing that I remember, Sam, is what an ugly red color that blood makes next to a sister's pretty red hair. The thing is; Maggie shouldn't have been riding the bus on that day anyway. It was another bad decision by our father. That particular day happened to be senior 'skip' day. Dad wouldn't have any of that nonsense. He and Maggie argued fiercely the night before, but Daddy won. Maggie fought so hard to fit in at school but Mom and Dad just didn't understand us kids. I guess I shouldn't blame them. Hell, they only finished the fifth and seventh grades in school themselves. They spent most of their lives scratching in rocky ground, trying to eek out a living raising tobacco down in the Cumberlands. They didn't have time for their kid's problems. They themselves came from 'kids should be seen not heard' households. Sometimes Maggie would rebel against my father, but she didn't this time."

"Maggie was built for playing basketball. She lettered in it earlier that year. Back then the girls wore their letters on school sweaters and the boys wore the jackets. Maggie begged my parents to buy her that sweater but they thought it too frivolous. She so wanted that sweater to wear to school so she would fit in. I remember Maggie being buried in that gold letterman's sweater with the big maroon and white letter sown on. She looked so proud in it. I guess they thought it not so frivolous after all."

"Did your parents sue the man that hit your sister?" asked Samantha.

"No, we settled out of court. Maggie got two thousand dollars for dying, I got two hundred for mental trauma, Mama got sick and Daddy got taken; those damn Jews!"

"Aren't you being a little hard on Jewish people for what one man did?"

"You're right, Sam. Hell, my best friend in 'Nam, Mike Klassel, was a Jewish kid. We even went on R&R together. I guess what bothers me most is that a Jew killed Maggie and the Jews killed Jesus. Maggie always believed that when you die you go to a mansion on a hill. I've often wondered if she made it." Sonny smiled, "I can still picture her at home on that first day of suspension from school, sitting there with that ice bag on her eye. She looked laughable, but she was proud of her fighting trophy. Anyway, she looked at me with her good eye and said, 'Sonny, I think a man has to stick up for what he believes in, don't you?' I proudly agreed. She went on, 'Sometimes life is a war with many battles. The way I see it, is that we'll be judged on how many battles we've fought, not on how many we won.' That was her credo. Maggie taught me a lot of life's lessons. God bless Maggie Mae."

"As a young man, I was frightened of the world. I didn't have a clue on how it was run. Now I know. I'm disappointed with it, but at least now I know how it works."

"But are you still frightened of it, Sonny?"

"Even more so than before," he said somberly. "There is no mansion on a hill, Sam. It's an illusion."

"Oh, Sonny, you poor dear, the mansion on the hill is our goals, our aspirations. The fun part, darling, is our journey to get there. That's called life. Let's take that journey together."

"I don't know, Samantha. Why would a classy chick like you take a liking to someone like me? What I've shown you here and what all I've told you is all that I have."

"Listen to me, Sonny. I want you. I know that these woods are your home, your mansion, but you're living in the past."

"But, what about Tremont Inn?" he asked.

"You told me yourself that they are going to tear it down. Sonny. Please listen to me. I love you darling. I want you, I want all of you! I've agonized for nearly a week over you, Sonny. Please!" she begged.

"What about the boys at the prison?"

"We were not encumbered with saving the world, that's for the preachers and politicians. Incarceration is too late anyway. You've got to move to higher ground. Go to the streets. Meet the kids before they go too far. Listen, my dad has connections. He can help. Come back to Indy with me, Sonny. You can make a difference there. I'll be your confidant. Oh, I know that you're a maverick, but I won't fence you in, darling. I just want to feel you near. Take me in your arms my handsome one and hold me. Hold me tight."

Drawn in by the redolence of Sonny's male musk, Samantha adhered to his body and fervidly worked her soft mouth, sucking and licking on Sonny's neck, savoring his wild flavors. "I must know the taste of a man, a real man," she whispered in his ear.

Meanwhile, Sonny's mind was in battle with guilt versus passion, and love versus hate, with fear as the referee. "Sam, this home has been my safe haven ever since I was a kid, scared of life. I was forced out into it everyday. Then I came back to my home, here in the woods, by the tracks where I felt safe."

"I understand, but you embrace martyrdom like you're its lost prodigal son. You've got to pull yourself out of this quagmire. I have a quest for life, Sonny, and you're part of the mix. I'll commit myself to you, but you'll have to leave Paradise Woods behind. I can't compete with ghosts of the past, Sonny. I just can't. All of me for you, but you have to leave the mansion, that's the deal. I've never felt this strong about anything in my life. It means a commitment, a commitment that you won't regret."

Sonny's procrastination was becoming unsettling for the redhead in her heat of passion. With her womanhood ablaze her eyes danced with anticipation. "You're still playing the game, baby."

"What game, darling, I don't understand?

"You're the mystery, Sonny. That's right. You're like a mystery train, not knowing where you're headed." she said, her voice quivering.

Samantha broke from his grasp and bolted to the area where the house once stood. Without warning, she slowly raised her skirt, exposing her meager panties, fringed with her own natural red velvet. She then slipped her thumbs inside the elastic waistband and artfully slid out of the wispy garment, holding the sheer panty out in front of her for Sonny to see. Overwhelmed with desire, Samantha delivered her fervent message, "Come on Sonny, I'm ready, let me ride your mystery train. I want to ride your mystery train!"

She flung the delicate undergarment; then dropped her skirt, exposing her burning bush, and unbuttoned her silk dress shirt and let it fall to the ground. She introduced her ripened passion fruits to the warmth of the sun as their pale-red tips pointed upwards with altitude and attitude. She started dancing artfully as if in a ballet, toe dancing, leg kicks, pirouettes and all. The young danseuse looked chameleon-like as she moved through the woods. In the forest shadows she looked like a sylph. When she bounded in the sunlight she looked like the beautiful swift Impala whom Sonny referred to early on. But her slender naked body, with her ultra-thin waist, and hips that sat high on her legs, made her look more like the jaguar; beautiful, sleek, and dangerous. Her raw beauty held Sonny spellbound. The impudent young reporter looked scintillating prancing and dancing in the forest's light with her bright red curls bouncing freely and her buoyant breasts jiggling, generating her giggling.

Sonny became overwhelmed with Samantha's sprightly teasing. He rushed to meet her, and she ran to him. She laid siege to his body, crashing her twin peaks into his chest and assailing his neck with her hot succulent mouth in a wild embrace. She groped for his scepter and he savagely fondled her womanhood. "I'm tired of running down desolation alley, darling, it's a dead-end street," Sonny cried in desperation.

"You are such a mystery, my darling. Where you're headed I don't know, but if you lead I will follow. I want to ride your mystery train," she purred.

She kissed him long and hard, and open, with her reptilian-like tongue exploring deep, trying to reach the hot passion within his soul. She slid her hands up his chest, raising the cotton shirt with her thumbs and buried her face in the fur between his breasts, biting with little stinging nips into his chiseled brawn. Samantha then slowly slid down Sonny's chest, along the way releasing his trousers with her nimble fingers, and immersed her face into his dark silky growth while removing his coverings. She was met with a meteoric rise of his sexual passion. It was huge, not a prerequisite for a young collegian's quest, but an obstacle that she feverishly endeavored to over-take.

With sensual rage tearing at her insides she fell back onto her elbows, pulling Sonny on top of her while soulfully searching his eyes. With her breath brushing against his lips she whispered, "Take me to heaven, lover. Please, take me to a higher ground," she begged. She wrapped her hand around his huge circumference and guided him into her narrow secluded valley. Sonny plunged, and pierced a thin membrane, causing the red-haired virgin to roll her eyes back and gasp loudly as he broke through the keeper of the gate. Sonny stopped abruptly with the realization of his exclusive discovery. "Don't stop," cried Samantha; just on the brink of her sexual euphoria. "Take me, lover. Take me hard!" she demanded while scooching down lower to allow easier passage and a larger entry. Her virgin blood mixed amicably with her moist love. What were once gentle, fleshy folds amid her legs were now doors wide open, stretched taut against the pounding, massive intruder. The engorged ram-rod tested the suppleness of the straining twin lips while striving to bore an even deeper well. From the friction heat immerged her cobra head, swollen trice its size, ready to strike from within the depth of her fiery undergrowth. Samantha's svelte body shook violently from Sonny's powerful long thrusts. With her eyes open and shutting in cadence, her quivering lips spewed forth matching grunts of rapture, harmonious to his. To Sonny's repeated thrusts, Samantha's long legs were introduced to the rhythm of making love, and in this case, making life. The constant pounding was bruising the young reporter's pubic knuckle and was chafing her thighs, but their lovemaking had taken on incendiary proportions. Her incessant moaning wasn't from her raw wounds on the outside, but from her ecstasy created by Sonny's large protuberance stretching and probing the sensitive tissues inside her body. The forest mulch that supported her backside was now embossed in her tender skin, as she was scooted along by the force of her strong virile partner. There was no small talk now, just too lathered bodies in hard-driving carnal pleasure. Samantha's moans and pleasure groans culminated into shrieks of joy as she begged her lover along. While accumulating the last vestiges of their love making, the woman-child climaxed into one lasting explosion when Sonny spewed forth the hot molten lava of sex into the chambers of her love glen. Samantha arched her back, and her sleek figure quivered and shimmied as convulsing rhythms of ecstasy undulated throughout her body. Sonny withdrew blissfully in retreat. Samantha's fiery womanhood was ablaze and her over-filled vessel sizzled, creamy moist love.

Through Samantha's innocence, and loss of innocence, she had released Sonny from the tortures of life. He emerged out of his own dark recesses to find his demons gone. Samantha's quest for womanhood was met. She had lost her puritan ways but gained in moral strength. She came to Paradise as a "babe-in-the-woods" and would leave with one in her womb. As they lay naked in each others arms the glowing red-haired beauty softly stroked Sonny's head. The animals of the woods curiously gathered around to examine the new-born Adam and Eve. They were as one with Sonny in their Paradise woods, but cautious of the girl with the red mane and the alabaster breasts. She had made them skittish with her screams and moans of her ecstasy, but was now deemed acceptable as family as she sputtered little whimpers while cooing to her lover.

When Sonny tapped into her forbidden fruit the infusion of their two worlds created for them a new universe. He had taken her to the mountaintop, Beulah land. It was the place where her blood seeped and love flowed. Samantha wondered aloud, "Is this fate? Fate is such an easy answer. This must be providence. Yes, it is providence!" She softly closed her eyes in reverence. The stars shone down on the clandestine lovers as dusk permeated the evening.

"Mother, wake up! I'm afraid you've fallen asleep," said Danielle. Samantha awoke and rose up from her bath.

"Oh Mother, what a beautiful story," exclaimed Danielle, while helping her mom on with her bathrobe. "It sounds like a fairytale like Sleeping Beauty or Snow White."

"It *was* enchanting," mused Samantha.

"Did you ever go back to those Paradise woods, Mother?"

"Oh yes, my dear," said Samantha. "After you were born, you and I would return every year on the very day that you were conceived. It was our little ritual, yours and mine. That is, until you started school. We would have a little picnic, and I would tell you how wonderful your daddy was, and of the stories about his childhood growing up in

Paradise Woods. The last time that I visited Paradise Woods was six years ago after Sonny was almost killed in that motel raid."

"I remember. That was such a scary time. It was horrible," said Danielle. "Why then, Mother?"

"I guess that I went out of guilt of not being there for Sonny when he needed me most. I was in D.C . . . doing my thing. You know, reporting Washington politics and such. Paradise Woods just wasn't the same when I was there last. There was no enchantment, no magic, no . . . Sonny. I once remembered a time when the wind would slice through the trees and you swore that the woods were alive and singing to you, almost symphonic. It was magic, Danielle. Everything seemed mystical, but not the last time. The woods seemed so forlorn, abandoned, with little hope. It was as if it had lost something or someone very dear. I felt unwanted there."

"Did Sonny ever go back?"

"No, your dad came with me to Indianapolis and never looked back. He left his memories, his friends; left it all for me."

"I wish Matt felt that way about me," moaned Danielle.

"Oh, I wouldn't worry about Matt, my dear. He's just a pup that needs to be disciplined, now and again."

"I guess that's my job, huh?"

"Look," laughed Samantha, "Sonny is as tough as they come, but even he needs nurturing at times. Besides, if Matt has any mettle in him at all he'll straighten out."

"I certainly hope so," Danielle sighed wishfully.

"What separates Sonny from most other men is that he's got mettle. He is the boldest man I have ever known."

"Mom, what's the secret of the longevity of your and Daddy's marriage?"

"He made me into a woman and I let him be a man. Plus we are both very adventurous. We'll try anything, once."

"Are you still in love with Daddy?"

"What makes you ask that?"

"Oh, I've noticed slight changes between you and Daddy ever since he got fired from the police force."

"Your daddy didn't get fired from the police force. He was retired as an honored hero."

"Look, Mom, he retired at the age of 42 with 18 years of service.

What did he get, an early-out?"

"Yes, he did, as a matter-of-fact. Besides, where do you get all of this nonsense?"

"Words get bandied about."

"Well, lay that rumor to rest because your dad is a good man."

"You still haven't answered my question, Mother."

"Am I still in love with your dad? I don't know anymore. I think so. There are no red flags yet. A few caution flags maybe and some speed-bumps along the way these last few years. Oh, we fell in love alright, there's no doubt there, but in love with? Oh, how he used to make me laugh. Now I have my silent joys."

"Do you still make love to each other?"

"Oh yes, but not with the same fervor. Look, Danny, changes take place in our lives that we have no control over. I'll never stop loving Sonny. Sonny has changed since Centralia, but it's not because he left the force. He left part of his soul back in that motel room. Sonny once told me that as we walk down life's highway, you never know what fork in the road you'll take. You just pray that it's the right one. I picked lucky, Danny. I found providence. I can't imagine my life without Sonny Rafferty in it."

"That makes me feel good, Mom. Thanks for sharing that with me."

Mother and daughter shared warm hugs as Samantha kissed a tear sliding down Danielle's cheek. "I've go to go now, but before I do, I would like to know what became of Genevieve and Sir Charles of Tremont Inn? Did she make it, Mom?"

"Genevieve spent three years in a psych ward, and the last we saw of her she was picking peaches from her orchard in Paw-Paw Michigan. She married a nice farmer and thanked Sonny for being there for her. Sir Charles, on the other hand, couldn't come to grips with leaving Tremont Inn. He once told me that he didn't participate in life anymore, he was just a spectator. Verna found him in his room, dead from a gunshot wound to the head. On his writing table, where his head lay, was a bottle of Pinot Noir and a note to Sonny. Sonny gave me the note and I've kept it over the years in my Bible, right next to the Lord's Prayer. If you could wait a bit longer I would like to get it and read it to you."

"Oh, yes Mother, please do."

Sonny,
I caught a falling star, seems like yesterday
I'm sorry but I let her slowly steal away,
You loved her too I once heard you say.
So have a drink with me Old Chap,
Let's celebrate today
If you do this my friend, your debt to me is paid
Sir Charles of Lancashire (Tremont Inn)

"Go home now, Danny, and good luck tomorrow."

"Thanks Mom. Thanks for making me feel wanted after all."

"You're welcome, but the next time you come over late in the evening, little girl, use the front door. You scared the shit out of me tonight."

"Okay," laughed Danielle as she closed the door.

Samantha disrobed and slid her warm body between the cool sheets of her mansion bed. Concerned over Sonny, but enormously tired from the long day's events, she soon fell into peaceful slumber. Impala jumped up onto the mansion bed and lay at her master's feet, for she too sensed that something was amiss.

R-i-n-n -n-n-n-g, R-i-n-n-n-n-n-g, R-i-n-n-n-n-n-g!

"Hello?"

"Is this Mrs. Rafferty?"

"Yes it is."

"I'm sorry to wake you at this late hour, but it's about your husband . . . ."

Chapter Eleven

The Devil's Bone Yard

The countryside shone silvery on this warm summer's eve as the Hoosier crops bathed brightly in the night's celestial light. The thirsty corn silently consumed the moisture from the thick heavy air that hung about, while oblivious to the black stealth marauder barreling down the paved trail that ran among it.

Two country rubes spilled out of the corn onto the county road that was healing from the day's treacherous sun, unsuspecting of their impending rendezvous with an even darker side of nature than the blackened night.

They said that Travis Bowles was the "catfish king" of Jefferson County. They also said that Travis wasn't wound too tight. If that was the case then his nephew and long time fishing buddy, Po Daniels, wasn't wound at all. Travis, the larger of the two, walked at a smart pace while carrying his fishing tackle and catch bucket. On his heels was Po, his simple-minded but affable sidekick. Their voices filled the night like a couple of magpies at a berry festival.

"Nary a fish tonight, how do you figure that, Travis? We had a full moon, no wind, nor rain, I don't get it," complained the befuddled, Po Daniels.

"Ain't no figuring to it, Po, it's just plain bad luck. Why, this morning I was hauling some gravel down to Clifty Falls and a black cat ran out in front of me. Sure enough, as I was driving through that S-curve on Hwy 62, I had a blowout and dumped the load. Lucky I wasn't kilt. That cat was a bad omen. It took half a day to get a wrecker out there to right that truck. The boss gave me heck. Said I was driving too fast. Put me on probation he did. That's not all," babbled the fishing genius, "This afternoon, while driving home, I saw a terrible car accident in San Jacinto where a woman plowed into the back of a hay wagon. Kilt her dead. I saw her before the police arrived. She smashed the windshield with her face. Cut her up real bad. I hadn't seen a person messed up that bad since 'Nam. Then, this evening we couldn't even catch a fish. That ain't never happened to us at Meyer's Pond. No siree, I see a bad moon a rising, Po, a bad moon I say."

Travis sensed that Po wasn't following him anymore. He impatiently turned around to see what he was up to. "What in tarnation are you doing, Po? If you keep straggling behind, Della Rae's goin' to give me what for and skin you alive, boy! We're already two hours late in a gettin' home. Hopefully she'll be snoring away like she usually is."

"I'm trying to catch me a fish out of Meyer's ditch, here," claimed Po.

"You ain't gonna catch no fish out of that ditch, Po. The best you can do is to hook a minnow or a frog. Pull your line back in and let's go," pleaded Travis.

The pole suddenly bent, "Wait a minute, Travis. I caught something, and it's big!"

"Congratulations Po, you just hooked a muskrat and he ain't happy. Cut the line before he takes a nip out of ya!"

Travis noticed a set of headlights coming toward them, "Po, stand up and take heed!"

"Why, what's wrong?" asked Po, snipping the nylon filament.

"There's a car comin,' and the way our luck is going he'll probably run us over," quipped Travis.

The men watched curiously as the black sedan screeched to a halt. Travis sensed trouble as he stared into the bright beams of light. "Po, go see what they want!" ordered Travis. Po nonchalantly walked up to the driver's side of the automobile. Travis raised his hand in front of his eyes, blocking the intense glare as he strained to watch his simple pal conversing with an occupant of the dark vehicle. He could see Po, wide-eyed and talking nervously. That disturbed Travis because when Po got nervous he would babble incoherently, and then nobody could understand him. Po suddenly bolted from the car window with a look of terror on his face. He quickly waved for Travis to rescue him from his dilemma. Travis sensed danger and walked abruptly towards the black ford while sliding his right hand into the back pocket of his overalls to secure the 25-caliber hand gun that he carried for shooting vermin.

"Hello, mister. Can I help ya?" asked Travis.

A strong gruff voiced erupted, "Stop right there farm boy. If you pull anything but a handkerchief out of your back pocket you won't live to see the sun come up! Do you hear me, boy?"

"Y-y-y-yes sir," snapped Travis.

"As a matter of fact, take that palm pistol out of your back pocket, drop it on the ground, and kick it under the car."

"Yes sir, I'll do that now," said the obedient oaf.

From his glances at the configuration inside that car, Travis perceived a lone male occupant sporting a wide-brimmed hat pulled down low, and he derived from the tone of his voice that he was desperate and dangerous, and maybe somewhat demented. Travis knew that the stranger meant business.

"I tried to pry some information from your lain-brained friend there, but he just started talking stupid shit, couldn't make him out."

"Pay no attention to Po, mister. He's a retard. It weren't his fault though. His mother was a whore. Heck, she used to spread her legs every time she caught the scent of a boy. Then one night she latched onto Paylo Daniels —"

"I get the picture," said the disgruntled stranger. "What I need to know is where the hell am I?"

Travis glanced at Po and Po at Travis with a puzzling look. "Why, mister, you're somewhere between Paris Crossing and Clifty Falls, said Travis. Po and I come from Scoville, but we live just up the road apiece. Where are you headed, mister?"

"Indianapolis."

"That's over two hours north of here. Where did ya leave from?"

"Centralia," said the stranger.

"Centralia? Geez, mister, you've been going in the wrong direction if you're headin' towards Indianapolis."

A sigh of frustration came from the dark silhouette that sat before them. "Well, I need a drink. Do one of you boys have a bottle on you; whiskey, moonshine, anything?"

"I ain't never acquired the taste for drink, myself," spouted Po. "Travis used to drink but he got saved last year so he don't drink no more."

"Saved? Saved from what?"

"Saved from hell-fire and damnation," bragged Po.

"He means that I got saved from the evil of drink," said Travis sheepishly.

"Well, would either one of you do-gooder morons happen to know where a fella' could get a drink around here if he *wasn't* saved from the evils of this world?" growled the stranger.

"Oh yes," answered Travis. "Drive about two and half miles up this road and turn right onto Rattlesnake Highway. It's a gravel road but they named it Rattlesnake Highway 'cause they've found so many rattlesnakes in that vicinity, which is rare in these parts."

"Yeah, I saw one myself," added Po. "Was walking down that road one day collecting aluminum cans when I came across a big diamondback sunnin' himself right there on the gravel. I would've kilt him but all I had was a can-hook."

"Anyway," continued Travis, "Rattlesnake Highway will lead you straight to a roadhouse called the 'Devil's Bone Yard.' It sits right on the edge of an old limestone quarry. They call it the 'Bone Yard' 'cause it's been rumored that there are more than a few bodies buried in that old water-filled quarry. It's a dangerous place, mister. The locals all hang out there but the Bone Yard seems to attract a lot of outsiders, also."

"Yeah, Travis used to go there to date girls. One night the outsiders beat him up so bad they almost kilt him. That's when he got saved," said Po.

"I think the man has heard enough of your foolishness, Po. We ought to let him be on his way," urged Travis.

From the dark recesses of the black cruiser came the guttural utterances of, "Homer, you take Jethro on home now, and get rid of that little palm pistol before you shoot your little dicks off!"

"Okay. Yes sir. I'll do that. I sure will."

"Good evening, gents," said the dark stranger as the big ford squealed out, leaving its mark embedded in the warm pavement.

The two bumpkins picked up their gear and began strolling home.

"That man really scared me," admitted Po.

"Yeah, he scared me too. I'll tell you somethin' Po, that man has either seen the Grim Reaper or he is about to meet him. You could see it in his eyes!"...

"Hey, Travis."

"What is it, Po?"

"I think I wet myself back there."

"Po, that's alright."

..."Hey, Travis"

"What is it, Po?"

"When I die will I go to heaven?"

"Sure, you have a free voucher, Po. It's the unlucky stiffs like me that have to worry."

"Don't you think I need to be baptized first?"

"Heck, we tried to baptize you but you bit the preacher's hand when he was putting you under."

"He was trying to smother me, Travis. I couldn't breathe."

"You couldn't breathe because he put his hand over your mouth so you wouldn't drown, you idiot."

"But I nearly drowned anyway, Travis."

"Po, you beat all I ever saw. I can't believe you came out of my dear sister's womb. Nope, you couldn't have. You must've been one of them asshole babies."

"I was not. Take that back, Travis!"

Travis enjoyed toying with his slow-witted nephew, as Po was good company to him. But this time he sensed that he hurt his feelings as the boy fell behind and sulked. "I didn't mean it, Po, I was just joking with ya," Travis apologized. "Come back up here and walk with me."

Po rushed back up and hung his arm around his uncle as they walked down the road like a couple of school chums.

"You should have seen that preacher's face when you bit him. Boy what a sight. He was howlin' like a banshee, and you were flailing around in that water. Heck, I had to wade into that old pond myself and save you from drownin'."

"Did you, Travis? Was that you that saved me?"

"You're dern tootin' it was."

..."You know, Aunt Edna once told me that I must have crawled out from under a rock."

"Did she really?"

"Yes she did, quite a few times," said Po, nodding his head.

"Well, I wouldn't take stock in anything that Aunt Edna said. She's dead now anyway. Her third husband did her in for mouthing off so much.". . . Sniff, sniff, "hey Po."

"What is it, Travis?"

"Take your arm down. You're startin' to smell."

"Oh,". . . Po smiled oafishly.

The air lay heavy with the stench of stale cigarette smoke, along with the pungent smell of Columbian Gold. The muffled prattle in the background was that of the clannish locals unwinding from the workweek. The sound that the juke-box blared out was none other than the infamous "Steve Earle", the country outlaw rocker, singing a cult favorite, "Copperhead Road."

Harlan Tweeter was small but wiry. His dossier read as a round robin of violence and failures. When he drank too much, Harlan got quite pugnacious. The majority of the time he took his hostilities out on the barroom harlots. Most of them steered clear of the scurrilous Tweeter because he was too abusive for their liking. There was one tart, however, a little hellion by the name of Lori Burns, who hung with the likes of Tweeter and his friends when she wasn't hustling.

Tonight Lori was hangin' and Harlan was playing, pool that is, a game of eight-ball with his nefarious friend, Jimmy Tompkins; Jimmy Tom to his friends and relatives. Completing the four-some around the pool table was the lowbred, rawboned, Dirt Weaver; as vile as they came, for he was known for being the dirtiest barroom brawler in three counties.

To the right corner of the tavern sat two members of the Devil's Disciples' motorcycle gang. The bigger of the two was a huge man known only as Pig Eye. Pig Eye was a skinhead and a hulk of a man, topping 400lbs easily while sporting several piercings on or about his head. Sitting next to him was a big burley fellow, lesser in size than his friend, but never-the-less a strapping man with bulging biceps, who went by the name of Blue Nose. He once dabbled in pugilism in his earlier years before joining the biker gang. He derived his name from a broad tattoo of a dragon sweeping across his face, camouflaging most of his beak with the blue dye. Blue Nose and Pig Eye were hired by the powers-that-be to help guard the Devil's Bone Yard from interlopers, and to act as bouncers when the barroom brawls got out of hand. Most of the time they treated the bar fights as sporting events until someone was about to meet their demise. That's when they stepped in. There was no love lost between the bikers and the locals at the Bone Yard.

To the far end of the room from where the bikers co-existed, and across from where the profligates were playing pool, was an L-shaped bar boasting 20 stools in length and four stools wide at the end, next to the door.

Yes, the Devil's Bone Yard was alive tonight just as it was every late Friday night, except . . . for the stranger sitting stealthily next to the door.

"Barkeep, a shot of "Jack" and a beer," ordered the voice from under the pulled down fedora.

Tommy Mack gave a nod at the wayward stranger with no eyes. Tommy was always amused at the variety of people that allowed him to enter into their lives from behind that bar. Some came begging. Others just wanted to be entertained. A few wanted a confidant, most just wanted a friendly plate to spoon their troubles on. Tommy was a pro. In his 30 years of keeping bar he'd seen it all, at the big houses, the swank houses; in Chicago, Cincinnati, New Orleans, and then to Hicksville, USA. Some called it a step down, but Tommy Mack worked for the money. He knew how to listen and when to keep his mouth shut, and he knew how to deal out the liquor.

Tommy promptly returned with the stranger's order to slake his thirst. "Mr., you look like someone who has a bad memory of something that he wants to kick loose," he said inquisitively.

"Mind your own business," snarled back the stranger while slamming down the shot glass onto the mahogany counter.

"Yes sir, I'll do that. I sure will," assured Tommy. "I just thought that maybe you needed someone to talk to, that's all. Give me a yell when you want another drink, Mr."

"Keep the whiskey coming," said the stranger.

"Gotcha!" nodded the barkeeper.

"Ha-ha-ha," guffawed a slattern old hag from four stools away. "Mind your own business! Mind your own goddamn business! I guess he told you, Mack," taunted the gaunt lantern–jawed woman. "Hey stranger; how about buying an old gal a drink, how about it Mr. Huh?"

"Shut up, Thelma," snapped Tommy. "Pay no attention to that spiteful old shrew, Mr. She's just a Bone Yard alky. She's like a bad penny. We keep getting rid of her but she keeps coming back."

From behind Tommy's back came a loud cry of, "Fuck you, Tommy. I need a goddamn drink!"

"Get her a drink," ordered the stranger.

"Make that a double-vodka," sneered Thelma.

Lori Burns searched the barroom in hopes of finding a new customer to milk. By this time of night she had usually serviced most of the men that wanted her action. Star Cargile was Lori's sole competitor for the evening, but she was slowly becoming a fallen' star what with that prominent white belly of hers bulging from underneath her short tee, and getting larger each week. Any other competition would come from beyond the black wall. The black wall led to the rear portion of the establishment, which was properly called, "The Devil's Lair".

The Devil's Lair actually consumed most of the roadhouse. The barroom was more-or-less a front for the mysterious goings on in the rest of the Bone Yard. From the outside there was a side entrance to the Lair where luxury sedans and limousines stayed parked. There was no back entrance to the club, but in keeping with the local code there was a rear exit, and if one were to leave through that exit they would fall into the abyss, the bottomless gulf, so they say, and would most likely meet their demise, for the Devil's Bone Yard sat on the very edge of a water-filled quarry pit. Many rumors existed about what was in that black hole.

The Lair boasted of a gambling room with a roulette wheel, several one-arm bandits, and two high-stakes poker tables. The Lair also encompassed a bookie's den and the boss's office. Upstairs were a-half dozen suites for the ladies of the evening and their gentleman friends. Those were the places where a man could imbibe in his favorite fantasies, where a sensuous strumpet could showcase her wares, where she could bump and grind into a man's heart, feed his voracious imagination, and then open herself up to him. The more she opened up the more he opened his wallet; very good for business, and good for the nurture finders.

At the far right end of the bar there was a door that led to the Devil's Lair, but it was kept locked. Only Tommy Mack could enter. Occasionally a high-class hooker would emerge from the Lair to retrieve a particular liquor from the bar. And if her business was slow, and a local barroom patron caught her eye, she might solicit him to sell her wares. That infuriated the local trollops, especially Lori, but she couldn't do much about it because "the man" gave his approval; "the man", being Miles Pergosi, the manager of one of the county's most profitable businesses. "Greasy Palm Pergosi" was what his adversaries called him but they were far and few between, or in hiding, for the roots of corruption run far and deep.

"Hey, Harlan"

"Don't bother me girl, I'm about to make a very important shot," he answered while staring down the long tapered rod that was poised to hit the white ball on the felt table.

"I just saw Nabob Williams come in and I'm going up front to do some business with him," interrupted Lori.

Frustrated, Harlan backed off his shot and gave Lori a scowling look. "Okay, go take care of the old man, then skitter your ass back here with some beers 'cause I think the waitress must of died or somethin'."

Hardly anyone noticed the scarlet dressed woman that slipped into the haze of the beer parlor from the Devil's Lair, for the music was loud, and so was the barroom banter, as Friday night's were long and festive at the Devil's Bone Yard.

"Hey, Tommy, business is good tonight eh?"

"Hi, Candy. Yeah, we're fairly busy, how about you?"

"Nah, my man cancelled tonight, some Logansport banker. Got any prospects for me tonight?"

"Not really, sweetheart," he replied. "There is this stranger at the end of the bar that Lori hasn't seen yet. He's kinda hard to talk to. I think he has some major problems."

"I'm good at problem solving. That's my greatest asset."

"That's not what I've heard," teased the bartender.

"What did *ju* hear about me?" she said with a sly smile.

"I've heard that you've got a mean swing on your back porch," quipped Tommy.

"That's right, honey. Swing it or don't bring it. Shake it and don't break it," said Candy as she swiveled her hips back and forth. They both shared a laugh. "Actually, I'm here to get a bottle of Champagne for Jamaica Red."

"Champagne? I delivered a case over to the Lair yesterday!" exclaimed Tommy.

"Jes, but Jamaica Red wants the "primo" stuff. I guess she's entertaining a high roller from Indianapolis tonight, some wannabe politician or somethin' like that. Pergosi okayed it."

"Why does Pergosi hire those high-baggage whores for anyway?" said Tommy.

"First of all she's not a 'ho.' She's a call-girl, and a very high-priced one at that, and Pergosi knows that high-baggage reaps high profits."

"Yeah, I know," admitted Mack. "To me she's an arrogant bitch. Why couldn't she be more like you? You're cute, and you make good bread in the Lair."

"Be like me, a Puerto Rican?" laughed Candy. "Let me tell *ju* somethin', Tommy. The high-rollers like '*Rican poosy* but we're too trashy for show."

"Well, you look fine to me."

"Why don't *ju* cross over sometime and take a taste?" she flirted.

"It's not my style to make it with the help, nor is it Pergosi's policy."

"I'll give *ju* a cut rate, Tommy."

"Thanks just the same, sweetheart. I'll go get the Champagne for you now. It might take awhile. It's packed away in storage somewhere."

"Take your time, Tommy. Jamaica Red's got all night with her man, and besides, I want to check out that stranger at the far end of the bar," she said provocatively.

Candy sneaked up on the unsuspecting stranger and softly pressed her firm breasts into his side while smoothly caressing his back. She felt him relax, for his body was in the now but his mind was six years past. She whispered softly in his ear, "Hello mister. My name is Candy Adams. *Ju* know, Candy, as in candy shop. I sell sweets of all kinds for *ju* my lover. What's nice about me is that I'm open twenty-four-seven. *Ju* can enter the front door or come in the rear, whatever your preference is," she murmured in her soft Puerto Rican drawl.

Her voice seemed warmly familiar to the stranger, but not recognizable. He raised his head and looked at the glowing face of the young courtesan but still didn't make a connection. She then gazed into *his* eyes as they danced furiously with the past.

"Hey, I know *ju!*" cried the young Hispanic. "*Ju're* the cop that took my sister off the streets and helped her get off drugs."

The stranger was nonplussed by the Spanish harlot.

"*Ju* must remember her, mister. Her name is Angie Garza. I'm

Candy Garza, her younger sister. She was 16 at the time and I was only 10. Remember? *Ju* even got her a job on the police force. I don't know how *ju* did it, with her drug record and all. I do know that she is very grateful to *ju*, sir. Shit, she had a crush on *ju* for the longest time. Now she even owns her own business, thanks to *ju*."

"Look, that's all very nice, but I'm not a cop."

"But, but—"

"You seem to be a nice girl, Candy, and I'm sure that you are good at what you do, but I don't want any. I just came in here tonight to wash away some old memories. So thanks for your offer, darling, maybe some other time."

"You heard what he said. He don't want no Mexican whore. Go on back to your ghetto and have a whole passel of kids. That's about all your good for anyway," screeched Thelma.

The stranger had just about had it with Thelma's caustic remarks and cast a glare her way. The old woman retreated into her drink. He then pushed his hat forward and slugged down some more brew. Meanwhile, Candy sadly retreated back to the other end of the bar to wait for Tommy's return. She was bewildered by the stranger in the drawn-down hat. She was sure that he was the man who had previously saved her sister, Angie, from a certain demise, and he was the cop that the Indianapolis Hispanic community once held in very high esteem.

It wasn't unusual seeing men coming out of the women's bathroom at the Devils Bone Yard, especially when Lori was on duty. They usually emerged light on their feet and lighter in their wallets.

Nabob Williams slipped out first and stumbled oafishly to his barstool. Lori soon followed looking none the bit ruffled as she had made short work of Nabob. He was one of her favorites. He would loose his seed quicker than any of the others, even the virgins.

Nabob's wife was Lori's high school guidance counselor and 10th grade algebra teacher; flunked her too. Mrs. Williams, in a way, was now helping to support Lori's career choice.

Lori did a double-take as she caught sight of the stranger at the end of the bar. "How did I miss that big fellow?" she said to herself. "He must've slipped in while I was in the john doing Nabob. Doesn't matter, he looks like a hunk, unlike the rest of these barnyard dogs. Come on girl, let's turn up the charm, have some fun and make some big bucks here," she declared.

The stranger sensed Lori skulking up to him even before the acid-tongued Thelma started her ranting.

"You cheap hussy, go back to your squalor!"

"Up yours, Thelma!" said Lori.

"Go sleep with your dogs you fornicator, you devil's foot!"

"Shut up you old witch," cried Lori.

"Leave the stranger alone you sorry slut."

"Fuck you, Thelma!"

The stranger winced as the bawdy young girl grabbed at his crotch.

"What do you have slithering in your pocket, mister?" asked Lori.

No answer.

"Well, I'm going to make you a happy man tonight. What do you say to that?"

No answer.

"You don't talk much do you, mister?"

Still, no sound came from the stranger.

"Let me give you a little sample then," said Lori unabashedly, pulling up her tee and exposing her breasts. "How do you like these beauties, mister," asked the bumptious young hooker.

No answer again.

"Goddamn it, mister, are you going to look at me or not?" she moaned.

"I don't need to look at you. I can smell you," growled the outsider.

"Smell me, smell me? Then what do I smell like, big guy, lilacs or roses?"

"You smell like male sweat and stale ejaculate."

A tempest was beginning to stir inside the young hellcat as she asked again, "What did you say I smelled like?"

"You smell like sheep dip and mule sperm. Now go away and leave me alone," said the voice from under the hat.

"Do you know who my boyfriend is, mister?"

"Apparently every man in this room," he replied.

"You're an ass. You know that? Tonight you shall feel the wrath of Harlan Tweeter, and believe me, stranger; you're not going to like the results. Nobody makes a fool out of Harlan Tweeter's girl. Do you understand?" Lori turned abruptly to rush back to Harlan, but instead, ran into Jimmy Tompkins.

"Where the hell you been, girl? Harlan's gettin' pissed, he wants his beer," scolded Jimmy.

"This guy right here has been giving me a hard time, Jimmy," she said referring to the stranger.

"Do you mean that old guy with the hat?"

"Yeah, that old fella, he's been treating me like yesterday's garbage. I reckon he can't get it up is his problem," said Lori, loud enough for all to hear.

"You run back and fetch Harlan. I'll take care of this guy," said Jimmy. "Hey, mister, you messin' with Harlan's girl?" he yelled out.

No answer.

"I'm talking to you, asshole!" said Jimmy, moving closer to get in the stranger's face.

Without hesitation the stranger grabbed the aggravating Tompkins by the hair of his head and slammed his face against the polished hardwood counter, breaking his nose, all-the-while not leaving his barstool. Tompkins fell to the floor, out like a light.

Thelma Jenkins had just relaxed into a drunken stupor when the commotion around the stranger stirred her. Aside from the fact that she was able to pry a couple of drinks out of him, there was something about that stranger that drew her to him. She couldn't quite figure it out. It didn't feel like a kinship or anything like that, but something from the past maybe, a common thread of some kind.

The room suddenly turned cold to Thelma. She felt a strange entity creeping about. She became fearful, not just for herself, but for everyone within the room.

"He's coming to. Lori, go fetch a wet towel and clean him up. Dirt, help Jimmy Tom to his feet while I go take care of this fella!" ordered Harlan.

"Hey, stranger, why did you slight my girl for?" yelled Harlan, walking up to the outsider.

No answer.

"Hey, Indiana Jones, I'm talking to you!" snapped Harlen. "Lori Ann told me that you tried to humiliate her. She said that you grabbed her in places that you shouldn't grab a lady. You hurt her pride. Do you know that? O-h-h-h, I forgot. She's a whore isn't she? And whores ain't got no pride do they, Jonesy? I'll forgive you for that, Jonesy, but you hurt my friend, Jimmy, and Jimmy don't like that. I don't like that either, Jonesy, not at all. I'm gonna' have to hurt ya, Jonesy, hurt ya real bad!"

The crowded room grew quiet, and the jukebox sat silent while the tension in the air became stifling. Even Blue Nose and Pig Eye gathered around as evil crawled from its ugly darkness. But the brown-hat mystery man just sat there minding his own demons with his head down and his hand holding firmly to his glass of whiskey that sat atop the polished bar. His silence was deafening. Suddenly, the snappish sound of a switchblade cut through the tension.

"Harlan, don't, please, he just came in here to drink away his troubles. He doesn't mean any harm," pleaded Tommy Mack, just back from the storeroom.

Tommy's pleading just antagonized Harlan more, as the shiny blade began vacillating back and forth. He was now joined by Jimmy Tom and Dirt Weaver. All were poised and ready. Harlan had that crazed look in his eyes and an evil smile across his face as he grew ever so closely to the brawn of the stranger's back.

Thelma stood up suddenly, and spewed forth with the clarity of a skilled orator;

"I looked and there before me was a pale horse
Its rider was named DEATH
And hell followed close behind
Behold the pale horse and his rider come by
Feel the hot breath of hell tonight."

The stranger suddenly spun around, and with his left hand, blocked the knife coming at his neck. He then stood up to face Harlen. And for one split second Harlan saw it. He saw what every human fears the most. He saw the death mask of the Grim Reaper—He saw the steely eyes of Sonny Rafferty! In one powerful stroke the heel of Sonny's right hand smashed Harlan's nose back into his brain causing instant death.

Panic stricken, Jimmy Tom took a timid swing and missed while Sonny came back with a furious left hook to his mouth causing a red vapor to fill the air, taking him down like a crushed puff-ball. Meanwhile, Dirt Weaver caught Sonny with a hard left to his right ear, knocking him to his knees. Sonny tried fighting back from his weakened position but several more hard blows from Weaver put him down, spread-eagle on the wood flooring among the smashed cigarette butts. Dirt gave him a swift kick to the ribs to make sure that he was out. The body flopped lifelessly. Clad only in a muscle shirt and sweat pants the fiendish Dirt Weaver straddled his lifeless opponent, and while gloating to the onlookers, pulled down his sweats, exposing his manhood. He grabbed his hose and started pissing on his victim, a tradition among many of the Bone Yard degenerates.

Lori Ann, Blue Nose and Pig Eye spurred the champion on in his degrading of the outsider while others walked away in disgust. Tommy Mack just shook his head, while Candy cried shamelessly. Thelma smiled. She just . . . smiled. Suddenly, Sonny bolted up, grabbing a grape and plucking it from its vine, bringing the screaming ex-champion to his knees clutching his damaged ball-sac. He then dove headlong into the big belly of the ursine-like Pig Eye. He knocked him back but not down. The fat man grabbed Sonny around his lungs and began squeezing. Sonny gritted his teeth and constricted his body while pummeling Pig Eye's hard cranium. It wasn't working. The Pig man was winning and Sonny was weakening. Sonny then jammed his thumb into the big behemoth's eye. Pig Eye screamed out but squeezed even tighter. Sonny could hear Blue Nose's wicked laughter in the background.

"Come on, Pig Eye, crush him. Kill that son-of-a-bitch!"

Sonny was desperate now so he jammed a second digit into the eye and plucked it out clean. The fat man dropped him and grabbed at his eye socket. Sonny quickly sidestepped a wild lunge from Blue Nose while shoving him into a table and chairs. He then gave a hard kick to the side of Pig Eye's right leg, popping his kneecap, sending the fat man sprawling on the floor in great pain. Sonny turned, only to be peppered by three straight rights from Blue Nose who was now in his boxing stance. Sonny assumed his boxing stance, but kept getting peppered by his larger opponent's right hand. Sonny was a brawler, not a boxer. He knew that he had to use his cunning if he was to prevail against this one-time pugilist. Blue Nose continued beating Sonny's face into a bloody pulp. Sonny finally got a shot into the big man's ribs, making him wince, causing an opening, allowing Sonny to plow into his body, smashing him up against the bar. Blue Nose was somewhat shocked by the resiliency of the indefatigable stranger. He wrested out of Sonny's tight grip and shoved him away, but the Bone Yard stranger came storming back. Blue Nose mustered all of his strength and used his leverage to flip the crazed madman over his head and over the bar behind him into the bottled liquor and the bar-length mirror, causing shards of glass to fly in every direction. Blue Nose wearily climbed over the bar only to be met with Sonny's left hook. The irate Disciple started peppering Sonny with punches again but Sonny kept spinning his way down the bar isle receiving mostly glancing blows while trying to wear the boxer down, and it worked. When his fatigued opponent reached the end Sonny righted himself and landed a quick right jab into his adversary's throat, busting his larynx. The troubled boxer grabbed at his throat gasping for air as Sonny delivered another crushing blow to the big guy's ribs. You could hear the sound of his bones cracking throughout the barroom. Sonny then grabbed him by his legs and shoved him back over the counter onto the floor. He followed after to deliver one last death-blow to the man's throat. He reached down and pulled him up by his bloodied shirt, raised his fist and . . . heard this voice in his head, an old friend, the voice saying, "Sonny, Sonny stop! What's the matter with you? This isn't how you taught me to do our job. Take it easy. This is Junior speaking. This is Junior speaking. This is Junior . . . ."

Sonny didn't feel the chair crashing into his skull. His eyes rolled back into a deep sleep while his head met the floor. There he lay, next to death's door, while the crimson face of Jimmy Tompkins spluttered incoherently.

The light appeared, then dissipated. It reappeared now and again getting brighter each time. "Where am I?" asked Sonny to himself. "I can't hear myself breathe. Hell, I can't move! Am I dead; in suspended animation? Wait a minute. I see something. It's a shadow of some kind. It's fuzzy but getting clearer. It's a woman. I can tell by her long bare legs. She must be Samantha. But why is she standing over me? Wait. Someone else is joining her. I know him. That's Chance! What's he doing with Samantha? Wait a minute. That's not Samantha. She's too dark-skinned. Where the hell am I? Oh man, it's getting fuzzy again, and the pain in my head is killin' me. Samantha. . . . ."

"He's not carrying a piece so he isn't a cop," said Pergosi after frisking the stranger.

"Oh, he's a cop alright," said Chance Taylor. "Don't you know who this guy is?"

"No sir, but I've got his wallet right here. Let me check. It says . . .

Sonny Rafferty."

"That's right, and my sister's name is Samantha Rafferty. This guy is my brother-in-law. He's up to no good. He was a vice squad detective for Indianapolis Metro until he fucked up and got his nigger partner and a young girl killed. Metro discharged him of his duties so he then became a private dick. There's no tellin' what he's doing here. I personally can't stand the guy myself. Neither can my ol' man. Rafferty has always been big with Niggers and Spics. They treat him like he's their savior or somethin'. Hell, he's got three of 'em damn near living in his house right now."

"Oh, I'm sorry, my lovely. Don't take this personal. You are above all that aren't you?" asked Chance of the elegant, burnished skinned Jamaica Red.

Jamaica Red didn't say a word, just held her head high. She knew that Chance would pay for his remarks with his green in due time. Besides, Jamaica Red didn't care about race, politics, or religion. All of that was too mundane for her. Sex was her game, and Chance was a major player, as was his father before him.

"So what do you want to do with him, Chance?"

"I want you to finish him off," he said callously. "Use a shiv. It's quiet that way. Then dump the body into the quarry."

"But Chance, it's been years since I've iced someone," said Pergosi.

"He's almost dead anyway, Miles, but don't worry. If I'm not mistaken, that's the dead boy's girlfriend leaning against the wall over there with his stiletto hangin' from her hand. She looks to be a bit stressed to me. I think she should be the one to finish off Sonny."

Miles at one time had some cold blood in him and diced a few people, but he had never seen anybody as cold-blooded as Chance Taylor.

"Hey, sis, come over here!" yelled Chance.

"What do you want?" said the tearful hooker.

"How would you like to get revenge for your boyfriend's death?"

"What do you mean?"

"Why don't you take that pick that you have in your hand and run it through that man's ribs a couple of times. That ought to make you feel better," said Chance.

"Sure I will Mr. I'd love to kill that bastard," she said with hate in her voice. Lori knelt down beside Sonny and smiled as she drew the knife back.

"Hold it right there, drop that knife!" shouted Deputy Zeke Doughtry, nervously pointing his revolver at Lori.

Lori rose up slowly.

"Hold on a minute, Lori," said Miles hastily. "Zeke, what the hell are you doing here? You know that you're not to be at the Bone Yard unless you're called."

"I was called, Miles," said Zeke, still holding his sights on Lori.

Miles and Chance looked at each other and then toward Tommy Mack at the bar where he was cleaning up debris. Tommy raised his hands and shook his head, "It wasn't me boss."

"Look, Zeke, this stranger came in here, tore my place up, killed a man and crippled four others. He killed Lori's boyfriend and she wants her just revenge. Besides, the man is almost dead anyway."

"I can't let you do it, Miles," said Zeke, moving in closer. "Now drop that knife, Lori Ann," he said.

"Hell, I bet the sheriff only gave you one bullet, and it's in your shirt pocket," taunted Chance. "I can see right now that you're so nervous that you're about to piss your pants, boy."

Zeke glanced nervously back and forth between the men and Lori. Pergosi slowly reached inside his jacket.

"Hold it right there, Pergosi," came the slow Florida drawl from within the dark recesses of the room, "Or you might find yourself with another button hole in that fancy suit coat of yours," warned Jewel Mullins, Sheriff of Jefferson County.

"Why, Sheriff, fancy meeting you here tonight," said Pergosi. "You should know by now that we handle our own minor skirmishes here at the Bone Yard, so that you can tend to your sheriffing duties in more appropriate venues."

"From what I see here, it looks like you've done a slip-shod job of it tonight, Miles," drawled the portly Sheriff.

"Enough of your buffoonery, Sheriff, you get paid good money to stay away from the Bone Yard, so what the hell are you doing here tonight!" snapped Chance.

"Well, sometimes I get a little bit of religion in me, you know, and a little bit of religion comes in handy now and then. Ain't that right, Zeke?"

"That's right, sir," smiled the deputy.

"Now, Miles, why don't you slowly reach inside your coat again and gently pull that nine-millimeter out of your shoulder holster by its butt and slide it across the floor to me. And Mr. Taylor, it looks like you might have a belly pistol in your waistband. Take it out please and slide it over in the same way. Thank you. Now, both of you pull up your britches legs so I can see if you have any ankle weapons. You see, this way, gentlemen, I don't have to come over there and get personal with you."

Chance was seething! "My dad has squashed bigger bugs than you, Jewel!"

"That may be, son, but your daddy's not here right now and I am, and I'm still the law in these parts."

"I assure you, Mr. Mullins, that your tenure will be short."

"Don't threaten me, Junior! It's not good for your image."

"Neither is being at the Bone Yard, but I shall survive, Sheriff. You can bank on it."

"I'm sure you will, son. I'm sure you will."

Jewel turned to Jamaica Red, "Okay, ma'am, how about you. Are you concealing any weapons?"

The tall Jamaican reached behind her and pulled the zipper on her French gown, dropping the strapless dress onto the floor, revealing her large, dark-nippled cones and gold-trimmed briefs. "Does this answer your question, Sheriff?"

"Uh, yes it does," said the red faced lawman. "I believe that's more than I need to know, but thank you, ma'am, for sharing this Kodak moment with us. Zeke, call us a backup, and call Susie at base, and have her send us all the medical units that she can muster up. Then we will all walk through this mess to check out the injured."

Minutes later, after examining Sonny, the Sheriff declared, "This ol' boy has quite a lump on his noggin, but he ought to be all right after we get him to a hospital."

"Hey Sheriff, we've got respiratory failure over here! Come and take a look!" yelled Zeke.

"When I found him he had already turned blue and was holding his throat," said Zeke upon their arrival.

Jewel put his head to Blue Nose's chest and then checked his eyes. "This man is at death's door. We've go to hurry! Give me your pig sticker, Deputy. Miles, you got any quarter inch to half inch tubing

143

anywhere? I need to make a trach tube."

"I don't know of anything except maybe a straw from the bar."

"No, a straw won't do, it would only collapse. Get Jamaica Red over here! Hey Red, get me one of your tampons quick!" said the sheriff.

"Tampons?" answered the bewildered beauty.

"Yeah, a tampon, you do bleed don't you?"

"Do you prefer the one that's shoved up my cunt or would you like a new one?" she said sarcastically.

"Please, ma'am, I don't mean to insult you, but I can use the tampon applicator as a trach tube. Hurry please. Okay, Zeke, hold him down while I make a hole in his trachea."

Jewel held the point of the Bowie knife against Blue Nose's throat, and with the palm of his right hand forcefully popped the knife butt, forcing the blade into the man's trachea. He twisted it, then pulled it out and grabbed the tampon from Jamaica Red's hand. He pulled the cotton out of the applicator and inserted the tube with a twist into the opening. He then commenced to breathing into the tube and then pumped the chest, doing this maneuver several times until the lungs were expanding properly again.

Jewel stood up and held up the big steel knife for Miles and Chance to see. "You may think that Barney Fife here carries only one bullet, but I guarantee that he can carve y'all a new asshole with this baby. I've seen him do it before," boasted the Sheriff.

After the rest of the injured were checked out, Zeke led the Sheriff to the dead man. Jewel flinched upon looking at the smashed face. "Damn, I can't recognize that boy, Zeke. Who is he?"

"That's Cora Tweeter's boy, Harlan."

"Oh, lord, not Cora's boy. He's the only one she had left, what with her ol' man in prison and her youngest runnin' off with that tent revival preacher last summer."

"Yeah, I know what you mean," said Zeke. "You know, Cora got the holy-ghost last week."

"Nah, did she?"

"That's what Annabelle told me. Her and the kids were at the church that night."

"You don't say. Well, I reckon this will set her back some. Call Dr. Brady and get him out here. We need a coroner's report on this boy. And tell him to put the boy's eyes back in his head. We can't let Cora see him like this. It would kill her."

"Okay, Jewel. I'll get right on it."

As the last red light disappeared from the Bone Yard, the sheriff and his favorite deputy stood in the doorway, staring at the morning sun's approach on the deep pink horizon, while pondering the night's events.

"Zeke, did you find out who the stranger is?"

"Yeah, I ran the plates on that black Crown Vic out in the parking lot. It belongs to a Sonny Rafferty of Indianapolis. He's a private investigator."

"I remember him. He used to work for Indianapolis Metro, and got involved in a botched raid or somethin' in Centralia a few years back. I remember it was all over the television. You know, Zeke, there's something very mysterious about that Rafferty character. Did you notice the damage that he inflicted on those boys? We're talking about one big bad-ass here."

"Yeah, he definitely walked through the Reaper's grin tonight."

"I don't trust Pergosi or Taylor for that matter, so I'm going to assign a man to guard the stranger until he's released from the hospital. The sooner he gets out of there the better. I'll personally call his family and get someone up here to get him tonight."

"What's going to happen to Pergosi and Taylor?"

"Probably nothin', they both have concealed weapons permits. Heck, the girl was the one with the knife in her hand. Even that would be a weak case for attempted murder. No, they'll go free, but at least we did our best, Zeke."

"Hey, Jewel."

"What is it, Zeke?"

"Why, *did* you come by tonight?"

"My hypocrisy only carries me so far. You know that, Zeke."

The deputy and Sheriff both shared smiles.

R-i-n-n-n-n-g, R-i-n-n-n-n-g, R-i-n-n-n-n-g!

"Hello?"

"Is this Mrs. Rafferty?"

"Yes it is."

"I'm sorry to wake you at his late hour, but it's about your husband . . . .

Chapter Twelve

A Walk Thru the Reaper's Grin

It was a gray, dismal morning in greater Indianapolis, but even more so in the Rafferty household. Myra didn't hear her sister Mary enter the room, for she was engrossed in the careful tending of the many wounds of her unfortunate son. Oh, she knew that Sonny wasn't really her son, and Samantha wasn't her daughter, but she had adopted them in her heart.

"Land to Goshen girl, what happened to Mister Sonny?" exclaimed Mary.

"A lot that you care, gallivanting around all weekend with that man," chided Myra.

"That man happens to be my next husband if you must know. Besides, I'm Mister Sonny's housemaid not nursemaid," she said defensively.

"Mind your tongue girl," scolded Myra with a cold glance. "Sonny's been very good to us, and very liberal with you, I might add." She glanced again, this time stretching it into a stare, startled by her big sister's ruff appearance. "Sister, what happened to your eye? Where's your patch?"

"Aw, the strap on that old eye-patch broke, and I was trying to put my glass eye in when Rufus and Napoleon began their usual rough-housing and knocked it out of my hand. Those two ornery pranksters rolled it around awhile then took off with it. I'll probably never see it again," said Mary.

"Well, I suggest that you sew that eye-patch back together because right now your face would scare the paint off the wall," fussed Myra.

"I'm fixin' to, I'm fixin' to, as soon as I get a chance," said the annoyed housemaid. "You rushed me over here with that note that you left, scaring me half to death, telling me there was an emergency at Samantha's house and all. I'm still trying to catch my breath."

"Well, while you're catching your breath can you tell me, did you see Shauna downstairs?"

"Oh yeah, Shauna's busy cuttin' out paper dolls or somethin'. She helped me look for my eye for a little bit; said somethin' about making angels for Sonny. Has she seen him yet?"

"Nah, I couldn't let our little darling see him in the condition that he was in. She thinks so much of him and all. Why, yesterday his eye was swole' shut, and he had a lump on his head as big as my fist. Nah, I told her that when he wakes up she could talk to him." Myra smiled, "Shauna said that she was goin' to make somethin' for him. Lord knows she adores him like he was her daddy."

"Well, she'll find different when she grows up and notices that she's black and he's white."

"What are you talkin' about, sister? Shauna's not a baby anymore, and she's not stupid either, and you ought-not be tryin' to stir up trouble such as that."

"You know what I'm talking about, Myra."

"I know of no such thing. Now, did you come over here to help out today or are you goin' to keep talking nonsense?"

"Calm down little sister. I didn't mean nothin' by it. I like the Raffertys too; Samantha anyway."

Myra gave a sisterly smile. "Well then, maybe you can give the house a little extra cleaning today since I'm sure that Sonny will be having visitors."

Mary started to voice her opinion on her competency to do her job, when she caught her sister's soft smile. It was contagious. She was aware of and sometimes amazed at her younger sister's uncanny ability to defuse arguments and other disagreeable uprisings. "Tell me, Myra, what happened to Sonny?" she asked.

"With the information that I got, Sonny got into a skirmish at a bar, down-state somewhere. Now, from readin' between the lines and from eavesdropping on Samantha's phone conversations, the fight may have had something to do with a hooker, and I think Sonny may have killed someone. Samantha called me early Saturday morning. She was almost in hysterics talkin' about Sonny being hurt in a fight, and about it being too dangerous to keep him in the hospital there. She was going to transfer him to Indianapolis General but her father contacted her and told her to bring him home so as to keep things quiet from the press. He's a newspaperman so I guess he knows what he's doin'. Mr. Taylor has assigned his own personal physician to look after Sonny and has hired a home nurse to care for him at night. Mr. Taylor is a dear man for all the support he has given to Sonny and Samantha. So it's been one big mess around here, Mary. I'm at my wit's end."

"Where's Ms. Samantha?"

"I sent her off to work today to get her out of the house. She cried all day yesterday and last night, worried and confused about Sonny's dilemma. Sonja doesn't know about Sonny yet, and neither does Danielle. Danielle's been away to her softball tournament all weekend. She'll be back today sometime.

Samantha fears telling the girls about Sonny being hurt 'cause the last time he was in this predicament the girls were traumatized for quite some time."

"That was back when J.R. was killed wasn't it?" asked Mary somberly.

"Yes it was. The doctor says that Sonny is sufferin' from a concussion, and that he will be coming in and out of consciousness for awhile yet."

"So Sonny's gonna be all right?"

"Yeah, the doctor says that he'll recover. He just needs some rest and rehab right now. I just finished bathin' him and changin' his bandages. The IV tube and catheter tube can come out as soon as he regains full consciousness."

"Do you know how to take them out?"

"Oh yes. I carefully watched the nurse put them in, and she instructed me on how to take them out if need be."

Mary ambled over to where Sonny lay. "Boy, he sure took a mighty whoopin'," she said, curiously examining his cuts and contusions while pulling the sheet away, searching for more damage. "M-m-h-m-m, not bad for a white boy," mumbled Mary.

"Ain't you got enough respect to leave the man with his dignity?" scolded Myra. "Didn't our Mama teach you better than that, girl?"

"Oh yes, sister. I was just checkin' to make sure Mister Sonny's dignity was still all there," said Mary.

"I assure you that all of his parts are intact. Meanwhile, I'm going to leave you here to look after the boy while I go downstairs to check on Shauna and to fetch some clean linen, if that's alright with you?"

"Oh yes, I'll look after Mister Sonny."

"And leave his private parts alone!"

"Oh no, I won't mess with his dignity anymore," said Mary, innocently replacing his covers.

With Myra downstairs Mary hovered over Sonny, studying his swollen features, using her good eye to closely inspect his disfigured face. She remembered how nicely his pretty blue eyes once set in his handsomely chiseled face. Mary never trusted Sonny as Myra did. Sonny had too much power, too much control over women, as far as she was concerned. She assumed that it was in her inherent nature to distrust men. "It must be in my genes to not trust men," she said aloud to herself. "Mama was like that, you know. Myra dotes on you," said Mary to Sonny as if he could hear her voice. "Samantha adores you and your daughters idolize you. You must have cast a spell or somethin' on them with those pretty blue eyes of yours. Yeah, those pretty blue eyes, she mused, just like the pretty blue eyes staring at me now. Pretty blue . . . E-e-e-e-e-e-e-k!" screamed the startled housemaid.

"Ah-h-h-h-h-h-h-g-h!" cried Sonny simultaneously while grabbing the generous fleshy pillows that hung from the disfigured shadow.

Shocked by Sonny's sudden resurrection, Mary jerked back, stretching her soft mammaries into tubal-like protrusions before snapping them loose from their newfound moorings. She then quickly turned and sped out of the bedroom.

Hearing the commotion, Myra dropped her linens and quickly hurried up the stairs fearing the worst. Mary rushed past her sister on the way down, sputtering, "Lordy-Lordy, save me from that peckerwood! Sa-a-a-v-e me Lord, Sa-a-a-v-e me Lord, save me from that peckerwood!" Myra gave her a short look of worry, then, headed up the stairs to Sonny's bedroom.

Myra softly thanked her maker when she entered the bedroom, for Sonny looked beautiful to her eyes, even with the scowling frown on his fight-weary face.

"Myra, what the hell is goin' on?" asked Sonny.

"Well, Sonny, I think you just scared the bejeezus out of Mary."

"Well, she scared the hell out of me. I mean, goddamn, all I remember is waking up to an ugly black Cyclops staring down at me. And where the hell is Samantha, anyway, and what am I doing here, and why the hell are these tubes stuck in me?" he said angrily while ripping out the IV from his left arm. It wasn't until Sonny grabbed for the other tube that Myra decided to intervene in Sonny's ranting.

"If you pull on that tube, Sonny, you'll be in a much bigger hurt than you are now," snapped Myra with authority.

Sonny looked at Myra in stunned confusion. With a mother's touch, Myra reached under the sheet and grabbed the shaft of Sonny's penis into which the tube was inserted. "First of all, young man, you do not use the Lord thy God's name in vain in this household! You have a home filled with ladies and they deserve better, and so does the Lord. Second of all, Samantha's at work where I sent her. She's been taking care of you for over two days now, crying her eyes out and worrying over you. Besides, it's Monday morning and that's where she belongs. Thirdly, you're here because you got your narra' ass into some kind of ruckus in a roadhouse down south somewheres. And fourth of all, you have these tubes inserted into your body to keep it functioning properly so you can survive this ordeal. Now, if you behave and can relax for a bit I'll take this other tube out before you really hurt yourself."

"Yes, ma'am; I'm sorry Mama, for talking to you the way that I did. I apologize for my rude behavior, but could you please loosen up on your grip a bit? It's really starting to hurt."

Myra copped a tinge of a smile at Sonny's request for forgiveness. He was back to calling her "Mama" again, a sound that brought joy to her heart. Myra relaxed her grip on Sonny's penis, then pulled back the covers and retrieved a pair of scissors from the nightstand. She then snipped the port end of the tube, releasing the saline solution that inflated the bulb that held the catheter in his bladder. With the bulb deflated, Myra slowly pulled the tube through the urethra until finally it popped out of the purplish mushroom-shaped head. Up until now Sonny was too confused and astonished to be embarrassed. That was, until a surprise visitor burst into his presence.

"Sonny, Sonny, look what I've made for you," blurted out Shauna as she rushed into the room. Sonny grabbed for his coverings and brought them to his middle.

"Geezus, Myra, can't you find me some shorts or somethin'?"

"Shauna, you go back out and knock on that door like a proper young lady does while I fetch some britches for Sonny," directed Myra.

"Mama, my head is killin' me," said Sonny, trying to stand up.

"It ought to be with all those lumps you have on it," said Myra, holding open a pair of boxers for Sonny to step into.

"I feel a little dizzy. I may have to sit back down," said Sonny, his legs wobbling.

"You just lean on me, son, and lift one leg at a time while I slip these drawers on you."

"Thanks, Mama. I don't know what I'd do without you," said Sonny.

Myra studied Sonny's face carefully as she assisted him back into his bed. "Sonny, can you tell me what happened?" she asked in earnest. "What got you in this fix, son? You've got us all worried sick about ya."

"I don't know, Mama. If I could remember I would tell ya. I don't know what I've got myself into," he said, shaking his head. "Hell, I've been beat up before, but I could always remember what happened."

"You know I love ya like you was my own. I've done lost two boys. I don't know if I could stand to lose another," she said, tears welling up in her eyes.

"I love you too, Mama," replied Sonny.

"You've probably just got a little amnesia or somethin'. Maybe when Samantha returns home this evening she'll help you get your memory back. She's got the lowdown on what went down but she's keepin' kinda quiet about it 'cause I think she's fearin' for your life, Sonny."

"Well, don't worry yourself sick, Mama, because whatever happened, I'm going to get to the bottom of all of it and straighten things out." Sonny smiled, "It's in my nature, you know. Now, where the heck did big Mary run off to?"

"She's probably changing her drawers," said Myra with a sillyish smile. "You've got her all in a tizzy. You know, she was already upset because she dropped her glass eye on the floor downstairs and Rufus and Napoleon ran off with it. Grant it she's quite a sight with just one eye in her head, but she don't mean to be."

"Aw, she just caught me by surprise, that's all. Would you fetch her for me, Mama, so I can apologize to her for the scaring that I gave her?"

"Okay. I'll go look for her and I'll tell Shauna that she can come in and see you now."

"Thanks, Mama."

As Myra shut the door behind her she met Shauna waiting in the hall. A wide smile encompassed the little girl's face and her big brown eyes sparkled with anticipation while two bushy tails waved sprightly from the sides of her head.

"Okay, Missy, you can see Sonny now," smiled Myra.

Shauna giggled.

Knock, Knock, Knock!

"Who's there?"

Shauna put her hand up to her mouth and giggled again. "Shauna," she managed to sneak out of her laughter.

"Shauna? Shauna who?" came the reply.

"Shauna Robey!" she squealed.

"Come in Shauna Robey."

She quickly ran in and jumped into the arms of her beloved Sonny.

"How ya doing, Baby Girl?" said Sonny, trying to put on a happy face.

"I'm fine," she said distinctly.

"Hey, I see that you've lost another tooth. How many does that make now?"

"Three," she giggled, while holding up three fingers to Sonny.

"Wow, the tooth fairy is gonna' make you rich and I'm gonna' to have to call you snaggletooth. Is that all right with you?"

Shauna quickly shook her head no, "I'm not snaggletoof. I'm Baby Girl," she said.

"Ok then," smiled Sonny, "you're still my Baby Girl. Hey, whatcha got in your hands?"

"I made you some angels," she replied.

"Angels? Let me see them."

Shauna released one side of the stack of folded paper and let it fall downward in accordion-like fashion, revealing ten white paper angels.

"Did you make those angels just for me?"

"Uh huh, when you were real sick Grandma told me to pray for angels to come and fly you to heaven."

"Well, you've got quite a few angels here. That should be enough to get me there," teased Sonny.

"No, silly, these angels can't fly, they have only paper wings."

Sonny smiled, but a sad thought suddenly entered his mind. What if angels really did have paper wings? Or what if they didn't exist at all? He quickly dismissed that thought. Shauna's right, you are being silly, he thought.

Just then, Myra walked through the door pulling on Mary who seemed a little embarrassed and somewhat reluctant at being there.

"Sonny, Mary has something to tell you," said Myra.

"I'm sorry, Mr. Sonny, for being so nosy and carryin' on the way I did," apologized Mary, innocently glancing away.

Sonny took her hand in his. "No need to apologize, Mary. You were just being curious. Heck, I must have been having a nightmare while I was out. I kept dreaming that a big blue-faced monster was chasing me and trying to beat the crap out of me, and all-the-while I had this pounding headache. Then, when I woke up and saw you standing over me, I guess I just freaked. So you see, Mary, you got rid of the monster for me. Unfortunately, I still have that pounding headache. No, I apologize to you, Mary. Did I hurt you any?"

"No sir," answered the plump housemaid, her face flushed,

"You know, I think that I might be able to find your eye."

Mary and Myra looked at each other befuddled.

"Baby Girl, how would you like to do me a favor?"

"Huh?"

Sonny cupped his hand to Shauna's ear and whispered into it. Her eyes widened as she listened intently to his instructions. "And take Impala with you," he said aloud as Baby Girl jumped to the floor.

Out the door she went, followed closely by the red-coated matriarch of the Rafferty animal kingdom. While descending the flight of stairs Impala took over the lead, through the foyer, through the kitchen, into the pantry, and out the side door to the storage room in the garage, ending with Impala pushing through their famous canvassed covered hole in the wall. Shauna carefully crawled on her hands and knees through the narrow opening, being extra careful not to damage her favorite chiffon dress that Sonny had recently bought her. This was a route well traversed by the spunky little girl, as she used it for play-hiding from her great auntie Mary who babysat her at times when Myra was at Sonny's office.

As Shauna rummaged through Napoleon's stash he gave a sudden snarl, but Impala backed him off with a growl and a show of ivory. Napoleon would never harm Shauna. It was just that he was so proud of his treasure of collectables. But due to Impala's insistence he was willing to part with any item of Shauna's choosing. To his dismay, Shauna chose the small, roundish item that he, with the help of Rufus, had just confiscated an hour or so earlier. It was a small sacrifice for the mischievous dachshund as he tried to lick her smile while she softly stroked his head.

The Times Taylor building wasn't as flashy as its owner, Big John Taylor, but it didn't have to be, for Big John had the inert charisma that most powerful men were born with. His slant on life was to achieve an empire by sliding gracefully between the laws of the land. His law was to pick one's pocket before they picked his. He didn't detest his adversaries, but challenged them. One would not find John Taylor's name in the "who's who" of crime and corruption, but in Indiana's business society he was on the front page. He was well versed on politics of the big man and of the little guy. Nobody could straddle a political fence as well as Big John Taylor.

Though Big John had yet to arrive, Samantha and her staff waited patiently around the big conference table discussing why the big guy pulled their final editorial on the nursing home debacle. Gaining their notoriety for digging and searching in diverse places for a good story, Samantha's staff, with the cognomen of "The Fab Four", ardently protested to Samantha against her father for killing the story that they had feverishly worked so hard and long on. They were a proud bunch, handpicked and molded by Samantha herself. The Fab Four was headed by Merle Bullock, a 28year old African American woman, married to Darryl, a nose guard for the Indianapolis Colts. She was an intellectual, and was the brightest of the bunch. Then there was Larry Crowell, computer expert, and Jessie Coltraine, a seasoned investigator. Last and least was the mousey looking Lisa Dawson, a.k.a. Jitterbug. Along with Samantha they toiled together, partied together, laughed together, cried together, and sometimes slept and showered together; just to get the gospel according to the Times. They formed together like a perfect dovetail joint.

Samantha listened carefully as the Fab Four spewed forth their complaints and comments.

"What's gotten into your dad, Sam? We have Losch and his cronies dead to rights, and Big John won't let us put him away," complained Merle.

"I've traced their nursing home profits going to a puppet corporation called Miramar," added Larry.

"And they're purchasing a lot of their goods and services from this company. But Miramar is a dummy corporation as far as I can tell,' spouted Jessie.

"So that means that they are paying themselves for goods and services not rendered and getting reimbursed by the government all the while. That's outright fraud!" charged Jitterbug.

"The only assumption that I can come to is that maybe Dad thinks that we're moving too fast on the case," replied Samantha.

"Too fast!" protested Jessie. We've been on their asses for three months now, and they've only made a few minor changes in their employment. That's supposed to make everything alright?"

"Don't get me wrong, guys. I'm just as vexed by Big John's actions as you all are. I'm just trying to take an optimistic approach to this problem. Dad's never really crossed lines with me like this before. He should be here soon to explain himself."

When Big John entered the room, eyebrows raised and ears perked. Actually, the editor-n-chief didn't enter the room. He engulfed it. At 6 foot 5 inches and 255 pounds, he was an imposing figure. That, along with his boisterous personality, made him most intimidating. Following close behind him was the Times managing editor, and Big John's personal mistress, Margo Solsta.

It didn't bother Samantha so much that Margo was sleeping with her dad, for infidelity was one of Big John's greatest vices, in which he had many. No, it was the arrogance and condescending attitude of Daddy's whore that rankled the spicy redhead. She was offered the managing editor's job many times herself, but turned it down due mostly to her loyalty to the Fab Four. Samantha knew that any one of them could perform Margo's job better than she. It was said to be quite an accomplishment for a young girl of 30, as was Margo, to be the managing editor of a large newspaper. Samantha was convinced that Margo's meteoric rise to the top came from humming "I'll Fly Away" while flapping her legs back and forth like wings while lying on the boss's couch.

"Sorry I'm late, everyone," apologized Big John while hastily opening his briefcase. "I've been in St Louis all weekend at the request of John Losch of Waverly Enterprises." With a forced smile the big guy looked around the room, "So how is my favorite reporting staff doing today?" he asked, hoping to ease the verbal barrage that he knew was coming.

"We're not doing well at all, Daddy. As a matter-of-fact we are all highly pissed!" seethed Samantha.

"How could you do it? How could you pull Samantha's editorial out of Saturday's edition like that?" questioned Jessie.

"Yeah, Mr. Taylor, we feel betrayed," blurted out Larry.

"Yeah, betrayed, we feel betrayed," the others chimed in.

"Whoa! Wait a minute," said Big John, holding his hands out as if pushing back an angry mob. "As you all know, we at The Indianapolis Times do not do things in an irrational manner. We think things through. We do what is best for our community. That's our motto, and that's what's printed on the front page of every paper that we send out. That is why Margo and I decided to stop the bleeding, now."

"But, Dad, how about all of the Medicaid money given to Waverly for falsified records? That money is the government's money, and the government's money is the taxpayer's money that is being wasted on these profiteers."

"Goddamn it, Sam, we are not the frigging F.B.I." boomed Big John in a momentary loss of patience. "Look, everybody, we have a sweetheart deal here. I spent all weekend with John Losch and associates, and they promised that they would cooperate fully with the state to try to attain a 100% proficiency rating for every home by year's end. That means zero tolerance, Sam. Waverly's facilities in Portage, LaPorte, and Chapel Hill will be on probation for two years, and the state board will inspect them every three months. In addition, Waverly has agreed to build nine new nursing homes in our state, two of them in the Indianapolis area. And they will start breaking ground this fall. It'll be great for our city, great for our state and great for our elderly. So, you see, that's why I backed off on Waverly. And oh yeah, John Losch gave you high praise, Sam, for being such a gutsy reporter. When he found out that you were my daughter he nearly flipped. He said that you were a chip off the old block," Big John chortled.

"I understand all of that, Mr. Taylor, but the fact is that Waverly is still buying goods and services from a dummy corporation, and that means some crook is making a lot of money," said Jessie.

"What do we care how much money is being made and where it goes as long as they adhere to our rules and restrictions and provide quality care for our elderly? Look, guys, corporations straddle that thin gray line of right and wrong everyday. That's the way it is and that's the way it has always been. The local and federal governments work in the same way. It's called politics. And sometimes they cross over that line, but that's the nature of the beast." Big John turned to Margo. "Do you have anything to add?"

"Just one thing, John; with the strides that they have made I think that Waverly has pretty much succumbed to our demands. Besides, if we were to pursue them any further they would just probably sue us for slander and we would be tied up in the courts for years. That would be messy. So just put your best foot forward and work just as hard on your next assignment, people."

"Thank you, Margo," said John.

"You're welcome, sir"

"Okay, if there are no other questions I've got to run. I have an appointment with the Rush advertising firm at Adam's Mark in 45 minutes. Then I have to go downtown at 11:30 for a ribbon cutting ceremony with Kitty. I promised her that I would be there. Sam, I want you and Merle in my office in five minutes please. And I think Margo wants the rest of you people in her office to discuss your assignments for this coming week. Thank you all for coming."

"So what do you guys think?" asked Samantha.

"It makes sense I guess, but it leaves a bad taste in my mouth," said Merle.

"Yeah, me too," agreed Jessie.

"What do you think, Jitterbug?"

"I hate that fucking bitch!"

The rest all laughed heartily at their cohort.

"Are you talking about Margo?" chortled, Samantha.

"Yeah, I hate that fucking condescending bitch!"

"My, my, Jitterbug, I didn't know you had it in you, being a staunch member of the First Baptist Church of Chapel Hill," teased Jessie. "And a choir member to boot," she laughed.

"I get tired of being fed to the lions."

"I know what you mean," said Merle in a more serious tone.

Whatever the reason, guys, Big John's made up his mind. So let's move on and go about our business of reporting," said Samantha. "Merle, let's you and I go see what Daddy wants now."

Even after the jousting they had in the conference room, Samantha warmly hugged her father at entering his office. "Oh Daddy, I was so scared when I first heard about Sonny. I thought he was dead," she said, tears rolling from her eyes. "Thank you so much for helping us out. I don't know what I would have done without you."

"Now now, little girl, don't you cry. That's what daddy's are for. I'm always here for you, little darling."

"I just thought that, you know, Sonny and you never really hit it off so well, and I thought that maybe . . . you wouldn't want to help us again because of that," she said, wiping her eyes with her palms.

"No, darling, don't think such things of me. I would never let you or your family do without. As far as Sonny goes, let's just say that I've grown accustomed to his shenanigans by now. Hell, I pulled him out of that Centralia fiasco a while back, so there's no reason I can't help him out of this mess. That boy seems to find trouble in all the wrong places."

"Hey, Dad, just how did you find out about Sonny? Heck, you called right after the sheriff called me from the hospital."

"Oh, you know how word gets around, Sam. Hell, I know people all over the state. One person tells one person and that person tells another and so on. Kinda like that begettin' thing in the bible. Besides, bad news travels fast."

"I wonder if you could tell me what really happened, Dad, because the sheriff was supposed to fill me in, but when I got to the hospital he was replaced by a state cop and he didn't know the sheriff's whereabouts."

"I can tell you what I heard, darling, but not right now. It's essential that I get over to Adam's Mark for that advertisement meeting right away. How about meeting with me for lunch at Lucrecia's at say, one-thirty?"

"Sure, Dad," replied Samantha.

"Okay, good. Your prodigal brother has finally returned to his office after being away for two weeks, and he wants to speak with both you and Merle, and it seems important."

"Okay, Dad, we'll go right in. Say, Dad?"

"Yes, what is it, dear?"

"Isn't Chance still in charge of the advertising department?"

"Oh yeah, Sam, but he's into politics now, and you know how those politicians are. They're lazy bastards."

Samantha exchanged smiles with her dad, as did Merle.

Samantha and Merle were met with open arms as they entered into Chance's office.

"Hey, little sister, how you been doing," greeted Chance with a hug.

"Are you getting skinny or what?" teased Samantha.

"Six foot two, a hundred and sixty-eight pounds; same as always, sis, give or take 10 pounds."

"That's what I thought. Isn't Liz feeding you enough at home?"

"Oh, Liz is still a good cook but I've been on the road for 18 days, and you know how I hate that hotel food."

"Oh yeah, you always were a picky eater," kidded Samantha. "You're nothing more than a bean pole."

"That's alright, Sam. I can still whoop the ol' man's ass, though."

"Pshaw, you never could whoop Daddy's ass. Now that I think of it, you never could whoop mine."

"Come on sis, let's get it on," joked Chance, taking a fighting stance.

"Oh no, not today," she said.

"Well, why not?"

"I'm on the rag, and my belly hurts."

"Hey, that's the same excuse that you've always used."

"Yeah, I know, and it always worked too." Along with Merle they both laughed heartily.

"How are you, Merle," asked Chance, awkwardly embracing the pretty black reporter.

"Doing just fine, Mr. Taylor," said Merle, somewhat embarrassed, since he had only spoken to her once before.

"So, what can we do for you, Chance?" asked Samantha.

"As you both know, I'm running for the U. S. Senate. And as you also know, I won in the primary by quite a good margin. But now my opposition is that rat-bastard republican, Troy Charbonau."

Samantha's heart raced and her face blushed.

"You know who he is don't you, Sam? Sam?"

"What? Oh, yes, yes I know the senator. I mean, I've heard of him," said Samantha weakly.

"Are you all right, Sam? You look a little flushed."

"I'm okay," said Samantha, feeling weak in the knees.

"She'll be okay," answered Merle, grabbing Samantha by the arm and leading her to a chair. "She just needs to sit down. She's been under a lot of stress lately and not getting much rest from taking care of Sonny."

"Oh yes, I heard about Sonny from Dad. You give him my condolences Sam," said Chance.

"Condolences hell, he's not dead yet!" said Samantha peevishly.

"I'm sorry. I mean, give him my best. I always did like him, you know."

"I didn't know that you liked Sonny."

"Oh yes. I always considered him as my big brother. Don't you remember when we were kids how I always wanted for a big brother?"

"No, I don't remember that either."

"Sam, you must be getting old, 'cause, you're losing your memory."

"You might be right, Chance."

"Anyway, you say Sonny's gonna be all right then?"

"Yes, the doctor says that he'll be up and about in a few more days."

"That's good news, Sam. It really is," said Chance, his voice denying his eyes.

"Merle," said Chance.

"Yes sir."

"You're the girl that I want to talk to. As I was saying, my opponent is Troy Charbonau, a staunch republican in a republican state. These damn biased farmers won't let a good democrat into office. They don't care about the inner city youth, the poor, the blacks and other minorities. Nah, all they're interested in is lining their milk-fat pockets with money. I need you, Merle. I need you to get the urban vote. I want you to be my campaign manager."

"I thought Lou Stevens was your campaign manager," questioned Samantha.

"Oh, he still is. He's gonna get me the rural votes. Whaddya say, Merle? I'll pay you twenty thousand on top of what you're receiving now, and it's only till November."

"I don't know, Mr. Taylor. I've never done anything like that before," said Merle nervously.

"Look, Merle. You're black, you're beautiful, you're intelligent, and your husband is a professional football player. All you have to do is travel to the big cities, Terre Haute, Fort Wayne, South Bend, Gary, Michigan City; lunch with the Mayor, start fundraiser dinners, and get your beautiful mug on camera a lot. We'll take care of the newsprint. Just think, Merle, if I become senator, how much more money I can get for our inner city youths here in Indianapolis. Lord knows, we could use it."

"I'll need to discuss this with my husband first," said Merle.

"Sure. Talk to Darryl, but remember that he'll be away playing football the rest of this year. Who knows, maybe we can run a commercial with him in it too. And Sam, I need your okay to let us borrow Merle from your staff."

"That's totally up to Merle."

"Good, I hope you choose well, Merle, and be my manager. I would love working with you."

R-i-n-n-n-n-g, R-i-n-n-n-n-g, "Hello, this is the Rafferty residence, Myra speaking."

"Hello. Myra, this is Sam. How's Sonny?"

"Hello dear. Sonny's been up and about some today. He's still pretty weak but the doctor saw him earlier and said he'll be fully recovered within a few days, except that his amnesia might last a little while yet."

"That's really good news, Mama. Has he had any visitors?"

"My lord yes, Danielle was here most of the mornin', and a Mr. Lujak and Brogan were here, and so was Father Harrington."

"Oh yes, Father Harrington. He was Sonny's chaplain when he was with the force. They used to be fishing buddies. Has Sonny asked about me?""

"Yes, darlin', he's been asking about you all mornin'."

"Can he talk now, Mama?"

"Well, he has a Spanish-looking girl talkin' with him right now."

"Don't bother him then. Hell, maybe she'll put a little spark back into him. It wouldn't hurt."

"You are joking aren't you, Samantha?"

"Aw, lighten up, Mama. Of course I'm joking. Hey, I've gotta' run and meet Dad for lunch, so I'll probably be home late. Give Sonny my love."

"I will, dear."

"Bye, Mama."

"Goodbye dear."

"Angie, long-time no see. What've you been doing with yourself, kid?" said Sonny in mild surprise.

"The question is what have you done to yourself?"

"Well, my muscles ache, my nose is broken, and I have 11 stitches in the back of my head, I'm told. Apparently I was in a brawl. Where, I don't know, and why, I don't know. Nobody seems to know anything around here except Samantha, and she's at work. You've met my wife haven't you, Angie?"

"Yes, I met her at a Christmas party, years ago, when I was a rookie."

"That was a long time ago, Angie."

"Yes it was, but I vividly remember it. I remember that I hated that redheaded witch that you were married to. I remember at the Christmas party, you giving me a kiss, a real kiss, a lover's kiss, and I fell in love with you. I had a crush on you for years, and I still do, some."

"Is that all that we did?" asked Sonny.

"Yes. You were hopelessly in love with your wife at the time."

"Who told you about me being laid up here, Angie? I'm trying to dig up some answers. So far I've been unsuccessful."

"That's what I've been meaning to tell you, Sonny. My little sister called me from Cincinnati and told me about the fight that you were in. You remember my sister, Candy, don't you?"

"Not right offhand."

"Come on, Sonny. I was 16 when you pulled me off the streets, and Candy was just 10."

"Oh yeah, she was the little girl with the white bows on her head and used to jump the double jump rope real good."

"That's the one, Sonny. She became a whore at age 14, the same year I became a cop. She didn't like that, so she ran off with a guy to Cincinnati and worked at a topless bar. Somehow, through that topless bar work, she became a call-girl. Can you believe that, Sonny? My sister becoming a goddamn call-girl! Well, anyway, she called yesterday from her apartment in Cincy to tell me about seeing you in the bar where she worked. She wouldn't give me the name. She sounded scared, real scared. She said you were ganged up on. She called the cops, Sonny, even though the bar prohibited her from doing so. She told me that if the cops hadn't arrived when they did that you would have been knifed to death. They wanted you dead, Sonny."

"That's the break that I'm looking for, Angie. Let's call Candy back and I'll talk to her."

"I've already tried, Sonny. She won't answer. Now I'm scared for her."

"Do you know where she lives?"

"Somewhere in Cincinnati is all I know."

"Well, when I get to feelin' better we'll go down there and find her. She's got the pieces to my puzzle, Angie. Something strange is going on, and I aim to find out what it is. I fear that she might be in danger also."

"How about the cops, Sonny; think we could we get their help?"

"Being a cop yourself, you know as well as I that they won't be of any help in a case like this. No, I'll go down there with you and we'll find her if she's in the city. I promise you that."

"Thank you, Sonny. I knew I could count on you."

"Of course, darling,' as always,"

"I've got to go now," said Angie.

"Stay in touch, Angie," he said.

"I will, Sonny."

Samantha arrived at Lucrecia's a bit early, but she didn't mind because the owner was a good friend of her and Sonnys. Lucrecia was the bohemian girlfriend of Jaques Tuqua LeBlanc, the French artist that painted Samantha's nude portrait that hung over her bed. Samantha spent a lot of time with Lucrecia and Jaques back when Sonny was doing all-nighters with the Metro Police force. They taught her the art of nude yoga, total relaxation, and channeling, which she later gave up for naught. She even did lesbian poses with Lucrecia for Jaques at time, but with little seriousness. Jaques and Lucrecia were now just two old hippies staring at the past, yet loving each other ever more.

When Big John arrived, Samantha was seated with her two friends at a corner table. "I'm sorry I'm late, darlin'. Those ribbon cutting ceremonies can be quite lengthy. I had to do a lot of handshaking and all that good stuff," said Big John.

"That sounds like fun," kidded Samantha.

"Believe me, it wasn't," chided Big John.

"That's okay, Daddy, for I was just chatting with my friends here. Dad, this is Jaques LeBlanc and Lucrecia."

"Hello, Mr. Taylor. Samantha has spoken often of you," said Jaques in his usual polite manner.

"Well, I don't remember Samantha mentioning the both of you, but I do like your German beer here," said Big John.

"Very well then, Lucrecia, serve Mr. Taylor some of our best import." ordered Jaques.

"You should try some of their pirogies too, Daddy. They taste terrific," said Samantha.

"Sounds great, let's do it," replied her father.

Lucrecia moved quickly toward the kitchen.

Big John pondered, "LeBlanc, LeBlanc. That name sounds familiar."

"Oh, it should, Daddy. Jaques is the artist that painted the portrait of me that hangs above my bed at home."

"So, this is the fellow that painted a picture of my naked daughter when she was just a youngster," said Big John, somewhat disgruntled.

"Now, Daddy, I was 23 years of age and old enough to need no one's consent at the time, except for Sonny's, that is."

"Oh, so it was Sonny's idea, huh?"

"Mr. Taylor, all your daughter is trying to say is that she has a beautiful body, and a woman's beauty should be admired and cherished. She wanted a painting to remind her lover of what a beautiful woman that she had become. Don't deny her that, my friend," said Jaques.

"Well, maybe you're right, Jaques. My wife likes these, uh . . . abstract paintings. I can't make head nor tails of 'em, but she loves 'em.

So if she loves 'em I'll hang 'em. To each their own I say; to each their own."

Big John and Samantha enjoyed their lunch of beer and pirogies as John told Samantha of Sonny's fate on that previous Friday night. Of course, he skewed it to his liking to keep Sonny in check and Samantha from prying too deep. So Sonny was made the culprit again. He was the bad guy, and it would be quite awhile before anyone would believe different, except for Sonny himself . . . and the Garza sisters.

"What the hell were you doing down at the Bone Yard, son?" boomed Big John.

"Take it easy, Dad. I have everything under control," Chance said calmly.

"I just spent the afternoon lying to my daughter, trying to convince her that Sonny is the bad guy and a murderer, just so neither would get too nosey and find out things they shouldn't know. And you say that you have everything under control, bunk!"

"You worry too much, Dad. You're going to have a heart attack or stroke if you don't watch out."

"Listen, Chance. I've been running this business for quite sometime now and I don't need anyone to show me any different. Did Sonny see you there?"

"Of course not, hell, he was nearly dead by the time I got involved. And if it wasn't for Jewel Mullins, he would be."

"Well, Mullins has already been taken care of. I don't think his deputy will squeal either. Now we have to find out who called the cops in the first place. That type of person is a danger to us."

"I can do that," volunteered Chance.

"No, you stay put!"

"But, Dad, I wasn't gambling or anything. I just went to see Jamaica Red again."

"That big Amazon whore's the ruination of every man she fucks. You've got to stay away from her."

"But, Dad, you've got to see her in action."

"No, son, a woman like that has no place in our business. Why don't you take your magic stick home to your wife? I'm sure she has a need for it by now."

"Why, that whiney pig's still breast-feeding, and I'm lactose intolerant."

"Still breastfeeding, what's wrong with her? That kid's got to be two years old by now!"

"I tried talking to her, Dad."

"Hell, Liz has become addled from you slapping her around so much. Have Sam talk with her. Maybe she can talk some sense into that woman. And for God's sake, pull that boy of yours off that tit!"

The house was quiet as Samantha softly closed the front door. It was a long day at work, and the saucy redhead had lost her zip, and was in great need of some precious sleep. Myra, Mary, and Shauna had left by now. Even the dogs were put away, except for Impala, Samantha's most trusted friend, who gave her a light nudge, seeking soft recognition to the top of her head. While ascending the curved stairwell Samantha whispered sweet nothings to her canine companion while stroking her red silky mane. Samantha silently slipped through the bedroom door, trying not to wake her husband. Only a small lamp gave light to where the home nurse sat reading.

"Hello, Mrs. Rafferty. How are you tonight?"

"I'm totally worn out," said the sleepy redhead. "How was Sonny today?"

"He's doing fine. His hematoma is almost gone, and the swelling in his eye has gone down considerably. He'll need those stitches in his head for another week. Sonny walked around some today, and felt pretty good. He had a lot of visitors which tired him out at the end of the day though."

Samantha began peeling off her clothes as Barbara Fugate chatted on about Sonny's condition. The last two nights she had worn her peignoir to bed, but tonight she just wanted to lie naked next to her lover. Barbara couldn't help but stare at the long-legged redhead while she slipped off the last of her clothing. Even through the gloomy darkness her body seemed to shine through like an evening star.

Samantha slid ever-so-tightly against Sonny's backside while reaching around and skillfully massaging his manliness. Suddenly, warm passion rushed from her loins through her love chamber, as an undulating ripple sent shock waves through her body. Barbara feigned indifference at Samantha's sudden gasp of reaching her zenith, yet softly cried as the sleepy redhead so sorrowfully begged, "Sonny, oh Sonny, why are you so different? Why must you travel down the road less taken? Is it martyrdom? Must you always be the martyr? Why are you the maverick, the lone rider, the defiant one? Why must you taunt the Reaper? She wanted to moan mournfully, but just whimpered in soft quietude.

Chapter Thirteen

Body Perfect

Body Perfect by Angelina was a quaint little place on the north edge of town. Angelina's was more than a gym. It was a meeting place of sorts, where women of business, professional women, and ladies who wanted to spruce up their vanities, or women who just liked to be with other women gathered to rehab their minds and bodies.

"Hey, girlfriend" was a phrase that seemed over-exposed in Midwestern vernacular, but between Samantha Rafferty and the wickedly humorous Gina Pirelli, it was a most sincere and provocative greeting.

The red and raven-haired beauties both collided with a hard kiss. Not of lovers, but as long lost blood-sisters, newly reunited. After their warm embrace, Gina backed away at arm's length and examined her ecstatic friend while squeezing Samantha's hands in hers.

"Gee, Sam, you haven't changed a bit in six years, except maybe you've grown taller. You know, you always were giraffe-like," said Gina facetiously.

"Aw, come on, Gina, I'm not that awkward looking am I?" asked Samantha.

"Of course not, my dear, what I meant was that you are elegant like a giraffe, with your streamline body and those legs of yours. I know men that would pay a lot of money to have those long stems of yours wrapped around their middle. In a different state of mind, I think that I might enjoy that myself," she japed candidly.

Samantha blushed awkwardly.

"And you also have those few well-placed freckles that I think so adorable," added Gina. "Actually, I'm envious of your body, Rafferty. Can you tell?"

"Why, thank you, Pirelli. I must say that you look quite ravishing yourself. I myself have often dreamt of lying on the beach as a smooth, olive-skinned beauty such as yourself, soaking up the sun, especially after my own pallor covering has turned red from the hot rays of Old Sol. You know, after living with you for nearly two months, and learning your ways, I still can't figure out the spell that you cast on those beltway boys. They were drawn to you like ants to a picnic."

"It's my Sicilian heritage, girlfriend. 'I gave them an offer they couldn't refuse,'" Gina uttered in her best Godfather imitation. Hey, get your clothes off and your sweats on, Rafferty. Let's hit those treadmills and glute machines. I need to firm up my fat ass."

"Your ass isn't fat," disagreed Samantha, pulling off her clothes.

"Don't kid yourself, Sam. My caboose has been dragging ever since you saw me last. I think I need a butt-tuck," she said, examining herself in the dressing room mirror.

Samantha smiled at Gina's vainglorious ways. Gina was, at times, self-absorbed and self-aggrandizing, but to Samantha, always kept her heart of gold.

"Hey, I see that you still haven't succumbed to the convenience of panty hose," quipped Gina

"Nah, I like my freedom down there. Besides, Sonny like's my taste in hosiery," smiled the redhead.

"Well, you won me over back in D.C., Sam. I realize now that my twat was never meant to be encased in any restrictive garment, including that convenient mesh prison known as pantyhose. Besides, it is very titillating for my male friends as they watch me slowly remove my hosiery. There's something about a garter belt and nylon stockings that turns a man into putty. That's something that I learned from you, Sam, and that's quite kicky coming from a normal Midwestern girl."

"Normal is now quite passé for the modern woman of Indianapolis," said Samantha while tying her cross-trainers. "Say, Gina, I invited two of my friends from work to meet with us here today, but since I arrived a little late I seem to have missed them. You didn't happen to notice a young black woman about your size and a kinda mousy looking girl in here today did ya?"

"As a matter-of-fact I did, Sam. They've already gone out into the gym."

"Good, I can't wait to introduce you to them. They're pretty good reporters themselves, and of course I told them all about you. So, girlfriend, let's go do some jogging. Maybe we'll run into them."

"Sounds like a plan, Sam. Let's go," said the ebullient news reporter.

And run into them they did, Merle on the stair stepper and Jitterbug toiling away on the stationary bike. Samantha made the proper introductions. They automatically took to one another like ducks to water. After all, they were all journalists of the same nature. Even still, with Gina's drolleries, she could turn any insipid evening into a joyous occasion.

The four modern women of Indianapolis cavorted through the gym like kids at an Easter egg hunt, finally ending up on the treadmill. Merle prattled with Jitterbug, while Gina was in breathless babble with Samantha. Being an ex-track star, Samantha could easily outrun her loquacious friend in a foot race, but chose a speed on their artificial tracks that Gina could keep up with. Even still, it was a good pace, as Samantha noticed the perspiration dripping from Gina's nose, and the sweat line running from the middle of her tee covered back down into the butt crack of her running shorts. Samantha was lathered up like a thoroughbred racehorse, herself. Nevertheless, Gina didn't complain or beg-off, for it would not be in her competitive nature. Her competitiveness was man-like, the only male trait that she had. Samantha surmised that was the reason that she was so successful in her career. She admired her for that.

"Gina, how did you come across this place anyway?" inquired Samantha

"Our sound girl back at the station told me about it. I told her that I was looking for a place that I could unwind, relax, and workout, so she directed me here to Body Perfect. She said that she knew of a women's-only gym where a girl could get a good workout without some muscle-bound ape looking up her butt every time she bent over to pick up a weight. She said that they have a good masseuse too. A big blonde Swede named, Eva. I saw her when I first got here. She's huge all right. She has a man-like body, but not bad looking in the face."

"Yeah, I noticed her myself, earlier tonight, walking around in the weight room. She's a big girl alright."

"Hey, Sam, what do you think of this place?" asked Gina, her voice cracking while struggling to breathe and talk at the same time.

"Oh, I really like it here. I like the fact that there are no men to worry about."

"Yeah, me too," agreed Gina, "I don't like to smell a man's sweat unless he's on top of my body pumping his loins into me."

"Why, that's kind of a surprise. That's not like you, girl," kidded Samantha.

"Listen, all of us Diva's need a rest now and then," countered Gina.

Samantha noticed that Gina was now really laboring on her treadmill. "Hey, Gina, are you about ready to stop yet?"

"Hell no, girl, we've only run two miles. I should be good for two more."

Samantha knew better. "Gina, let's slow down to a fast walk because I feel one of my legs starting to cramp up and I need to walk it off," lied Samantha.

"Are you sure?"

"Yeah, I should've stretched more before we started."

"Okay then," agreed Gina, thankful but not revealing it.

"Hey, you guys," came the voice of Merle Bullock from the third treadmill over, "Jitterbug and I are calling it quits. We're going to soak in the jet-pool for awhile, and then maybe take a steam, how about you two?"

Gina checked with Samantha. "We've got to do our pecs yet, Merle. We'll meet you guys for a steam later, if that's okay with you," said Gina.

"That's fine with us," agreed Merle. "See you in the steam room."

Gina and Samantha headed to the weight room to work their chests. They opted for the regular style bench, as they figured the Olympic was a little out of their league at this stage of their lives. After all, they were just there for fun, firming, and frolicking with their friends. They all represented the Midwestern new-age *kaffee klatsch*. It worked just the same, but was caffeine free.

It didn't matter anyway because the Olympic bench was occupied by the big Swede masseuse along with a smaller, but well-built Hispanic, who happened to be the owner, Angelina. Angelina was standing at the head of the big Swede who was on her back pushing the barbell up off her chest in many repetitions. The Hispanic stood poised and ready to grab the bar in case of default. There was a lot of weight on that bar for a woman, but the Swede seemed to have no trouble with it. She would hoist even more before she was through doing her sets for the evening.

Gina and Samantha's planned workout on the bench press was to lift four sets each, starting at 50 pounds, adding 10 pounds each set. One lifted while the other rested.

Samantha couldn't hear Gina yelling encouragement at her, for she was too focused on finishing the last three repetitions of her final set. It was a struggle for her, a greater struggle than running a mile uphill, which she was more accustomed to. She had a system, and it consisted of blowing air out at a fairly rapid pace while pushing the heavy weight off her chest. It was a procedure that she used in delivering her two daughters. Samantha surmised that if the act of blowing air out rapidly could help push two eight pound balls of life through her stretched vagina then she ought to be able to push 80 pounds off her chest eight times. Gina had a different method. It was called grunting. Grunting was usually a man's game, or a pig's, but in a women's gym, with only other females around to hear, it seemed okay, for Gina anyway. Yes, she grunted. On her last set she grunted like a Russian weight-lifter doing the clean-and-jerk. But that was okay, because Eva grunted too. The big Swede grunted like a man though, and she was lifting a man's portion of weights.

"Com'on, Sam, you can do it. Com'on, don't be a pussy. Push, push, push!" commanded her Italian friend.

With a new blue vein popping out on the side of her head and rivers of sweat pouring from her body, the flush-faced redhead finished her last set. Samantha then sat up to face a high-five from her energetic friend.

"*You can do better than that,*" came a voice from behind the bench where Samantha sat.

A bit perturbed by that statement, Samantha turned around to face her foe. "I don't think so!" she said stoutly while in the process of retrieving her normal breathing pattern.

"I don't see how either," added Gina.

"First of all, let me introduce myself. I'm Angie, the creator of Body

Perfect. I am also a certified trainer. I do apologize for my rude entry, but I noticed the both of you over here on the bench doing some serious lifting. I thought I would come by, introduce myself, and offer a few free tips to make sure that your efforts produce the most positive results."

"Hi, I'm Samantha Rafferty, and my friend here is Gina Pirelli."

"This is our first time here," said Gina.

"Well, I hope it won't be your last," said Angie, glancing hard at the redhead. So that's Mrs. Rafferty, Sonny's wife, she thought to herself. She looks the same as she did many years ago at that Christmas party. She is still very pretty. I wonder if she realizes how lucky she is to be married to a guy like Sonny. I wish it were me. While coming back to reality Angie noticed Gina staring at her for an answer.

"Oh, I'm sorry. I didn't hear what you said," answered Angie.

"I said, what is your secret for us to bench-press more weight?"

"There's no secret, really. You just need to do a better job of spotting one-another, and to have better form when lifting. That's all."

"Do you mean something like you and that blonde were doing, earlier?" asked Samantha.

"Exactly," said Angie. "By the way, that blonde girl is Eva, my masseuse. Anytime you need a good massage, she's the gal to see."

"I bet she does give a mean massage with those man-hands of hers," said Gina.

"Give her a try. You won't be disappointed," smiled Angie.

"So, Angie, what tips can you give that will be of help to us? I must admit that lifting cold heavy steel off my chest is not my favorite form of exercise," said Samantha.

"I noticed you arching your back on your last set, Samantha. That's not using proper form."

"But that's the only way I could get it up."

"When you arch your back you are using more of your legs and back instead of your chest. You will be surprised how easy it is to bench-press when someone spots you properly. Let me demonstrate. Gina, why don't you take your position on the bench to do another set?"

Gina took her position, lying supine on the padded bench. She reached upward with both hands, and using a wide grip, grabbed the barbell, waiting for Angie's cue before lifting. Angie then positioned herself at the head of the bench; legs spread shoulder-length apart, while grabbing the middle of the bar with her right hand.

"The trick, girls, is for the spotter to stand directly over the head of the weight-lifter. I call this the 'Head-to-Snatch' method. This way the spotter has more leverage to help the lifter and less chance of doing injury to herself. The spotter's main job is to help the lifter push the barbell from her chest in proper form. The rest is up to the girl on the bench. So, Gina, let's get to know each other," cued Angie.

Gina lifted the bar out of its channel and brought it down to her chest. Then, with a grunt and a burst of strength, and Angie's right hand, she shoved the steel upward, and repeated that same movement several times more as she pumped out another set. Samantha soon exchanged places with Gina and did the same.

When they were finished, Angie, Gina, and Samantha all congregated around a much desired water fountain, quenching their thirst while chatting about the workout center and such. .

"Angie, if we were to work out regularly using heavy weights would we get muscle-bound like . . . like your friend, Eva?" asked Gina.

Angie sniggered, "Muscle-bound, that's a phrase from the past, and somewhat of a myth too, I might add. Here at Body Perfect there is no such thing as a muscle-bound person. Muscle-bound is a term suggesting too much exercise causing enlarged muscles with little elasticity for proper body movement. We have none of that here for we preach stretching as much as exercise. You can pump iron all you want, and if you stretch properly you won't get muscle-bound. We have stretching exercises for each muscle group and we have them plastered all over the walls of this gym. So, 'take heed and read,' is our motto. As far as Eva goes, she *is* very muscular, but I must tell you that she is a professional body-builder. She takes supplements, works out every day, and is on a vigorous low-fat diet most of the time."

"No kidding," said Gina with growing interest.

"Yeah, you probably noticed Eva's large chest. She has huge pecs but no boobs."

"Yeah, we noticed that too. Why is that?" asked Gina.

Samantha, slightly embarrassed, gave Gina a light nudge with her elbow. Angie noticed and smiled.

"That's because she has very little body fat. Breasts, of course, contain a lot of fat. But don't worry, girls. Working out your pecs once or twice a week with progressive weights will not diminish your bust line, but enhance it. Just remember that you want to build those chest muscles beneath your breasts. It'll make those tits stand tall, and every woman wants that." Samantha and Gina nodded their heads in agreement.

Gina lifted her arm and took a whiff, "Hey, guys, I've got to hit the showers. I'm starting to reek, how about it, Sam?"

"Yeah, me too, Gina, I stink like a horse's butt. Thanks for your advice, Angie," said Samantha.

"Yeah, thanks Angie," echoed Gina.

Angie studied the two women as they headed to the locker room to shower up.

Body Perfect's turquoise tiled steam room had heard many a conversation in its short history, but this evening's friendly confab between the four lady news journalists would soon turn risqué enough to make the blue room blush.

The hot fog seemed to bring about a most sensuous euphoria, and along with Gina's anecdotes and friendly banter, created a rare excitement to which the girls of newsprint had never before seen the likes of. Gina was the most uninhibited of the bunch as she cavorted around naked in front of the others while the vapor from the 105 degree steam caused little rivulets to flow down her flawless body, emitting an olive glow. A white club towel hung loosely around Samantha's middle while covering her private stock, at least for the time being. Merle preferred basking in the heat and humidity topless, her deep brown breasts showing like black gold in the steamy mist with her body's sweat dripping steadily from their ebony tips. Meanwhile, Jitterbug wore her terrycloth folded tightly around her as if she was hiding the treasured gold of the Sierra Madres.

The primary question of the evening, which was asked by Jitterbug and directed at Gina, was what was it like to spend half a year in Iraq, Iran, and Saudi Arabia? It was a question that she had encountered many times since her return back to the states. She also answered that question many times on public broadcasts and various functions around and about the city. Her opinion was highly valued by experts and politicians alike. But this evening was about play, not politics and war. Gina was clever enough to know how to ease out of one subject and segue into another.

"Let me tell you one thing, ladies. You can put to rest the notion of dashing young sheiks riding around on their white Arabian horses rescuing women in distress. The sheiks that I saw were, either, fat, old, or both, while Rolls Royce's and limousines were their mode of transportation. And they had large harems of women bought and paid for by the U.S dollar. That's not what I had envisioned for myself."

"What were the other men like over there?" asked Samantha.

"What men? We were stuck out in the sandy wilderness most of the time. They don't like western women journalists, per se. Our moral character isn't up to their code. I must say, I don't see how they have so many children because sexual activity seems to be taboo to the Muslims. They must just keep it all under wraps, no pun intended. All that male jism must be going into sperm banks somewhere. I did notice a lot of the camels walking around with smiles on their faces though," she jested, causing a laugh.

"I didn't think I was ever going to get laid. Then one day I ran into a French journalist. He made my tenure in the desert worthwhile. Oh, those Frenchmen, they do have a way about them, you know. Ooh la-la!"

"Sam told us that you have a way with men," said Merle.

"Why, Samantha, you are the flatterer aren't you?" said the ostentatious reporter.

"And these are men of distinction too, I might add," said Samantha.

"Well, those politicians of Washington are the reason that I drive a red Jaguar today," boasted Gina.

Suddenly, the door opened. Into the little heat-soaked rotunda appeared Angie, walking hand in hand with Eva. They all greeted and nodded respectively as the couple headed to the far side of the room. Except for the sound of new steam hissing from a small port-hole in the wall, the room stood quiet while prying eyes watched the odd couple remove the white towels from their bodies. Angie looked womanly with her legs crossed one atop the other while laying her head back on the top tier, welcoming in the fresh steam to cleanse her body. Eva, on the other hand, sat with her legs splayed, exposing her huge genitals for all to see as she stroked Angie's right breast with the back of her hand. Jitterbug, who sat to the right of Eva, nervously edged away ever so slightly so as not to disturb the big Swede. It was quite a sight, one that none of them had experienced before. Angie turned and gave Eva a kiss on the lips. She then laid her head in Eva's lap and stretched her legs along the tiled edge, revealing her well-trimmed Venus triangle. Eva now fondled Angie's ample breasts while softly kissing her face every now and again. Angie would occasionally reach up and caress the manly but long-nippled breasts of her lover in return.

Gina sat down next to Samantha and broke the quietude with a whisper, "Does that Swede have a dick, Sam? Is she one of those hermaphrodites or something?"

Samantha snickered at her friend, "No silly. She's all-woman. She just owns an oversized clitoris, and her inner labia are quite large also."

"How do you figure she got that way, Sam?" asked Gina curiously.

"She probably uses male enhancement drugs of some type. You know, steroids maybe. She is a professional body-builder. You heard Angie say that. They'll go to all kinds of extremes to compete. She's a girl alright, and I have to say that even though it sounds pretty kinky, seeing Eva and Angie together like that sort of turns me on. You know what I mean, Pirelli?"

"Yeah, I kinda feel the same way," admitted Gina.

"She does have some large flaps hanging," declared Samantha.

"Flaps hell, those are Dumbo's ears!" exclaimed Gina, a little too loud, while staring straight at Eva's blonde undergrowth.

Samantha laughed aloud and struggled to suppress it. Merle caught sight of Samantha's laughter and began to snicker. Gina, suddenly realizing the hilarity of what she said, began laughing also. It became contagious as even Angie sported a smile at their jocularity while her obtuse partner sat stoically; caressing her lover's wet skin. Jitterbug looked dumbfounded by it all as she was still intimidated by the odd couple doing their shenanigans next to her. Soon, a new burst of steam dulled the laughter.

"Hey, how did that date go with you and your old friend the other night, Gina?" asked Samantha.

"It was a wash. He took me to a nice nightclub downtown but he drank too much so I went home without getting laid."

"Oh, that's too bad."

"To be truthful, the best sex that I've had since I've been back was yesterday when I went to the clinic for my annual Pap smear and breast examination."

"You've got to be joking," said Merle.

"No, my doctor may be an old gent but he does have nice soft hands," said Gina with a glint in her eye. "I always say, when you are needy don't be greedy." Everyone shared in another laugh.

"Wait until you turn 40 and have to take the mammogram. That'll change your tune," warned Samantha.

"What's so difficult about a mammogram? All they do is take an x-ray of your breasts, right?"

"I'm afraid it's a little more complicated than that," said Samantha.

"Pray tell me, what is it about mammography that has you so skittish, girlfriend?"

"Let me run you girls through the procedure, then, you can draw your own conclusions," said Samantha with a devilish smile. "After the gynie has his way with you he sends you to a modern day torture chamber where you are greeted by some nice lady, an older woman in my case, and very cordial, whom you soon discover is really a sadomasochist guised as a technician. She then presses pasties onto the ends of your tits to protect your nipples from radiation exposure, she says. Then the fun part begins. She has you step up to the machine, the vice I call it, and then grabs one of your honies and lays it on a cold slab of steel and tries to flatten it out. But she says that's not good enough so she tugs and pulls and tugs and stretches on your boob until she has half your chest on that cold steel plate. She then lowers the top of the vice down onto your stretched-out mammary and tightens it and tightens it and tightens even more until it hurts like hell. You just grit your teeth because the only thing you can think of is that she's going to do the same thing to your other honey."

"Yikes! That doesn't sound like too much fun, Sam."

"No shit."

"What did you feel like when they were through with you, Sam?" asked Jitterbug, her curiosity abounding.

"You feel like you have two pancakes hanging from your chest with pasties dangling off the ends, but don't fret, Jitterbug, you're still young yet. It'll be awhile before you have to go through *the torture chamber!*"

"Well, thank you Sam, for you have enlightened us to the drudgeries of becoming a 40year-old female," said Gina.

"You make me sound like I'm ancient."

"Oh no, not at all, Sam, but I do believe that we have all learned a lesson here."

"Oh yeah, what is it?" asked Merle.

"Cherish your breasts ladies, for they are what distinguish us apart from one another. Man is ultimately searching for the elusive clam, but he always negotiates with your breasts first. Look, girls, we were all born with like equipment between our legs. I mean, shave the beard and we all look the same down there, with few exceptions," she said while glancing at Eva. "It's our boobies that we are so proud of and that men are so fond of. We all have different kinds, big ones, small ones, fat ones, skinny ones, droopy ones, and they come with short nipples, long nipples, small nipples, and barrel-head nipples such as mine have," she said while proudly squeezing her ample breasts together. "They're like fingerprints. No two sets are alike. Of course, some are bogus, but that's alright too. Hell, if they needed it, I'd have no qualms about enhancing these babies either."

"Sonny thinks that breasts should be revealed not revised, revered not altered," said Samantha unabashedly.

"But Sam, you're an anomaly. There is no sag in your body, even though you're in your forties," said Gina.

"I'm 43 to be exact. Exercise and diet is the reason that I stay in shape. How do you keep in shape, Gina?" asked Samantha.

"Sex, red wine, and more sex, that's what works for me," boasted Gina.

"Seriously now; sex may be a good workout for a man, but I think not for a woman," said Samantha.

"You've got to ride the wild stallion, girl, not him ride you," replied Gina, sharing a smile with the room.

The little blue steam room heard several more rounds of loose talk before spewing out the lady journalists for their evening cool-down.

The walls echoed the laughter from Samantha and her friends as they poured into the shower room. The hissing showerheads emitted a comforting cool spray that replaced their jocularity with sighs of relief. It had been quite a lobster-fest for the girls, what with Gina's entertaining stories of her misadventures abroad, and with the staged performances of Angie and Eva. The sight of Eva's considerable attributes alone had a strange, voyeuristic appeal that captivated her audience.

The cool rush of water soon turned Samantha's tangelo complexion back to its tawny glow. While she lathered her red mane, Gina, who was showering nearby, stared at her friend in anticipation.

"Hey, Sam, after the governor's ball next month I'm being reassigned to D.C. again."

"Congratulations Gina. I'm happy for you. That's what you wanted all along isn't it?"

"Very much so, but it would be twice as nice if you were to go with."

"No, Gina. As much as I would like to, my place is here with the Times."

"Well, I wouldn't want to take you away from all of your friends at the Times, but if you were to change your mind I could easily find you a job in Washington."

"Thanks for caring, girl, but I'll just stay right here."

"You know, Sam, you never did say goodbye to Troy properly when you left. You broke his heart and never told him why."

Samantha quickly rinsed the lather from her eyes as the pace of her heart quickened. This was the one moment in her life that she hadn't hoped for. "I just couldn't, Gina. I didn't know how to say goodbye on such short notice. It was an emergency. I had to get back to Sonny right away. I called you several times after and told you about it. Didn't you say anything to Troy?"

"Sure I did, Sam, but it wasn't the same. He loved you, not me. He needed to hear it from you."

"I didn't mean to hurt him, really I didn't," she said, her voice lowering with her eyes. Samantha didn't notice, but the curious brown body of Merle Bullock slipped out of her spray to join the mix.

"Troy! Does she mean Troy Charbonau, Sam?"

The harshness of Merle's voice snapped her eyes up to meet her glare. Samantha froze.

"Let me get this straight. I've been hired as the campaign manager for your brother, who is running for political office against an incumbent that you've had an illicit affair with. Is that correct?"

Samantha's skin flushed. It was more than just embarrassment that flooded her face. She nodded, then lowered her head and answered with a muffled, "Yes." She then lowered her eyes even more because of the guilt and shame that she had kept inside for so long.

"That's just great! That's just fucking great!" fumed Merle. She did an about face and walked out, grabbing a clean towel along the way to dry off with in the locker room.

"Gee, Sam, I didn't know that you kept this a secret all of this time," said Gina.

Samantha didn't hate her friend for exposing the truth, but at this moment she didn't like her. "I'll say one thing, Pirelli. Your timing sucks!"

"Your right, Sam, I'm so sorry. I have a big mouth, and sometimes it gets me into trouble. I feel really stupid right now. Are we still friends?"

"Yeah, yeah," answered Samantha coolly, as she pondered on what to do next. "Look, Gina, I've got to go talk to Merle and straighten things out."

"Okay, Sam. Can I call you in a couple of days, and maybe we can do lunch or something?"

"Sure, give me a call."

Samantha felt besmirched. Worse yet she had to win back her friend's confidence, not only for herself, but for Chance and the Times. Merle was her confidant, and Samantha figured the best way to win her back was to be truthful with her.

"Please don't be angry with me, Merle," begged Samantha.

Merle was sitting on the bench next to her locker, half-dressed and still shaking her head in disbelief. "How could you do that Sam? I don't get it. I always thought of you and Sonny as such a great couple."

"We are, Merle. Don't think any different. I made a serious mistake once, and that happened a long time ago."

"Did you tell Sonny about your affair?"

"No."

"How about Chance, did you tell him?"

"No, of course not," replied Samantha.

"You do know don't you, if word gets out about your affair with Troy Charbonau that it would become quite a scandal for sure?"

"It won't get out, Merle. Just you, Gina, and I know about it. We have got to keep this our own secret."

Disappointment masked Merle's face. "What happened, Sam?"

"What happened? I'll tell you what happened. I fell in love, Merle. I didn't fall out of love with Sonny, but I fell in love with the young senator from Indiana. I must have been crazy or something. I acted like a young, naïve schoolgirl. Washington was just too big for me, too powerful. It devoured me, Merle. It took my soul," cried Samantha.

Merle stood up and warmly embraced her friend, for she now had discovered Samantha's fragile zone, the anxiety of a secret past love affair, and her fear of losing Sonny. "Don't worry, honey. I will always stand by you. You'll always be my friend," said Merle.

Samantha held to Merle tightly as they shared tears together.

Sitting between rows of lockers and out of sight of the embracing couple was Angelina Garza, listening to every word that was said. She had come in to retrieve used towels and other left out articles of the day, as she did every evening. She always performed this task very stealth-like, for she liked to eavesdrop on unsuspecting women to hear the latest gossip. Tonight was no exception, but tonight was different then the rest because the conversation dealt with a man that was very important in Angie's life. That man happened to be Sonny Rafferty. He was the man that rescued her from a childhood of bad memories. She had a crush on him for years, and still did somewhat. When he was around her, he still made her feel like that same kid. What Angie heard his wife talking about tonight enraged her. How could any woman betray a man like Sonny in an illicit affair, thought Angie. She doesn't know how to treat a man, but I do. Maybe, when the time is right, I will tell Sonny about his cheating wife. He might want *me* then. But the time is not right. We both have too much on our plates right now. But when that time comes, I will tell him, and then I will be his." She smiled at that thought.

The storm had passed, but Sonny's mind was still cloudy. He had found solitude on his patio in the backyard, searching the star-studded sky with an old telescope of the kids. During his recovery, Sonny had searched his mind long and hard but could not remember much about that night, especially after leaving Centralia. Keeping him company in the backyard were his canine friends, Napoleon and Rufus. Impala would poke her head out of the hole-in-the-wall every once in a while to check on the boys, but her real loyalty lied with Samantha whom she always waited for at the front door of their old colonial two-story. Sonny was in a melancholic state of mind tonight, proving that a man who can't retrieve his memory is indeed a lost soul. Oh, he conjured up faces and some background, but couldn't piece them together. It became very frustrating for him, for he had always been the problem solver.

Sonny could sense Samantha sneaking up from behind by the heavy, exuberant panting from her sidekick, Impala, who was by her side.

"What are you doing, looking for your lodestar?"

Sonny turned around and greeted his wife with a friendly kiss. "If the north-star was my lodestar, life would be simple because it's so easy to follow."

"So, how have you been feeling today?" asked Samantha warmly.

"It's not the ache in my body that bothers me. It's the ache in my heart. I feel like I can't do enough, Sam. I feel like I've been given this huge job to undertake, and I'm losing ground in my quest for what's right. It's like a burden to me, and I've felt like that since I was a kid. Oh, I've had my respites now and then. Maggie May when I was younger. You and the girls until lately, but it doesn't seem enough, Sam. I just don't understand it. I keep trying to pull things together, but all I get are flashbacks now and again. And then you and your dad seem to know more about what happened to me then you let on. I'm perplexed, Sam."

"Let's just put that all behind us tonight. Take me to bed and make love to me, darlin'."

"I don't know if I can fulfill my obligations as a husband and father anymore."

"That's okay. Come lie with me then. I just want to feel you next to me."

Sonny hesitated.

"Kiss me, goddamn it!" cried Samantha in desperation.

Sonny embraced her and kissed her warmly.

Samantha pulled her hot yearning lips from his. "Don't kiss me like we're married. Kiss me like we're lovers!"

Sonny kissed her hard and deep. Samantha kissed back with unbridled passion.

The silvery moon slipped from behind the Hansen's big oak and shone brightly through the castle window that harbored the Lady Godiva astride her stallion, with her crimson mane bouncing happily against her pale shoulders.

"There's something about the intrusiveness of your big, hard penis that excites me. It almost scares me," she giggled.

Their bodies did not betray them, as their life of Camelot was still alive and well. Oh, it had been broken somewhat, but the mending had now begun. Unless something else major would interfere, the Prince and Princess were back together again. It was a fairytale romance surviving all odds, trying desperately to have a fairytale ending.

Chapter Fourteen

Our Little Corner of the World

Knock, Knock, Knock!

"Yes, come in."

"Did you wish to see me, Mr. Taylor?"

"Yes, Merle, sit down, please," gestured Big John. "I just wanted to link up with you to make sure we are in-sync on Chance's senatorial campaign. First of all, I appreciate you for accepting this challenge. If we win this thing, I'm sure it will be very beneficial to us all."

"I believe so too, sir."

Big John pulled out a long cigar from his coat pocket, clipped the end off, and prepared to light it. "Do you mind if I smoke?"

"No sir, not at all."

"So what's your take on all of this?" he asked as the rich smoke billowed above his head.

"Sir?" she asked.

"What's your strategy, your game plan?"

"Well, sir, I figured that we would campaign in the northern part of the state first. You know, Gary, Michigan City, South Bend, Fort Wayne, and then work our way down."

"That's good thinking, Merle. They have a strong African-American influence up there. That's what we want."

"But I must admit, sir, we don't have much money left in the campaign coffers."

"You just let me worry about that. In the meantime I've got an itinerary made up for you to meet with certain party affiliates in these cities, and they will coordinate with you on campaign dinners and such."

"Excuse me, sir, but I really think that we need Chance at these functions to make them work."

"Precisely, my dear, you set things up now, then in several weeks, after the Governor's Ball, you take Chance with you through those cities."

"The Governor's Ball, why wait till then?"

"Well, Lou Stevens has Chance doing county fairs right now to get the milk votes. Besides, you need to be here for the Governor's Ball because you all are up for an award on the Waverly project."

Merle turned her eyes, "Oh, I wish you hadn't brought that up. I don't think we're going to win anything for that."

"Oh ye of little faith, I don't believe you or Sam, or the rest of the Fab Four know the breadth and scope of what you accomplished on that Waverly project."

"Maybe your right, sir," she said, feeling belittled.

"Hell. I know I'm right," boasted Big John. "You'll see. So, after your respite from the Governor's Ball you can then take Chance and show him the ropes."

"Are you giving me the authority?"

"Oh yes, my dear, and I'll make sure that Chance knows it. Take him under your wings and clip his. Chance's biggest problem is women, one in particular right now, Jamaica Red. Whatever you do, Merle, keep Chance away from that goddamn Jamaica Red."

"I don't even know who she is."

"Oh, you'll know her when you see her. She definitely stands out in the crowd. Look, Merle, Chance isn't stupid. He just does stupid things at times. He's smart enough to be a senator. Hell, he's held several political jobs already. Once he becomes a senator, he'll know what to do. I guarantee it."

"I want to be upfront with you, sir. I think we've got a long-shot at best."

"Hell, young lady, I've been taking long shots my whole life. John F. Kennedy was a long shot, but I helped him get elected, yeah, first catholic president. If they hadn't killed him he would have squelched that Vietnam thing and this country would be a lot better off today. Look, Merle, I've crunched some numbers, and I believe that if we can get a sixty percent black voter turnout in these major cities then we can beat that right-wing son-of-a-bitch."

In a puff of smoke Big John abruptly stood up and offered his large hand to Merle. "How about it, Merle; are you in?"

Merle returned his gesture and confidently answered, "Yes sir, I'm in"

"Thanks for coming by, Merle."

"Your welcome, sir, I'll do my best."

"I know you will, darling. I surely do."

"Ms. Rafferty, you have a call on line two," said the sprightly secretary.

"It's not that nurse again is it? I can't be bothered with her. I'm too busy. Hell, we finished that Waverly article a month ago. That's a dead story now."

"No, it's not her, Ms. Rafferty, but she has been quite persistent though."

"Well, if she keeps calling, tell her the story's dead, and that's it. And get rid of that person that's on the line now!" she said irritably.

"But, ma'am, he says he's your husband."

"Oh . . . well, why didn't you say so to begin with?"

"I'm sorry, ma'am."

"That's okay. I'll take it in my office."

"Is this my lover speaking?" she asked with last night's sparkle in her eyes.

"No, Highpockets, this is your husband, Sonny."

"You big lug, don't tease me like that."

"Geezus, getting through to you is like trying to talk to the President."

"We're really busy here, what with Merle changing jobs, Jessie calling off, and me being stuck here with a temp taking my calls for me today."

"So, I guess going out to lunch with me is out of the question, eh?"

"I'm sorry, baby, but I'm swamped. I probably won't even eat lunch today. So, what have you been up to this morning?"

"I'm here at the office sorting through my mail and returning phone calls."

"Do you have any good job offers?"

"I've got a couple of small ones, nothing substantial."

"Well, I've got some good news for you. Daddy wants you to direct the security force again for the Governor's Ball next month."

"That's good. Can I pick my own men?"

"Oh yes, he says that you have full control."

"That's great, honey. I can use the work. So, if lunch is out how about dinner tonight? I received a five-hundred dollar check from Mrs. Weiler today, and I thought that it would be nice to take a lovely redhead that I know out to dinner at Deiters Nasch this evening."

"That sounds delightful, but I won't get out of here until at least nine tonight. I'll tell you what. I would prefer a nice, quiet, romantic little dinner at Lucrecia's at say, nine thirty; how about that, darling?"

"Okay, yeah, that sounds good."

"Hey, Sonny," said Samantha in a softer, sexier tone.

"What?"

"I bet you're sitting behind your big oak desk, aren't you?"

"Why, yes I am."

"Do you remember when we bought that old used desk and put it in your office?"

"Yeah," laughed Sonny. "We christened it before we even got the dust wiped off of it."

"Well, after our intimate meal at Lucrecia's I want you to take me up to your office and do me again."

"Do me. Oh, that's a nice choice of words coming from a lady of class and grace."

"I can't help it. You bring out the nasty in me, lover boy. You had me sizzling last night, baby. You know, you sent me to heaven seven times, lover. I want to ride those wings to paradise again tonight."

"Okay. I'll do my best, sexy lady."

"See you tonight, then."

"Yeah, tonight at nine thirty then," agreed Sonny.

"Till then, lover," she said with a kiss.

"Till then, baby."

Samantha smiled while closing the glass-embedded office door behind her. The remembrance of last night stood out fresh in her mind. It had been an excruciatingly long day knowing that tonight she would be rendezvousing with Sonny to exchange pleasures of the flesh. Sonny hadn't quite reached the point of being reborn yet, but he and Samantha were making great strides into regaining their old forms.

A blanket of dusk covered the city as Samantha left the Times building and walked toward her car that was parked along the street. While driving away she noticed another car pulling out behind her. She thought it quite odd since there were no cars parked along the curb. She made several turns but the car still followed. She began to tense up. She was being tailed but she didn't know why. Finally, she decided to hit the main thoroughfares hoping to lose the shadow that followed her. At least then she could tell what kind of car it was from the streetlights. But as she drove, the car backed off and stayed back. Samantha saw a chance to shake 'em off. She floored the red Impala and blew a red light and hit the entrance ramp to the expressway.

"By God, I'll either lose you now or find a cop," she said aloud as the needle on the speedometer approached 90 miles per hour.

After traveling several more miles down the highway, Samantha noticed two little lights growing larger in her rearview mirror. She knew that it was the same car as before because one of the headlights was dimmer than the other. "Where's a cop when you need one!" she exclaimed. Then a thought crossed her mind; a cop, cell- phone, Sonny! Samantha rummaged nervously through her purse for her phone as the lights loomed larger in her mirror. Suddenly, the 10th street exit sign appeared. She had to turn on that exit to get to Lucrecia's. She quickly grabbed the wheel with both hands and slammed on the brakes, throwing her purse and phone to the floorboard while trying desperately to guide her Chevy through the exit. Samantha heard the terrifying sound of screeching tires as the mystery car fish-tailed around her. The lucky Impala squealed safely down the off-ramp before easing onto 10th street.

"Whew, that was a close one," she said, her voice quivering. "Just ten more blocks, then I'm home free."

As Samantha turned onto 6th street, she noticed another car falling in behind her. It had one bright light and one dim. "Damn! What the hell's going on here?" she yelled. With about a block to go Samantha yanked her wheel sharply to the right into an alleyway, a shortcut to

Lucrecia's pub. She jumped out of the car, ran down the sidewalk, and around the corner to the basement pub. She stepped nimbly down the stairwell until she was hidden in a dark shadow. She heard only one car door slam. She then heard the footsteps coming in her direction. Samantha's first thought was, Stupid me, if only I would've brought my purse, I have pepper spray in there. Her next thought was to take a couple of more steps down and open the door leading into the safe-haven of the little restaurant.

But she had that inquisitive mind, whether be it from her job, or from living with a cop for so long. She wanted to see who was so intent on following her to this destination. The footsteps were right there now. She could hear their hard breathing. It was a woman, to Samantha's surprise. The woman stopped and stared out into the street, nervously searching. She then slowly turned around as if she was distracted by a noise or—Crack!

"Here, put this against your eye, it'll make the swelling go down," said Lucrecia, handing the blonde an icepack.

The blonde looked up and scowled, "Who the hell are you?"

"Oh, I'm just an old woman who runs a bar," replied Lucrecia.

"The question is who are you, and why were you chasing me all over hell's half acre?" snapped Samantha.

"My name is Loni Jacobs and I'm in trouble, big trouble. I need your help."

"Why do you need my help?" asked Samantha.

"Because I think they're going to kill me."

"Who's going to kill you?"

"Who do ya think? The powers that be," she said with a mock smile.

"Why do you come to me? Why not go to the cops?"

"Huh, you got rocks in your head or somethin', lady? The cops, what are the cops going to do for me? I'm a 34year old nurse with four kids from three different men, and I've been arrested twice for drug possession. Fuck the cops! They're not going to help me."

"So, Loni, what makes you think that I can help?"

"I'll tell you the reason why, because you, the media, owe me. I'm the one that called in the information about the nursing home violations, and I know how they cook their books. I'm the whistleblower!"

"But that information came in from a series of anonymous phone calls."

"Yes, I know. I'm the one that made 'em. If they'd found out who-dunnit they would've killed me already. Now they know, I think. Now they're trying to quiet me. I fed you all the information that you needed, but you quit on me. You didn't put them away, goddamn-it."

"Yes, we closed on the story early because Waverly was cooperating with us. They even closed down Ginger Hills for two weeks and put them on probation until they get up to speed. They're hiring more staffing to meet the national standards."

"So, you believe all that bullshit?"

"We have to draw the line somewhere, Loni."

"Draw the line? Hell yes, draw that fucking line, Rafferty. You've got to hide the truth someway. Look, I'm a floor nurse at Ginger Hills. I'm the only experienced nurse left that hasn't been fired or let go. Why? Because I've got the goods on the company, that's why. They want to keep an eye on me until they get rid of me for good."

"Come on, you're getting a bit ridiculous now, aren't you?"

"You're right, lady. It is ridiculous for me to think that a pompous ass like you would want to help the common folk like me and the other nurses?"

"I take offense to that!" snapped Samantha.

"Well, good, at least that shows that you're not brain dead." Loni said boldly.

Samantha smiled. She may have decked her good out on the sidewalk, but Loni gave a good account of herself in the battle of wits. "I like you, Jacobs, let's talk some more; how about some red wine?"

"How about a good beer?" retorted Loni.

"Lucrecia!" called Samantha.

"Right at ya, Sam, a German beer for your friend and some Bordeaux Merlot for you, coming right up," said the barmaid.

"Let's go sit in a booth out front," suggested Samantha.

"Can I take a piss first?"

"Yeah, go right ahead, out the kitchen door and to your left."

"You know, Rafferty, you've got a pretty good right hand," she said while taking the ice pack off her cheek.

"Yeah, I guess I do. Thanks."

"You know that was a sucker punch, don't you?"

"Well, yeah, I guess it was but—"

"Cause if it wasn't I would have cleaned your clock," said Loni, as she walked out the door.

"I guess you would," mused Samantha while watching her walk away. "I guess you would."

Sonny hadn't arrived yet as Lucrecia delivered the wine and the beer to the girls, but that was okay with Samantha because she was sidelined right now with a new exclusive on the Waverly scandal.

"So, what's the story on the barmaid? You two seem like pretty good friends," said the blonde.

"We are. She kinda took me in when I was a kid, just married, pregnant, and my husband working nights as a cop. She's good people. Lucrecia's a true Bohemian from the Czech Republic. She came to the United States when she was twelve. She's an original hippy, you know."

"Oh yeah?" said Loni.

"Yeah, she was at Woodstock when she was just 15years old. She told me that was where she first experienced the squirt of male sperm into her bowels, as she put it. She's kind of poetic, a flower child of sorts. Heck, she hasn't worn a bra since Woodstock either, and you can tell," said Samantha with a grin. "So what's going on at Waverly that's got you in such a huff?"

"They've fired most of the experienced nurses at all the homes and replaced them with unskilled nurses from the Philippines and Venezuela. They're over here on ill-gotten work visas and start out at minimum wage. Their sponsors take half of that money. In other words, they're pretty much importing slave labor and firing all the experienced nurses on trumped up charges, but really for making too much money. It's taken over the whole industry, especially Waverly. I'll give you one quick story, which is the reason that I started investigating things. My sister is Barbara Fugate. Do you remember her?"

"Why yes, she was my husband's home nurse when he was ill awhile back."

"That's right. Do you know why she's a home nurse now?"

"I presume because she likes it."

"No. It's because she got fired by Waverly two years ago. They claimed that she let a lady fall and break her hip and didn't record it. It was all made up. The company's lawyers even went to her unemployment hearing to stop her from drawing unemployment. They blackballed her to where no other home would hire her. Finally, she got on with a home health care agency."

"Couldn't you take it to court and fight it? Don't you have contracts with these homes?"

"When you first hire in, they kiss your butt, say you've got this, you've go that. Then, when you read the fine print, you find out that you have no contract for yourself at all. That booklet with all the rules and regulations and do's and don'ts isn't for your protection. They make you think that you have a legal contract, but you don't have a contract at all. It's a big lie, Samantha. Nursing is supposed to be a profession, but it's not. It's all about slave ownership. I bucked the system. I probed, broke into records, and got passwords for the computers. I know their system, Rafferty. It's ugly. It's real ugly. As you know, all of their profits go too Miramar, as does the Medicare. It's not spent on the patients or the nurses."

"Well, we knew about Miramar being a bogus company, but we don't know who's raking in all the profits."

"I do, Samantha. I know exactly where it's going. That's why they want to kill me."

"Tell me, Loni, I'd like to know."

"Well, let's not get too carried away here, Rafferty. First of all, you have to promise to print this story. That's the only thing that will save my ass. If you agree to that, I'll get you the proof. I have it on paper and I will deliver it to you tomorrow. But you have to promise to get the truth out."

"I promise I'll print it as soon as I find out exactly who the money's going to."

"Tomorrow night I will come here at about the same time and show you proof on who Miramar really is. You're not going to like it 'cause it hits close to home. You'll fill your little lace panties when you find out," boasted Loni.

"You were our voice from the beginning, Loni, so you give us Miramar, and I'll print it. I promise," said Samantha.

"Thanks for listening Rafferty. I feel like I've got one friend left in this world that I can trust."

"I'll do my best."

As Sonny opened the door to Lucrecia's he was greeted by a roughed up blonde on her way out. They exchanged pleasantries and soon she was gone. The air was filled with the scent of ginger as the strange sound of a Hindu's sitar came from a corner of the pub. Nothing surprised Sonny when he visited Lucrecia's pub, for she and Jaques did not quite mix into the fabric of this society. They were most unconventional, what with Jaques being a French artist in a Midwestern state capitol, and she an old world Slavic running a German pub in Bohemian style. But they were good friends to he and Samantha, and good friends were a scarcity nowadays for the ex-cop.

"Hey, Sonny, your wife has been waiting for you," was Lucrecia's greeting as she grabbed his hand and pulled him to the booth where Samantha sat. "Here, talk to your pretty wife. Tell her how she needs to eat. I tell her that she's too skinny, but she doesn't want to listen to me. I'll go to the kitchen and bring back something to fatten her up," she said in her broken English.

Sonny greeted his wife with a kiss. Then sat down opposite of her in the booth. Samantha grabbed hold of his hands while staring at him with love sparkling in her eyes.

"So, how's your day been, Highpockets?"

"It's been a long day, Sonny, too long without you in it. You ignited a fire in me last night that won't go out."

"Gee, Sam, I don't know what to say."

"Tell me that you'll take me to your place and make wild passionate love to me tonight, you big ape," she said while poking at his chest.

"All right, but first lets eat. Here comes Lucrecia with our food. We must put some meat on your bones. I wouldn't want to break anything tonight, dear," Sonny teased.

"Don't worry. I bend. I don't break."

"And bend you shall, my dear, tonight on that old oak desk in my office."

"Oh, what suave talk; I can tell you were out in the park again today, watching the dogs mate, right?"

"Yes, and they seemed to be quite happy at it."

"Sonny, you're incorrigible."

"Here you are, my good friends. A round of fresh cheese of goat, a marble rye, and of course, a bottle of Bordeaux Merlot," said Lucrecia while serving their meal.

"Lucrecia, sit down and have a drink with us," requested Sonny.

"I mustn't interrupt two young lovers as you."

"Yes you must. We insist," implored Samantha.

"Besides, we're not that young anymore," added Sonny.

"You're young at heart. That's where it counts, in here," she said, pounding her sternum. "You young lovers, you excite me. You remind me of Frenchie and me when we were young. Oh, he was somethin', that Frenchie," she said with a gleam in her eye. "Oh how we used to make love," she reminisced. "But we got old. Now we just roll around like two hedgehogs in the bushes. But o-h-h-h that Frenchie, he was somethin' else," she said with a loud smile.

Sonny and Samantha smiled with her, for they thoroughly enjoyed the little woman's European style of humor.

"Hey Lucrecia, is Jaques around?" asked Sonny.

"No, he ran off for awhile today. We argue this morning. He called me an old shrew and left with some artist friends of his today," she said nonchalantly while slicing the cheese. "He come back late tonight though, trying to crawl into my bed, but I lock the door. He will sleep on the couch tonight. Tomorrow he will love me again," she said most assuredly.

"Lucrecia, your food is excellent as usual, and your wine is tasty," praised Sonny, "but the music in here tonight, I must say, sounds kinda strange."

"The cheese we buy fresh from the farmer, and this morning I bake for you the bread myself. Bread, cheese, and wine are the food for lovers, to eat under the moonlight, or at Lucrecia's," she smiled, "As for the music, different maybe, but strange? There is nothing strange if your mind has an open door to it, my handsome friend."

"That's what I like about you, Lucrecia, you have all the right answers," said Samantha.

"Life is not about having all the right answers, my dear, but answering all the right questions." Lucrecia stood up, "I must go now, and so must you soon. I have work to do. It was my pleasure to break bread with both of you again."

"It has also been our pleasure," said Sonny.

"Yes, it has," added Samantha.

"Oh, Sonny, you must get Samantha to tell you about her boxing prowess tonight." With that, the smiling Bohemian barmaid disappeared into the kitchen.

"What did she mean by that, Sam?"

"When you first walked in this evening did you happen to pass a blonde with a shiner going the other way?"

"As a matter-of-fact I did."

"Well, she's been stalking me lately, so I set a trap and ambushed her in front of the pub. I gave her that black eye."

"Who, you?" said Sonny with a grin.

"Yeah me, I knocked her out cold, I did."

"You've got to be kidding, Sam."

"No I'm not, and you thought I was just a panty-waste all these years."

Sonny sat there looking stunned.

"Quit staring at me with that silly grin. I am capable of defending myself, you know."

"So those years of kick-boxing lessons must have paid off, eh?"

"No, I just clipped her one right under the eye, knocked her right on her ass," boasted Samantha. "Come to find out, she had some important information on the Waverly nursing home scandal."

"Whoa, wait a minute, time out here. I thought you finished that article weeks ago. Remember, you had that tussle with your dad over it?"

"Yeah, but something really big has come up that I think important, and she has some valuable information to give to me on it."

"I don't think that's such a good idea, Sam. You don't want to piss off the ol' man."

"Sonny, she's got information that will blow the lid off that story!"

"If you ask me you should just let it be, Sam."

"I didn't ask you."

"No, you didn't. I'm just giving you some sound advice 'cause I know how Big John is."

"Screw you and your advice," she said with a glare.

"Okay, Okay, screw my advice. I can deal with that."

"Let's get up and go. I want to make love while I'm still in the mood. Does that seem like sound advice?" she mocked.

"Oh, yes. I enjoy frolicking with the opposite sex now and then . . . I mean with you of course."

"That's more like it," she said with a half smile. "You take the wine glasses and Merlot, and I'll gather what's left of the bread and cheese. I get mighty hungry after having sex, you know."

"Won't Lucrecia mind us taking her wine glasses?"

"Lucrecia!" shouted Samantha.

"What is it, my dear," she shouted back from the kitchen.

"Sonny and I are going to take two of your wine goblets with us tonight. I'll bring them back tomorrow. Is that okay with you?"

"Sure, Samantha, you two lovers just go make love under the moon tonight," she replied.

"Gee, Sam, what did you tell her about us?" asked Sonny as they walked toward the door.

"Nothing."

"Yeah, right," he said, shaking his head.

Sonny opened the door for his sassy redhead. As she exited she looked at him, and with an impish grin said, "On the way to your office I'll tell you how I drove a hundred miles-an-hour on the expressway, and how I blew seven stop lights getting here tonight." She then rushed out, and Sonny quickly followed. As the front door came to a close, some of the few patrons that were left could hear their faint voices as Sonny asked, "Hey Sam, you did pay the car insurance for this month, didn't you?"

"Yeah, sure, why?" she replied.

"No reason."

And the sitar man played on.

The old building had never before heard this much ruckus, what with all the bantering and carrying-on by the two lovers as they made their way to the top floor. The top floor was occupied by Sonny's office, and tonight would become Samantha's pleasure palace.

The closing of the windowed door reverberated throughout the antiquated structure as Samantha crushed Sonny's body against it while feverishly tongue-kissing him. Without uncoupling, they worked their way through Myra's office, and on into Sonny's, where they finally nestled in his black leather sofa. Samantha still hung around his neck, smothering him with hot, wet kisses while his arms were around her waist, clutching two wine glasses in one hand and a bottle of Bordeaux Merlot in the other.

"Hey, darlin', let me get up and pour ourselves some drinks," suggested Sonny.

"Okay," she said releasing him, "You know that red wine is my sex drink of choice, don't you?"

"Yes, darlin' and it does you good," he replied.

Samantha slithered out of her "Bill Blass" business suit while Sonny poured the drinks. He handed Samantha her drink and then sat next to her.

"I want to make a toast, Sam."

"Okay baby. What will we toast to?"

"I want to make a toast to you."

"Well, I'm flattered, but what for?"

"For being so damn beautiful; but mostly, for always being there for me when I needed you."

"I don't think I deserve accolades for that," she said coyly.

"Oh yes you do. If it wasn't for you I'd probably be dead by now. You helped me recover from Centralia, and you have stood by me after this last incident. I couldn't ask for a better wife, or a better friend than that, Sam."

Suddenly, guilt flooded her mind. They then touched glasses. Sonny took a sip of his wine. Samantha chugged hers straight down.

"Whoa there lady, there's more where that came from," said Sonny with a smile.

"Get me another, please!" she said. Samantha ached inside. She so wanted to expose the truth of her infidelity, and she wanted to expose her soul, but she just couldn't. Sonny was too fragile. He must never know, or that would be the end of their marriage, the end of Camelot. He turns me on so, she thought. Why must I be so haunted by my past sins? It seems so long ago, but it keeps raring its ugly head.

Sonny returned with her Merlot, and then opened the blinds and reached for the light switch.

"No! Don't turn out the lights! I want you to see me, all of me, tonight. Come here, lover, and kiss me," she said. They came together in a wild embrace. "Your kisses, they set me on fire," said Samantha while catching her breath.

"I can't help it, darlin'. Your lips, they're so soft and full. They taste of wine . . . red wine."

They kissed again, and in the heat of passion, Samantha slid off the leather and stationed herself in front of the old oak desk. The tall naked redhead then turned around, and with a "Lolita" pout asked, "Do you have the Bolero?"

"Yes I do darlin'. I'll play it for us," he said.

"Set it up to replay, will you, honey? I want this to last awhile."

The doleful sound of a single flute started the sleepy rhythm of Ravel's Bolero. Sonny slipped his sinewy body behind Samantha's, and together they formed slow, rhythmic movements between them as his skin meshed with hers. For several moments they danced as if in a trance, matching movement to movement to a crescendo. Their hypnosis continued as the orchestra grew stronger along the way.

Samantha lowered her soft breasts against the cool hardness of the desk top and made herself open for her lover's gift. Sonny filled her openness. Oblivious to everything around her, Samantha felt his pulse, in one rhythm with hers, and to the hypnotic rhythm of Bolero. Soon, the whole orchestra came together and culminated into a thunderous climax, causing passions to burst in the two lovers. The song then played again and again, as did the lovers, until exhaustion overcame them.

Angie didn't recognize the sound of the phone ringing even though the nightstand was next to her side of the bed. She had worked double duty, splitting her time between Body Perfect and the Metro Police Department. When finally arriving home, to Eva's dismay, she had flopped into bed and fell into a deep slumber.

Eva reached over her lover and picked up the receiver. "Hello,"

"Let me speak to Angie. Please hurry!" said the voice.

"Hold on, I'll wake her, said the Swede. Angie, Angie, wake up," said Eva, shaking her briskly.

"What's wrong?" said Angie.

"I believe your sister is on the phone and she sounds desperate."

Angie grabbed the phone. "Hello, Candy? What's wrong, baby?"

"Angie, I'm scared. I'm really scared," cried Candy, her voice trembling. "They're going to kill me!"

"Who, Candy, who's gonna kill you?"

"I don't know. The mob I guess. The word is out that I'm the one who made the phone call that night of the big fight. They're still pissed off about the bar fight that Sonny was in. Angie, these people really scare me. I've been gettin' phone calls, and I answer them but nobody's on the line! I think I'm being followed, Angie. I feel like they've got me in a cage. I feel like I'm going crazy! Please, ju've got to help me!"

"Candy, shut up and listen to me! I'm coming down to get you. Are you still living with your friend, Tracy?"

"No. Tracy kicked me out because of all those strange phone calls."

"Candy, tell me where you live. What's your address?"

"I live at . . . wait a minute Angie. There's someone at the door."

"Candy, don't go to the door! Candy . . ."

"Angie, are you still there?"

"Yes, of course."

"Never mind me, Angie. It's just Tommy, my friend. I feel safe with him here. I'll be alright, sister. I'm sorry to have wakened *ju.*"

"No, listen, Candy, I don't mind. Please tell me where you live!" pleaded Angie. Angie listened intently to the voice in the background. She couldn't make out the prattle, but did hear Candy talking to the male voice.

"Listen, Angie, I've got to go. I'm alright, really I am."

"But Candy, tell me where you" —– **Click!** Angie slammed the receiver down. "Goddamn it! That little bitch!"

"What's wrong, Angie? Is Candy in trouble?" asked Eva.

"Yeah, she's in trouble, big time I'm afraid. I'm going down there and bring her back home with me."

"Good. I'll go with you," said Eva.

"No, I'm going to call Sonny up."

"Sonny, who is this Sonny that you talk of?" asked the Swede.

"He's Sonny Rafferty, an ex-cop that broke me in many years ago at Metro. He's helped me out a lot over the years. His wife was that tall redhead at the club last night. Remember?"

"How could I not? I do not think I like her."

"Well, I don't either, but Sonny's all right."

"Men are no good for you, my dear. I'm better than him. You know that," said the Swede.

"Don't get all in a huff. I need you at the gym while I'm gone. I need you to run the place. Besides, Sonny is somehow involved with Candy in all of this. So do me a favor and make me some coffee while I get dressed. I'll need it."

"I will, but I don't like this at all. Not one bit!"

"I'll make it up to you, Eva. I promise," said Angie while dialing up a number.

"Yeah, what is it?" answered the groggy voice on the other end.

"Sonny, I need your help."

Chapter Fifteen

Taking Candy from a Baby

It was a quaint, but rundown little clapboard sided house that sat betwixt and between the Ohio River and the town of Newport. It seemed the perfect place for Candy's sanctuary. The house was all but hidden by the overgrown arborvitaes. How could anyone find her there?

"Boy, am I glad that *ju* came along, Tommy. To tell *ju* the truth, I was getting pretty scared."

"Who was that on the phone?" he asked curiously.

"Oh, that was my sister. I called her up because I feel like people are watching me, following me or something."

"Is she coming to see you?"

"I don't think so. I told her that everything is fine now, with *ju* being here and all. Tommy, how did *ju* find this place tonight?"

"Pergosi gave me the day off and sent me looking for you."

"What for?" asked Candy nervously.

"He wants to know where you've been the last few days. He said that you left a suite empty, and that he isn't making any money from it while you're gone."

"Does he want me to come back, really?"

"Of course, my little Spanish devil, he needs you."

"Well, I heard that he was pissed about that big fight of a month ago."

"He was pissed, but I think that he might be over it by now."

"I heard that he was looking for the person that called the cops, and he was going to rub 'em out."

"Candy, you've been watching too much television or something. Why would he want to lose you? I mean, you bring in a lot of money for the Bone Yard."

"Oh man, I feel so relieved, Tommy. I was so sure that he wanted to kill me. That's why I'm hiding out here. By the way, how did *ju* find me here? I don't remember telling *ju* about my moving."

"I'll tell ya, baby, it was hard, but I kept asking around until I got the right answers."

"*Ju* must have met my best friend, Tracy then, right?"

"Yeah, right, she was very helpful. She's a nice girl that Tracy is."

"Actually, she's one of the reasons that I moved, really. She was scared from all of the phone calls and hang-ups that we were getting."

"Did you ever think that maybe she's the one that's in some kind of trouble?"

"No, not Tracy, she's a good girl. She just dances. She never fools with the men that she entertains. Tracy is just trying to earn enough money to get her through college."

"So, this is your hideout, and no one knows where you live, eh?"

"That's right, just *ju* and me, Tommy, and of course, Tracy."

"Tell me, Candy, are you the person that called the cops that night? This is just between me and you, honey."

"*Jes*, it was me, Tommy. They were ganging up on Sonny."

"You know this Sonny character?"

"Oh *jes*. He was a cop that helped my sister a long time ago. My sister was stupid when she was younger and became a street whore, and not a good one. The men kept abusing her. She was just too shy to say no. They almost killed her. Sonny took a liking to her though. He busted the pimp and his bunch and put my sister in rehab. She had become a hopeless heroine addict, but he saved her. So, *ju* see, I just couldn't let anything bad happen to him."

"So, why didn't he save you from all of this?" asked Tommy.

"Save me? I like what I'm doing, Tommy. I like men. Besides, my body is better equipped to take in men. Better than my sister's. And thanks to *ju*, I can go back to the Bone Yard and work it. Do *ju* wish to stay with me tonight, Tommy?"

"What do you think, honey?"

"Well, *ju* can sleep with me, but I'm on my period and bleeding quite heavy, so I'll use my mouth to your satisfaction. I'll make *ju* come quick."

"No. Remember what I told you before. I don't mess with the hired help."

"But *ju* are my friend, Tommy. Besides, we are not at the Bone Yard."

"You are a beautiful, sexy girl, honey, but coming here for sex was not my intention. Before I lay with a woman I want to wine and dine her, treat her like a proper lady. Know what I mean?"

"But, Tommy, *ju've* given me such relief tonight. What *can* I do for *ju*? I would give *ju* a drink, but I don't have any liquor in the house."

"I didn't come here for a drink either, my dear. I come to you as your good friend, and perhaps, someday, who knows?" said Tommy while shrugging his shoulders. "But I'll tell ya, for some reason or other, late at night I sometimes get a craving for fried potatoes."

"No problem, Tommy. I have five pounds of russets in the bottom of the fridge. I'll gladly cut 'em up and fry them for *ju*," said Candy cheerily.

"You must eat some with me," Tommy insisted.

"I don't know about that, Tommy. I must watch my weight. When *ju* have a job like mine *ju* have to watch your weight, carefully."

"Oh, don't you worry about your weight, Candy. One night of good eating won't hurt you. Besides, I don't like to eat alone."

"Okay, Tommy, I'll do it just for *ju*," she smiled. "But don't be surprised if my ass gets big and fat because that's where I put it on when I gain weight."

Tommy laughed, "I always did like the swing on your back porch."

"That's right, honey. Swing it or don't bring it. Shake it and don't break it," said Candy, swiveling her hips back and forth.

Tommy snickered at the young Hispanic whore as she sliced the potatoes.

"Why do *ju* sit at the kitchen table and laugh at me for?" asked Candy.

"Oh, I was just amused by you, my dear. Here you are, one of the top fillies in Pergosi's stable, slicing and frying me up some potatoes at 2:00 o'clock in the morning, wearing pajamas saying, 'I'm a little angel' on 'em."

"I am an angel," pouted Candy, "I just don't have my wings yet."

"Do you think that you'll ever get any?"

"Hey, I'd settle for paper wings. At least that way I would look like I could fly," she joked. "*Ju* should see my winter pajamas. They are made of flannel and have little, pink booties that go with them. I can't stand the cold, Tommy. Can *ju*?"

Tommy didn't answer, but looked distant as Candy deposited the potatoes into the hot grease. "Why didn't you tell Pergosi that you were the one that called the cops?" queried Tommy.

Candy wasn't paying much attention to what Tommy Mack was saying now, for she was concentrating too much on making his potato feast. Who knows, if he likes my potatoes the two of us might just become an item, she mused. Hell, he liked me well enough not to want to bang me right away, plus I really like him. This might just work, she thought, blissfully. Through her little stint of daydreaming, the kitchen knife slipped off the potato and sliced a deep gash into Candy's left forefinger. "Ouch! Damn it! I cut myself," she cried.

"Let me look at it," replied the estranged voice.

It was a hot August night that watched the black super-charged Ford streak down the tranquil streets of the big city and propel itself onto the long stretch of Interstate 74, destination: Cincinnati.

As soon as Sonny received Angie's call he knew that there was big trouble at hand. They had no time to lose. They both said goodbye to their partners that loved them, and headed out hoping to find and rescue Angie's little sister, wherever she was. Sonny drilled Angie for all the information on Candy that she could garner, which was very little. But they had worked together many times in the past when she was a rookie and assigned to partner with her tough mentor. They felt comfortable with each other. With very little to go on, they decided that when they arrived in Cincinnati their first visit would be to the Top Hat, the last known place of employment for Candy.

"So, how about you, Angie, how's your business doing?"

"Just fine," she said.

"And how's your love life?"

"How's yours?"

"Mine's just fine. I want to know about yours."

"What do you mean?"

"I mean, you know, do you have a significant other?"

"Do you mean a boyfriend?"

"Yeah, or a husband," said Sonny.

"I don't like men. They are dogs."

"So, what do you mean? You prefer women?"

"Yes."

"Come on, Angie, I've known you since you were 16. You're not like that."

"Women treat me nice. They don't hurt me."

"Listen, Angie, all men are not like the ones that you grew up with. I assure you of that. There are some nice young men in this world that you can trust."

"You don't get it, do you, Sonny?"

"What's there to get? I know that you're not a lesbian. If you were that would be fine, I wouldn't care, but I know that you're not. I just think that you ought to stretch your boundaries a little more and get some male friends. That's all I'm saying. I just don't understand why you have such a hatred for men all these years. You're such a pretty girl, Angie."

"I'll tell you why. You haven't had rectal reconstructive surgery!" stressed Angie, staring away.

. . . "No, I haven't," said Sonny quietly. "I'm sorry Angie. I didn't know. It's just that seeing you grow up from a young girl into a woman, and the way that you've made something of yourself, has made you very special to me. I apologize for being so nosey. I just wish the best for you, always. I mean that," he said, staring at the road ahead.

The sadness in Sonny's retreat stunned Angie. She wasn't used to being coddled, not by a man, anyway. She thought how strange it was, Sonny Rafferty apologizing to her. She was once a broken young teenager, forsaken by all others, when this cop with the giant heart swooped down like an angel from heaven and snatched her from the depths of despair. Angie felt ashamed of herself, talking to Sonny the way that she did. It was true though, she hated men, feared them, all but Sonny. She loved him, real love. Not the kind that goes away after a few years. It's funny, she thought, how you can discard love, but it keeps coming back. That's the way Sonny was to her. It was an unrequited love. She knew it, but it was real to her. Angie knew the chances of getting Sonny were next to nil. Hell, he had been married to that redheaded witch for centuries, it seemed like. It didn't matter though. Angie knew that life was a series of moments, and that happiness was moments of joy. She just wanted her moment.

Angie cut her eyes toward Sonny. She searched for his non-flinching, cobalt-blue eyes. She was determined to remove that stern look from his face. She had long since put sadness behind her. This was her chance for at least a moment of joy, and she wasn't about to miss it. Angie broke the silence with, "Sonny."

"What."

"You look unhappy. I love you Sonny Rafferty. Marry me."

"What?" he said in mild surprise.

"I don't like men, Sonny, except for you. You know that to be true now. So marry me Sonny, and I will make you happy. I promise," she said, partly in jest but mostly in truth.

"What do I do with the wife that I now have?"

"That redheaded witch, she's no good for you, Sonny. Get rid of her."

"I don't think so. Besides, I'm too old for you. I've got hair growing in my ears for Crissakes!"

"You swear too much. That shows that you are not happily married."

"It's hard work, keeping a woman happy in a marriage. It's stressful," he replied.

"Not if she's a good woman."

"Oh, Samantha's a good wife. She would never mess around or anything like that, though she can be stressful at times because she listens to her father far too much instead of me."

Angie quit listening. She slid up next to Sonny and started playfully tonguing his ear.

"Don't do that! Come on, get your tongue out of my ear," he said, pushing her away. "Can't you see I'm driving? You'll cause a wreck. Now stay put!"

Stay put, she did, for awhile. She gave Sonny just enough time to gain back his road concentration. Then, with a sly smile she slithered her hand up to Sonny's shoulder; then further, and started fingering Sonny's ear. "Fuzzy ear, fuzzy ear," she teased.

"Damn it, quit messin' with my ear!"

"Fuzzy ear, fuzzy ear, fuzzy ear," she jested.

"Get your finger out of my ear!" stressed Sonny, shoving her aside with his strong right arm.

"Sonny," she said with a pout.

"What."

"I'm tired. Can I snuggle up to you and go to sleep?"

"Yeah, but don't stick your tongue in my ear again," he said gruffly. "It gives me the cold chills, goddamn it!"

"Okay, goddamn it," she said softly with a smile.

As their bantering ceased, worry and fear crept into their hearts. Sonny pondered their journey while Angie clung tightly to his arm, whispering a silent prayer for her little sister.

Tommy grabbed Candy's finger and quickly stuck it under the cold tap water of the sink. "Yeah, you cut yourself good, girl. Why are you so stupid?" he said in a strange tone of voice.

Candy looked up to him with nervous eyes. She sensed eeriness in her Bone Yard buddy.

"You know, Candy, maybe you're not as smart as I thought you were. We had it going, you and I. Why'd you mess it up?" cried Tommy.

Candy looked at him hurtfully, as tears began to form in the big brown eyes of the Puerto Rican beauty. "But *ju* told me that everything was okay with Pergosi, remember? *Ju* told me that. *Ju* did!"

Tommy pushed her away in disgust. "Go turn the potatoes before you burn them," he ordered.

"But, my finger," she said.

"Shut up about your finger, and go fry the potatoes, I said!"

Candy adhered to Tommy's commands and stationed herself behind the big skillet on the gas-fired stove. She lifted the lid as splattering hot grease escaped in all directions. She took a spatula and began turning over the layers of sliced potatoes. All the while blood dripped from her injured finger into a hand towel that she had wrapped it in.

Tommy sat directly behind her at the kitchen table with his back against the wall, glowering at her. He was in a quandary. He had lied to Pergosi about Candy being there, out of the Lair, watching the fight, and about seeing her at the phone, calling the police. He lied for her because he liked Candy. She wasn't crude or brash like the other girls.

She was unpretentious and always smiling, having fun. She gave what she had and asked for little in return. Tommy had the doors to his heart closed to her. That's the way he had always played it with the working girls, but somehow she found a way to enter his heart against his will. He became disjointed by the dilemma that he was thrown in, choosing between the loyalty to his employer of many years, and his unfulfilled love of a young Spanish harlot. He himself would surely be cast to the lions if he did not take on the task at hand. Tommy didn't realize the severity of his agony. Even he did not recognize the Jeckyl and Hyde that he was becoming on this night. His shame turned to fear, and fear turned to hate. He needed somebody, anybody, to blame for this transformation. Rage clouded his mind. "You're right, Candy. You do have a big ass. That's what your johns come to you for, because you're so goddamn free with it."

Candy was too frightened to turn around, for his voice was now of some stranger, a voice that sounded so sinister and vile that she didn't want to listen to, but had to. She continued to repetitiously turn and salt the frying potatoes, not feeling the searing sting of the hot oil against her skin or the throbbing pain in her left hand. Candy wept quietly as she feared that there was no way out of this bad dream.

"You know, we were a good mix, you and I. Sooner or later we would've ended up together, Candy, but you had to mess things up. You had to save your sister's friend. He meant nothing to you. You knew Pergosi's rules. You caused your own demise, all for some stupid, mixed-up stranger. Aren't those potatoes done yet?" snapped Tommy.

"Oh, *jes*," she answered while trying to stifle her tears. "Here they are, Tommy. I make them special, just for *ju*," she said, scooping them onto his plate.

"Boo-hoo, boo-hoo, it's too late to cry now little girl. Sit down and sup with me."

As Tommy ate, Candy sat there in despair, with her head down, chin in hand, and nervously whimpering as big tears rolled down her cheeks. "What's wrong? Aren't you hungry?"

"No."

"Why not, is your hand still hurting you? Let me see it."

Without looking at him, she raised her toweled hand for Tommy to see. Tommy slowly unwrapped it. "Geez, Candy, I believe you'll need stitches. You'll be lucky if you don't lose that finger."

"I don't care about my finger, Tommy. I just want to tell *ju* that I'm sorry if I have caused trouble between *ju* and Pergosi."

"It's a little late for apologies, don't you think? Do you know why Pergosi didn't go after you right away? Well, do ya?"

"No."

"I'll tell you why, because I was lying for you. Yeah, I lied all this time because I didn't want to see you get into any trouble. But, you know what? It didn't work. He found out someway that it was you. I don't know how, maybe from one of the other girls. It doesn't matter now."

"But, Tommy, I've only been working at the Bone Yard for little over a year now. I didn't know how strict Miles was with his rules."

"That's right. You're just a yearling aren't you? Hey, I'm thirsty," he said abruptly. "I'm going to help myself to a glass of water if you don't mind. Do you want some water, Candy?"

"No, I don't want no water." She heard him go to the sink and fill a glass with water. When he came back she looked up at him. He had his glass in one hand and a couple of knives in the other. Candy sat upright, stiff from shock.

"Wh-what are *ju* going to do with those?" she stammered.

"I'm going to give you a much needed lesson," he said with a wicked grin. "Do you see this small knife that I hold here?"

"*Jes,*" she said nervously.

"Well, this knife is called a paring knife. It has a short blade for peeling things like apples, pears, and potatoes. If you would've used this knife while peeling your potatoes you would not have cut your damn finger halfway off. Now, this other knife is the one that you used." He held the long blade in front of Candy's face. "This piece of cutlery is made for cutting meat, like chicken, steaks, or whatnot. See the row of notches in the stainless steel blade?"

Frozen with fright, Candy barely shook her head.

"That's for sawing through chicken bones and such. Let me show you an example."

Candy was suddenly startled as the blade sliced through her face from her right ear to the hinge of her mouth. She didn't feel the pain of the knife, for she was in an analgesic state caused by the terrifying transformation of her friend. Stunned by his actions, Candy stood up and backed into the stove. Tommy slashed again, this time her other cheek, the same cut. Red blood oozed from her cuts and her mouth as she stood there in disbelief. He made another sweeping stroke with the knife, this time cutting deep into her forehead near her hairline. The thin, white cut soon changed to bright red, as blood appeared and dripped down into her eyes. Before he could swing the shiv again she fell toward him on her knees, pulling frantically at the zipper of his slacks. "Tommy, let me love *ju!* Please let me love *ju!*" she begged with blood spewing from her mouth.

In his own disbelief, Tommy backed away while shoving her aside. "I told you that I didn't come here for sex, and I didn't even come here to eat your fuckin' potatoes! Pergosi sent me here to kill ya! Yea, to kill ya! You leave me no other choice, Candy."

"But *ju* don't have to do this, Tommy. *Ju* already hurt me. I'm really sorry about the way things are. Hurt me some more if *ju* want, but don't kill me. *Please!* Just tell Mr. Pergosi that I'm dead, *okay?*"

Tommy gave her a scowling look, "**We had it going, you and I, but you messed it up!**"

"Please, Tommy, don't hate me, Make love to me." She grabbed for his fly again, but was greeted by the blade slashing through the middle of her face. Candy grabbed at her lacerated eye as blood spurted through her fingers. She squinted through her good eye, trying to catch a glimpse of Tommy's whereabouts. "Tommy, *ju* cut my eye. I can't see *ju* Tommy. Please don't cut me anymore. I have to look right for Mr. Pergosi. I have to make some money for him, *ju* know. He wants me back. *Ju* told me so. I heard *ju* say it. I did I did!"

Candy stumbled into the living room, but was closely followed by the crazed barkeeper. Using his fist, he cracked her hard near her spine, then again to her kidneys, the blunt trauma taking away her breath for a moment and temporarily paralyzing her from the waist down. "Look what *ju* made me do," she spluttered, "I peed my pants." She struggled to crawl away, but was grabbed by the red, matted hair of her head. In the throes of death Candy made one final plea with her assailant, "Please let me go, Tommy. I must go to the bathroom. I must make myself nice for *ju*. I've got to get ready for the Bone Yard tonight. I'll make myself pretty for *ju*. I promise," she gurgled.

Tommy yanked her head back, stretching her throat taut while mashing her vertebrae into un-forgiveness. He then pulled the seriated blade of the butcher's cutlery across her throat, her soft, defenseless throat. The little angel on the front of her cotton shirt soon turned red . . . blood red.

It is said that the devil was once God's most beautiful angel. Old wives tales have him pared down to just a wolf in sheep's clothing. Maybe hell is not the hot works that the clergy speak about, but instead, is the excruciating mind pain from the expectations of the dealing of the cards. For if life runs its course with the same odds as Vegas, Dante's inferno will claim more than its share of lost souls.

An old metaphor states that blood is thicker than water. For Candy Garza, that yet remains to be seen. But one thing's for sure. The blood runs warm in the valley along the Ohio tonight. Hell has its yearling.

Chapter Sixteen

The Face of an Angel

She forlornly lays amongst the hills, snuggled up next to the river Ohio, this city called Cincinnati. Considered to be Cleveland's red-haired stepsister, Cincinnati had taken some abuse over the years. There was the big brouhaha over the Robert Maplethorpe Exhibit, Pete Rose's fall from grace in the sports world, and an ex-mayor becoming the host of daytime television's biggest sleaze show. In reality, this city was not much different than most big cities. She just caught a bad rap, that's all.

None of that mattered to Sonny as he sped down the long slope of I-74 into the heart of the city. His interest now was with the sister of his partner whose head rested against his shoulder. She was sleeping soundly, for she trusted Sonny, and Sonny loved her for that.

When they arrived at the Top Hat the door opened as the last shift of dancers were making their way out of the club. As Sonny and Angie entered the building they encountered one of the club's bouncers, a big bald guy. More round than big.

"We're closed," he scowled.

"Yeah, I know. We're not here to have a good time. We're here to gain some information on an employee of yours," said Sonny.

"We don't give out information, mister."

"Just let us talk to your manager," insisted Sonny.

"Maybe you didn't hear me right, bub. We don't give out information here, comprende?"

Sonny pulled out his I.D., as did Angie. "Look, baldy, I'm a private investigator. My name is Sonny Rafferty, and this is Officer Garza of the Indianapolis Metro Police Department. We believe that you all might have some information that is pertinent to us. So just let us talk to your boss. Then, we'll be on our way."

"I don't care who you are, asshole. You're not gettin' in here!"

Losing his patience, Sonny grabbed the bald man and slammed him against the wall and pressed his arm tightly against the man's neck.

"May I be of some help?" came the announcement from the inner smoke-filled room.

He appeared to be a slim man, with thin hair and wearing dark glasses while drawing deep on a cigarette. "I'm Jackie Schurch, the proprietor of this establishment. I see that you have met my doorman. You can let Curly go now. I assure you that his bark is much worse than his bite."

The bald man gasped for air as Sonny released his hold.

"I happened to overhear your conversation while in the other room. So you are looking for one of our girls, I take it.?"

"Yes, Candy Garza, we believe that she may be in grave danger. But we're having trouble locating her," said Angie. "We do know that she used to work at the Top Hat a while back, and thought that maybe you might know of her whereabouts."

"Yes, Candy Garza worked here previously, but she left us two years ago. From what I hear, she became a female escort of sorts. Very independent she was. Haven't heard from her since."

"Well, all I know is that she shared an apartment with a girl named Tracy who works here at the Top Hat," said Angie.

"Sorry. There's no Tracy that works here, and if she did we couldn't tell you. Employee privacy laws, you know."

"Are you sure? Because this could be a life threatening situation," insisted Sonny.

"I assure you, there is no person working here with that name," said the man with the thin hair. "There are several other clubs around here that you might want to check with."

Sonny and Angie headed out to the parking lot to regroup their thoughts. "He may be right. Maybe we should try the other clubs," said Angie.

"That bastard's lying. I know he is!" seethed Sonny.

"Hey there," came a voice out of the darkness. Suddenly, a young woman's face appeared. Sonny recognized her as one of the departing workers from the Top Hat. "My name is Ella. I'm a bartender at the Top Hat. I couldn't help but overhear you guys asking about Tracy's whereabouts. Do you think that she might be in any trouble?"

"Yes, she could be," said Angie hastily. "Do you know where she lives?"

"Wait a minute now. We girls here at the bar don't just go around giving out each other's addresses for no good reason. I know Tracy personally. She only dances to make money for college. If her parents found out what she does she would never forgive me."

"Don't worry. What she does for a living doesn't concern us. We're worried for Candy's safety. I'm Candy's sister. Here's my proof," said Angie, while showing Ella her police I.D.

"Did you know Candy too?" asked Sonny.

"Oh yeah, I knew her real well. She was an excellent dancer, but Jackie forced her back into prostitution. He felt that Candy didn't bring in enough customers with her dancing, alone. Last time I saw Candy was about a year ago at Tracy's apartment. She had gone independent as a call-girl, and seemed quite happy with it. Tracy didn't work tonight. We get personal time off each month, and this is her week. She should be home tonight. Her full name is Tracy Robbins, and she lives at: 268 Connelly Street, just off Batavia Rd. It's close to the airport."

"Thanks a lot, Ella," said Angie.

"I hope Candy is okay. I really liked her."

As Sonny pulled his black sedan in front of the apartments where Tracy lived he noticed Angie stretching over the back of the seat reaching into the sports bag that she had brought with her. She pulled out a large hand-gun and checked the clip.

"Damn, Angie, what do you plan on shootin', an elephant?"

"I just might be," she said, nuzzling the barrel against her cheek.

"Hell, that 44 magnum is bigger than you are."

"I like big guns," she said, kissing the barrel.

"And all this time I thought you had pajamas in that bag."

"Hell no, Sonny, I figured if you and I were to stay over that I would sleep naked."

Sonny smiled at his sidekick.

215

"What kind of weapon are you packin', Sonny?"

"A flashlight," he answered.

"A flashlight, who are you trying to be, Andy of Mayberry?"

"I've never used a handgun since I left the force. My piece is at home, locked in a desk drawer. But I do have a night-stick in the trunk."

"Is that all the protection that you have?"

"Well, yeah, that and my wits."

"Oh, that really makes me feel safe," she said, reaching into the back seat again. This time she pulled out a 357 magnum. "Here, you can carry this, Sonny."

"What've you got, an arsenal back there?" he said somewhat amused.

"Well, yeah, Sonny, somebody's got to protect you."

"No thanks, darlin', we shouldn't run into much trouble here."

"Suit yourself. Better to be over-armed than under protected is what I say. You told me those very words when you trained me. Do you remember that?"

"Did I say that, really?" They shared a quick smile to ease the tension as they got out of the car and headed toward Tracy's house.

Sonny knocked on the door but received no answer. He tried again, still the same. He then turned the knob and the door fell open. The lights were out so Sonny entered cautiously with his flashlight held shoulder high, scouring the walls and the corners of the room. He knew that something was amiss because of the unlocked door. Angie followed close behind with her weapon drawn. Wherever the light shone, so was the barrel of her 44-magnum pointed. Suddenly, Sonny heard a moaning coming from a bedroom. When he reached the bedroom he flipped on the light switch. "We have a person down," he whispered loudly to Angie. "Check her out while I search the rest of the apartment."

When Sonny returned back to the room he found Angie on the floor cradling Tracy Robbins in her arms, trying to revive her.

"All is clear, Angie. What have we here?"

"This seems to be our girl. She's been struck hard in the face a couple of times. She winces every time I try to move her, so she might have some bruised or broken ribs." Angie probed cautiously along Tracy's pelvic area. "Her lower abdomen seems to be fine. She should be alright when she gains full consciousness."

"I'll find some cold water and a towel to help revive her. She's got to tell us where Candy is, and fast," said Sonny.

Sonny soon returned and quickly applied the cold compress to Tracy's forehead.

"Where am I? Who are you?" asked the dazed brunette.

"I'm Officer Garza, Candy's sister. Can you tell us what happened?"

"Oh, you must go to Candy as soon as possible. There's a crazy man that's looking for her. He asked me where she was. I said that I didn't know. He broke the chain lock on the door and started beating on me. I had to tell him where she lived or he was going to kill me. I'm sorry, but I had to tell him."

"That's alright. I understand," said Angie.

"Can you give us a description of him?" added Sonny.

"He had black wavy hair, forty, maybe forty-five, about five-ten, two-hundred maybe. Was strong, very strong, never got his name though."

"Tracy, can you give us Candy's address?" asked Sonny.

"She lives across the river at 301 West Lake St. in Newport. Am I going to be okay? My mouth is really hurtin', and when I try to move I can hardly breathe," she said weakly. "Did he knock any of my teeth out? I must know."

Angie reached her fingers inside Tracy's mouth, "No, your teeth are all still intact, but you do have a couple of loose ones. They should heal up in time. I think you might have a couple of cracked ribs though, Tracy. That's why you're having trouble breathing. My partner and I are going to lift you to your bed. It's gonna be painful, but you should be able to rest better that way. My partner's going to call 911 to get you some help. Is there anyone in this apartment complex that can look after you? We need to leave as soon as possible."

"Yes, in apartment #11, two doors down is a Ms. McKinney. She's an older woman. Probably is asleep. She'll look after me if you can wake her."

A cold chill filled the hot summer night as Sonny's retired police cruiser pulled up in front of the white clapboard-sided house.

"I'll take that 357 magnum now, Angie."

She quickly retrieved the firearm from the bag and handed it to Sonny. There was no friendly bantering going on now as the prospects of Candy's demise weighed heavily on their minds.

The house was hidden by a row of large arborvitaes. As they skulked up the walkway leading to the house, Sonny noticed dark footprints on the concrete coming from the house. It was too dark to tell what they were caused from, and Sonny didn't want to flash any light to tip off any possible suspects in the house, plus, the sickening feeling that he had in the pit of his stomach suggested to him not to expose the tracks for his partner's viewing.

Angie herself was no novice at this. The sight of those tracks didn't sit well with her either. Following close behind Sonny, she struggled to keep her imagination from running wild. She felt her throat closing and her pulse racing, and started sweating profusely. Angie thought the heat to be stifling for this late of night.

As they approached the front stoop Sonny noticed that all the lights in the house were turned off. He sensed that to be a portent of things to come, the same as it was at Tracy's place, or worse.

Sonny turned to Angie, "Listen to me carefully," he whispered. "You go around and cover the back door. I'm going in the front. Don't come in. Listen to me now. Don't come in until you hear from me. Do you understand?"

"I understand, Sonny. Don't come in until you call. I got it," she said nervously. "But Sonny, you don't think that—"

"I don't think anything, Angie. I'm just taking all precautions. Okay?"

"Okay, Sonny, but I don't like the feel of this. I sure don't."

Sonny clipped her lightly under the chin, "Keep your guard up, girl."

"Okay. I will, Sonny," she said with a forced smile.

Sonny slowly turned the knob on the solid wood door. It was locked. The door was equipped with standard hardware, so Sonny soon had it open as he jimmied the lock. With his flashlight held high in his left hand, and the 357 in his right, Sonny pushed open the door with his foot. He quickly entered the foyer and dropped to one knee, all-the-while carefully searching the room in hopes of finding nothing out of the ordinary. He felt strange, in an eerie way, like he shouldn't be there, almost as if he was imposing on some young girl's nakedness, her soul. The heat from the room was suffocating to the private-eye. He acquired a humming noise inside his head. He could hear little buzzings all around. He chillingly realized that there were flies everywhere. The air was filled with the stench of death. As he got up to walk, Sonny felt his trouser leg sticking to the floor. There was blood, dark blood, leading toward the living room and beyond. He followed the path to where the buzzing grew louder. There was blood everywhere, on the couch, puddled on the hardwood floor, and on the coffee table. The grim air of the Reaper was stifling. Then he saw her, an arm at first, then her leg; then the rest of her bloody body. That is, everything but . . . her head! Sonny gasped at the body. He reached down to touch the torso. She was still warm to the touch. She hasn't been dead long, he thought. He was aghast at the heinousness of the crime. He was having trouble with the ugliness of it all. He shook his head to clear it of the demons trying to enter. "What am I going to tell Angie?" he said to himself. "What the fuck am I going to tell Angie!" He recovered somewhat from the shock and quickly checked the other rooms, with the last one being the kitchen. It smelled heavy of grease, and blood. The rear of the kitchen faced the back yard. Sonny peeked through the window curtain to check on his faithful companion. She was pacing nervously back and forth holding that big 44 between both her hands. She seemed to be muttering something, probably praying, probably in Spanish. She caught sight of him looking out the window and threw her arms up. He could see her mouth "What's going on?" Sonny quickly closed the drapes, wishing that he hadn't looked at her. He turned away from the window, and there she was, sitting there, atop a plate of fried potatoes, just staring at him like a bloody Medusa. Across from Candy was an empty plate, probably where her killer last ate. As he stared at the strange table setting Angie started pounding on the back door.

"Sonny, let me in! Let me in! I know something's wrong, Sonny!"

"Go away, Angie. You can't come in!" cried Sonny.

"Let me in, goddamn it!"

"No, Angie. You can't come in!" Sonny yelled back, all-the-while-staring at Candy's head.

Soon everything became quiet. Angie stopped pounding on the

back door. Sonny snapped out of his trance. She's going to the front door!

"Get out of my way, Sonny!" demanded Angie. "I'm coming in!"

"No, Angie. You don't want to."

"I said get out of the way, Sonny!"

"Please, Angie. You don't want to see her like this," he begged.

"Move over you son-of-a-bitch. I'm going to see my little sister!" she ordered while pushing her way past the big guy. He tried to hold on to her but she broke away and turned on the lights.

"Oh God, Oh G-o-d!" she screamed. She ran to where her sister lay and fell in the blood with her 44-magnum sliding to the wall. Angie crawled to the arm sticking out from behind the couch. She raised the lifeless hand to her face, and let out a blood-curdling scream when she noticed the headless torso.

"Angie, Angie, you mustn't disturb the body," pleaded Sonny.

"What do you mean, Sonny?" she cried.

"You can't, the police, the evidence, we've got to find out who did this."

"Leave us alone Sonny! Just leave us the hell alone! I want her face—I need to see her face, Sonny!" she screamed in her delirium.

"You don't want—"

"Bring me her face!" she screamed.

Sonny brought the head from the kitchen and gave it to his crazed partner. What he was doing now was against all police regulations, but Sonny didn't care anymore. All he cared about now was helping Angie survive the hell that she was in; to pull her from the abyss.

Sonny left Angie with her sister and searched throughout the house for some clues. Any clue as to whom this maniac was that killed Candy Garza.

Sonny called the cops and stared out the bedroom window, and watched the sun rise to morning's early light. Angie kept to her own hellish world.

It is said that it's always darkest before the dawn. Candy Garza would never see dawn's early light again, nevermore.

Chapter Seventeen

The Devil's Lair

Samantha was sleeping well past her normal wake-up call. Then again, she wasn't at home either. She was sleeping the good sleep, dreaming the good dream. This always happened after a night of power lovemaking. Two nights in a row had her drained. It had been sometime since she and Sonny had been this in-tune with each other. She was quite a sight, lying on the big leather sofa with her face buried into the cushions, covered only by her suit coat pulled up around her shoulders. It was a humorous fit that left her white bottom hanging out over the edge of the couch.

Shauna was the first to see the sleeping beauty. She always ran into "Sonny's room", as she called it, when Myra would bring her to work with her. Sonny would always have some candy, a toy or whatnot waiting for her in his desk.

At the same time, Myra was plugging in the coffee pot in her own little office when she discovered a pair of Samantha's gold-trimmed briefs hanging on her computer monitor. She knew that the panties belonged to Samantha, for they had the signature name of her favorite clothier on them. Myra folded the scanty undergarment and smiled to herself as she speculated on what might have happened in the office that previous evening.

Shauna burst back into the room with a chocolate bar in her hand. "Gramma, Gramma!"

"Whatcha doin' with that chocolate bar so early in the morning,' girl? You know I don't allow that," said Myra.

While ignoring Myra's ranting, Shauna took another bite of her chocolate bar and nonchalantly announced, "Samantha's sleeping on the couch."

"What did you say, girl?"

"I s-a-i-d, Samantha's sleeping on the couch, Gramma. I was quiet. I didn't wake her up."

"Oh, lord, she must've overslept. Let's go wake her up, Shauna."

It didn't take Samantha long to realize the voice that was coaxing her to get up was not that of Sonny, but of the little pixie, Shauna. Samantha abruptly jumped up. Embarrassment flooded her face when she realized that she was standing there, butt naked, in front of Mama and Shauna. Shauna gawked, but Myra paid little attention to the redhead's lack of coverage.

"Aren't you supposed to be at work this mornin', dear?"

"Yes, Mama," answered Samantha, clutching her suit-coat to her chest. "What time is it?"

"It's 8:30, dear."

"Oh no, I'm running late! Sonny and I were out late last night so we decided to spend the night here instead of driving all the way home," she said while frantically searching the room for the rest of her clothes.

"You go freshen' yourself up, dear. I'll gather your things," said Myra, handing Samantha her folded panties and bra that she picked up along the way.

"Thanks a lot, Mama. I appreciate your help."

"Go on now."

Samantha headed toward the bathroom, then stopped abruptly and turned around. "Mama, have you seen Sonny this morning?"

"No, ma'am, I haven't. He wasn't here when we arrived. Maybe he left a note or somethin'." As Myra looked around she noticed a folded piece of paper on the otherwise barren desk. "This must be it," she said while picking up the note. "It has your name on it. That's not right of Sonny not to wake you when he ups and leaves like this," she explained.

"I do recall Sonny mumbling something early this morning, but I was too out of it to remember what he said. You know Sonny, he always has a case going on somewhere," said Samantha, rushing off to the bathroom.

Samantha looked in the mirror with a strong disapproval of her morning face. She opened the mirrored cabinet and took out Sonny's toothbrush. She squeezed a copious amount of paste onto it and commenced to brushing her teeth. At the same time, she sat on the stool, and with the gusto of a young mare, relieved herself from the spoils of last night's little soiree. Samantha then opened Sonny's note. It read, "Highpockets, gotta go, on a case, call ya later, Sonny. P.S. Great evening wasn't it?"

Samantha smiled warmly as Sonny touched her heart with so few words. Sonny's little notes seemed to have a calming effect on her, yet made her a bit nervous just the same.

Samantha took a couple of swipes, stood up, then spit and rinsed. She pulled on her briefs and then gently placed her tender breasts into their individual spandex casings. Oh, the price of ecstasy, she thought.

When Samantha exited the bathroom, she was met by Myra and her wee assistant with a cup of coffee and the rest of her clothes. She quickly dressed in her business attire and gulped down her coffee on the way out the door.

Samantha was anxious to meet with her staff to discuss her run-in with Loni Jacobs. To Samantha, it was always the rush, the story, whether hard at work or hard at play. Such was the life of a newsprint journalist.

For Sonny and Angie it had been a hectic morning all around, what with the gruesome death of Candy, and having to cope with the police. The precinct captain chastised Sonny for their disturbance of the crime scene. He then held them both at the station for several hours while running background checks. Sonny's contumacy didn't bode well with the police chief who didn't release them until midday. Angie's mind still wasn't right by then. Sonny checked the local hospitals, looking for Tracy's whereabouts. He found her location and picked her up after she was treated and released. Sonny then visited a local clothier and bought himself a new suit of clothes, for his was blood stained and he wasn't ready to go back to Indianapolis just yet. Angie clung to him, incessantly, but he understood. She was going through a tough grieving process. Not the normal kind of grieving that one goes through when they lose a loved one to an accident or disease, but the kind that leads a mind down different avenues, to different destinations, with vengeance as the point man. Sonny knew of it. He had been there many times himself. That's why he wasn't going back home yet.

They all finally ended up at Tracy's apartment. Sonny questioned Tracy about Candy, her work, her friends, phone calls, and so forth. She gave him nothing to work with. She said she knew nothing of Candy's affairs. They just lived together to split the rent. Sonny wasn't so sure, but that was her story. Eva, Angie's live-in partner, showed up, making things even more complicated for Sonny. She right away didn't like him. The feeling was mutual. Angie must have called her from the police station. He wished she hadn't. Tracy invited them all to spend the night. Eva and Angie decided to stay over until Candy's body was ready to be shipped back to Indy. Sonny politely refused Tracy's invitation, for it was too awkward a situation for him to be in. Besides, he had a different agenda, to find Candy's killer.

Sonny took Angie aside, "Look I'm going to go do some investigating."

"Good, I'll go with," said Angie.

"No, you stay here with your friends. You have to get Candy home and buried."

"Do you have anything to go on, Sonny?"

"Not yet, but I'm going back to the police station and see if they have a match on those fingerprints yet. After that I'll just play it by ear."

"Please stay here with me, Sonny. I need you," she begged.

"No, I can't. Besides, you've got somebody to be with now."

"Who, Eva? I don't want Eva. I want you, Sonny. I hurt so bad inside. I can't describe it."

"I know, honey. Come walk with me to the car."

Angie clung to Sonny's arm as they walked to his car. "I'm going to kill him, you know that, Sonny."

"Don't be talking that way, Angie. Let me take care of things."

"No, I'm going to kill him," she said coldly.

"Listen, that's foolish talk. You want to kill this man for vengeance. I understand. If you did that, it would tear you up inside. It would haunt you, Angie, for the rest of your life. Let me take care of this Tommy character. I'll see that justice is done. I've never let you down yet, baby. You go and make sure that your sister gets a proper burial."

"Sonny, would you just hold me one time before you leave?"

"Sure, baby." As they embraced, her lips found his. For the first time, they kissed. Angie's lips felt delicate to Sonny. So delicate, and so sad, the same as the tears rolling down her cheeks.

"Sonny, do you remember when you found me in that back alley, dying?"

"Of course I do."

"Do you remember what you told me when I came out of that hospital?"

"Well, yeah, I think."

"You told me that I was a free-bird. When I came out of drug rehab, you were there, and you told me the same. Remember? You called me free-bird for the longest. I felt as though I was reborn, Sonny. I don't feel that way anymore. I want to be that free-bird again."

Sonny kissed Angie goodbye, and with a heavy heart, watched the broken police officer walk out of his world and into another's.

The jealous eyes of Eva Swenson glared down at the black Crown Vic until it was out of sight.

"Rafferty, what gives you the audacity to show your face in this police station again?" grumbled Floyd Knobbs, the ill-tempered police chief.

"I came back to find out if you've obtained an I.D. on the Candy Garza murderer."

"As a matter of fact we have, but why should I tell you?"

"Well, because I'm the private investigator working on the Garza case, and I have a special interest in it since her sister, Angie, was under my tutelage when she broke in as a cop."

"Hell, I already know about all that, Rafferty. We checked both you and Angie Garza out with a fine-tooth comb. She checks out alright, but you, you're a "loose cannon", Rafferty. They said that you were once a good cop, or had the capacity to be, but that you would often extend your boundaries too far, and that you flaunted authority. Let's face it, Rafferty; you were just a rogue cop that got his tit caught in the ringer in that Centralia gig six years ago. Yeah, that's right. We know all about that too. Hell, I remember it well. It was big news at that time. You broke a child porno ring, received your accolades, and then retired. You became a private dick and ain't been worth a shit since. The way that you botched up my crime scene this morning proves that."

"Maybe, but there were extenuating circumstances there, Floyd. Candy was Angie's sister for chrissakes."

"Look, Angie Garza has been a cop for eleven years, and if you were her mentor like you say you were then you both should have protected the scene of the crime, even though the victim was related to one of you."

"You have no heart, Chief."

"Oh, I have a heart, but I also have a sense of duty. That may be something that you seem a little short on, my good man."

"Are you going to tell me who the suspect is or not?" said Sonny.

"I'll tell you, Rafferty. I'll tell you what you want to know, but you'll have to promise to leave Cincinnati and stay gone. We don't need your kind here."

"Why, Chief, I was just on my way out of Cincy when I decided to stop and say goodbye to my good friend, Floyd."

"I'm not your friend, so don't call me Floyd."

"Okay, Chief."

"We found the murder weapon under the couch in the living room. He used a carving knife on her. That's about the only untainted evidence that we found in the whole house. We did get some decent prints on a fork and a water glass. Apparently he and Ms. Adams, Garza, whatever her name, were sitting down to a late night supper of fried potatoes at the time of the incident. She must've really pissed him off about something. From the amount of blood all over everything, it took her a long time to die. The way that she was sliced up, we figure that he tortured her for awhile before decapitating her. The culprit's name is Tom Slattery, alias Tommy Slatts, and known in his circle of friends as "Mack the knife."

"And his circle of friends being?" said Sonny.

"The Irish mob of Chicago's Southside. I guess he started out innocently enough. Tom Slattery went to culinary school and became quite the chef. He opened a restaurant on Halsted Street, and that's where he became affiliated with the mob. His restaurant went belly-up. At least that's what the records say. Then, Slattery went to work for the mob under the guise of a bartender mostly, working at several clubs all over the country for the last 20 years. He got hooked up with Miles

Pergosi, a long time gangster from the Windy City. Miles is big in the numbers racket. He sets up clandestine gambling joints around the Midwest. I guess the F.B.I. has been on his tail but they haven't caught up with him yet. Nobody knows the whereabouts of either one of these guys. The last place that we traced Slattery was down in New Orleans back in '99. There, I've told you what we've got. Now you tell me what you know."

"I don't know anything, Chief. Remember, I'm not worth a shit anymore," scoffed Sonny.

"You didn't happen to see the victim's purse or personal items lying around the house did you?" questioned Knobbs.

"No, Chief. If you're thinking that I took her things, you're wrong. Hell, you searched us, and I know you searched my car. Isn't there something in the statutes about reasonable cause? Can't y'all get in trouble for that?"

"Don't push me, Rafferty."

"Listen, Chief, doesn't it seem kinda strange to you that this Tommy Slattery fellow takes off with Candy's purse and other belongings but didn't take the murder weapon with him?"

"Yes it does. Before we received the results on the fingerprints we thought that maybe the killer was some sort of crazed maniac, maybe a disgruntled boyfriend or john. But now that we know that Slattery did it, we figure that it probably was a mob hit, but they are usually quick and clean. This was truly a deranged killer that did Garza in. Taking her belongings tells me that someone is trying to hide her identity and the people that she's been working for. We don't have all the pieces to the puzzle yet, but we will soon. We just now found out that she was previously living with a stripper in Newport. We're going to bring her in for questioning."

"Don't bother, Chief. I just came from there. She claims to know nothing. I tried to get her to spit the bit but she won't give."

"Well, I believe that we might be a little better at interrogation than you are."

"Don't waste your time. She's too afraid of her parents finding out her place of employment."

"Oh, another stripper that doesn't want Mommy and Daddy finding out that she's showing her most private goods to strange men, eh?"

"Parents aren't such a bad sort, Floyd. Hell, you may have had one or two of your own at one time," jeered Sonny.

That befuddled Knobbs for a moment.

"Listen, Chief, why did you give me all that gab on Slattery for? I know it's not because you need a hug."

Floyd conjured up a smile. "No, Rafferty, I figure that you want Slattery really bad. You'll find him, and then you'll fuck up and we'll step in and finish the case."

"Thanks for your vote of confidence, Floyd."

"You're welcome. Now get the fuck out of my jail."

"But Floyd, can't I come and visit when you're in a better mood?"

"Hell, no, I never want to see you again."

On the way out, Sonny figured that would be the last he would see of the old police Chief, for Indiana was out of his jurisdiction. And the one thing that Sonny knew for sure was that Candy worked in Indiana, but where? If and when he found that out, he knew that he would find the killer, and maybe solve the mystery that his own mind kept so, recluse.

Sonny didn't stop at McDonald's because he was having a "Mac Attack". He just needed a place to gather his thoughts and what little evidence that he had, to put together a plan to find Candy's killer. At the drive-up window he ordered a black coffee and a chicken sandwich. When the girl taking his order asked, "Do you want fries with that?" Sonny answered back with a resounding "No!" It would be a while before he would eat any kind of fried potatoes again. Sonny pulled into the parking space, reached behind his seat and pulled out a road atlas. As he sipped his coffee he studied the map closely, hoping to recognize a town or a road that would jog his memory. He figured the place not to be too far across the river since Candy did live in Cincy. Sonny saw nothing that seemed remotely familiar. His memory at that moment was still nebulous on the goings on at the Bone Yard.

Frustrated, Sonny got out of his car and opened the back door. He then pulled out the middle of the rear seat, exposing a false bottom. From the false bottom he pulled out a plastic sack and carried it back to the front seat with him.

The bag was filled mostly with feminine hygiene products. Sonny knew from his years of detective work that a good detective leaves no stone unturned. He found a box of Tampons, noticed that two were missing, and started going through the rest of them, pulling out the cotton sponges from the applicators. Sure enough, he found two applicators with half a cotton sponge in them and a bag of a white substance which was most likely, cocaine. At least she had some class about her, thought Sonny. She stayed away from the rock version of the stuff.

Through his pilfering he came across a flip-top box of Marlboros. He opened the box and found four marijuana cigarettes rolled tightly at the ends. Also inside the box was a rather large book of matches that caught his interest. The matchbook cover was black, with a red and white letter advertisement on it. It read, "Love Sessions with Jamaica Red," on one side, and the other read, "Devil's Lair, Come up and see me sometime." How interesting, thought Sonny, no telephone number on it. That's a hell of a way to advertise. He set that aside and scrounged some more until he pulled out a box of condoms. How ironic, he thought, that Candy practiced safe sex.

All at once it started coming back to him. He imagined her face, warm and friendly with dark doe eyes like her sister's. He remembered her voice, with that soft, Puerto Rican drawl which was most unlike Angie's. But most of all he remembered the red dress that revealed the light brown softness of her breasts, and he remembered the words; "Hello, Mr. My name is Candy Adams. *Ju* know, Candy, as in candy shop. I sell sweets of all kinds for *ju* my lover. What's nice about me is that I'm open twenty-four-seven. *Ju* can enter the front door or come in the rear, whatever your preference is."

Sonny became very sad. She felt real to him now. He knew her well through her sister, and he remembered that little ten year-old that jumped the double rope like nobody's business. Sonny wanted to cry but he fought it off. He reached one last time into the bag. He pulled out a receipt. It was for the tampons and rubbers. It read, "Thank you for shopping Meyer's Drug Store, 105 Main Street, Scoville, Indiana." Sonny smiled as the tears returned. He had hit pay dirt. He had that feeling. He looked on the map again and found it. He laid the map down, backed the big Ford up, threw it in drive, and squealed out of Cincinnati towards Highway 50, destination Scoville.

Scoville proper amounted to no more than a post office with a strip mall next to it, followed by Meyer's Drugs. Sonny proceeded to the front counter of the drugstore feeling a little embarrassed asking the whereabouts of the Devil's Lair. On duty was a little old blue-haired lady with a powdered complexion looking more like 80 than 70. As Sonny approached her with his question she gave him the evil eye and answered with, "Did you come in here to buy something?"

"No, not really, ma-am," replied Sonny.

"Well, I know of no such place young man. You best try another town," she screeched. That went well, thought Sonny when walking out the door.

Sonny jumped in his car and headed on through town, trying to conjure up a new approach to finding the Devil's Lair.

The evening had turned to dusk as Sonny came upon some bright lights at a country intersection. On the left corner was an eatery called the Big Rock Cafe. Across the road from it was a convenience store. It was more like an old general store with two old gas pumps out front.

"What the hell. May as well give it a try," said Sonny.

He got out and walked up to the store's entrance. He noticed a rough-looking gal in heavy make-up leaning against the storefront smoking on a long cigarette. She looked too old for the mini-shirt that she was wearing, and too old to be a hooker, though she did look as though she once made those rounds. "Excuse me, ma'm," said Sonny.

"Yeah, what the hell do you want?" she snarled.

"I'm looking for a bar or nightclub called the Devil's Lair."

"Do I look like a whore to you?"

"No, ma'am, I just thought that you might know. That's all."

"Yeah right, you men are all alike. You see a good-looking woman and right away you're trying to bag 'er."

"No, that's not true, ma'am. I'm sorry if you thought that I implied that."

"You must be new around here, aren't you?" she asked suspiciously.

"Well, I guess I am."

"We don't need you city folk comin' out here, messin' things up, you hear?"

Sonny walked inside the store leaving the clownish looking termagant babbling to the night air. He scoured the building, looking for the most unassuming character in there, hoping to get some answers without all the flak. He spotted a little oafish fellow standing at the soda fountain helping himself to a Slurpy.

"Hey, buddy, I've got a question that maybe you can answer for me."

The little man quickly glanced up, and went back to filling his Slurpy.

"I'll give it a try, Mr." he said.

"I need to know how to get to the Devil's Lair," said Sonny.

Suddenly, the little man's head snapped up, looking straight at Sonny.

"It, it, it, it's you," he stuttered in fright, "Oh, you mean the Bone Yard down yonder ways," he stammered, while pointing with his thumb. "G-g-got to go, Mr." he said, running out the door, leaving his Slurpy behind.

Sonny shook his head in disbelief and frustration. "What kind of a place did I get myself into," he whispered to himself.

"I can tell you where the Devil's Lair is, Mr." said a pregnant girl appearing around a grocery aisle.

"And who might you be?" asked Sonny, now a little gun-shy.

"I might just be Star Cargile. I work at the Devil's Bone Yard which is right next door to the Lair. Don't worry about that little fella that ran out on you."

"What was wrong with him?"

"Oh, he's just a bit shy, that's all, and a bit stupid," she added. "He's Po Daniels, the village idiot. One of many in this town, I might add. What's your name, Mr.?"

"I'm . . . uh, Johnny, Johnny Carlisle."

"I can tell that you're not from around here, Johnny. That's okay though," she said, struggling with her grocery basket.

"Let me help you with that," said Sonny, relieving her of her groceries.

"So, is there anybody in particular at the Devil's Lair that you're lookin' for?"

"Yes, I'm looking for a lady by the name of Jamaica Red."

"A big spender, eh?" she said. "I'll tell you what, Johnny Carlisle. If you pay for my groceries and buy me supper, I'll tell you all I know about Jamaica Red and the Lair."

"Sure thing, darling," replied Sonny, walking her up to the counter.

"Hey Madge, toss in two cartons of Marlboro 100's will ya?" she said to the clerk.

"Aren't you afraid of harming your baby?" asked Sonny.

"Oh, no, Johnny, I don't smoke that often. It'll be all right. Thanks for the interest though."

Sonny paid for the groceries and carried them to Star's old Ford Escort. He then escorted her across the road to the café. Sonny was both excited and nervous, for his hard investigative work was now coming to fruition.

He found Star to be quite pretty in the face, and though seven months pregnant, she had a surprisingly slender body. The young brunette did seem to be a bit slow on the uptake, except when it came to taking a man's money. Still, Sonny was intrigued by her brazenness.

"I've got to squeeze into a booth if you don't mind, Johnny. My hemorrhoids are killing me. I have to sit sideways as it is."

They were interrupted for a moment when the waitress came and took their orders.

"Are you sure you don't want anything to eat, Johnny?" asked Star.

"Yeah, coffee is fine for me," said Sonny.

"I feel a bit embarrassed, ordering a big steak and all," said the brunette.

"Don't worry about it. You're eating for two," he said. "When is your baby due?"

"Oh, I don't know exactly. In a couple of months, I guess."

"You do see a doctor, don't you?"

"Oh yeah, sometimes," she answered. "To be honest with you, Johnny, I can't wait to have this kid so I can go back to working regular."

"What kind of work do you do?"

"I told you already. I work at the Bone Yard. I'm a pleasure girl. You know what I mean? I satisfy men's natural cravings, and I make a good buck at it because pleasing men is what I'm good at. What do you do, Johnny?"

"It doesn't matter what I do darlin'. Tell me about Jamaica Red and the Lair."

"First of all, the Bone Yard is the name of the roadhouse. It's a large wooden building that sits on the edge of a quarry. The bar's out front. That's where I work. The rear portion and the upstairs are called the Devil's Lair. I've never been back there, but I do know that they hire high-priced hookers and call-girls to come work there. They're pretty quiet about it all. I hear tell that Jamaica Red demands five thousand dollars an hour, or twenty thousand for all night."

"She must be somethin' else."

"She is quite beautiful, and they say that she can do things with her body that no other woman can do."

"How can I get a hold of her?"

"It's hard, Johnny. Most customers, I hear, are high rollers and make appointments on the internet. But for the right price, I might be able to get her cell-phone number for you."

"Okay. What's your price?"

"How 'bout a hundred-n-fifty," said Star.

"How 'bout a hundred," bargained Sonny.

"Look, Johnny, I need the bread if I'm going to be able to raise this kid properly. I don't even know who its father is."

"All right, one-fifty."

"Thanks, Johnny, you're swell," she said, clutching his hand.

After the food arrived their conversation died down somewhat until Star finished her steak.

"Tell me, Star, do you know a Puerto Rican girl that works there by the name of Candy Adams?"

"Yeah, she comes out of the Lair sometimes and tries to horn in on my customers. I don't really care for the bitch. She and Jamaica Red are good friends, I hear."

"Do you know—"

"Say, are you a cop or somethin'!"

"No, of course not, darlin'"

"You sure do act like one. Look, I told you more than I should have already. I can get into trouble for this, you know."

"Okay, okay that's fine. All I want is a date with Jamaica Red. Can you tell me how to get to the Bone Yard?"

Star just stared at Sonny.

"Okay, how much?"

"A hundred," she replied.

"You sure are expensive, girl."

"Not as expensive as Jamaica Red."

"Okay, a hundred bucks," said Sonny.

"Keep taking the main road until you get to 900-North. Then, turn right and follow the road for ten or eleven miles and turn left on 150-East. Take 150-East until you get to a gravel road called "Rattlesnake

Highway." Follow it to the end and you'll be at the Bone Yard. Got it?"

"Yeah, I got it. Thanks a lot, Star. You've been a great help," said Sonny, laying the bills out on the table.

"Listen, Johnny, don't tell anybody that I told you about any of this, okay?"

"My lips are sealed."

"Walk me out to my car, will you, Johnny?"

"Sure thing, doll," he said, helping her from the booth.

"I could go for a guy like you, Johnny."

"You don't want me, kid. My kind are a dime a dozen."

"Well, at least go home with me so I can pay you properly for supper."

"Do you live alone?"

"No, I live with my mother, but she won't mind."

"No thanks, darlin', you're too pregnant for me."

"Don't let that stop you, Johnny. We'll do it like the doggies do it."

"No thanks, dear," replied the detective.

"Well, at least kiss me goodnight," she said. Sonny bent down to give her a little smooch but she transformed it into a full blown tongue kiss while her hand fell to his groin. "My, you are a big boy aren't you?"

Sonny smiled and walked away.

With wine on the table and Jessie Coltraine by her side, Samantha anxiously awaited the return of Loni Jacobs to Lucresia's.

"Wasn't Jitterbug and Larry supposed to meet with us, Sam?"

"Yeah, I just talked to Lisa on the phone. They're still following up on a report from the police scanner of a car being pulled out of the Eagle Creek Reservoir. According to Lisa, it seems there might be suspicion of a homicide or suicide to it. That's why they're still there. Not too many people run off into the reservoir accidentally."

"What time are we supposed to meet with this Jacobs woman?"

"Between 9:00 and 9:30 or 'round there," said Samantha. "Why, are you in a hurry, Jessie?"

"Oh no, I need a rest after sittin' with a sick kid all weekend."

"Is Cassie all right now?"

"Yes, she's a lot better, Sam. Her fever finally broke. It's hell having the measles this time of the year."

"I bet it is. Who's watching her now?"

"Her dad, he doesn't mind."

"How's Jack been doing lately, Jessie?"

"Things have been going real well for him at work lately, but you can never tell about advertising. It's such a fickle business you know. How's Sonny been since his . . . accident, Sam? I know that you were really worried about him for awhile there."

"Yeah, I was, Jessie. I appreciate all of you sticking by me during those hard times."

"Well, we all have to help one another, Sam. That's what friends are for."

"For awhile there, Sonny just laid around like an old confused bull. He didn't know whether to chew his cud or pound his pud. I think Sonny's finally come out of his shell. Actually, he's been great the last couple of days, or I should say nights," said Samantha with a mischievous smile.

"Oh, I see. You guys have been gettin' it on hot and heavy, huh?"

"Yeah, he's really been great the last couple of days. I feel like I'm 20 years old again, Jessie."

"Well, share your formula with me, girlfriend, 'cause I've got some dead wood at home that needs energizing," said Jessie somewhat jokingly.

"Oh, I wish it were that easy," sighed Samantha. "Sonny hasn't really been the same since Centralia, six years ago. I believe you were in television then, Jessie."

"I remember it well, Sam. I reported on it too. I was there at the scene and saw all the blood and gore. I saw the agony on Sonny's face when they pulled the sheet up over the little girl's face. I guess Sonny never got over that. I guess you never do."

"He doesn't talk about that anymore. He never mentions it. But when you look deep into his eyes, he seems to be thinking about something, always thinking. Oh, he'll talk to you in the now, but his eyes seem to be thinking, watching, thinking; watching. It's as if he thinks the "Boogie man's" still out there, and he's going to get us."

"Ooh, that sounds really creepy, Sam."

"Yes, it does, let's change the subject, shall we?"

"Yeah, lets."

"Hey, let me tell you what happened this morning. Now, you've got to promise not to tell anyone what I'm about to tell you, because it was quite embarrassing, to say the least," said Samantha.

"I promise," agreed Jessie.

"Last night, after my run-in with Loni Jacobs, Sonny came by to have a late dinner with me. We got half drunk on wine and decided to go to his office to make love. We screwed our brains out, girl. Sometime during the night Sonny must've gotten a phone call and left. That's not all that unusual. He's done it before. His job calls for that sometimes. Well, I was dead to the world and didn't remember him leaving. So, here I am the next morning with my clothes strewn everywhere, laying in that big sofa in his office with my face buried in the pillows, snoring away, and only my suit coat covering me, and my lily-white ass hanging out over the edge for anyone to see. I mean to tell ya, girl, I had the whole laundry hangin' out there. And, of course, who walks in, none other than Myra Robey and her little granddaughter, Shauna."

"You didn't hear them come in?" asked Jessie with a wide grin.

"Nah, I was dead to the world, girl."

"What happened next?"

"I felt somebody poking me in the butt, telling me to get up. You know how it is when you have a good night of sex and you don't feel like getting up the next morning?"

"No, I don't," quipped Jessie, "but go on anyway," she said with great anticipation.

"Well, I just rubbed my legs together, stirring up our love juices again while reliving my previous evening of bliss. Of course, I soon realized it wasn't Sonny waking me up, but Shauna. I jumped up, embarrassed as hell, and there stood Myra and Shauna staring at me. I know I looked foolish standing there with that coat up around my chest trying to hide my tits, all-the-while not realizing that I was baring my big, red, bush for all to see. Little Shauna just stared, but thank God Myra kept her wits about her. She just handed me my underwear and sent me off to get ready for work."

Samantha smiled amusingly at Jessie while she laughed hysterically at the redhead's story.

As the laughter waned, Samantha nervously checked her watch. "It's, 10:00 o'clock. Something is wrong, Jessie. I can feel it."

"Oh, she's probably just running a bit late."

"No, she told me that people were after her. I believe her. And I wonder why we haven't heard anymore from Lisa and Larry." The sound of Samantha's cell-phone ringing put an abrupt ending to the girls' conversation.

"Hello, Lisa?"

Jessie watched Samantha's eyes turn down as she began talking on the phone.

"What? . . . No . . . It can't be . . . That's terrible . . . Those son-of-a-bitches! . . . I don't know Jitterbug. I guess we'll have to regroup. Have you called it into the paper? . . . Then you and Larry may as well go on home . . . Yeah, me too, see you tomorrow. Get some rest. Bye."

"They got to her, Jessie. Loni Jacobs is dead. She was the one they pulled out of the reservoir. Jitterbug said they found an empty whiskey bottle in the car. The cops are talking death by drunk-driving. I know that's not true, Jessie. Waverly was afraid that she would talk. They snuffed her out just like snuffing out a candle flame. I was just talking to her last night. She was sitting right where you're sitting, Jessie. How strange. What a shame. I don't believe it. It, it's so sad," Samantha said despondently. "Let's go home, Jessie."

"Are you going to be alright, Sam?"

"Yeah, I'll be alright. Sonny called me earlier. He should be at home waiting for me now. We'll go over this case again tomorrow. I really don't know what we can do about this now. We're back to square one."

"Yeah, back to square one," chimed, Jessie.

"Hi, darlin', how was your day?"

"It wasn't good, it wasn't good at all."

"Neither was mine."

"Hold me, Sonny. Please hold me," she cried.

"I prepared a hot bath for you, darlin'"

"Join me, will you, baby? I don't want to be alone."

"Me neither."

The mellifluent sound of Enya filled the air as they clung tightly to each other in the balmy waters of their little candle-lit haven, feeling sheltered from the ugliness of the outside world.

Two hearts of two lovers, two lovers yet two strangers, two partners yet far apart, for he was thinking about Candy and retribution and she thought of Loni, cast into the cold darkness of death.

They were two warriors of truth, yet they fought with two different weapons. But indeed tonight, they both were of the desperate kind.

Chapter Eighteen

Out of the Mouth's of Babes

It was an inauspicious occasion, Candy's funeral that is, but she didn't plan it that way. Most people don't. Sonny showed up and Angie showed her appreciation, but she had a different aura about her. Her eyes still perked up when Sonny was around, but he noticed that she wasn't kid-like anymore. She seemed more mature, sedate, and held her chin up at all times. She didn't bother Sonny about his investigation. She didn't seem to care at all. But she did give her kid sister a proper funeral.

A funeral was held on the other side of town also. This one was for Loni Jacobs. Samantha was there. She felt bad, real bad. Not for the swollen right eye of Loni. No, the mortician covered that up pretty well, but she knew deep inside that she, in someway, was responsible for Loni's death. She felt that if she would have stayed on the Waverly scandal and sought out convictions on the perpetrators that Loni would probably be alive today. But Big John was too convincing, too big a hurdle to jump. Loni was the Waverly snitch and she paid for it with her life. She had the key to "Pandora's box", but somebody closed "Pandora's box" for good.

After the funeral, Samantha sought out Barbara Fugate. Barbara wasn't angry with Samantha like her sister was. She had fought Waverly over two years ago and lost. She not only lost out to the powers that be, but she was also expunged from the nursing home community. It took her a year and half, along with a couple of lies on her resume, just to get back into nursing. She took her whipping and went on with her life. Loni, on the other hand, was different. She was the defiant one. As Barbara put it, Loni was born pissed off. Waverly became her enemy. She was going to make them pay for what they did to Barbara. This time, Goliath slew David.

Sonny stood and watched while Kitty took her laps in the pool. His mother-in-law was a graceful swimmer. She once told Sonny that as a kid in West Virginia she became a strong swimmer by swimming upstream in the rivers of the mountains. Though some people thought Kitty to be flighty and shallow, Sonny looked past all that. He saw more in Kitty than most. He saw her as an indigent child of a West Virginia coal-mining family, trying to escape the harshness of her childhood. She found her freedom all right, in the guise of Johnny Taylor. Big John was quite the philanderer, but that didn't matter much to Kitty, for he helped her climb that social ladder, and for that she would be forever grateful to him.

When Kitty finished her laps she shook the water from her face and rested her head in her arms atop the concrete edge at the far end of the pool. As she regained her breath she turned around to head back. A gleeful smile widened her face as she saw her son-in-law standing at the other end. "Sonny!" she yelled, and quickly swam to where he was.

Sonny helped her from the water and greeted her hand with a kiss.

"You are quite the gentleman, still," said Kitty.

"And you are still as beautiful as ever, Kitty," Sonny replied.

"Why, thank you, Sonny. You know how to make a woman feel special."

Kitty was beautiful for a 65 year-old woman. The only difference that Sonny saw in her now than when she was younger was a little more roundness in her belly and a little more sag in her seat. Her face and breasts were still of highest standards thanks to a few nips and tucks.

"I do believe you have bought yourself some new breasts," joked Sonny.

"Why yes, John bought these for me," she said, squeezing them together. "Dr. Carl Frances did the implantations. Have you heard of him?"

"I don't believe so, Kitty."

"He is a renowned plastic surgeon. You'll have to meet him sometime, Sonny. He is quite the fellow," she bragged. "So, what do you think, Sonny, do you like them? John says they're too large."

"No, I think they look just fine."

Kitty slipped off her shoulder straps, baring her breasts. "Here, Sonny, feel these and tell me if they feel real."

"I can't do that, Kitty," he said with a blush.

"Aw, come on, they won't bite."

Sonny squeezed her round mounds. "What do you think, Sonny?"

"Firm, real firm," he said.

"They feel real, don't they?"

"Why, yes they do, Kitty."

"I'm glad, Sonny. I value your opinion more than John's sometimes. He just tries to placate me. You always tell me the truth."

"That's me all right, ol' truthful Sonny," he smiled.

"I expected to find Samantha with you. She called this morning, telling me about the two of you going to funerals today, and about you both feeling down and out. That's why I suggested that she and you come by for a late afternoon swim. You know, to unwind and relax a little."

"We went to separate funerals. Hers probably lasted longer."

"Oh, do I know either of these people?"

"No, I don't believe so, Kitty."

"Well, you two can just make yourself at home here because John is on a business trip and won't be back until tomorrow. I've got to get ready to go now. I've got a date tonight."

"No shit, with whom?"

"Why, Dr. Frances, of course. Don't mention any of this to Sam. Okay?"

"Don't worry, Kitty. My lips are sealed."

"Good. I know I can trust you. I always could."

"Well, thanks, Kitty."

"Hey, Sonny, I apologize for not coming to see you back when you were laid up at home. I just couldn't stand the thought of your pretty face being beaten up and all. I was thinking about you, though."

"That's okay, Kitty. I understand."

"Look, I've got to rush. There's beer and wine in the kitchen. Help yourself. I want you and Sam to make an evening of it. Get a little drunk and go skinny dipping."

"I don't know," sighed Sonny, "We're probably too old for those kinds of shenanigans."

"Nonsense, you never get too old for that. Believe me, I haven't yet," smiled Kitty before disappearing into the house.

Upon Samantha's arrival Sonny was taking a swim in the pool.

"Hi, honey. Where's Mother?" she asked with a kiss.

"Oh, she had some function to go to. You know how she is."

"Damn her, she was supposed to be here. It's not that often I get to see her."

"But you talk to her on the phone most, everyday."

"Yeah, but that's not the same, Sonny."

"Well, anyway she told me to tell you that she gives you her love."

"I guess that'll have to do. Hey, baby; how about pouring me a glass of Merlot while I change into my swimsuit?"

"Okay, Sam," he said toweling off.

The water felt relaxing, almost soothing to the two lovers. There was no frolicking this evening, no skinny-dipping that Kitty spoke of, just snuggling, caressing, and reassurances. They were both beaten soldiers, both recovering. No, they were not lovers tonight, for they had too much on their plates to think about.

"Hey, Sonny," she said.

"What is it, darlin'?"

"I know that we have always agreed not to discuss our jobs at home but I'm really in a quandary tonight. I need your help, or at least an opinion."

"Tell me about it, darlin'. I'm listening."

Samantha commenced telling Sonny about Loni's story. About her kept secret that caused her demise. She also told him about the plight of the nurses at the Waverly facilities. About their mistreatment and their ill-construed firings, hoping for Sonny to give her a simple recipe to end those problems, at the same time realizing that it just wouldn't happen.

"Tell me about the accident, Sam."

"What do you want to know?"

"Was she drinking?"

"Yes."

"What was her blood alcohol?"

"It was point one-six; they found an empty whiskey bottle in her car. I talked to her sister today and she said that Loni received a phone call from someone claiming to be the press, wanting to meet with her at Flannery's Tap. The witnesses at the bar had her drunk and walking out of the place with two men that they never saw before. A half hour later she drove her car off into the reservoir."

"What did the autopsy say?"

"That she died from drowning."

"No signs of a struggle?"

"Not according to the police report."

"Was her car damaged?"

"According to Larry Crowell and Jitterbug it was, but she was driving an old car. It was banged up anyway. So what do you think, Sonny?"

"To give a professional opinion I would have to see the forensics and pictures of the deceased, and I would have to take a look at the car. I would also need to talk with the victim's sister, and that's just to start with. Just from what you have said leads me to think that it could have possibly been a homicide."

"Sonny, will you take on this case?"

"No, not me, darlin', let the police have a shot at it. Give them a chance."

"They don't care, Sonny. Loni told me as much. She wasn't exactly on their A-list. Come on, do it for me, baby. I've never asked you for anything like this before. I want this story. I want it bad!"

"Whoa, darlin', who's gonna pay for all this?"

"I'll pay for it Sonny. Out of my pocket if I have to."

"Wait a minute Sam. Isn't that like robbing Peter to pay Paul?"

"Okay, okay, I'll take it from the Times. We have a fund that will cover the expenses."

"Your dad would shit a brick if you did something like that, and you know it."

"The hell with Daddy, I'll bypass him."

"Look, Sam. You're just putting a tighter noose around your neck, that's all."

"But, Sonny, We can't let this crime go unpunished. I would never forgive myself."

"There's little else you can do, darlin'. This Waverly thing is becoming much bigger than a few nursing homes. You've done all that you're supposed to do. You belong to the print media, darlin'. You're an investigative reporter. You investigate and report your findings to the public. That's the good that you do for the people of the community. In that, you're like a guardian angel, but you only have paper wings. You can't do anymore than you are capable of doing. You have to let the law enforcement do their jobs. You can't chase down the bad guys and put them away. That's for someone else to do."

"But surely I can help the nurses in someway."

"In what way, Sam, they have no contracts with their employers?"

"What about discrimination?"

"Well, let's see. You have the big three, race, gender, and age. When it comes to getting fired, they are all hard to prove, and Waverly will drag the lawsuit out by using continuances and such until the plaintiff can't afford to carry it out any further. It's a corporate game and lawyers love to play it."

"They can't just up and fire them for anything at all?"

"Sure they can. This is Indiana, the fire-at-will state. Do you remember when Danielle was 15 years-old and working at that drive-in as a carhop?"

"Yes, the Purple Onion."

"If you remember correctly she got fired after only working there for three days because one of the other girls wasn't waiting on the customers fast enough. I went and talked to her boss because Danielle told us that she was doing her job and was fired for no reason at all. The woman agreed that Danielle wasn't the culprit, but since she had the least time there she fired her to set an example for the other girls. That was the most stupid reasoning that I'd ever heard of. The bitch told me that she could fire anyone anytime she wanted. She didn't even pay Danielle for the time that she worked. If you remember we took her to small claims court and lost. Why? Because Indiana is a fire-at-will state and you can be fired from a job for no reason at all. It taught Danielle a good lesson. That some people are real assholes, and that some of our laws really suck. But we got that ol' gal back though, me and the boys. We fixed her wagon."

"The weird thing about it all is that as far back as 1991 the National Labor Council put forth a bill to change the law to *fire with just cause*," explained Sonny.

"Then why don't we go by that?"

"The state legislature must vote it into law, and of course, the powers-that-be will never let that happen, for they must keep the proletariat class down. They're afraid for the working class to have any power. Much like a communist country, except that we hide it better. It would be nice for the nurses to organize, but it's not likely to happen either, with the hold that Waverly has on them. Besides, unions are weak nowadays, and don't seem to be all that interested in recruitment, especially where women are concerned."

"It is a sad story, Sonny, and I don't know how we can make it any better," Samantha sighed.

"There is power in numbers. What they need is some large group with some money and clout to go to bat for them."

"You're right, Sonny, but where are we going to get help like that?"

"I don't know darlin'. Your guess is as good as mine."

Samantha thought for a minute, "How about the women's rights organizations?"

"That makes some sense. They have plenty of money, and women's rights are what it's all about now. But the thing is, Sam, they're more interested in trying to infiltrate the men's workforce and disrupt their lives instead of lobbying for higher wages and equal rights for the jobs that their gender excel in. Nursing and office personnel are at the top of that list. That's where the National Association of Women's Rights ought to be directing their priorities."

"We've dealt with them before at the Times, Sonny. In the past they have bought ad space in our paper and we have donated to some of their causes. I know their president, Pat Fowler. I think I'll have a talk with her."

"It is a long shot, Sam. Don't be too disappointed if they aren't too keen on helping. They seem just like a group of men-haters to me."

"They're a large powerful organization that could be of some use if I could only somehow convince them to help." said Samantha.

"I'll tell you what, Sam. You work at gettin' the nurses some help and I'll get in touch with Frank Lujak in the crime's division at Metro and see what his take is on the Jacobs's drowning. That's the least that I can do for Mrs. Fugate since she was so good at helping me recover when I was laid up. Besides, Lujak got my job when I left. He kind of owes me."

Samantha put her arms around Sonny in a hug of appreciation. "Thanks, Sonny, I knew that you would come through for me."

"I would probably help you more, darlin', but I have a pretty busy schedule ahead of me for the next few weeks."

"I know it's none of my business, honey, but are you going to help that Garza girl find her sister's killer?"

"Well, I hope to. Why? Do you know Angie?"

"A little, I met her last week at the Body Perfect Spa."

"She owns that spa, you know. Plus she's a cop to boot. She broke in as my partner many years ago. You met her once at a precinct Christmas party, though I doubt that you remember."

"Do you plan on going back to, where was it, Cincinnati?" questioned Samantha.

"Yeah, I'll be going back down to that area in the near future."

"I want you to be careful this time, Sonny. The last time you left town like that you ended up back in Centralia and lord knows where else, and you almost got killed. I don't think I could handle all that again, darling."

"Don't worry about me, baby. I'm a big boy. I'm trying to figure my life out, I really am. I'm more concerned about you, because you're playing with the big dogs now. I'm afraid for you, Sam. Watch 'em, they bite hard. Just work it as we discussed. You get the nurses help and I'll get the cops on the Jacobs's case, okay, darlin'?"

"Okay," agreed the redhead. "Hey, darling, I've got to get out of this water. I'm starting to wrinkle."

"Let's swim awhile yet, Sam. I need the exercise."

"I don't think so. You go ahead, Sonny. I'm gonna' towel off."

"I'll race ya three laps down and three back," said Sonny.

Samantha smiled. "What's the stakes, big boy?"

"The loser cleans the kennel and walks the 'gang' for the next month."

"You're on!"

"Say, Sam . . . how 'bout a head start?"

As the front door opened, the noonday sun blasted through the

Bone Yard like a night train through a tunnel, and was followed by a seductive, dark-eyed creature in a short red dress. When the bartender caught site of her he quickly slid behind the bar. "Can I help you, ma'am," he asked in a polite manner.

"Yes, I'm looking for the manager of this establishment."

"May I ask what your name is?"

"Lana, Lana Darrah," she spoke.

"Do you have an appointment, Lana?"

"Yes, I do."

"Just let me give the boss a call," he said.

Lana looked around until she met Star Cargile's jealous stare. Lana smiled, a pretentious smile, while Star just snarled.

"Come, darlin', I'll take you back to the Devil's Lair to meet with Mr. Pergosi," said the bartender, grabbing her hand.

On Miles Pegosi's command, Lana entered his office. Pergosi had his eyes buried amongst a disheveled pile of paperwork on his desk while gorging himself with a kielbasa sandwich. With eyebrows raised he caught sight of Lana's beauty. "Say, you're quite pretty in the face," he blurted out, wiping mustard off his mouth.

"Why, thank you," she politely replied.

"I can't remember your name. My secretary put the information that you gave her on my desk, and I can't find the damn thing."

"My name is Lana Darrah," she said clearly and concisely.

"Yeah, yeah, that's it, like Lana Turner, right?"

"That's right, sir."

"Okay, so do you have some kind of proof or papers on what you do?"

"Yes, I do. Here is my resume," she said.

"You know, while observing your demeanor and looking through your resume, as you deem to call it, I can tell right away if you are a whore, a hooker, a call girl, or just a plain old slut. Do you know that?" he boasted.

Lana courteously nodded.

Pergosi noisily shuffled through her papers, "It says here that you worked the Grand Plaza Hotel in Vegas. How much did you make there for a trick?"

"I made a thousand for a one hour stint."

"One-thousand, that's not bad, not bad at all, even for Vegas. Let's see how your medical looks," he said, checking her file. "You seem to be all caught up on your shots . . . no diseases of any kind. Good girl. Okay, strip, let's see the goods."

Lana slowly undressed in front of the stranger.

"Come on, come on," he said hastily. "Off with the drawers, this ain't brain science girlie!" he scolded. "M-m-m, not bad, not bad at all, Lana. You're clean. You're trimmed nicely, and you don't have any fuckin' tattoos. That's great. I never could understand why girls want to defile their bodies in that manner. I have only one other girl that works for me that doesn't have a tattoo, and that's Jamaica Red, prettiest of the bunch, and that's the reason why. Turn around and let me see the rest, yeah, that's it. You show a little too much muscle for my liking, but you'll do just fine. You look like you might have a little Hispanic in you. You're not Puerto Rican are you?"

"Oh, no sir, I'm of Mexican decent."

"Call me Miles, darlin'. So what was your Mexican name before you changed it?"

"It was La Rosa Sanchez."

"Hey, that's not bad either, but men don't want to pay as much for Mexicans and Ricans. They think they're too slutty, I guess. Hell, we just let go a little Rican girl. She was pretty, and a popular little whore, but she just didn't work out for us."

"Why not, Miles, may I ask?"

"Oh, she had a big mouth. See, around here we have certain rules to follow. They're not hard rules to obey either. One is to keep your mouth shut. See, it's simple, fucking simple. How are you on the dance pole?"

"I'm good, Miles. I'm a good dancer."

"Do you have your own clientele?'

"Not really, not from around here, anyway," she said.

"Don't worry. I'll line up some customers for you. It won't take long. You can have Candy's johns.

"Whose?"

"Candy Adams, she was that little Rican that I let go."

"Oh," said Lana faintly.

"You'll have two tests to pass before you can work for us. One is that you'll come in at 5:30 tonight to meet the rest of the girls. You'll have to perform a lap dance, then a pole dance. If the girls like you, you're in.

Don't worry, my dear. They won't be jealous of you or anything 'cause they're every bit as beautiful as you."

"Now I'm going to tell you what the job entails. You start at five-hundred dollars an hour for your performance in your own suite. You'll have the amenities of a queen. During that hour you pleasure your customer anyway you see fit. You will make one-hundred dollars a customer, plus tips. The more you please him, the greater his tip. I assure you that these men will pay you well if you give them what they want. So, after the pleasure suite, bring your man down to the casino and spend some time with him there. If he wants you to stay with him it will cost him a hundred dollars an hour. If he takes you back to your suite he pays another five-hundred dollars. All these men know the rules so they won't cheat you. Sometimes they want you all weekend. That's where the big money comes in. Men love to have beauty hanging on their arms when they go to different functions. Do you have any restrictions yourself, Lana?"

"Yes. I don't do anal."

"No problem. Like I said, you satisfy the customer anyway you want. Just remember, the more fun he has, the bigger the tip. Do you have any more questions?"

"No, I'm fine with everything, Miles. Shall I put my clothes back on now?"

"Not just yet, honey. You have one more test to pass," he said, unzipping his fly.

"Do you mean—"

"That's right, baby. I have to know how you perform. This is your payment to me for letting you work at the Devil's Lair. Feel privileged, kid."

As she lowered herself, she took him in hand and showed him the ways of a desperate woman. Not desperate for love, or money, but for revenge. Tears slid down Angie Garza's face as her mind slid back to her childhood days in the back-streets of a big lonely city. Angie paid the piper, while the piper finished his lunch.

Sonny tried to touch base with Angie to see if she had extracted any information from Tracy about her sister when he left her down in Cincy. He never brought the subject up at the funeral, what with

Angie acting in such a strange manner. He was hoping to find her in a different state of mind. But find her, he didn't. Sonny did manage to seek out her partner, Eva Swenson, though she wasn't too happy to see him. According to Eva, Angie took some time off from Metro. Said she needed the rest and headed off on her lonesome. Eva claimed that Angie said something about flying to Puerto Rico to visit with some relatives for a while. Eva wasn't too happy about being left behind by her lover, but Angie had apparently put her in charge of running the health club. Sonny thought it strange for her to be off on her own like that. Besides, she never spoke of any relatives in Puerto Rico. If she had some there, they were distant He didn't like losing touch with her. It worried him because they had become close again, the little frightened girl in her and the caretaker in him. He just didn't want her to get lost in the shuffle of life again.

If only he could make contact with Jamaica Red, was his thinking, but she wouldn't return his phone calls. Apparently she wanted no part of a person known as Sonny Rafferty. That fact alone told him that he was on the right track in finding out what happened on that dreadful night, the night at the Devil's Bone Yard. Sonny knew that he was going to have to change his strategy. He was going to have to bring in his alter ego, Johnny Carlisle, and set a date with her at the Devil's Lair. And if that pregnant whore down in Scoville was telling the truth he was going to have to shell out five thousand dollars to meet with her. She must be quite the item, he thought. What the hell, I'll just add it onto the bill for the Governor's Ball.

Sonny again dialed the number that Star gave to him, and again he got the same recording. The soft sultry voice answered, "Hi there, handsome. Have a rough day? You called the right place. Let Jamaica Red take care of your needs, make all of your troubles go away. For one of my sessions, at the beep, leave your name and number so I can get back with you. Thank you for calling, lover. See you soon. See you *real* soon."

Sonny put in his request. Now all he had to do was to wait. The wait was short-lived as the cell-phone rang soon after he sat it down on the desktop. "Hello," he answered.

"Hi there lover, am I speaking with Johnny Carlisle?"

"Why, yes it is."

"What's your pleasure . . . Johnny?" she whispered.

250

"I would like to set up a session with you."

"Your name doesn't come up on my computer screen, so I take it that we have not met yet. Is that correct, Johnny?"

"Yes, I'm kinda new at this," he replied.

"That's alright, dear. I like virgins."

"I'm not really a virgin."

"You are until you've met me, darling. By the way, how did you come by my number?"

"I finagled it from a friend of mine."

"You wouldn't want to tell me his name, would you?"

"Not really. I don't think that he would like his name bandied about by the likes of me."

"That's alright, lover. Which session do you prefer?"

"I don't really know."

"Well, I have three sessions; the scorpion sting, the cobra strike, and the praying mantis."

"What's the praying mantis like?"

"Oh, you are new, aren't you? That's where I ravish your body until you can't take it anymore and you pray for me to stop. Then, I bite your head off." she laughed. "You know I'm just kidding, Johnny, don't you?"

"I certainly hope so."

"Actually, I give all my virgins the scorpion sting first."

"What's the scorpion sting?"

"I can't tell you that, Johnny. That would ruin the surprise, and surprise is what my sessions are all about."

"I hear that you are quite expensive."

"Just five thousand a session for the first-timers; that's very inexpensive for the experience that you will receive, lover. By the way, what kind of work are you in?"

"Oh, uh, I'm into home security systems."

"Are you in the selling or the installing of them?"

"I sell them, and install them."

"That's interesting, Johnny. Do you want me to set you up for a session?"

"Sure, why not?"

"Okay. Right now I'm working at the Devil's Lair, exclusively. Do you know where the Devil's Lair is?"

"Yes. It's behind the Bone Yard."

"That's right. When you get to the Bone Yard, go to the side entrance towards the back. You'll be met by one of our security men. You tell him that you were invited there for the Jamaica Red Extravaganza. He's gonna' pat you down, so don't be bringing any weapons, knives, or anything. He will then lead you to the gambling parlor where you can sit and wait for me, or you can participate in some games of chance. Do you have any questions so far?"

"Only when do we start?"

"Oh, you are a horny little boy, aren't you? I have an opening next Friday at midnight. Don't worry. I'll be fresh. How does that sound?"

"Sounds great," he replied.

"Now, all I need is your credit card number."

"I prefer not to use my credit card. My wife, you know."

"I understand darling, but I need to have some assurance that you will show up. My work hours are valuable."

"How about I send you a money order? Will that do?"

"That would be just fine, Johnny, just fine. Make it out to Miramar Corporation, will you? That makes things better for tax purposes for me and you."

"Okay, I'll do that."

"Hey, Johnny," she asked.

"What?"

"Bring a lot of cash with you, because you never know what you might want to get into here."

"Okay, I'll do that, darlin'"

"I can't wait to see you, lover. I'll be here waiting for you. Goodbye, for now."

Bernice Lujak was one of those women who could talk the leg off a horse, as they say. She and Frank were high school sweethearts at one time. They got married when she got knocked up her senior year. She was nursing her first born on the day that she graduated. Frank always wanted to become a cop and worked hard towards that goal, while Bernice worked at K-Mart and had three more boys. At least twice a summer the Lujak family, along with the Brogan's and Rafferty's, would gather in their backyard for a cookout. Frank was the quintessential backyard grill-master and Bernice was a great conversationalist. This had become a summer tradition over the years. That's the way it was with good cops, good family men.

The drive to the Lujak's was quite enjoyable for Samantha, as she was always delighted when Sonny chose to drive his big Crown Vic on such occasions. She felt safe and warm cuddled next to her man, as he would put his arm around her and playfully toy with the rigid nubs of her breasts. By the time they reached their destination, Samantha would be so inflamed with passion that they'd have to take several minutes for her to compose herself before exiting the car. Then, throughout their evening of socializing Sonny would inadvertently brush up against her breasts, or graze a hand against other intimate parts of her body. It was a game that Sonny loved to play and Samantha didn't rebuke him for it. By the end of the evening, when they climbed back into the car to go home, Samantha was so overwrought with desire that she would cross over into forbidden zones of erotica, and Sonny was none the worse for it. It was a most moveable feast.

The drive this evening, however, wasn't quite the same. Oh, it was for Samantha, but Sonny was feeling somewhat guilty for sending a five-thousand dollar money-order to pay a high-priced hooker for an hour of who-knows-what. His plan wasn't to find pleasure, but to find answers. Though somewhat reluctant, he still played the sensual game with his lovely wife.

Early on, Samantha cornered Frank at his grill tending to the steaks. "Hi, Sam, how's the most beautiful redhead in the world doing?"

"You better not let Bernice hear you talking like that, big guy."

"Oh, Bernice knows that she's my one and only. I flirt with all of my friend's wives. It must be the beast in me. Besides, it's not often that you and I are alone like this. What's up, Sam?"

"Sonny said that you were looking into that reservoir drowning of a few days ago. I have some interest in that. Could you tell me what you found out?"

Frank took a squirt bottle and doused some grease flames and then turned to Samantha with a grimace on his face; "We still have the case listed as death by accident due to drunk driving, but we're still looking into it."

"But, Frank, didn't Sonny tell you about my relationship with the driver the night before she died, and about her tie-in with the Waverly scandal?"

"Yeah he did, Sam. There was some damage to the driver's side of the car with some fresh paint on it, but that car had numerous dents in it already. We tried tracking the paint down but we came up with nothing. Look, she had twice the legal limit of alcohol in her body, and she was a known boozer and druggie. Did you know that?"

"Yes, I did. She told me herself, for crissakes, but—"

"It's hard digging up old news like the Waverly scandal. Which by the way, your paper exonerated them to some extent. And now you want to attach a murder case to it?"

"But, Frank, she didn't kill herself. I know she didn't."

"You might be right, Sam, and I haven't quit on you either. I'll keep searching for clues, okay?"

"Okay, Frank. I'm depending on you, as Sonny's friend."

"That's fine, darlin'. I'll let you know as soon as I find out anything different. I gotta' run. Bernice is calling me."

As the evening waned, Brogan and his wife went home while Samantha and Bernice cleaned up, leaving their husband's in the backyard drinking their beers.

"You know, Sonny, one thing that I like about our backyard is that we see a lot of sky at night. And, my god! What a beautiful sky we have tonight. It's as if God painted the heavens with stars."

"It is amazing out tonight. Enya sings a beautiful song called; "Paint the Sky with Stars. Did you ever hear of it, Frank?"

"Enya?" Frank said, scratching his head. "Is that Tanya Tucker's sister?"

"Hell no, Frank. Tanya Tucker's shit-kickin' music! Enya is . . . you know, romance, poetry, with a little bit of a heavenly sound. Don't you have any romance in you, Frank?"

"Of course I do, Sonny. I take Bernice line-dancing every week, and hell, at times I even dance the two-step with her."

"Why, goddamn, you do have some romance in you after all, don't ya?"

"Hell yes. I even take my boots off when we make love."

"You're all class, Frank, all class," laughed Sonny.

"Hey, Sonny."

"What is it, Frank?"

"Your wife confronted me on that Jacobs's case tonight."

"So, what did you tell her?"

"I lied to her, Sonny. I had to."

"I figured as much, Frank."

"What do you mean?"

"Hell, Frank, a blind man could tell that was a mob hit. I don't want Samantha to get involved in all that as much as you don't want to."

"It's not me, Sonny. It's the captain, and he gets his orders from the police commissioner."

"And he probably gets his orders from Big John Taylor, right?"

"I didn't say that, Sonny."

"I know it, but you know as well as I do that if there is a syndicate in this town, then Big John runs it."

"That is the common belief around here, Sonny. My hands are tied, you know. Hell, I remember when I was a uniform cop I would have a liquid lunch everyday to stay in shape. I would have a Slim-Fast or a protein shake, so I would be ready to chase down the bad guys. After I got your job and all the frustration that went with it, I still had that liquid lunch, but it changed to beer, and then booze. I don't know how you did it for all those years, Sonny."

"It caught up with me in the end, Frank," said Sonny, patting his friend on the shoulder. "All I ever wanted was to raise my kids and make love to my wife, but the powers-that-be won't let me. I'm just trying to get out of this world alive, Frank."

"I'm afraid that won't happen for either of us, friend. The one thing that I always admired about you Raffertys is that you're always trying to save the world. That's also your downfall. To defeat the enemy you must play their game. You have to get ugly. You can't play by the rules. You can't walk that thin gray line like you do, Sonny. You have to match evil for evil. You have to crawl in mud, and that's too much of a price to pay. It is for me, I know, and I believe the same for you."

"Hey, Frank."

"What?"

"Let's pop open another beer. I feel like gettin' drunk tonight. What about you?"

"I'm already there, my friend. I'm already there."

There have been many women's organizations over the years,

especially since the burning of the bra movement in the '60's. Some were legit, some not. Some proposed to free women from the bonds of domesticity. Some wanted to change everything to a woman's viewpoint. After all, men have been running this world since day one.

The National Association of Women's Rights, Indiana chapter, had humble beginnings in a storefront building on the lower west side of town. Eventually they grew. After years of recruiting new members, they emerged atop the social climate in their push for equality. As with most good movements, they got infiltrated with people who represented a different agenda. Samantha was hoping to change that.

She brought Lisa Dawson to the meeting with her. She felt that she needed some support in her effort to win over Pat Fowler and her followers. The setting was much like a school board meeting with the officers sitting behind tables on a stage, and Fowler in the middle. There were at least a hundred fold-up chairs facing the stage with about 60 of them filled with ardent members, while she and Jitterbug occupied another two chairs.

Pat Fowler was a lesbian. That, in itself didn't bother Samantha, for she considered diversity in society as now the norm. Pat was quite the speaker though, which Samantha surmised was one reason for her rise to the top of the organization. The first part of the meeting was pretty mundane as the group went over their finances and the latest goings on and such. Pat then turned the meeting over to the floor and accepted questions and grievances.

Then, finally, Samantha's turn came as Pat Fowler addressed the print journalist, "Ms. Rafferty, you may now have the floor."

"As most of you know, I'm Samantha Rafferty, investigative reporter and editor for the Indianapolis Times newspaper. I have faxed to everyone on the committee an outline on what has transpired within the last year in our state's extended care facilities, particularly, Waverly Enterprises. We at the Times went head to head with the Waverly people to make changes in these facilities for better care for the patients. We made a lot of progress but our nursing industry, I'm afraid, is suffering from the changes."

"In what way, Ms. Rafferty?" questioned Fowler.

"In the past six months, 177 nurses have been fired or forced to retire from these facilities. In the last two years that number is a staggering 404 nurses. These are all board certified, professional people that we are talking about. My staff has also researched two other companies that own nursing homes in Indiana and have found the same disturbing trend in their facilities. We are now talking about 76 nursing homes and over five-thousand nurses being affected. These nurses are arbitrarily being replaced by lesser-skilled nurses from foreign countries at half the wages. The foreign nurses are brought into the United States by sponsors who charge these people half of what they earn. So you see, these foreign nurses make slave wages while our own people are being denied the right to earn a livable wage. Nurses are the most underpaid and overworked professionals in the United States. At the same time, corporations are crying broke to the government while stashing away Medicare payments into a clandestine parent company. We at the Times have exposed Waverly Corporation as far as we can without getting into litigation problems. Our concern now is with the nurses."

"I understand the plight of the nurses, Ms. Rafferty, but I fail to see where it is any concern of ours," said Fowler. "They sign contracts. If their contracts are breeched, they should litigate."

"That's all a myth. They are lured in by what they think is a contract, but it is non-binding in a court of law. So, when the worker does sue for breech of contract the case is thrown out before it even reaches the courts. In the meantime, the injured party loses large amounts of money on expensive attorney's fees."

"They could organize a union. Then they would have a contract," stated Fowler.

"They are constantly living under the fear of losing their jobs, and the consequences of getting caught trying to organize would be disastrous for them," said Samantha.

"Look, Ms. Rafferty, our organization is all about women's rights. You're talking about worker's rights."

"You're right. I am talking about worker's rights, and 90% of the workers that I talk about are women, professional women who are denied their rights!"

"Ms. Rafferty, why did you come to us for help? There are dozens of women's organizations around."

"I know that. I come to you because the NAWR is the largest women's rights organization in the nation. You have the money and you have a fine track record. I did some research on your organization and was myself quite impressed. Last year you took 166 sexual harassment cases to court and won over half. You acquired 160 more jobs for women in construction and 106 more for the police and fire departments. Hell, you even have it where a woman can nurse her baby in the firehouse. Now we can even take a year off for maternity leave. That's all great, Ms. Fowler, but most of those are just bones thrown your way by our government to protect business interests and to distract you from the real problems."

"What do you mean by that!" snapped Fowler.

"I mean corporate greed, for which the government allows loopholes for."

"Well, I'll tell you right now that we are not in the position to fight big business."

"That's not what I'm asking for."

"Then just what do you propose, Ms. Rafferty."

"Look, Indiana is a hire and fire 'at will' state. It should be a hire and fire with "just cause" state. But it's not, because the legislature won't pass a bill for it, because big business would be subjected to litigation from disgruntled employees. That would cut into their capitol and they would lose their control over the peons. We do live in a slave-minded society, still. What I propose is that we lobby the state and federal legislators to create a bill that requires all medical facilities to hire nurses by contract only. They are professionals and should be treated as such. All professional athletes have contracts, and I think the medical field is a little more important than men playing kids games. We should also push for congress to check into our immigration policies on the cheap slave labor that enters the United States, which undermines our standard of living. As you know, my brother, Chance Taylor, is running for the Senate. If we could help raise votes to elect him into office he would help us on the federal level."

"What's in it for us?" asked Fowler.

"I'm sure that we can give you some free publicity in our paper, plus, we will help raise money to support your organization to fight this cause. Just imagine, getting a bill like this passed for the largest group of women workers in the United States; what it would do for salaries. These women would indeed have some rights then. The NAWR would be the organization credited. Just picture how much stronger that would make you."

"I'm quite intrigued by your idea, Ms. Rafferty. On the surface it seems plausible. I'll get together with the committee and discuss this further among ourselves. We'll get back to you with an answer. If we do decide to take this on, I will have to be the one in charge."

"I have no problem with that," said Samantha. "Thank you for listening to me."

Samantha left feeling relieved that the ordeal was over, and Jitterbug assuring her that she presented herself well. They were both confident that they had the NAWR on board for the long haul. While exiting the building, Samantha ran into Eva Swenson, Angie's girlfriend.

"Why, Eva, fancy meeting you here. Are you a member of the NAWR?" asked Samantha awkwardly.

"I'm the Sergeant at Arms," she said with a glare.

"Is Angie a member too?"

"No, she isn't."

"By the way, how is Angie doing?"

"I wouldn't know. She left home after Candy's funeral and I haven't heard from her since. Maybe your husband knows. He and Angie seem to be quite tight with each other."

"Nah, they're just good friends, Eva. They have been for years," assured Samantha.

"It's more than that with Angie. I can tell. She knows about you hiding your infidelity from your husband, and she doesn't like it."

Samantha was stunned by the big Swede's revelation. "I beg your pardon. How do you know about that?"

"Angie told me that she overheard you telling your black friend all about it at Body Perfect. All I know is ever since he returned into her life again she has changed, and that is my business. You need to put a reign on your man and keep him out of my backyard. You ought to stay home a little more often, and then maybe your husband would lose his urge to roam." With that, Eva briskly walked away.

"Sam, what's she talking about?" asked Jitterbug.

"Aw, it's a long story. I don't want to get into it now. Let's just keep our focus on our job at hand. Shall we?"

"Okay, Samantha."

"Let's go eat, my treat."

Chapter Nineteen

Jamaica Red

The big Ford sedan cruised down the gravel road churning up the limestone into a long, billowy cloud of dust as it reacquainted itself with the likes of Rattlesnake Highway. Things were starting to become familiar to Sonny, the wind in the road, the silvery corn in the moonlight, and then the wooded rolling hills. He felt that he had seen all of this before, though he wasn't sure when, but it had to have been on that fateful night after leaving Centralia and Peggy Sue. He remembered Peggy Sue, and he remembered mostly what she was about, warmth, love, and need. Those things you don't forget about. It's the wickedness of the world that a man tends to hide in the deep recesses of his mind.

For six years the ghosts of J. R. and Mindy had let him be. But a previously unknown entity now haunted Sonny from the grave. That entity was Ray Jenkins. Peggy didn't have to tell Sonny about Jenkins, but she did. Why did she do it? He didn't know. That answer lies beyond anyone's grasp.

As Sonny closed in on the Bone Yard, he peered into his rearview mirror like a vainglorious woman in pursuit of the perfect look. He searched meticulously for flaws in his makeover. He couldn't afford any slip-ups again, not this time. He was too close to finding the right answers, the answers that Big John was hiding from him and Samantha. And he had to find Candy's killer. He owed her that much for saving his life while losing hers in return. And he owed Angie.

When Sonny crested the hill the Bone Yard came into view, sticking out in the night like a 300 pound French whore at a church picnic. She wasn't pretty but she stood out. Sonny parked his car near the entrance to the Devil's Lair. He noticed that the Lair had a sentry guarding the entrance, a big guy, Buddha-like in physique.

Sonny made it past the big Buddha all right, by giving his fictitious counterpart's name and showing a fake ID. He walked right into the foyer and they sat him down in a deep-cushioned settee. Jamaica Red was right. It was quite an extravaganza. Where Sonny sat, it looked like the inside of a casino, brightly lit with rich carpeting, and having a noisy party atmosphere about it.

The sound that filled the room was that of loud and boisterous men, along with the sound of women who had the giggle of little girls in their voices while pleasing their male companions in a variety of ways.

Sonny stroked his beard nervously, hoping no one would recognize him in his thin disguise. He was assured by Jaques LeBlanc that only someone that knew him well would be able to detect his true identity.

A yellow-haired girl appeared supporting a serving tray atop her shoulder that held a complimentary whiskey sour for Sonny. She was naked except for a bright colored sarong around her waist. Her freckled body showed her being the outdoor type, if not now, a short time ago. She wasn't beautiful but she was pretty, a natural pretty that required no make-up. She had one thing that was unique about her that most people wouldn't covet. She had only one arm. "Hello, Johnny, welcome to the Devil's Lair. My name is Suncerie. Most people call me Sunny," she said through a smile. "I'm your hostess for tonight. I have for you a complimentary drink. If you do not like it I will exchange it for another, on the house."

"Thanks, darlin', this will be fine," he said, taking the beverage from her tray. While doing so he noticed a sniffling of her nose. "You better put on some clothes, dear. It seems like you might be coming down with something," he said to her.

"Oh, I'm alright, Johnny. It's the smoke in here. I'm allergic to it."

"Sonny knew better. He had witnessed this too many times before, years ago with Genevieve. Both she and Genevieve were young, blonde, and had a passion for the white powder. They both had that distant look in their eyes. He wondered what her story was. He glanced at the stub where her right arm used to be, and figured that to be part of it.

"I'm sad to say that Jamaica Red has been delayed for awhile. I am to entertain you until she's ready. She told me to tell you that she regrets the delay and that she is paying for your bar-tab tonight. So help yourself," said the waitress.

"So, what's the delay?" asked Sonny.

Suncerie sat down by Sonny and leaned her face toward his and whispered, "I'm not supposed to say anything but we had a couple of limos of Japanese customers arrive unexpectedly tonight, and they have first priority because they pay twice as much as everyone else. Quite frankly, Jamaica Red is pissed at the boss. She doesn't like anybody messin' with her schedule."

"My job tonight is to get you ready for Jamaica Red, and she demands a lot. So, why don't you walk around the Lair and check out our little casino here, and see if any of these games of chance interest you. If they do you can buy your chips at the finance window around the corner. The poker games are in the back rooms, but they're all filled up tonight."

"I'm not really interested in gambling tonight, darlin'"

"Well, follow me then," she said, leading him into the den of voices. "Do you see that red curtain on the far side of the room, Johnny?"

"Yeah, I see it."

"I want you to go on over there and sit yourself down on the bench behind that curtain. I'll freshen your drink, and when I return I'll show you how a one-armed broad can lap dance."

Suncerie loosened the sarong and let it fall to the floor, and just as quickly stepped out of her scanty briefs joining in the rhythm of the music. She was built like a swimmer. She had a wide chest, with no mounds to speak of, and her taut belly funneled down nicely between her narrow hips into a sparse, corn-silk valley. With his hands held firmly around her waist, Suncerie did the bump-and-grind in Johnny's lap until she awakened his manhood. She then turned around and rhythmically fed him her gold nuggets just long enough for a tease, causing even greater passion between the two of them. As he nibbled, she moaned, a low moan, not from her throat but from deep inside. Soon she was gleaming in sweat with her chest heaving deep and fast. Sonny reached down and felt between her succulent tenderloins, causing the surfer girl to release her passion and collapse into his arms.

"I'm sorry, Johnny, that wasn't supposed to happen," she said, weakly. "I don't know what came over me."

"Not bad for a one arm broad," he teased.

Suncerie checked her watch, realizing it was time to go upstairs to assist Jamaica Red in setting things up for her next customer, Johnny Carlisle.

That was fine with Sonny. It gave him time to investigate the joint. He wanted to get a layout of the building, just in case. He learned from early on in his investigative career that you're better off getting too much information than too little. He knew by now that nobody in the room recognized him. So either his disguise was working or maybe he hadn't met everybody yet. While searching the room he noticed a door leading to what he presumed was the Bone Yard. He didn't notice anyone going in or out of it so he looked around to see if anyone was watching. He opened the door slightly and slid through it.

It was quite a transformation going from the rich, plush Devil's Lair to the Bone Yard. The Bone Yard was more of a honky-tonk, filled with a mélange of young rednecks, bikers and wanton women. The dress code there consisted of jeans and a tee-shirt with any kind of stupid saying on it. Sonny found an opening at the bar and quickly slid into it, trying not to draw too much attention since he did stick out somewhat.

"What'll ya have, mister?" asked the bartender.

"I'll have a beer on draft," said Sonny.

"Say, you seem out of place in here. Did you come over from the Lair?"

"Yeah, I snuck through the side door. Is there something wrong with that?"

"It don't matter to me, mister, but I ought to warn you that some of these boys in here don't care too much for strangers. I don't want anybody startin' anything. The last time we had a fight in here it got pretty nasty. We had to shut the place down for a week to clean up the mess."

"Don't worry, I'll leave right after I have a beer," said Sonny.

"Let me know when you want to leave, stranger, because that door locks from the other side. I'll have to unlock it for you to get back into the Lair."

"Okay, Mack."

Sonny looked around to see what was going on. On the stool to his right was a young man with dirty blonde hair sticking out from under a NASCAR baseball cap. He was laying a line on a long-nosed girl in a short leather skirt, hiked up damn near to her waist. She was swiveling back and forth on her stool, showing off the white crotch of her panties to the boy, and to Sonny.

"That'll be two bucks, mister," said Tommy Mack, snatching Sonny's concentration from the girl's Venus triangle.

Sonny gave him three and then grabbed the cool glass of beer. "What about me?" shot the voice of a haggardly old woman sitting to his left. Sonny looked curiously at the woman.

"Now, Thelma, what did I tell you about begging from the customers? Guess I'll have to kick you out again," said the bartender.

"I'm sorry, Tommy. I wasn't cussin' or yellin' or nothin' like that," she said, lowering her eyes.

The ol' gal smelled of piss and body odor, but for some strange reason Sonny felt compelled to buy her a drink. "Go ahead and get her one, barkeep. I'll pay for it," he said.

"Are you sure, mister?"

"Yeah, no problem," said Sonny.

Tommy gave Thelma *that* look and poured her a double-vodka.

Suddenly, a playful couple accidentally fell up against Sonny's backside. "Hey, watch it, you guys. You almost made me spill my beer," warned Sonny.

"I'm sorry, man," apologized the big-eared fellow.

"Nabob, you go in and wait for me in the men's room," insisted the little hellcat that was with him.

"But, Lori, what do I do until you come?"

"Geezus, Nabob, take it out and play with it if you want. I don't care. I'll be there shortly to finish it for ya." She then put one arm around Sonny's neck, and with the other, grabbed his crotch. "Hey, big fella', you came in from the Lair, didn't you?"

"Yes I did," said Sonny politely.

"They're quite expensive on the other side, aren't they?"

"I guess they are."

"Look, baby, I can do you better. For two bills I'll spend the weekend with ya as your own personal sex slave. I'll do anything you want and anyway you want to do it. And I'm clean. I just got checked out three days ago."

"Nah, not today, thanks."

"Just let me go take care of Nabob first, then I'll come back and we can leave. How about it big guy? I'd like to try out that big tool of yours," she kept on.

"Not tonight, darlin', I've got a date with Jamaica Red."

"Jamaica Red, shit, I'm better than that bitch, and a hell of a lot cheaper," bragged Lori.

"No doubt, but I'm already committed for tonight."

"Suit yourself," snapped Lori, walking away in a huff.

Sonny went back to drinking his beer, feeling an odd familiarity towards the little slut.

"**The Indian has your hat,**" said Thelma, giving Sonny a quick glance.

Sonny wasn't sure that he heard her right. "Did you say something?" he asked back.

"I said the Indian is wearing your hat."

"I have no idea what you're talking about, Thelma. What Indian?"

Thelma pointed over her shoulder, "The Indian that guards the record machine," she said soberly.

Sonny got up and walked back a ways, and sure enough, around the corner sat the juke-box with an old cigar-store Indian standing beside it, and Sonny's brown fedora sittin' on his head. Damn, thought Sonny. This is the place. This is the fuckin' place that I got my ass kicked. And that's Daddy's hat, but I sure can't take it, not now. Hell, knowing these people, that Indian's probably some kind of God or something to them. Sonny was worried now. If that old barfly of a woman knew who he was, how many more people would find him out? He quickly returned to his seat and leaned in close to Thelma, "How do you know that's my hat, Thelma?"

"I saw them take it from you," she replied.

"How did you know it was me?"

Thelma smiled a little and showed Sonny her empty vodka glass. "Sure, sure," said Sonny hastily. "Hey bartender," he yelled, "another double-vodka over here please. So go on Thelma, tell me. How did you know it was me?"

"Your name is Sonny Rafferty, isn't it?"

"Shhhhh! Not so loud, Thelma, please. How did you know my name?" Sonny whispered.

"I got it from the grave."

"You what?" said Sonny.

"I got it from the grave. You killed my kids. You know that."

"Who told you that I killed your kids?"

"My husband told me."

Sonny hesitated while frantically searching through his mind. He then carefully asked, "Thelma, who is your husband?"

"Ray Jenkins."

Sonny's blood chilled with his mind scattering in all directions.

"I must go now," said Thelma. "No, you can't go, Thelma! I need to talk to you some more," stressed Sonny.

"No, I can't stay. I must leave you, and you mustn't follow me."

"Tell me, Thelma, when will you be back?"

"I can't say, but I must go now. Do not follow me," she said sternly. With that, the old woman got up and walked out the door.

"Hey, barkeep, I'm ready to go. Let me out of here!" shouted Sonny, somewhat shaken by Thelma's revelations.

Sonny was hoping to find Suncerie waiting for him in the Devil's Lair, but she wasn't there upon his return, so he opted for the small cash bar to get himself a free drink, compliments of Jamaica Red. When Sonny reached the bar he waited in line behind a club waitress who was clad only in a white thong that disappeared deep into her fabulous round ass. She was about Sonny's height in her super-high heels and had rich brown hair reaching to the middle of her back, reminding him of Angie.

When her order was filled by the bartender, the brunette picked up her tray and turned around.

"Angie!"

"Sonny!" she said startled. "Is that really you, Sonny?"

"Hell yes, it's me, but what the fuck are you doing here?" he snapped.

Angie's look of surprise turned into a false coolness. "What's it look like, I'm having a drink with my friends. Look, Sonny, I've got a handle on things here. Why don't you go back home to your wife and family, I can take care of myself. I'm a big girl now."

"I've got to talk to you, Angie."

"I can't, I've got friends waiting for me at the blackjack table."

"I can't let you go. I've got to talk with you now," insisted Sonny, grabbing her wrists.

"Don't do this, Sonny. You'll get us both in trouble. Don't you know there are eyes everywhere in this room watching us right now?"

"I don't care. I'm not going to let you do this to yourself."

Suddenly, out of nowhere a large man in a black suit grabbed Sonny by the back of his jacket collar. "Is this man bothering you, Lana?" he said gruffly.

Sonny made no attempt to resist, or to say anything for that matter, because he could automatically tell from the man's grip and the fact that he himself was on his tiptoes, that the big guy, at the moment, had the upper hand on him.

"No, Champ, he's not bothering me, really. We were just discussing a lap dance that I owe him. As a matter-of-fact, as soon as I deliver these drinks I'm going to pay up. Isn't that right, mister—"

"Carlisle, Johnny Carlisle," said Sonny.

"I'll meet you in the red room, Mr. Carlisle," she said putting on a smile.

As Angie left to deliver her drinks the bouncer released Sonny and warned him, "I'm watching you, mister, and I don't like you. So don't fuck up, hear!"

"I understand, Champ. You won't have anymore problems with me," said Sonny, pulling on his cuffs to straighten out his ruffled suit.

Sonny had never seen Angie in all of her naked grandeur. Oh, she had flirted with him plenty, and if he would have shown just a little passion toward her she would have bedded down with him easily. It didn't matter to her whether Sonny was married or not either. Hell, she knew Samantha's deep dark secret that Sonny didn't know about. She could ruin their marriage anytime she wanted now by exposing that secret. But she hadn't thus far. Why? She didn't really know, herself. It was probably because Candy had been her main concentration since her recent connection with Sonny. Or maybe it was because she had too much respect for Sonny to divulge to him his scarlet woman's affair.

Never-the-less, Angie stepped out of her meager panty and bared herself to the man she had always longed for. She bent over and mashed her soft pillows into Sonny's face.

Even in her naked womanhood, Angie was still a little girl to Sonny, and he was still just a wild dream of hers. The closest that he had been tempted into infidelity, up till now, was with Peggy Sue, but she was just a figment of his imagination as far as Sonny was concerned. Sonny's plan was beginning to unravel. What the fuck is she doing here? She'll ruin everything! thought Sonny. He grabbed her by the waist and pushed her from him. "I can't do this, honey. I just can't." he said. "It's all wrong for us."

"I understand, Sonny. I don't blame you, but don't blame me either. I can't help how I feel about you."

Sonny began helping Angie back into her thong. As she held onto his shoulder he noticed a couple of red marks on the inside of her arm that seemed familiar to him. He grabbed her arm and straightened it out and commenced rubbing off the taupe-colored make-up. "Goddamn it, Angie. Are you doing smack again?"

"No, I'm not doing drugs, baby. You know that."

"Bullshit! You've got the needle tracks right there in your arm for chrissake!"

"You're not in charge of me anymore, Sonny. I came here to take care of business, and you're not going to stop me!"

"It's just that, it's just that I can't bear to see you like this again, honey. You've worked so hard to get away from all of this. Don't throw your life away. I'm begging you."

"You're too late, Sonny. I just finished servicing four men at the same time just before you showed up. I'm out there now, baby, way out there, and I'm not coming back until Candy's killer is in hell!"

"Listen. Listen to me carefully now. I'll avenge her death for you, sweetheart. I promise. Just give me one more day, Angie; just one more day to find the murderer. You don't want to ruin your life like this. I'm experienced at revenge. Trust me, how about it?"

"I've got to spend tonight and tomorrow with this Japanese fella'."

"Forget about him and leave now," insisted Sonny.

"I can't Sonny. He's already paid for it. Besides, what's one more blow-job more or less at this stage of the game?"

"Okay, but tell me, where are you going to be after you finish up tomorrow?"

"I've been staying with Tracy, in Newport."

"All right, wait for me there Monday morning. Okay?"

"I'll be there waiting, Sonny."

"Angie, have you found out any information that might help in finding the killer?"

"No, Sonny, I haven't," lied Angie, "I've only been working here a week."

"Okay, darlin', but watch yourself. And stay off the horse, okay!"

"Sure, Sonny, I won't do anymore smack."

Sonny and Angie embrace, with Angie heading back toward her friends under the guise of Lana Darrah, and Sonny slipping through the curtain where he was met by the one-armed surfer-girl.

"Why, Johnny, you've been cheating on me. I'm supposed to watch after you. You didn't waste yourself on the likes of her, did you? Jamaica Red would really be pissed at me if you came to her depleted, you know."

"Don't worry, darlin', I've got enough to go around," said Sonny, still thinking about Angie.

"Well, come on then. You're in for the ride of your life," she said excitedly.

Suncerie led Sonny upstairs to a room called "The Lion's Den."

"Why is it called the lion's den?" asked Sonny.

"It's Jamaica Red's doing. You see, in the lion kingdom the female is the fierce hunter of the species. The large-mane male struts around, roars, and flaunts himself until the lioness gets home with his meal. He then succumbs to her. It's quite an ironic twist of nature, what with the male being the pussy and the pussy taking on the male persona. Jamaica likes that."

Suncere opened the door, leading Sonny into a large, darkened room that featured a small stage at one end. There were lots of large plants along the walls, and the air was heavy with humidity, giving it a jungle atmosphere. Suncerie then directed Sonny to a black, high-backed chair that swiveled. She helped him take his jacket off and then removed his shoes. It was when she pulled on his belt buckle that he balked.

"Whoa, wait a minute there, darlin'. What are you up to?" he asked, grabbing her hand.

Suncerie became a bit confused at Sonny's trepid response to her fondling. "But Johnny, I'm just preparing you for Jamaica Red's session," she said.

"Why you?" he asked.

"Because I'm her buff girl, silly; don't worry, it's my job."

"Buff girl? I don't get it."

"I've got to get you standing tall for Jamaica Red. She requires it.

Besides, as soon as you're ready, you'll be rid of me."

"Oh no, we're not having any of that, sister. Look, you're younger looking than my own daughter, and I already feel guilty enough about our previous encounter with the lap dance."

"Okay, Johnny, suite yourself, but she ain't gonna like it."

"You let me worry about her, darlin'. You just skitter for now."

As Sonny released her wrist, she fell away and the room suddenly went pitch black. It became quiet. A nervous quiet, like when you think someone's watching you but you can't tell for sure. Then suddenly, from out of nowhere came this hissing sound, as from a snake, or a strange ground creature of some kind. It sounded far away at the beginning, but crept closer and closer until the sibilant serpent slithered its way up to Sonny's face. Sonny's mouth turned to cotton as he wanted to seek Suncerie but couldn't. It wasn't that Sonny scared easily, because he didn't. It was just that this hideous hissing sound sent chills up his spine. It was a beyond the grave type of sound. Up till now the night had already become quite bazaar, but this went beyond that limit, thought Sonny. Then a voice cut through the stillness as the fragrance of jasmine filled the air.

"Hey, lover, what gives? Don't you like my girl Friday?"

The sharpness in her voice caused Sonny to jerk his head back. Jamaica Red was so close that he could feel the hotness of her breath against his face. There was not physical contact, just the heat from her breath. Sonny's rods and cones searched desperately for some kind of light so he could focus on this strange entity that lurked before him. He could barely make out the dark outline of the mysterious image that confronted him.

"I was under the impression that I had a date with Jamaica Red tonight, not some unbridled, young surfer girl not yet old enough to support breasts," he bravely responded.

"You amuse me, Johnny Carlisle. Most men would love to have a young ingénue such as Suncerie service them in some fashion. Let me assure you that she is of age, and I think that you ought not to be so shallow as to let the size of a woman's breasts deter you from sexual gratification. What is it Johnny, is it because she has only one arm?"

"No, that's not it. It's just that I have a daughter that looks older than her, and that makes me feel very uncomfortable," admitted Sonny.

"That's even more amusing, Johnny. You seemed to have had no problem ramming your fingers into that young girl's honey pot earlier tonight," chided the voice from the darkness.

Sonny was stunned by Red's knowledge of him.

"See, I know about your hidden reserves of sensuality, Johnny."

"You know, it would help me immensely if I could see your face," complained Sonny.

With a snap of her fingers a light flashed and flashed and flashed, exposing to Sonny a horrific face! Jamaica Red fell back into a slow, rhythmic dance. As the strobe light splashed against her face, Sonny realized that she was wearing a macabre mask, the dance of death face. At the same time music filled the room. The sound was familiar to Sonny, though he couldn't quite make out the song. It was a Carlos Santana tune, he thought. "I like your style of music," he said through the bright flashes of light.

Every movement that Jamaica Red made in that strobe seemed magnified and spasmodic. As she swayed to the sound of the music she looked as if she was dancing vigorously. When the song ended, she ceased dancing and came face to face with Sonny while leaning on his thighs, burying her two exaggerated points into his chest. Though she still wore the hideous mask, her voice seemed very enticing, almost hypnotic.

"Do you wish to spoil my routine, handsome?"

"No, not really," he said.

"Then don't."

"But Jamaica Red, I didn't really come here for sex. I just wanted to talk with you about something very important."

"Sex!" she exclaimed, "You go to whores for sex! You come to me for a love session. Do you understand?"

Sonny was a bit taken aback by the wild-woman's fierce tirade. She emitted a charge of energy that he'd never seen in a woman before.

"By the way, you can just call me Jamaica, and I'll call you Johnny," she said in a more forgiving tone.

"I apologize, Jamaica, but I don't really mess around on my wife, you see."

"And, your wife?" she asked.

"No, she doesn't cheat on me either."

"Never?" she asked.

"No, never," insisted Sonny.

"I can't believe that you, or your wife, haven't tasted some of the good life by now, my big handsome one. You ought to be on the endangered species list."

"It may seem a little archaic to you, but it works for my wife and me."

"You know they call me the human vacuum, don't you? When I wrap my legs around you I can suck your sexual life-force right out of you in a matter of minutes."

"I don't doubt that one bit, but I'm committed to this love thing, you know. Thanks for your generous offer though."

"Don't thank me. You paid for it," said Jamaica.

"I would just disappoint you," said Sonny.

"What do you mean big guy? You've already got me wet between my legs from anticipation." She slowly slid her hands up Sonny's thighs. "Hey, is that a pistol in your pocket?"

"I don't carry a gun," said Sonny, tensing from her touch.

"You could have fooled me. It feels like a magnum 44. I lo-o-o-v-e that long-barreled 44," she moaned. "It shoots big bullets. I like a lot of lead in my lovemaking, I like it when the barrel gets hot, real hot," she said in a soft, sultry tone. "Look, Johnny, you just sit back and relax. I'll play some Santana. You like him, right?"

"Yeah, I like Santana, but how did you come to like him, Jamaica?"

"Oh, Johnny, he plays my music. He plays to my soul. I'm half African and half Polynesian, you know. I grew up in Rio and Jamaica where Samba became my trademark dance. I add a little African twist to it of course," she said as the lights stopped flashing and Santana's "Europa" filled the air. "I just love Carlos Santana."

For some reason, unbeknownst to Sonny, the room became a lighter shade of darkness. Jamaica Red slipped off her mask and nuzzled up to Sonny to the weeping sound of Santana's guitar. Sonny couldn't fight the feeling any longer and kissed on her long, slender neck. It tasted to him as sweet as the redolence of the jasmine that filled the air. Even in the darkness Sonny could see Jamaica Red's nostrils flare open and then close, and do the same again, and again, as her breathing became heavier with each moment in their lustful embrace. Then, Jamaica broke away for a moment to inhale on a strange pipe that appeared out of the darkness, and then turned back to Sonny and kissed him open-mouthed, forcing the narcotic deep into his lungs, followed by her own serpent-like organ. My God, she has the tongue of a snake, thought Sonny. She repeated this little venture several more times until Sonny was in the same euphoric state that she was in. Red knew that she had tricked him good, and she felt a bit sad about it because she liked him. She liked what he was made of on the inside. She also knew that he wasn't who he said he was. He could disguise his face but he couldn't disguise his voice. She was also interested in what he had to say, since the guy went through so much to speak with her.

Jamaica broke away from their necking, "Listen to me, Johnny. I'm gonna do my dance of death first, then the scorpion's dance, and then the scorpion's sting. That'll be the first half of my routine. Then we'll take some champagne and hit the hot-tub until we get our sea-legs back. After that, we're supposed to make love to your satisfaction, but since you want to talk, we'll talk. Talk for the rest of the night if you want because you're my last customer, and I like being with you, big guy. Is that okay with you?"

"That's okay with me," said Sonny, still in his opium stupor.

Jamaica Red disappeared to the small stage while Sonny sat relaxed without the realization that Suncerie was working feverishly below, bringing him to life to face the scorpion's sting. The spotlight shined brightly on Red as she entered the stage in full African regalia. A superimposed hologram of her was plastered on the wall behind her with laser lights shooting in every direction. Santana's, "Jingo" was her song of choice for her dance of death.

She was tall, and looked even taller in her African headdress, while sporting an array of gold bangles along her arms and ankles. She danced to the conga drums as wildly as her lithe, copper-toned body would allow. Her breasts were adorned with exaggerated gold cones while her writhing middle was covered only with a girdle made of gold chain links. She moved around the room screaming like a banshee until finally stopping in front of Sonny at song's end. She then retreated back behind the stage curtain. Next, came the scorpion dance, to "Black Magic Woman."

Jamaica Red stripped off her gold cones, revealing her own deep-crowned breasts, the most perfectly formed breasts that Sonny had ever seen. They were so supple, they had no sag, and protruded out almost as far as their gold coverings did earlier, or so it seemed. She worked her way up to Sonny and then dropped her girdle of gold, showing off her deep-ridged belly above a slick shiny valley that funneled to the deep crevasse that lay between two of the longest and sleekest legs that he had ever seen on a woman. Her labia splayed like a corolla, with several gold rings hanging from each lobe.

The possessed Jamaica Red then stared passionately at Sonny's package while showing off hers, and then declared, "I am the Amazon woman, the African queen, a Mayan goddess, and a Polynesian princess all rolled into one." At the same time, the music changed to a song appropriately titled, "Open Invitation", drawing Jamaica Red into a deep backbend. She then began a human phenomenon that Sonny had seen only once before in a circus type act performed by young Chinese girls. Ever-so-slowly Jamaica bent backwards, further and further underneath herself, opening herself wide, forcing her head and shoulders through her legs, and then raising her face to meet Sonny's stare while obscuring the gold piercings of her gaped love canal. It was a feat that only the supplest of being could perform, as she resembled a crustacean from some far-off island. Then, with the high-pitched cry of Santana's guitar, the alluring temptress crab-walked up to Sonny's rigid protuberance and flicked her long tongue along its sensitive underside, causing it to spurt forth a stream of passion-juice with a force that he hadn't felt since his boyhood. That was the scorpion's sting. Love session one was over.

Jamaica Red still had Sonny's glaze on her when they both eased into the hot-tub. Sonny relaxed in the warm water allowing his narcotic high to wear off. The salubrious Suncerie soon joined them. She looked like a little cygnet with her short-cropped hair, as she floated around, observing both Sonny and Jamaica Red, ready to service any request that they asked of her. She was innocent looking yet she was a veteran, conditioned by the harshness that life dealt out. Yet the one-armed girl seemed happy, even contented with what she was now about. One could say the same about Venus De Milo.

The high-ended Jamaica Red, on the other hand, seemed to glow in the water like a sea nymph, with her two large buoys holding her afloat. Her rich, black hair and unblemished face shimmered in the light, matching a diamond tiara on her head with a sparkling necklace of the same around her neck.

The warm water felt soothing to Sonny's body. The jet streams felt invigorating, but not nearly as exciting as the two lovelies that floated around with him in the over-sized tub. The drugs were wearing off, and he didn't need any help coming to life again.

The almond-eyed enchantress eased over to her peculiar male friend. She had never known a man to come to the Lion's Den and not take advantage of what she had to offer. Sonny was an enigma to her, but she liked the challenge of trying to figure him out. She was smart that way and had more than enough physical attributes to pull a man out of his vagaries. She knew who Johnny was. He was a different breed, a junkyard dog, fightin' for seconds his whole life, and he had the scars to prove it. She knew he wanted to talk, and she knew that he carried bad news with him. She could see it in his demeanor.

"I think I know why you're here, Johnny," she said. "I know that you're not Johnny Carlisle, but instead, Sonny Rafferty, a private dick from Indianapolis."

"How did you find out," Sonny asked. "Was it my disguise?"

"No, not really; I knew you'd come back. You're the chosen one. But why me?" said Red. "I'm just one of the many whores of Babylon."

"No, you're much more than that, Jamaica. You're a woman of substance, and that's why I'm here. I need some information on a friend of mine, Candy Garza, Candy Adams to you."

"Why? Has anything happened to her? Is she in any trouble?"

"It's worse than that. Candy's dead," said Sonny.

"Candy's dead, my little Candy? No, you're lying to me Sonny!" cried Red.

"No, I'm afraid it's true, Jamaica. She was brutally murdered in her home by some knife-wielding maniac. I discovered her decapitated body in a pool of blood in her living room. I found her head sittin' in a plate of potatoes on her kitchen table."

The beautiful courtesan gasped with fear as sheer horror crept across her face. "Why? Who would do such a thing?" she asked in disbelief.

"I was hoping that you could help me find that answer. You were her friend, I hear."

"We were more than friends. We were lovers," she said sadly. "It's got to be Pergosi. I knew something was up. I hate that son-of-a-bitch!" she declared.

"Why would Pergosi want to see one of his girls dead?"

"Because she broke one of his goddamn rules; she called the cops and saved your life. That's why. Hell, she wasn't even supposed to be on the other side of the wall that night, but I sent her over there for some champagne. It's my own fault that she's dead."

"No it's not your fault, Jamaica. If it's anybody's fault that she's dead it's mine. I shouldn't have been here that night. Tell me, darlin', what do you know about the fight? I, myself can't remember much from that night. I still have amnesia from where somebody knocked me in the head."

"From what Candy told me, a local whore by the name of Lori Burns started a fight between a stranger and her boyfriend, Harlan Tweeter and his derelict friends. That stranger was you."

"I think I ran into Lori already tonight. I slipped into the Bone Yard earlier to see if I could remember anything. Say, do you know a woman by the name of Thelma Jenkins? She seems to know a lot about me, but I don't know her very well."

"Stay away from Thelma Jenkins, Sonny. She's no good. Some people think she's a witch. They say she can put a voodoo curse on you. I think she's just a woman that's done something evil in her past and has been walking around in her own private hell ever since. There have been bar fights at the Bone Yard before, but not to the magnitude of that night. I was at the roulette wheel with Pergosi and Chance Taylor that night. When the ruckus got too loud they decided to check it out. Of course, I went with them since I was Chance's date."

"Chance Taylor? He's my wife's brother! What's he doing down here?"

"He's been doing me, mostly. So, you're Big John's son-in-law. This is a small world after all," said Jamaica, somewhat astonished.

"How do you know of Big John?"

"He's Pergosi's boss. Big John is also Miramar."

"You're kidding! How do you know so much about Big John?"

"I've known Big John for years. He helped me get into the escort business, and then this. I was his mistress back when I was working as a model. I was just 19 at the time. He became my sugar daddy. Now I do his son. He's nothing like his daddy."

"So Big John is Miramar Corporation. What all do you know about that?"

"I usually don't bite the hand that feeds me, but if it helps find Candy's killer, I don't care anymore," said Jamaica. "The Devil's Bone

Yard isn't Big John's only venture. He runs six more of these houses throughout the state. The reason I know that is because I've worked at them at one time or another. See, the Devil's Lair isn't my home. Hell, I wouldn't live in this little jerkwater town of Scoville for anything. I'm a call-girl by trade. I work where the money is, and where prostitution is hidden from the law. That used to be here until you showed up. I always felt that John Taylor was just a player in a much bigger picture. Just to ease my curiosity, one day I tried to find out, but the information on Miramar was locked out and I don't have the password."

"I'm beginning to get the picture now, darlin'. The local cops must've been paid off to leave the Bone Yard alone, but because of the phone call from Candy they showed up. That's bad for business. I don't think Pergosi killed Candy. He's too high up on the ladder. He must've ordered one of his henchmen to do it. Who does he have that's loyal to him?"

"Well, most of the casino workers are locals. His bouncers come courtesy of the Indiana Chapter of the Devil's Disciples. There could be some killers in that bunch, Sonny."

"I don't think so. I doubt that a mob guy like Pergosi would put his trust in someone like the Devil's Disciples gang to pull off a hit like this. The Cincinnati police matched fingerprints to a Tom Slattery or a Tommy Slats. He's affiliated with the Chicago Irish mob. His profile fits the bartender downstairs at the Bone Yard.

"Tommy Mack? No, couldn't have been him. He and Candy hit it off big. She really liked him, and I think he liked her. Candy used to talk about him a lot."

"Didn't that bother you?"

"No, that didn't bother me at all. I said that we were lovers; not married."

"Do you know if she had sexual relations with the man?"

"Boy, you are sounding like a detective now. I'm pretty sure they didn't have sex. He knew that she was sleeping with me, plus he had this hang-up about not screwing the working girls. He was always nice to the girls though. He didn't like me much, but that was because I was screwing Candy. Even the sluts that worked the other side get along well with Tommy Mack."

"So have the cops been cracking down on this place any?"

"What cops? Ever since that night there hasn't been any law

enforcement around. The sheriff disappeared, and his deputy is too despondent to be of any use. It was the deputy that saved your life, Sonny. I remember you lying there half dead and Chance goading the Burn's girl to finish you off with a knife that she had. She was just about to do it when the deputy appeared. He was just a little skinny fella'; scared shitless too. Pergosi was getting ready to plug him. That's when Sheriff Mullins arrived on the scene. He arrested both Chance and Miles, but Big John got them both out the next day. The same day that Mullins disappeared. They must've gotten to the deputy too. No one's heard a peep from him since."

"What's the deputy's name?"

"Zeke Doughtry, why, do you plan on looking him up?"

"I just might give him a visit. Do you know where might I find him?"

"You might find him at the county jail. If not there, he lives at Bryantsburg, just on the outskirts of town."

"Say, darlin', what about Chance, do you think he could be involved in any of this?"

"That pencil-dick doesn't have balls enough, Sonny. I ought to know, I've been his woman on many occasions. He's a real loser. But he likes to spend his daddy's money. That's why I stay with him. Pergosi's the one you want. He's no good Sonny. You just leave him to me. I'll take care of him. I owe him."

"How's that?" asked Sonny.

"He's a control freak. I don't like the way he treats the new girls. He's such a cold bastard. He just hired a new Hispanic girl. She's a very nice girl, keeps to herself and all. Get this. He has her come up to his office every day at noon to perform oral sex on him while he eats his lunch. I would've told him to go to hell, but she says that she needs the money, so she puts up with him. I want to see him go down!"

A frightened Suncerie quickly floated over to Jamaica Red, as the strong words of the one she loved was scaring her. She nuzzled up against Jamaica's breasts, finding the needed security that she sought.

"Listen to me, Jamaica. Don't lose your head and get carried away. I know you're a strong woman and all, but let me take care of Pergosi. You keep doing what you're good at doll; making men happy," said Sonny.

Sonny felt a kinship with the two girls. He didn't know if it was from their newfound friendships or the job that lay before him. He didn't want to leave the warmth of the jet tub just yet, but he did. He bid the ladies farewell and let himself out, for they were deeply involved with each other's lust.

They were all caught up in the trappings of life. Tonight, three friends unselfishly shared each other. The land of the lioness can be very amusing.

Chapter Twenty

Flight of the Wrecking Ball

Samantha Rafferty was awakened by the incessant hissing of the jet spray from the shower at the far end of her boudoir. She could only perceive that it was Sonny, for she also heard the bluesy sound of Clapton's guitar escaping through the bathroom door. She glanced at the clock and it read 12:04, just after noon. Samantha didn't know what time Sonny got in that morning but it was quite late, for she was up late herself, watching Bogart and Bacall. Never-the-less she was asleep long before her wayward husband returned home. But she remembered feeling his warmth up against her back sometime during her slumber. She reached over and felt now the warm spot where he once lay, for her reassurance. Samantha slipped out of bed and entered into their bath. The room felt hot and sultry, like a Tennessee Williams play. She fixed her eyes on the naked body behind the foggy glass. Sonny was leaning forward with his head down in thought, letting the harsh spray massage his neck and back. Samantha was drawn to his raw nakedness. She let her chiffon peignoir drop to the floor and slid in behind the well-worn but well-formed body of her husband and lover. She leaned into him, pressing her breasts against his back while enjoying the warm spray of water against her face. Sonny didn't move. He just stayed in his fixed position, his mind far away. Samantha had seen him like this many times before, but this time it felt different to her. She sensed that he wasn't just meditating, or searching for his lost memory, but was instead, scoping out his itinerary for the day; maybe the rest of his life. She couldn't tell what lay ahead. She never could before, but she did have a strong feeling that he would taunt the reaper once more before the day was through.

Samantha lathered herself up and rubbed her slippery body against his, stirring her sexual passions. She wanted desperately to pleasure him, to touch, probe, and explore every part of him. She longed to know him like never before. Her hands roamed his body, searching. Searching vigorously for his old battle scars from all the battles and wars that he had fought. She wanted to kiss them, and she wanted to feel his roughness against her soft lips. She felt like a shameless hussy, but she didn't care, for she had become drunk with fear of losing Sonny again.

Sonny turned around and was met by a fervent open mouth kiss from his wife. He succumbed to her tonguing. Samantha suddenly pulled her mouth from his and slipped past him to take her turn under the shower-head. She widened her stance, poised to receive the brunt of the hard spray to cool her passion fires. With a sudden gasp, she received the brunt of Sonny's hardness to stoke her fires back up again. Samantha's passion soon flooded her loins and mixed fondly with his in an elongated climax. The hard stream of water coursed through the redhead's crimson locks, drowning out her delicate moans of pleasure.

Samantha regained her composure and turned around to face her lover. She smiled at him with her lips, but not her eyes. Sonny sensed her fear.

"You know, Sam, crazy things make the world go 'round, and no matter how messed up things get, it never stops turning, never."

"I know, darling, I just want to savor this moment in our own little heaven," she said, burying her face into his chest.

She knew that wherever Sonny's lodestar directed his course, he would follow.

Sunday was literally a day of rest at the Bone Yard. Tommy Mack had the day off, and usually spent it down in Louisville with one of his girlfriends. But today he was in his popular perch at the corner of the bar, dealing out cards to his gin-playing friend, Star Cargile. Star was a popular Bone Yard strumpet and a good gin player. She wasn't the kind of whore that one dreamed about at night, but she was the kind that made good best buddies when things were slow.

"Goddamn it, Star! Quit blowing smoke in my face. I can't concentrate!" griped Tommy.

"You don't need to concentrate, Tommy. You've already taken four out of five sets. Besides, I have to smoke to keep my weight down. You know, the baby and all," she smiled.

"Well, it ain't workin', doll. What do you weigh now, a hundred 'n fifty . . . sixty maybe?"

"None of your business!" she snapped. "Damn it, Tommy, I don't need you to be a pain in my ass, my hemorrhoids are already driving me crazy as it is."

"Didn't you bring your donut with you today? You know these bar stools can be pretty uncomfortable on a pregnant girl's ass."

"Hell yes, I brought my donut. I'm sittin' on it right now. My ass don't hurt that much, but it itches like hell. Why don't you get rid of the itch for me, Tommy?"

Tommy snickered at the trollop's raw humor. "Shut up and play your hand. I'm on a roll."

The voluptuous Angie Garza appeared as Lana Darrah in the doorway of the bar with an air of confidence about her. She right away caught Tommy's attention and received an ugly sneer from his card-playing friend. She sashayed up to the bar to join them, her tight red dress clinging to her every curve.

"Well, if it isn't Lana Darrah, sneaking over from the other side. Boy, you Spanish-girls sure do like breaking Pergosi's rules," declared Tommy.

"Fuck Pergosi!"

"We had a little Puerto Rican girl working here awhile back who broke one of Pergosi's rules, and she paid for it, dearly."

"Oh yeah, what happened to her?" she asked.

"Let me put it to you this way, Lana. She don't work here anymore because of it."

"So, what rule did she break?"

"It's a long story. I don't really want to get into it right now. Let's talk about you."

"Hey, are we going to play cards or what?" spouted Star.

"That's enough gin-rummy for this afternoon, darlin.' You go on home now to your mama."

"But I'm down to ya for six bucks."

"I'll call it even for today. We'll take it up again next week," he said, staring at Angie.

"So, what can I do for you, my lovely?" he said to Angie.

"Fix me a bloody Mary, Tommy. I've got to wash Pergosi's stink out of my mouth."

"Oh, you had lunch with the boss again, eh?"

"Yeah and I don't like what's on his menu. You would think the son-of-a-bitch would take a weekend off now and then."

"Why should he when he has you here willing to please him."

"Fuck you too, Tommy. Why don't you just marry me or something and get me out of this dilemma?"

"If I did that you would just be in a greater dilemma, my dear. I have demands too, you know."

"Yeah, but I would enjoy pleasing you, Tommy. You're more my type. You'd treat me like a woman, you would."

"Of course I would, baby. A broad as easy on the eyes as you are needs special treatment, like a queen or somethin'" he said, handing her the tomato concoction that she had requested.

The cool, thick drink felt good sliding down Angie's throat. She didn't need the liquid eye opener just to clear her throat from the putrid taste of Pergosi, but also to clear her mind of last night's festivities and drugs, for it was now time to spin her web to trap Candy's killer before Sonny gummed up the works.

Angie slammed the empty cocktail glass down on the heavily shellacked counter and requested Tommy to mix her another. He did so, obligingly. She then leaned against the counter, showing off the deep cleavage separating her prominent breasts that strained to gain their freedom from the form-fitting dress.

"So how about it, Tommy, you and I. Lets do a girl and guy thing today. I need a friend, a real friend."

"I'd love to take you out to wine and dine, darlin', but I've got to run some errands for Pergosi today, and I won't be back until tonight sometime."

"I'm staying here at the Lair tonight myself, so why don't you come up and see me when you get back?"

"No, I can't do that. Those suites are for making money only. No male friends allowed. That's one of Pergosi's rules. You ought to know that."

"Well, then, how about I come and visit you at your place?"

"My place, how do you know about my place?"

"Oh, I've been back there before. You have a room right behind the Lair. Your place seems so quaint, up high, away from everything, and so close to the deep quarry. It's kinda breathtaking."

"I-I-I don't know about that idea," he said hesitantly.

"Look, Tommy. Are you going to let Miles reap the rewards while you just receive a pittance in comparison?"

"You have a point there, Lana."

"I'll even sweeten the pot for you, baby. I've got a matching bra and panties that go with this outfit. I'll wear 'em, sans the dress, just for you tonight, how about it?"

"That sounds like an offer I can't refuse," smiled Tommy. "What kind of wine do you like?"

"A good Chardonnay or Chablis will do. Oh yes, I'd like to have some candles also. I'm a helpless romantic, you know."

"You must be," kidded Tommy, "anything else, lady?"

"No. Just make sure that your big, brawny self is there," she said with a wink. "See you tonight, baby. I've got to go and make myself ready for you."

"Okay, see ya tonight, honey."

"You won't be disappointed," said Angie with a sexy wave goodbye.

Sonny didn't find Zeke Doughtry at the Sheriff's office. He didn't come upon the young deputy at Bryantsburg either. He found his house alright, but it had been abandoned. Sonny did manage to talk to an elderly neighbor lady who wasn't at a loss for words, though she didn't want to divulge the whereabouts of the Doughtry's. But through his cajoling, the blue-eyed sleuth wangled the information out of her.

With the disappearance of Jewel Mullins, and the responsibilities and pressures of filling in for the popular Sheriff, Zeke had sought the seclusion of his sister-in-law's farm near Sedgewick, at the far-end of the county. Sonny met up with the deputy at his sister-in-law's farmhouse, but Zeke didn't want to talk in front of his wife, so the two men took their business outside to the front porch.

Angie stared at her face in the bathroom mirror, in deep thought. This was her day of reckoning. This was the day that she had longed for since Candy's death.

Angie had been an Indianapolis cop since she was 21. She trained hard and honed her skills to be the best that she could be. The one thing that she was taught early on by Sonny Rafferty was how to keep that mental edge that a cop needed. He told her that the secret to the <u>edge</u> was found in two words, vigilance and diligence. He said to learn those two words, their meanings, inside and out, and apply them to her job as a police officer, and also to her own personal life. If she did just that, she would persevere, always. Angie had grown up on the wrong side of the street, and when given the chance was eager to learn, so as never to go back to where she came.

Like a good cop, Angie had her uniform all neatly laid out on her bed, waiting for her. Instead of a shirt and tie with trousers and a pair of oxfords, her uniform of the day was a red lace bra and matching briefs, and a pair of stiletto heels.

Angie snapped out of her stare and pulled open the vanity drawer. She reached in and took out a small make-up case and opened it to find that she had one more ampule left. She stared at the drug and sighed with relief, for Angie had lost her edge. She needed a crutch. She needed something to fog her conscience, for she had never before attempted to take another person's life, no matter how vile they were. Heroine was her drug of choice. It helped her to get through the daily ritual of oral copulation with her slimy boss, Miles Pergosi. "Just one more time," she said with a smile, "then I'll quit." She grabbed the ampule and the syringe out of the case. She broke the top off the ampule and inserted the needle. She aspirated the fluid, then turned the syringe up and squeezed the plunger, forcing the air out. Angie's eyes glistened while staring hungrily at her soul candy. She then made a fist and eased the needle into the blue vein that popped up in the bend of her arm. She pushed steadily on the plunger, forcing the heroine into her vein.

Angie felt a sudden surge of heat rushing through her body. With her head swimming and her stomach churning from the mind-bending drug, she lunged to the toilet where she hung her head while her diaphragm undulated violently, trying to rid her body of the demon drug. After a while she fell back spread-eagled onto the floor, with nasal mucus sliding down the sides of her bronze face. She watched in awe . . . at the soft clouds that floated through her mind.

It was a lazy Hoosier evening at the farmhouse, with the wind dying down and the frogs and crickets beginning to sing. The north-star shone in the high sky as a reminder that dusk was about to set in. Toward the west the reddish sun fought desperately to stay in the sky while steadily losing its battle.

"Do you mind if I smoke?" asked Zeke, leaning on the porch railing, staring out into the trees.

"Nah, go right ahead," insisted Sonny. "I tried taking up the habit once myself, but it didn't suit me."

"Well, I've just started up again. Lately it seems like a man needs some kind of vice."

"Yeah, I know what ya mean," agreed Sonny.

"Do you have any vices, Mr. Rafferty?"

"Oh yeah, I probably drink too much, and, let's see . . . I like naked women. Is that a vice?"

"No," snickered Zeke; "Not unless you have sex with 'em."

"Well, I was at the Devil's Lair last night, you ever been there?"

Zeke rose up from the railing and gave Sonny a slanted look. "I've been there once, and it wasn't for sex," stated Zeke. "I was there the night you were involved in that fight at the Bone Yard. They just about killed you."

"So, you're the one that took the scythe out of the reaper's hand. I'd like to thank you for saving my life."

"We were just doing our job."

"We who?" asked Sonny.

"Sheriff Mullins and I," Zeke replied.

"Sheriff Mullins? Wasn't he the fella that came up missin' the next day?"

"Yeah, he skipped out and went to Florida somewhere. He left a note. I found it."

"So, you are the interim sheriff now?"

"Well, I was, but I gave it up to another fella. Too much hassle for me, you know."

"Didn't a substantial pay raise come with that job?"

"Yes, but it would only have lasted until the next election."

"I know, but still, you've got five hungry mouths to feed, not including you and your wife's. I would think that you'd be happy to take on a raise."

"What are you driving at, mister?"

"What am I driving at? I'm saying that the Sheriff mysteriously disappeared, and he sure as hell didn't go to Florida, and I believe that you know what happened to him."

Zeke nervously took a long draw from his cigarette and shook another out of the pack and lit it from the one in his mouth.

"What are you scared of, Zeke?" asked Sonny.

"I don't get it man. I don't get what you're talkin' about, Rafferty. I told you all I know!"

Sonny got into Zeke's face. "Look, I talked to some girls last night. They said that there hadn't been any cops out there since the night of the fight. What the fuck is going on around here, Doughtry! The Devil's Bone Yard is an illegal whorehouse and gambling joint, and you're the cops. What are you hidin', goddamn it!"

The slight deputy finally broke. "I can't tell you. They said they'd kill my wife and kids," he sobbed.

Annabelle came running out to see what the commotion was about. "Zeke, you alright, darlin'?" she asked, looking curiously at Sonny.

"He's alright, ma'am," Sonny assured her. Zeke had his head down but waved her away insinuating that he was okay. Though skeptical, the young mother retreated back into the house.

"Tell me what you know, Zeke. I've got some scores to settle, myself. Work with me. We won't let anything happen to your family. I promise."

"It was horrible," he said, gaining his composure.

"What was so horrible, Zeke?"

The young deputy took a long draw off his cigarette. "Let me start from the beginning. The sheriff and I were on the take. He was gettin' a hundred a week and I was gettin' fifty for staying away from the Bone Yard. We were coerced into taking that. Everything was fine until one of the whores called us one night about a big fight that broke out. I drove over to check it out and found that you had kicked everyone's ass; even sent one boy to his maker. Lori Burns, a local whore, had a knife to your throat, and a fella' by the name of Chance Taylor was eggin' her on to run it in ya. Mullins showed up about the same time. You were in pretty bad shape, but not as bad as the others. We arrested Pergosi and Taylor, but they were freed the next day. Jewel Mullins was standing watch over you at the hospital because he was afraid for your life. He was relieved by a state cop. At least that was what was told to me. Anyway, the next day I got called out on an accident out in the county and was jumped by a couple of gang members from the Devil's Disciples. I was taken to the quarry and found the sheriff there also. The rest is a nightmare."

"Go ahead."

"They tied me up, but they nailed Jewel to the utility shed with a nail gun in crucifixion style. They made me watch."

"Who all was there?" asked Sonny.

"There was a Disciple there by the name of Crank Williams who did most of the torture. There were two others there from Kansas City, I believe. One by the name of Rico Constantine, and the other was Dominic Dattilo."

"I've heard of 'em. They're mobster hit men. Who else was there? Was Pergosi or Taylor there?"

"No, they weren't there. The way I heard it, Constantine and Dattilo were sent to the Bone Yard to straighten things out because of Pergosi's screw up."

"So what happened, next?"

"I used to carry a bowie knife with me; a real keeper, you know. It made me feel confident. Heck, the sheriff, he used to brag on how I would use it on the bad guys. He kinda gave me a reputation for being a bad-ass. I liked the idea, but of course none of it was true, I'm sad to say. Crank took it from me. He and his buddies used Jewel as target practice for the afternoon. The sheriff never screamed out. He only cursed at them now and then, but never screamed out until Crank got pissed off and castrated him. Then he screamed. Heck, he couldn't bear the pain. They dumped his dead body into the quarry and told me that if they ever saw a cop at the Bone Yard again that my family would join the sheriff in the quarry."

"Which one told you that?"

"Constantine and Dattilo both," said Zeke.

"Then they let you go?"

"Yeah, that Disciple bastard kept my knife though. I hated that. So, what are ya going to do, Sonny? Kill 'em all?"

"If need be."

"Look, let me help. Jewel was my best friend. I really want to get that Disciple bastard!"

"You stay here and take care of your family."

"But I want to help. I've been such a failure here."

Sonny patted him on his back. "You're not a failure, Zeke. I know. I've met your family."

Angie's alter ego, Lana Darrah, stumbled along gracefully as she followed the roadhouse's long shadow around the corner toward the wooden stairs leading up to Tommy Mack's apartment. Scantily clad in her silky red coverings, the sexy Puerto Rican shone through the dullness with rare beauty, rivaling that of the red Spanish rose.

"Hey, baby, where ya headed?" came a menacing voice out of the darkness.

Angie was startled by the sound and stopped abruptly in her tracks.

"You've got a lot of ass there, honey. How 'bout sharing some of it with us?" said another voice.

"Yeah, we'll play wishbone with ya, how 'bout that? That way we'll both get a piece of ass," taunted the owner of the first voice as they came into view.

Angie recognized them both as a couple of Pergosi's biker thugs, getting a bit feisty, probably from drinking too much beer. They must've come from the utility shed, where they sleep at night, was her thinking. As they approached closer, Angie gave a baleful stare toward her annoying subjects. "That sounds fine with me, boys. I haven't been tag-teamed in a long time, but let me check and see if it's okay with Tommy Mack. He's expecting me, you know. I'll just see if he'll let me do you boys first. Or better yet, let me ask Pergosi," she said sardonically.

"Okay, Okay! We get the picture. Forget about it," scoffed the agitated hoods while retreating back into the darkness.

Angie smiled nervously while making her way to the back stairs leading to Tommy's place. She stood at the bottom of the long set of stairs for a moment to gather her courage. The pale light-bulb that hung above the door seemed so far away to Angie. What little wind there was this evening felt like it was scorching her skin, but inside, she felt a cool mix, as of a fresh tossed salad. Heroine, it's such a sweet addiction. "I'm sorry Sonny. I really am. I hope you forgive me," said Angie prayerfully. She crossed herself and said, "This is for you Candy. This is for you, baby," and then began climbing the long set of stairs, gingerly, for she did not want to dislodge her secret weapon.

"I didn't know whether you were going to show up or not," said Tommy while anxiously opening the door.

"Why, Tommy, I don't welsh on my dates," said Angie, brushing up against him on the way in.

He reached out and grabbed Angie's arm pulling her back to him. He kissed her hard, too hard, painfully mashing her lips. Lana quickly pulled away, "Hold on there, big boy. Where's my wine?" she said.

"We don't need any wine, baby. We just need each other's bodies," said Tommy.

"I beg to differ. I distinctly remember you saying that you were going to wine and dine me tonight. You know, treat me like a lady."

"You're right, baby. I apologize. Sit down here at the kitchen table while I pour us a drink," he said, pulling a chair out for her. While Tommy clamored through the cabinets for glasses, Angie looked over his apartment. It was a quaint little place and kept rather nice for a bachelor pad, thought Angie.

Tommy, himself, had a nice look about him, standing just under six-foot tall with a good head of hair, though thinning at the crown; broad shoulders sitting atop a barrel chest, and had a fine manner about him. Never-the-less, that didn't soften her resolve, for she came here not only to kill Tommy Mack, but to make him suffer like he made Candy suffer. Her plan was to lead him down that primrose path where, at the end, she would unleash her deadly fury.

Tommy came back to the table with his hands full of glasses, candles, and matches. "Here, let me help you, darling. I'll take these into the living room. That way we can sit on the sofa while you serve the wine," she said sexily.

"Okay," agreed Tommy. The brawny bartender was a bit embarrassed at being such a klutz in his own home in front of his special date, whereas he was so smooth and suave behind the bar in public.

Angie sat back on the couch enjoying her wine while staring at Tommy, watching his movements, his demeanor, marveled by the unusual shyness in him. The flickering candlelight turned the room into a special love nest for the two potential lovers.

The night had a mystical feel to it as suspense hung in the air, with the many eyes of the woods staring out in anticipation of the arrival of the emancipator to free the whores of Babylon. He soon revealed himself under the smile of the moon. Crank Williams, the keeper of the gate, didn't see what the woods saw. Crank sat against the gate, his head slanted from the deep gash in his neck; his eyes staring dead set at the moon. He had a mouthful of himself, and a fuzz pocket where his manhood once hung. He held tight to a blood-covered bowie knife. It was a real keeper; a gift from the revelator. The revelator smiled; then walked on.

The boys from the shed also rested now, at the bottom of the deep quarry, along with Jewel Mullins and the others.

The silent night welcomed in the angel of death.

To Angie, time seemed to stand still. She didn't know if it was from the haziness of her drug induced mind, the candlelight setting, or Tommy's unexpected shyness. She hadn't felt this totally relaxed since she was in the arms of Eva, just previous to Candy's frantic phone call the night she was murdered. It was probably all of them combined, she figured.

Tommy took Angie's hand in his and kissed it softly, while glancing at her eyes. He then set his wine glass down and caressed her arm gently, every now and then brushing against the side of her bra-sculpted breast, all-the-while taking little glances, insuring Angie's approval.

"See, Tommy, even a whore likes a little romancing now and then," said Angie, breaking the silence.

"Don't belittle yourself, Lana. Your beauty transcends all others," said Tommy.

"Even Jamaica Red?" she asked.

"Why, that tall, arrogant, walkin'-stick. You've got to be kidding, Lana. There's no comparison between the two of you."

"I feel flattered, Tommy." Angie leaned forward and planted her painted lips against his and kissed him longingly while caressing the rise next to his thigh. She then backed away abruptly and stood upright, reaching behind her back and popping off her brassiere, freeing her breasts. In the room's reflection her breast crowns shown like jewels, each perched on a pillow of flesh, ready to be suckled. She then slipped her thumbs into the waistband of her frilly red panties and slid them down past her hips, slowly revealing her black, silky goodness. Tommy pulled his eyes from Lana's breasts to feast on the sprig of her Venus mound that begged for his attention. In the heat of the moment Lana rushed forward, almost hurling herself at Tommy, and pressed her hot mouth to his while her hands rummaged passionately through his dark brown hair. Meanwhile, he kneaded her soft pillows until they were swollen red, then, slipped down to suckle their delicate bronze protrusions as she pressed her chest hard into his face, spurring him along.It was all Angie could do to keep his prying hands from between her thighs, for she was on the verge of climax herself.

Then Tommy suddenly spit the tit and declared, "I've got to have you, Candy! I've got to have all of you!"

The harsh knock on the door startled Miles out of his catnap. He lifted his head from his desk as the creaking door opened slowly. "What the hell, do you want!" he demanded with a scowl.

"Haven't you heard, Miles? It's ruination day."

"Fuck you."

"I don't think so," came a bone-chilling reply.

Zip! Zip!   Zip! Zip!

Miles slumped over and fell gently to the floor.

Dying from a four-shot pattern of a silenced Lugar is such an easy way to go, so simple, almost serene; too good for the likes of some men.

The sound of Candy's name startled Angie back into reality. Between the confusion from the cravings in her loins and the fogginess from the drugs, Angie strained hard to focus her mind on her preconceived plot. The time for Tommy to die was close at hand. With her body glistening from sweat she gave Tommy one more hard kiss and then helped him off with his trousers, releasing his distended tuber. She quickly went to work on it, while with the nimble fingers of her free hand, pried open the passion-seeped folds of her tender loins, allowing passage for her secret weapon to slide through. She had to hurry, for she could feel his seed rising up inside him. The impudent young cop relaxed her vaginal muscles and released the brass-knuckle knife into her hand. She quickly slipped her fingers through the holes and with the flip of her thumb pried-open the four-inch steel blade. At that moment, his spigot opened and spewed forth, and she spat him out, while in one sweeping motion slashed his face. "This is for Candy, you deviant son-of-a-bitch!" screamed Angie.

Angie caught a glimpse of horror on his face before he brought his arms up as a buffer. She smiled and then plunged the blade deep into his prize, puncturing his ball sac. Tommy reacted by lunging forward into her mid-section, knocking her to the floor and falling on top of her. His face was bleeding profusely with his blood dripping onto Angie's face, stinging her eyes, and blocking her vision. With his body covering hers, she was still swinging the knife, trying to stab his back, but barely cutting his arm due to little range of motion. Angie tried thinking like a cop. She tried to think of what Sonny had taught her, but her mind was in a haze, too much heroine, too much rage. She was over the top and couldn't get back. He was the one that was injured, not her. She had the advantage but she wasn't thinking straight. All she wanted to do was to slash his body like he did Candy's.

Tommy raised himself up and came down with a hard right fist to Angie's jaw. The hardwood floor had little give to it, but her head bounced from the mighty blow anyway. She was still stabbing but he swung again. This time the impact from the blow sent her dental plate skidding across the floor as blood poured from her mouth. She kept stabbing his arm, but they were small stabs, doing little harm. Tommy's look of horror changed to blind rage as he kept pounding on Angie's face, again and again and again, smashing her face into a bloody mush, crushing her eye socket, causing a gray gelatinous liquid to ooze out. Angie's stabbing motion slowed, then, stopped. The knife finally fell from her quivering hand as the crazed maniac kept pounding.

Suddenly, Tommy grabbed for his throat! There was a cord around it, pulling taut. He couldn't breath. He grabbed his neck. It was a garroting. Someone was trying to kill him. Even though he was injured Tommy felt strong. He reached back behind him, grabbing the intruder's arms, trying to throw him over the top. They stumbled around for a bit, but Tommy couldn't get an advantage, but he did get one gasp of air as the cord slipped some in the hands of his attacker. The stranger was strong, maybe stronger than he was. The stranger re-gripped. Tommy was getting desperate now. He lost some of his strength in that last effort. His only hope now was to get to his feet again and back the intruder into something to cause him to release the cord. It was already cutting into his neck. Using all his strength Tommy made it to his feet, dragging the intruder around behind him. With the rest of his strength he lunged backwards, ramming his adversary into a stereo cabinet, knocking it over, then into his television, knocking it over. The stranger then fell backwards, still pulling hard on the garrote as Tommy laid on top of him, chocking and gasping for his life. His last effort had failed.

Soon, the only breathing heard in the room was the heavy panting from Tommy's killer. Finally, when assured of his death, the stranger shoved the body aside.

Tears fell on Angie's mangled face while cradled in the arms of the mystery man. "You're a free bird, darlin'. Free at last."

I awoke from my slumber
For I heard a doleful prayer
I got up and I searched
Found nobody there
It shall go down in the annuls, not of defeat
But of victory for the mild and the meek
I may be mighty or I may be small
If providence be with me
I'll crush the wall
So goes the flight of the wrecking ball

Chapter Twenty-One

Monster's Ball

We dare not believe a righteous man or any solid person to be a visitant to such a place as the Devil's Bone Yard, yet that belief transcends none of man's own will power. For his sins of the flesh are from his inherent nature. He breaks not the rules of nature but the rules of man.

It made the front page of the local paper, the fire that is. The fire department didn't receive the call in time. They didn't receive a call at all that night, yet the Bone Yard burned to the ground. People kept quiet about the other things they found. Once a plague leaves a community, no one talks about it. They just pick up the pieces and go on with their lives.

There were no witnesses to the demise of the Devil's Bone Yard, none that were believable anyway. However, there was Po Daniels, but everyone in Scoville knew that he was suspect at best. Po was among the prying eyes from the woods that night. He visited the Bone Yard often, from afar. The curious dolt had been enticed by Travis Bowles' tales of naked women in the parking lot, performing all kinds of lewd sexual acts. The licentious parking lot behavior from the likes of Lori Burns and Star Cargile had often drawn Po to boldly sneak by the guards and enter the arena to view the shameless hustlers in their lurid sex acts.

The easily confused imbecile told his story to anyone that would listen. In one version he saw the shadow of a lone man carrying the limp body of a woman out of the burning building and through the gates towards Rattlesnake Highway. Then, in what seemed to be a more contrived version, Po spoke of a band of angels leaving the fiery furnace, led by a giant angel, wearing nothing but a wide-brimmed hat, followed by the same man as before, carrying a lifeless body in his arms; then followed by a one-armed cherub, and another about the same size but with both limbs attached. He made no reference to any wings, though it didn't matter anyway. But his story did make good fodder for the likes of Travis Bowles and his storytelling.

The paper had it right. The Bone Yard burned to the ground. End of story. Nothing was even said about the wooden Indian that guarded the jukebox. The old chief didn't burn. As-a-matter-of-fact, he wasn't even singed, though the brown Fedora that he wore was missing. Nor did anyone give notice to a small article stuck back next to the obituaries of the same paper. It read, Local resident, Thelma Jenkins, commits suicide by ingesting copious amounts of rat poison. No suicide note found.

Sonny's day of reckoning had come and gone. He knew that he wasn't above the law. He was well beyond it. It was like an affliction that he was born with. The things that Sonny did to right the wrongs in his life felt good to him, if not good, satisfactory. Any alternative to his way of interpreting the law was incomprehensible. He didn't plan it that way. He just evolved into that line of thinking. Evil tends to put a slant on things that can bend a man's mind into illegitimacy.

When Sonny returned from his latest excursion he became listless, almost melancholic for awhile. At night, Sonny took on an introversion that he hadn't often exposed to his partner. He became as a child, sleeping in Samantha's arms instead of she in his. It was as if he was a little boy who got into trouble at school and was seeking shelter at home. For a few short nights, Samantha became Sonny's Paradise Woods.

But today was a new dawning for Sonny and Samantha. It was the day of the Governor's Ball, which was a misnomer, for this once a year soiree had little to do with the governor. However, the governor did attend, along with the city's mayor, council members, and various politicians. Also invited were numerous bankers, clergy and stodgy aristocrats, along with several people of the arts.

During the event, the banquet room was home to an award ceremony for the print and television media. All in all it was quite an extravaganza hosted by Big John Taylor.

As Dickens would have it, it was the best of times and the worst of times at Taylor Manor on the evening of the Governor's Ball. While Kitty was downstairs, forever being the gracious hostess to the early arriving guests; Big John was upstairs, imprisoned in his own billiard room. A cold, somber mood encased the smoke-filled parlor as some of the inhabitants enjoyed a game of nine-ball while discussing the affairs of the day. The usually boisterous Big John Taylor was taken aback by the message and the messengers that were sent to him from Victorio Delveccio. In the gaming business, Victorio was to Big John what Losch was to him in the extended care business, partners in crime.

The meeting was set-up by Delveccio but Big John insisted on having it held at his place. He didn't trust the Italian Godfather. Ever since their beginnings together they'd had several ego clashes. This day was no different. Rather than showing up himself, Delveccio sent two of his henchmen, Constantine and Dattilo, to represent him. It was quite a slap in the face, but the message he sent was even more demeaning.

Glasses of Johnny Walker were poured and Big John's best Cubans were passed around to cut the ice while the two families went through their formalities. Losch, Big John and Dattilo imbibed in the smoke and the liquor, as Police Commissioner Nick Parmalay and Rico Constantine shot a round of pool.

"Delveccio's pissed, real pissed," stated Dattilo firmly. "The Bone Yard's your responsibility, Big John. It was bad enough that we had to close it down for a week earlier this summer because of a fuck-up, but now this. We've got five dead bodies, and two were family loyalists. We can only cover up so much before the Feds start jumpin' down our throats. That's what Delveccio is concerned about right now, that and losing 17 million dollars a year income."

Rico Constantine rose up from a shot he was about to take and gave Big John a slanted look. "Yeah, we don't know what the hell happened this time. All of our witnesses are doing the six-foot under shuffle tonight. My personal guess is that someone didn't care for us cuttin' the sheriff's nuts off. I figure that bony-ass deputy played a part in all of this, but we can't touch him now. He has too much exposure. The Feds would be all over us."

"Delveccio wants to know what your take is on all of this, and what you propose to do about it," interjected Dattilo.

Big John took a serious puff off his Cuban cigar while pondering his answer. "Well, gentlemen; the first shut down of the Bone Yard was a breach of security caused by one of the whores breaking the rules and calling the cops to an ordinary bar brawl. The cops had been paid off, so they weren't even supposed to show up, but they did. So we eliminated the problem. We took out the whore and you took out the sheriff. End of story. Things like that happen, you know."

"Wait a minute, Big John," said Dattilo. "That's not quite the end of the story."

"What do you mean?"

"What Dominic's trying to say is that we have a breakdown in the network, and all the arrows point toward you, Big John," snarled Constantine. "First of all, that just wasn't an ordinary barroom brawl. Your son-in-law detective came in and annihilated the place while putting two good bouncers in the hospital for major surgeries, plus he killed a local. It's been noticed that your son, Chance; you know, the one that's running for state senator, has been bonin' this Jamaica Red broad for the last year and a half while gambling away thousands of dollars in your own establishment. This doesn't bode well for you, Big John. You, Losch and Mr. Delveccio are Miramar. As we all know, Miramar has interests in 12 states, and in each of those states we are personally supporting new senatorial candidates to change the gaming laws to our benefit, and to lobby for more Medicare for our health facilities. You're responsible for getting only one senator elected, and he doesn't look too viable right now."

"Hey, who do think you're talking to?" snapped Losch. "This is the man that got President Kennedy elected, for crissake!"

"We haven't time for niceties. Besides, time marches on, my good friend," retorted Dattilo.

"Hold on everybody. Let's back off from each other and take a breather before we say something we can't take back," boomed Big John. "I'd like to clear one thing up right now. With the exception of Chance, I have told nobody about Miramar Corporation. As a matter of fact, I have told no one about my business dealings whatsoever. I have no idea how Sonny Rafferty stumbled into the Bone Yard that night. I do know that he received a pretty bad head injury from it himself. Hell, he's got amnesia so bad that he can barely remember where his dick is, so he should be no problem now. Neither will Chance. He's stopped seeing Jamaica Red and is concentrating solely on his political career. I assure you that I will make every effort to get him elected. As far as what happened last Sunday night, I'm just as bewildered and distraught over that incident as you all are. Miles Pergosi was a good friend of mine. He was my right hand man down there. We'll just have to move on and rebuild, since we have no witnesses to the crime scene."

"Delveccio said that we can't rebuild the Bone Yard, not there. The area's too hot now. We're going to turn it into a landfill. Maybe that way we can recoup some of our losses. We need to fill that quarry up anyway. There are a lot of secrets in there that need to remain there," said Dattilo. "Delveccio also wanted me to tell you to find out who burned down the Bone Yard, and for you to deal with them in the proper way."

"But I have no clues, no way of knowing who the culprits were," insisted John.

"Well, Rico and I did a little investigating on our own. We found that there were three girls that stayed over at the Devil's Lair on Sunday night. One girl by the name of Lana Darrah, we couldn't find. She was relatively new and apparently gave a bogus home address. The other two we caught up with at L.A.X. airport. One was that tall, Amazon island girl by the name of Jamaica Red, and the other was a one-armed youngster from San Fernando Valley. According to her, Jamaica Red was taking her back home to her mommy and daddy."

"So, what did you do with them?" inquired Big John.

"We tried to extract some information out of them but they balked."

"So, what happened next?" asked the big man.

"We drove them out to the desert and I let Rico interrogate them."

"Yeah, I interrogated them," Rico sneered. "That Jamaica Red, she wouldn't talk, no matter what I did to her, but that little blonde girl, she squealed like a pig. She squealed on Jamaica Red and everybody. But mostly, she told of a man by the name of Johnny Carlisle, and described him as if he were your son-in-law, Sonny Rafferty."

"Who knows, could have been an alias," added Dattilo.

"I don't understand," said John, confused. "I just talked with Samantha last week and she said that he still didn't have all his memory back."

"You know, John, if you would have only paid better attention, that little girl would be alive today," added Rico.

"Do you mean you killed her?"

"Yeah, I really hated to because she was really nice to me. Even though she cried and begged me not to, I put a bullet in her head just to make an example for Jamaica Red."

John stared at Rico in disbelief.

"That Jamaica Red, she was something else, John. She wouldn't talk, even after that little one-armed girl squealed on her, and even after I busted her kneecaps. Finally, she just got me so pissed off that I cracked her in the spine and left her in the Mohave Desert, crawling 'round on the ground with the scorpions. She's been plucked clean by the buzzards and coyotes by now, I suspect."

"Why are you so cruel to women?" questioned Losch.

"Because they are fuck-ups," replied Rico coldly.

"We're getting off the subject here," warned Dattilo. "Look, I know you two guys go back a ways and all, but let's cut to the chase, gentlemen. Sonny Rafferty is a one-man wrecking crew. He's a loose cannon. He's dangerous for our business. He has no weak points, and he takes no quarter. He must be eliminated. Also, your daughter Samantha, single-handily wiped out half of Waverly's profits this year with her scathing news reports. She almost pulled the plug on the industry, as far as Miramar is concerned. You have to get her off that job, now!"

"We eliminated her source of information," replied Nick Parmalay who had been silent up until now.

"How's that?" asked Dattilo.

"Samantha was getting all of her information about Waverly from a disgruntled nurse by the name of Loni Jacobs. Loni had somehow broken the code to the Miramar account. She had the goods on all of us, so we wasted her. We ran her off into a reservoir and made it look like an accident."

"We also have another problem that we believe Samantha may be involved in. It seems that the NAWR is headin' up a campaign in Washington this week for nurse's rights in the workplace. We think it quite odd that the women's organization is lobbying for worker's rights. They're usually off on some tangent about discrimination or sexual abuse. It is strange that Pat Fowler, the chairman of the NAWR, is from Indianapolis and has been seen several times meeting with Samantha, and that's not good. Delveccio wants her fired. Let's face it Big John, you're getting' too old to perform your job properly. You're too soft."

"I think John Losch and I deserve a little more recognition on what we've built here. It was Losch and I that started the Miramar Corporation in the first place.

"You tend to lose a little face when you let 17 million clams go down the drain," cracked Constantine.

"You let me worry about that. And let me handle Sonny Rafferty and my daughter!"

"If you don't take care of them, we will." replied Rico with a smirk.

With fire in his eyes, Big John grabbed the lanky Italian hood by his lapels and slammed him hard against the wall. "If you touch one hair on my daughter's head, I'll make sure *you'll* crawl with the scorpions too, you slimy Wap mother-fucker!" vociferated the big man.

"Maybe you ought to have a talk with Delveccio," stated Dattilo.

"Maybe I will, but not now."

"If not now, then when?"

"When, I'm damn good and ready. This meeting is over, gentlemen," announced Big John in disgust, releasing his choke hold on Constantine. "Everyone is invited to stay for the ball and have some food and drink. Dominic, if I don't talk to you before you leave, give Victorio my best and tell him that I will contact him soon, and we will work together to get these problems straightened out."

"I'll tell him that, Big John," he said, departing with a handshake.

"Nick, you stick around. We have to go over this evening's events."

As the last man left, John turned to Nick. "I want you to keep an eye on those two Dagos this evening. They're supposed to fly back to KC tonight. You watch them until their plane leaves the runway. I don't trust them. I don't trust them one bit."

"Okay, Big John, I won't let them get out of my sight."

"Good. Thanks. Come on, Johnny, we have a ball to attend."

It was the shank of the evening when they finally arrived at the ball. Sonny was met with an affectionate kiss by the elegant Ms. Kitty Taylor while Samantha settled for some friendly scolding for not visiting her mother often enough. Sonny gave his mother-in-law a secret wink of approval as he tactfully eyed her new bosoms that overflowed their banks even more so than Samantha's did theirs. Like mother like daughter, he thought. Sonny surmised that they both must have those rubbery tug-nubbins of theirs either tied, taped, or tacked to the inside of their sequined encumbrances so as not to allow them to pop out like corks a bobbin' in water. He approved of both, for he loved them both, in different ways.

Next, was the arduous task of being introduced to several dignitaries and their partners, plus other lesser known, but highly aristocratic couples. It was the procedure that Sonny detested, more than the people. To Sonny, it was like running the gauntlet. If he could survive this beating, he could survive the rest of the evening. He reminded himself of the payoff at evening's end, a rendezvous with his lovely wife on the old oak desk in his office.

After the greetings and formalities, Sonny and Samantha split apart. She headed to the banquet room to meet with the Fab Four for the award ceremonies while he went searching for Frank Lujack to get a situation report.

"Hey Frankie, clue me in, what's been going on so far?" asked Sonny, grabbing a drink from a passing waiter's tray.

"It's the usual round-robin of sophisticates, same as last year, but a larger crowd this time, Sonny."

"Yeah, I just made it through the gauntlet myself. You know, rubbing noses with the likes of the Wellingtons, Grissoms, Laslows, Duponts, and all."

"So, how did you like it, Sonny?"

"Oh, it was alright. I just made sure that I washed up afterwards."

"I kind of like this lifestyle, myself."

"This don't suit you, Frank. It's too much of a circus for the likes of you and me."

"It seems to suit Sam quite nicely, though."

"Yeah, but she was born under the big top, Frank. She doesn't know any better."

"Speaking of Sam, where is she now? I haven't spoken with her at all tonight."

"Oh, she's in the banquet room, getting primed for the media awards ceremony. You don't want to see her anyway. She's a little miffed at you for not keeping her informed on the Loni Jacobs case."

"Hell, Sonny, that investigation is dead. I don't know how long I can keep up this charade with Sam."

"Don't worry, Frankie. I think I've steered her in another direction. Besides, I told her that the case is in the hands of Parmalay and the prosecuting attorney. That should get her off your back. By the way, where is Bernice this evening?"

"Aw, she decided to stay at home tonight."

"I specifically told Big John that all the security personnel were allowed to bring their spouses to the ball. It's in the contract that I signed with him."

"Nah, that's not it, Sonny. Bernice decided, on her own, not to come."

"I wonder why not? I thought this type of thing was every woman's dream. Heck, Sam preened herself in front of the mirror for at least an hour today getting ready for the ball."

"Bernice doesn't think she's pretty enough to attend a function like this. You know, she never could get rid of the weight that she gained after having the boys. She prefers to just run around in a pair of blue jeans and one of my old shirts."

"That's not like Bernice. That's not like her at all!" exclaimed Sonny. "She's always been the life of the party."

"Yeah, but that's always been in a backyard environment."

"That's too bad. Bernice would get a kick out of this bash. This is where women strut- their-stuff. It's all about the competition between one another."

"What causes women to be that way?"

"Oh, that answer is too convoluted. We'll never understand. It's just meant to be. They don't even care about the men that brought them here, not tonight anyway. This is about, their own pretentiousness. It's about the biggest diamond brooch, the greatest cleavage, and the most arrogance. As for their men, they just stand around and gloat over their accomplishments of the past year."

"Bernice just doesn't think that we are affluent enough to participate in such an event as we have here tonight. She sees it as being hypocritical. She's been kinda down lately. It costs a lot of money to send our boys to college and all. She fears that we'll spend it all on them, and not have enough to retire on. She wants that good life now, Sonny. She wants a life that I can't give her."

"But, Frank, you make a good buck as a detective, plus, you'll be making five bills from this gig tonight. I didn't know you were that strapped. If you need some money we can help you out."

"Oh no, Sonny, it's not like that. We're not destitute. It's just that Bernice is going through a phase. She just dreams too big. She'll get over it."

"We all dream larger than real life, Frankie. Are you sure everything is okay at home?" asked Sonny.

"Yeah, pretty much. Why?"

"You guys are still, you know, doing it?"

"Yeah, of course, Sonny, we still get together every so often. What about you and Sam. Is everything going okay for you two?"

"Oh yeah, as a matter of fact, we're going to rendezvous at my office tonight to have our own private party after this one. You know, Frank, there is something about seeing my wife's white naked body against the backdrop of oak veneer that changes her into a sex goddess, I can't explain it. Maybe you and Bernice ought to try that sometimes. At least think about it. It'll be my treat."

"Thanks, but no thanks. We do just fine without all that kinkiness."

"Okay. Suit yourself, buddy."

"Say, Sonny, there is one thing that I felt quite strange tonight."

"What's that, Frank?"

"A little while ago a couple of unsavory characters came from the upstairs billiard room. I've seen their faces on wanted posters back at the precinct. One of them, I believe, is Rico Constantine, a hit man out of Chicago and Kansas City. The other one I can't quite place right now, but he goes by the name of Dattilo. Shortly after they left, Big John and his associate, John Losch, soon followed, and they looked none too happy."

"Rico Constantine. Yeah, I've heard of him. He's a low-life mob thug. I'll keep an eye out for these fellas. Sounds like there's a storm a brewing and it just might be heading our way, Frank."

"I hear ya, brother."

Big John trudged through the crowd like a rock star on a British tour, frantically greeting his fans and shaking hands until he came upon Rick Jamison of WYNG, TV. Rick was enjoying himself with his lovely companion, Claire.

"Claire, may I borrow Rick for a moment? We need to discuss some important business in private. I promise it won't take long," said Big John.

"Sure, of course," answered Claire, "but don't get him drunk. I want him dancing tonight."

"Thank you, dear. I must say you look ma-velous tonight," said Big John while leading Jamison to the quieter and saner atmosphere of the men's room.

While stepping up to the urinals to relieve themselves, Rick asked, "What's up, Big John? You seem to be a bit rushed tonight."

"I know you've always coveted my daughter for your TV station. Well, Rick, I'm offering her to you now."

"What? Have you gone loony, Big John? Why would you want to ship her off to me? Hell, John, I'm one of your rivals. Besides, word is out that Samantha's going to win an award tonight for best investigative reporting this year."

"The thing is, Rick, Samantha's investigation of that Waverly scandal went over the line. She crossed over her professional boundaries and pissed off the wrong people. We've caught our tit in the wringer. You know what that's all about, I'm sure."

"Yes, but we've always managed to steer clear of big trouble, though."

"Well, if you could find an opening for her I would sincerely appreciate it as a favor. Of course, the Times will compensate any hardship caused by this untimely request. My only stipulation is that you offer her a job tonight and preferably out of this state, or even better, the country."

While Big John washed his hands, Rick rubbed his chin, pondering the big guy's request.

"Well, Gina Pirelli is my foreign correspondent, but by request I'm shipping her back to Washington to cover the beltway boys. Jessica Marlow, my anchorwoman, is going to take her place, while Lori Jung was going to get Marlow's spot. Though she agreed to make the move, Jessica doesn't really want to leave her anchor post here at WYNG, even though it would mean more money. She's a homebody type, you know. What I can do is leave Marlow as anchorwoman and use Jung for weekends and give the foreign correspondent job to Samantha for the time being. We have a three to six month opening in Iraq. It's pretty hot right now. Do you think that would interest her?"

"I like her chances there better than here right now," replied Big John.

"I take it that she doesn't know about this idea yet?"

"That's right. She doesn't."

"Well, I can even sweeten the pot for her, Big John. Once our mother station, CSN, finds that we've landed Samantha Rafferty they are gonna' want to steal her from us, and they will. They have long coveted her for the anchor desk at their New York facilities. Sam would be a prized catch for them, and we are talking seven figures, Big John. It's the big time."

"That would be great. That would be perfect. The main thing is to get her the hell out of Dodge as soon as possible."

"I'll do my best for you, John."

"Anytime you need something, let me know. I owe you big time, my friend."

"I will, John. I will."

It was quite a charged atmosphere inside the banquet hall for media members and their guests. Everyone was filled with anticipation of the upcoming awards.

The Times was well represented at Samantha's table with the likes of Lisa Dawson, Larry Crowell, Jessie Coltraine, and Merle Bullock. The unpopular Margo Solsta was also there, though her boss and lover sat on the stage with the other luminaries. The mayor was the master of ceremonies, but he was off somewhere padding his ego. Samantha didn't mind the wait. She eased her tension with a good amount of champagne, as did the others. Since there was a delay, Samantha deemed it necessary to make a toast and tapped her glass to garner the attention of everyone at her table.

"Since we are at the mayor's mercy and have time to kill, I would like to propose a toast. No, make it two toasts. One is for the Fab Four who did such a wonderful job on the Waverly project this year. I know I put a strain on everyone. I guess I became obsessed with the case, and I apologize for that." Samantha lifted her glass, as did the others. "This is for you my friends."

"Here, here, cheers!" they said.

Samantha stood up once again, and this time spoke with more conviction, "Thanks to one special person that sacrificed her life for a greater cause, we have teamed up with the NAWR in a quest to create a bill in congress that guarantees that the caregivers of this great nation of ours, the nurses in particular, will be treated with the dignity, respect, and receive the goddamn pay that they deserve. This toast is for our sister, Loni Jacobs, may she rest in peace."

"Here! Here!" They all cried out.

Samantha continued on, "I'm going to tell you right now that it will be a great day for women's rights when the NAWR and you and I win the contract rights for all nurses in America. You all didn't know Loni Jacobs, but I did, for a fleeting moment. Loni was a tough broad. She came from the side of life that we don't even think about, but she wanted freedom in the workplace. She wanted to make a difference, and she did. And with that, the bill that will be proposed to Congress next month will have her name attached to it. It will be known as The Loni Jacobs bill. That will be all women's battle cry until we get it into law."

Everyone at the table stood up and gave an arousing applause to Samantha's speech. As they sat down, Gina Pirelli tapped on Samantha's shoulder. Samantha turned to Gina, while the others returned to their normal prattle.

"That was quite a speech, my dear. You always did have a gift of gab."

"Hello, girlfriend," replied the surprised orator. "I think you have it backwards, Gina. You were always the one with the mouth."

"Yeah, but when you speak it means so much more," said Gina.

"Hey, I heard that they sent you to Washington early."

"Yeah, it didn't hurt my feelings any. I love it there, as you know."

"So what are you doing back so soon?"

"I came back to win an award, what else? Actually, I came on a double-date with a friend of mine . . . and yours."

"And who might that be?" asked Samantha.

"Troy Charbonau," said Gina straight-faced.

"Gina, how could you! Didn't we have it out over him the last time we were together?"

"I know, Samantha, but he insisted on showing up. He wants to talk to you so bad. Everybody thinks he's here because he's Chance's opponent in the upcoming election, but that's not completely true. Sure, he was invited by the governor, but he only came to see you once more."

"I'm too busy. I haven't time for this bullshit," said Samantha irritably.

"He just wants closure, Sam."

"I wouldn't even know how to approach him, Gina. Hell, it's been six years."

"You let me worry about that, Sam, I'll set things up. If I can find you free later on tonight, then will you meet with him?"

"What about his date?"

"She's just arm candy. She's just a friend of his from the Pentagon. As a matter of fact, the guy that Troy set me up with works there too. At least that's what he told me."

"I don't know," said Samantha hesitantly, "Sonny's here tonight."

"If Sonny is the guy that you say he is then he won't mind you talking with an old friend. Look, honey, I know that you love your husband. Just tell Troy that. Tell him it's over. He just wants to be sure. He just wants closure, that's all."

"Well, Gina, if you can find me when I'm not too busy later on, then I might meet with him. Okay?"

"Good enough, Sam, Thanks. By the way, I hope you win tonight."

"I hope you win too, Gina."

As the ceremonies started in the banquet room, so did the band in the ballroom. Sonny had watched them set up. He and Samantha knew the musicians well. They were a nice band for this type of affair. They weren't to play contemporary music tonight. Just mostly waltzes with a tango thrown in every so often to spice things up.

"Well, well, if it isn't Sonny the raging bull Rafferty," greeted Nick Parmalay. "Better keep an eye on that band. They look pretty dangerous."

"Well if it isn't, Nick Parmalay, our city's most infamous police commissioner and most prolific butt-licker. I haven't seen you in a while. I don't even remember seeing you at last year's bash. Big John must have had you on an errand or something."

"You must have me mixed up with someone else. I work for the mayor."

"Oh, that's right, the mayor. I forgot."

"You know, I just remembered why you could never cut it as a cop, Sonny. You are too dangerous. You're too dangerous to yourself, but mostly, you're too dangerous for others around you. You have a dangerous mind, Rafferty."

"Yeah, I have a dangerous mind, and it's accurate too."

"Oh yeah, is it accurate enough to tell me how many lives you wasted in Centralia? Huh, is it Sonny?"

"Digging up the past, eh? You like swinging below the belt, don't you, Nick?"

"What do you mean, Sonny, that's where you played all the time, you and your street whores."

"I was just trying to better the community, Nick."

"You never did understand your role as a police officer," Sonny.

"Why, I thought it was to get the bad guys off the streets."

"You better the community by making sure the traffic flows properly, and assure our good citizens that they can get back and forth to their jobs and homes safely, instead of trying to resurrect the trash from the gutters. The only thing you can make out of mud is mud pies."

"What can I say, Nick. I like mud pies."

"Say, rumor has it that you're a private dick now."

"Yeah, that's right, Nick. I've heard rumors that you have climbed so far up the mayor's ass that you've turned into a Baby Ruth. Is that true?"

Parmalay smiled with rage. "I hear that you are now just a legal peeping tom, Sonny. That worries me. Do you find that watching others fornicating keeps your sex life going strong at home?"

"Oh yes indeed, Nick. You must try it yourself. It might spice up your bedroom doldrums some."

"Oh no, I don't need all that kinkiness to satisfy my wife. She is perfectly happy with the man that she married."

"That's not what I hear," said Sonny with a questionable look.

"Oh yeah, just what did you hear?"

"Can't say; it's confidential."

"Well, tell me from what source did you hear this?"

"From the rumor-has-it mill, Nick, gotta' go now. My wife wants me to mingle with the blue-noses tonight. She says it'll perk up my image. You know all about that," jested Sonny, walking away from the befuddled commissioner.

After eating from the French catered cuisine, Rico Constantine headed towards the ballroom while Dom Dattilo slipped outside for a quick smoke. Dattilo knew men. He knew men of subversive nature, and he knew that Nick Parmalay would soon join him for that smoke.

"Hey Dominic, you really got the ol' man pissed off in there tonight," greeted Parmalay.

"So what's it to you? What are you, his gopher or somethin'?" said Dattilo sarcastically.

"No, no, of course not," laughed Parmalay, trying to shed the Italian's slight. "Big John is the power guy but I'm your go to man. I put things in motion. Hell, I've worked for Big John for years. I know the ins and outs of this city's hierarchy. I know who's on the take and who we can't make," he boasted.

"So, what are you getting at, Nick? If you've got something to say, spit it out."

"What am I getting at? I'll tell you what I'm getting at. I'm talking about Sonny and Samantha Rafferty here. That tandem has crashed your party this year and Big John, ain't done nothin' about it 'cause Samantha is his precious daughter. He's blinded by nepotism. His mind is muddled. He's dropping the ball, and your Italian family is paying for it, big time."

"Since you're ratting out your boss, what's your proposal?"

"I'll take out Sonny and Samantha for you, tonight."

"Is that right, all by yourself?"

"I got people working for me."

"So, what's in it for you? You want money?"

"I want Big John's place at Miramar."

"You mean you want to topple Big John's regime and take over his spot? You've got some set of balls there, boy."

"That's my offer; yes or no?"

"I'll tell you what, Nicky, when you show us their names in the obits, we'll talk."

"No problem, Dominic. Once his baby is gone, Big John's house of cards will fall," said Nick with a wicked grin. With that, Nick left in search of Frank Lujack.

Dattilo lit up another smoke and took a friendly walk around the botanical gardens. He had done his job today. He delivered the mail. Big John didn't take it well but Dattilo expected that. But business was business, and the Italian Godfather wasn't liberal with his time or his money.

Dattilo had just eased back against a tree to rest his eyes for a moment when he heard a slight commotion coming from a couple entering into the backyard. He was hidden in the shadow of the tree as he watched the two would-be lovers grope and fondle their way to the little summerhouse. He noticed who the male was right away. It was Rico. That Rico, he's the quintessential Italian lover, he thought. He would tap anything that cast a vertical smile his way. Dattilo couldn't tell much about the girl from where he stood, except from her voice. She seemed quite drunk. Rico had her dress pulled down to her waist as Dominic could see her big, pendulous breasts flapping around, with Rico struggling to corral her into the gazebo.

"Okay, that's enough," came a loud, stern voice out of the darkness.

"Who the hell are you?" asked Rico.

"I'm the security here. We'll have none of this raucousness on these grounds."

"Sonny, is that you?" cried out the inebriated Liz Taylor.

"Yeah, it's me, darlin'."

"We're just having a little fun," she said, stumbling to get a better look at his face.

"Yeah, we're just having a little fun," said Rico. "Leave us alone mister security man. We'll be done in a couple of minutes."

"I can't allow that," said Sonny, walking into the light.

"So you are the great Sonny Rafferty that everyone speaks of. You don't look so tough to me," snarled Rico.

"I never said I was."

"Well, Rafferty, why don't you go crawl back underneath that rock that you crawled out from."

"I can't do that. You're going to have to take your hands off her and leave. I'm through talking."

311

Rage filled Rico's eyes. "Why don't you talk to this, big man," he said, snapping open the shiny switchblade.

Sonny slipped out of his tux jacket and twirled it around his left arm. "Come on, Rico. Since you feel a little froggy, start hopping," said Sonny, undaunted by the stiletto.

"Wait a minute, gentlemen," interrupted Dattilo, appearing out of the shadow. "I hate to intrude on your backyard roughhousing, but Rico, we have a plane to catch, and we must leave, now!"

Rico felt hesitant, but he knew from Dominic's stern look that he had to back out of the fight this time. "Shit, with those big udders of hers pissing milk, she must be suckling a calf anyway. I wouldn't want to steal a kid's meal," said Rico sarcastically. "I'll tell you one thing, Rafferty. You're lucky this time, 'cause I was fixin' to cut you from asshole to appetite," he said with his finger pointed at Sonny's face.

"Luck has nothing to do with it."

"We'll meet again another day, Rafferty," he said with a killer's stare.

"I look forward to it."

Constantine and Dattilo disappeared back into the building.

"Liz, what the hell is wrong with you?" scolded Sonny. "How come you're not with Chance?"

"He doesn't want me around, Sonny."

"Sure he does, Liz. Let's put your dress back on and get you up into a bedroom so you can sleep this off." As Sonny helped her, he noticed a large contusion on the side of her left breast, and another on her ribcage. "Did that son-of-a-bitch do this to you?" he snapped.

"No, Chance did that."

"Chance? I heard that he quit beating on you."

"No, Sonny, he still hits me, but not in the face anymore. He doesn't want anyone to know."

"Goddamn it. I'm gonna' kick his ass and show him exactly how it feels."

"No, Sonny, don't! Please don't. I don't wanna make him mad again. He only hits me when I make him angry."

"What did you do to him this time to make him hit you?"

"I'm still breastfeeding our youngest and he doesn't want me to."

"He's about two now, isn't he?"

"Yes, but I can't stop nursing. He needs his mother's milk."

"Well, I'm going to talk to him anyway, because we can't have this."

"Please, don't start anything, Sonny. I don't want to lose Chance. I love him, Sonny."

"Christ, Liz! Okay, I'll leave it go for now, but you're going to go upstairs to bed. I'll have Samantha talk to you about that nursing thing or whatever. Okay?"

"Okay. I guess so," she said reluctantly.

Nick Parmalay approached Frank Lujack with an offer that he couldn't refuse. Frank didn't like it. He didn't like it all.

"But Nick, I've known Sonny and Sam for years."

"It's either do this tonight or face jail time, my friend. Think of Bernice and the kids. How would they feel seeing you behind bars for the rest of your life? Besides, there's a good chunk of change in this for you, enough to finally pay off your gambling debts. You don't want Bernice to find out about that, do you?"

"No, of course not, but . . . Okay, I'll do it," agreed Lujack grudgingly.

"That's good. We make a good tandem, you and I. That's what I like about you, Frank. I can always depend on you."

Frank tried to force a smile but somehow he couldn't.

"Here's the key to the blow-out room. If the chief is there, tell him that I sent you and show him the key. He knows it's mine. He'll let you go in. Understand?"

"Yeah, I understand."

"I have to leave now myself. Big John wants me to follow those two Dagos to the airport. He doesn't trust them. I don't either. When you're through, don't come back tonight. I'll explain your absence to Sonny. Do a good job now."

"Sure, Nick."

It was a raucous crowd that spilled out of the banquet hall into the ballroom. While watching the people gather in, Sonny sidled up to Father Harrington, the Metro police department's chaplain.

"There's enough shit floating around here tonight to start a sewage

313

plant," scoffed Sonny, to rouse the Padre.

"Well, hello, Sonny, nice seeing you again," said Harrington.

"Save any souls lately, Papa?"

"I don't save souls. I just try to guide you all down the path to righteousness. We let God do the rest."

"It's becoming a long and winding road, Papa."

"That's the glory of it, my boy. If it were too easy, life would be such a bore wouldn't it?"

"You make sense, Papa. That's what scares me."

"I fail to see where you scare at all, my son."

"Samantha puts the fear of God in me every now and then," joked Sonny, sharing a smile with the priest. "Gotta' go, Papa. I see Sam over there, now."

"I'll pray for you, my son."

"Pray a little harder this time, Papa. The last one didn't take."

Harrington kept his smile as his favorite ex-cop headed toward the red-haired beauty.

Samantha was gathered with her friends in a tight circle chatting away when Sonny approached. "Hey pretty lady, care to dance?" he asked.

"Hello, darling," she answered back, her eyes smiling wide. "I would love to. Excuse me, everyone, while my husband and I go rub bodies for awhile," she said proudly.

They held each other tight as they waltzed to "Moonlight Serenade," and then opened up some to a more fanciful tune that followed.

"I didn't think I was ever going to get out of that banquet room, tonight. To start with, the mayor took his sweet-ass time getting there, and he was his usual winded self."

"Did you win any awards?'

"Oh yes, I won a plaque for best investigative story. My friend, Gina, won for best war correspondent."

"I don't believe I've met her, have I?"

"No, you haven't, but you would like her. She's a peach."

"Don't look now, but your mother is walking towards us with her new boyfriend," said Sonny while spying over Samantha's shoulder.

"Boyfriend? What boyfriend?"

"Shush! Here they come."

"Hello, Kitty," said Sonny.

"Why, hi, Mother," said Samantha.

"Hello, children, are you both enjoying yourself tonight?"

"Yes ma'am. How could I not have fun with your lovely daughter?" said Sonny.

"Yes we are, Mother," Samantha replied.

"I must say, Samantha, I'm so proud of you for winning that award, tonight."

"Thank you, Mother, but I don't feel I deserve it."

"Nonsense my dear, you most certainly do. My, where are my manners. I haven't introduced my good friend, Dr. Carl Francis, to you yet. He's a renowned plastic surgeon, you know."

"So you're the doctor that gave my mother-in-law her new breasts?" said Sonny.

"Oh yes. She seems to enjoy them well, don't you, dear?"

"Oh yes. He did a fashionable job."

"Mother, you never told me," quipped Samantha.

"You never asked. Sonny knew. Hell, I showed them to him."

"Samantha, if you would be interested in some breast augmentation, I would gladly set up a complimentary appointment with you to examine your needs," said the doctor obligingly.

"Looking at my wife right now, what would you propose for her, Dr. Francis?" asked Sonny with a smirk.

"It's not really for me to decide, Sonny, but I personally think Samantha would look rather nice with larger breasts."

"No thanks, Doctor. Unlike my mother, I am well satisfied with what nature has given me," said Samantha.

"We'll let you two go back to dancing. I must introduce, Dr. Francis to the Wellingtons," said Kitty.

"Nice meeting you both," said Dr. Francis.

"Nice meeting you, Doc," answered Sonny.

"Did you get a load of that guy, thinking that I needed larger breasts? What a jerk!"

"He might have a point there, Highpockets," snickered Sonny.

"Oh yeah, what do you propose, Pamela Anderson's boobs?"

"That would be nice."

"I don't think so. Remember what you once told me, dear? More than a mouthful is a waste."

"Oh yeah, I guess you're right."

"Why didn't you tell me that Mom had a boyfriend?"

"Your mom didn't want me to. She thought it would upset you if you found out."

"I haven't really had much time to think about it. Hell, if she's happy with it, I guess its okay. At least she's getting some, now."

Sonny is startled with a sudden tap on his shoulder.

"May I cut in?"

Sonny didn't know the tall, dark-haired man but he assumed that Samantha did. She knew most everyone anyway, it seemed. "Why sure, go right ahead," said Sonny, "I've got to make my rounds, anyway. I'll meet up with you a little later, baby."

"I must say, you look ravishing tonight," blandished Rick Jamision, while gathering Samantha in his arms for a dance.

"Why thank you, Rick. Its nice seeing you again, I must say."

"I don't see how I let you slip past me in all those years of college."

"As I recall, you were quite the lady's man back then, and didn't seem to notice that I was around."

"How could I have overlooked you? Sonny is such a lucky man. Congratulations on winning the award tonight."

"Thanks again, Rick."

"Contrary to how I feel about you, I'm not here to try and steal you from your husband, but I do have a sweet job offer for you with WYNG. And believe it or not, I have your father's approval, that is, if you were to accept."

"Wow, I don't know what to say," answered Samantha, a bit dumbfounded. "This is such a shock to me at this time. I don't know, Rick, I have a lot of irons in the fire right now."

"Look, it's a job offer that will lead you to what you have always wanted, becoming a TV anchorwoman. I'm not just talking WYNG, but CSN, baby."

"But, Rick, there's been a lot of water run under the bridge since I was last offered the job of an anchorwoman. You know, I am 43 years old now."

"Don't fret about that. They've changed the rules. You're not too old for that job. Besides, you look much younger than your age. Must be that good life, eh? The only catch to it, Sam, is that we want you to work for us first as a foreign correspondent in Iraq for six months. After that, CSN will have a spot cleared out for you at their New York station. You're going big time, girl. Believe me, they will offer you a major contract with all the goodies attached. As it is, you will receive a substantial raise from us."

"Well, how soon would I start?"

"Monday would be none too soon. Actually, we will have you work with Gina Pirelli for a few weeks in D.C. She'll fill you in on all you need to know about the Middle East."

"Yeah, I know Gina. She's a good friend of mine."

"That's perfect, Sam."

"But are you sure that Big John is okay with all of this?"

"I'm sure. Check with him if you like."

"How long is this offer open to me?"

"We can hold it open for a good week, but not much longer. To be honest, we could use you right now."

"I'm flattered that you want me still, but I have to talk to my dad, since he is my employer."

"Sure, go right ahead, Samantha. We would love to have you on our team. We'll anxiously await your answer."

"Thank you for the dance, Rick."

"The pleasure's all mine."

Sonny found Jaques Leblanc with his easel set up near the kitchen. Lucrecia was with him, observing the different types of people.

"Hey, Sonny, my good friend, come have a drink with me" said Jaques.

"I can't right now. My assistant has left the building on another assignment, and that leaves just me in charge of inside security. I need all of my faculties. So, what are you doing here tonight, Jaques?"

"I'm sketching people; mostly couples that want remembrances of this evening. It doesn't take too long to sketch, and I enjoy it."

"Say, Sonny, the painting that Jaques did of Danielle turned out real well. Have you seen it yet?" asked Lucrecia.

"No, I didn't know that she was having a portrait made."

"Oh yes. She had Jaques to paint her nude as he did her mother so many years ago."

"You mean you painted my daughter naked?"

Jaques and Lucrecia laughed generously at their bemused friend. "Sonny, don't worry. Jaques was very discreet about it," assured Lucrecia.

"Yeah, I only painted her backside just like in Samantha's portrait," he added. "You know Danielle is the same age that Samantha was when you wanted me to paint her. And just like Samantha, your daughter is very beautiful. You will like, I'm sure," said Jaques confidently.

"I think I'll have that drink after all, Jaques."

As Samantha exited the ladies room she bumped into no other than Troy Charbonau.

"Hi," she said weakly.

"Hello, Samantha. It's been a long time. My, but you sure look great."

"Troy, I'm really sorry about—"

"Would you care to dance with me, Samantha? I know it seems awkward but I assure you no harm will come from it."

"Okay," she said shyly.

Troy took her hand and led the dazzling redhead to the dance floor. They danced quietly to some soft jazz. She could not look into his eyes at first, but she felt his upon hers. She felt the softness of his hands while her nostrils sucked in the sweet smell of his musk; same as before but yet different. They danced close and were silent, yet their eyes spoke volumes; Troy, with his soft stare, and Samantha with nervous glances at his handsome face.

As the evening waned, the huge chandelier cast a festive glow on the ballroom floor, where booze flowed and inhibitions fell to the wayside, with the band serenading coupled lovers embraced in dance.

"Darling; let's go somewhere more discreet, so we can talk," said Troy.

"Meet me out back, at the summerhouse . . . in five minutes."

"Matt Glover had finally sucked down enough booze to garner the courage to dance with his lovely wife, Danielle. But a heavy tap on his shoulder sought different.

"Yeah, what do you want," he snarled. "Oh, it's you Dad, sorry."

"Sorry hell! I'm dancing with my daughter. You go over there with Kitty. She's looking for someone to dance with, I think."

"Okay Dad, sure thing." Off he went.

"Daddy, you don't have to be so rude to Matt," protested Danielle.

"He doesn't have to call me Dad either, but he does," growled Sonny. "Sam told me that the human jock-strap has been giving you a hard time."

"Oh no, Daddy, everything is straightened out now. I took care of that a while ago."

"Are you sure? Because I'll straighten him out for you."

"No, he's just fine. Mom gave me some good advice and it worked."

"Have you heard from your sister lately? She never comes home anymore."

"Sonja's growing up Dad. She prefers to be at college with her friends. I saw her last week. She's doing just fine."

"I have another question for you, Danny. Where did you get the idea of letting a stranger paint a picture of you naked?"

"I got the idea from Mother's portrait. You let Jaques paint Samantha naked, and it's beautiful art. I want to look beautiful too. Besides, I got Matt to pay for it. Don't look so pissed, Daddy. It's only my backside."

"I'm not pissed, baby, but I don't want to see your picture in any Playboy. Hear?"

"Oh Daddy, you're so silly," smiled Danielle.

Sonny smiled back and gave his daughter a hug. "I better let joy-boy back over here. Kitty's feet are starting to bleed."

"Oh, Daddy, you're too much," laughed Danielle.

Samantha entered the gazebo while coyly looking over her shoulder. "I wasn't expecting you here, tonight. Who is that lady that came with you? She's very pretty."

"Charlene's her name. I call her Charlie. She's just a friend, that's all. She's not as beautiful as you, Samantha. You can't hide your thoughts, Sam. Your eyes give you away. You are the most unique human being that I have ever met." Troy drew her in closer. So close that his warm breath caressed Samantha's red lips. "I have longed for you, Sam. I've dreamed of a life together."

With her mind in a quandary, Samantha turned away. But Troy pulled her to him, caressing her long soft neck with short kisses. Samantha grimaced, rolling her head back and forth, her mind writhing in the pain of adultery. Troy's wet lips searched even lower, to the tops of her alabaster breasts as they basked in the moonlight. Samantha became chilled on the outside, but on the inside, the hot embers of six years ago were stoked into a raging fire about to release its fury. But Troy stopped, for Samantha was struggling too much with her thoughts. "Let your love flow, Sam."

"I can't, Troy. I just can't. I'm married, and I love my husband."

"But, honey, don't you think you can love more than one person at a time?"

"No. Not this way. What we had before was great for a while, but that was D.C. and this is my home. I made a mistake before. I was mixed-up."

"We can always fly back to D.C., dear. I've got a place there. It needs a woman's touch. It needs you, Sam."

"I'm sorry, Troy, but it's over. It has to be."

"Can I feel your lips just one more time, Sam?"

"Sure."

They embraced like the lovers they once were, and then Troy pulled away. "I'll hang around just in case."

Samantha nodded her approval, for she feared she would cry if she spoke.

"If you change your mind, darling, I'll be at the Adams Mark for the next week."

"I won't."

"I'm sorry it didn't work out, you and I."

"Yeah, me too," cried Samantha.

Chapter Twenty-Two

Turn Out the Lights

Several times previously Big John had thwarted his daughter's attempts to leave the Times to attain her career goal of becoming a news anchorwoman. It had been her desire since her college days. This time he would do anything within his means to get her to take the job. He had to first, get her out of harms way.

The big guy had the unflattering task of wishing the governor and his entourage a pleasant evening while escorting them out of the Taylor mansion at evening's end. Half the crowd had left by now and most of the rest were drunk, in some sense of the word. His duties for the Governor's Ball were now complete. All the dignitaries were safely tucked away in their limousines, on their way home.

Big John retreated to his den to treat himself to a double-scotch whiskey and a Cuban cigar, and to wait for his daughter to appear, seeking his advice. He thought long and hard about the future of his tenacious daughter. Even the Italian mob would leave his family alone if they didn't interfere with business. But Samantha had broken the rules. She didn't know it. She was innocent in thought. John needed to protect her. He heard what Constantine said, and he knew what that cold-blooded killer was capable of doing. Samantha didn't know the gravity of the situation, and it was too late to disenfranchise Sonny from the family, but he would be dealt with. .Samantha must leave until the dust is settled, was Big John's thinking. She mustn't know the real truth; that her father had long ago fallen from grace.

"I suppose you know about the job offer I received from Rick

Jamison," spoke Samantha upon entering the den.

"Of course, my dear, he ran it by me first," replied her father, "I think it's a great idea. It's your chance to anchor a major news station. That's what you wanted all along, isn't it?"

"Yes, of course but—"

"It's time I let you spread your wings and move on to greater things, daughter."

"I, I can't go away for a six-month stint in Iraq. I can't leave Sonny like that. Look what happened when I left before. He damn near got himself killed."

"You know, Sonny has become a millstone around your neck, Sam. Love is blind and you've been blinded by love ever since you met him. Your mother and I couldn't stop you, and we weren't about to because we didn't want to see our little girl hurt. It's not because Sonny comes from the wrong side of the tracks. That's not it at all. He's dangerous, Sam. He takes the law into his own hands. If he would've done his job the way he was supposed to, Centralia would have never happened. Neither would have Scoville. He bypasses the law. He runs with the hookers, whores, and reprobates. He represents everything that you don't. I know you love him, but are you going let him keep on ruining your life like this?"

"You've never liked Sonny anyway, Daddy. I think there's more here than meets the eye. What is it, Daddy? Look, I know I became obsessed with the Waverly scandal, but you didn't have to shut me down on it. I so wanted to nail that crook, John Losch. Why did you stop me?"

"John's our friend, Sam."

"Yeah, right," she said.

"Do you remember the night that you got stood up at the prom and I picked up a little girl crying on the steps in front of her school?". . .

"Yes Daddy."

"I made two phone calls while in town that night. Do you remember who they were made to?"

"I know you called Mother, but I don't recollect to whom the other call was made."

"It was to John Losch. Johnny owned Bernie's Bungalow at the time. He was the one that helped me out that night. He served notice that when we arrived, the rest of the evening belonged to you. He made sure that every man in his club danced with my little girl. Do you know why? It was because he was my true and loyal friend. He didn't care about making money or losing customers that night. He only cared about you. Johnny's not a bad man, Sam."

"Why didn't he mention anything to me, Dad? Why wouldn't he call me at the Times for a rebuttal?"

"Because you're my daughter, and he loves and respects you as if you were his own. No, he didn't ask for a rebuttal. He just took his lumps from you and tried to rectify things as best as he could. But you wouldn't let him be. He finally had to go on T.V."

"But, Dad, they were siphoning their profits to Miramar, stealing from the government, from the patients. And then the mistreatment of the nurses; what about all of that?"

"I'm going to tell you something right now that I never intended to reveal to you, Sam. John Loesch is Miramar. When he started Waverly Enterprises he was legit. Along the way he somehow fell into bad company. He is still associated with them but we're trying to break him loose. Politics and business make strange bed partners, and their practices are not always fair to the public. His associates don't like people snooping into their affairs. That's why I had to stop you, Sam. These people aren't friendly people. They sent their thugs this evening to deliver a message. One was to get rid of you, and the other was to eliminate Sonny Rafferty. You see, darling, Sonny has crossed over that thin gray line. We can only save him so many times. As with you, things will blow over by the time you return from Iraq. By then you'll be living in New York."

"But, Daddy, I love him, can't you see? He means more to me than anything else."

"If you love him, Sam, then let him loose. Take Jamison's job offer and go out of country until things blow over. This isn't like Centralia, Sam. These people are big-time hoods. I can't fight them. Neither can you. Sonny thinks different, and he's going to get you both killed for that. Now, you tell me. Where is his love for you?"

"But, Daddy, we don't know his side of the story."

"What is his side of the story, Sam? What has he told you?"

"He won't say."

"How fair is that to you? What has he got to hide, Sam? If he really cared about you, don't you think he would've told you? Where was your husband last weekend, Samantha? Tell me."

"He was in Cincinnati with a friend investigating the murder of her sister."

"Who was that friend?"

"Angie Garza. She owns the Body Perfect health club. She used to work alongside Sonny as a cop years ago."

"Did you know that she was a prostitute and a drug addict?"

"That was a long time ago, according to Sonny. Besides, she looked to be in perfect health the last time I saw her at the club."

"I didn't want to tell you this, dear, for fear of hurting your feelings, but now I must. Nick Parmalay had his people at Metro investigate your husband."

"That's not right, Dad!"

"Now, hear me out, Samantha. He found Sonny and that Garza girl together on several occasions, embraced in lewd behavior. They've even spent nights together at cheap motels around town."

"That's a lie! She's just a friend!"

"Is she? Did you know that two years ago Sonny lent Angie Garza thirty-thousand dollars to start that business of hers?"

" . . . No, I didn't,"

"Have you checked your bank records lately, Samantha?"

"No, but he wouldn't do that without consulting me first."

"Do yourself a favor and check your account, honey."

"That just doesn't sound like Sonny."

"Cincinnati wasn't the only place that Sonny visited last weekend. He paid a visit to that bar down near Scoville, where he killed that boy two months ago. He won't tell you that he was visiting a five-thousand dollar an hour hooker by the name of Jamaica Red, but I will. Guess what, Sam. That place burned to the ground Sunday night, and I bet Sonny wasn't in bed with you, was he?"

"Nick's wrong. That's all there is to it!" said Samantha defiantly.

"Nick didn't tell me that, Sam. It came from the two thugs that visited me earlier this evening."

"I just can't believe Sonny would do that, especially after all the years we've been together."

"I'm not trying to drive a wedge between the two of you. I'm just trying to give you the truth, baby. Talk to Sonny; ask him what he did last weekend. Ask him who Johnny Carlisle is."

"Johnny Carlisle? I don't get it."

"That's the name he used when he visited Jamaica Red."

"I'm so confused, Daddy. Things started out so good today, and now it's all unraveling."

"Take the job, Sam. Let Sonny solve his own problems. We'll see about you and him when you return. Who knows what may happen."

"I can't just up and leave him, Daddy. I can't let anything happen to him, because the girls love him so," she said teary-eyed.

"It's not your choice, Samantha. It's his. Can't you see that? The word is out. They want him dead, and they want you with him. Who will the girls have to love then? Do you want them to know you by just putting flowers on your grave and wondering what you would have thought of your little grandbabies if you were still alive? Is that what you want, Samantha? Look, you and Sonny had a great life together. Let him go. He's not likely to change. It's too late for him, but not for you. Give your girls a legacy. Don't leave them behind to face life alone. They've just now grown into womanhood. They need you, darling."

"But, Daddy, who will look after the girls when I go over-seas?" asked Samantha.

"Your mother and I will, of course. They're our girls too. They will want not, Sam. I promise you. You'll only be gone for a short while before your return, anyway."

"I've got another thing that I have to talk to you about, Father. I've teamed with the NAWR organization to support legislation aimed at helping nurses nationwide to fight against workplace discrimination. It's a bit detailed but I promised their president, Pat Fowler, that I would give them editorial space in our paper. They, in return, would endorse Chance for the state senate so he can help in the cause."

"Does Chance know about this?"

"Oh yes, I've talked to him. He likes the idea. I know that I should have run it past you first, but it seemed like such an important opportunity that I agreed first-hand. So, how about it, Dad? We can go over the particulars on Monday. That's when Pat's meeting with me at the Times."

"Listen to me, Samantha. You need to leave as soon as possible. I'll meet with Pat Fowler and give her what she wants. I promise."

"I have to be there, Dad. She doesn't trust anyone else. She's the one in charge of it all."

"Do you mean that you don't have your name on this at all?"

"No, that was part of the deal. The NAWR gets credit for everything if we can get our bill into law."

"Okay. I'll go along with that if you'll take Jamison up on his offer."

"Okay, Daddy. I just don't know what I'm going to tell Sonny. I just can't believe that he has done all that, especially him cheating on me," she said, burying her face into Big John's chest.

"I know, baby. It hurts. Have a good cry. Things will turn out all right in the end. I'm here for ya. I won't let you down. You're my little girl," he consoled, while taking a long, satisfying puff off the Cuban.

Samantha left word for Sonny to meet with her in the drawing room. The saddened redhead grabbed some tissues to dry her eyes as she tried to make some sense out of what her father had told her. Everything in her mind seemed scrambled right now. She knew her husband to be a maverick, and, at times, defiant, but she never suspected him of being a libertine. She had spent many a lonely night in bed, wondering where her husband was, what kind of trouble he might be in, and was he missing her as much as she was missing him. Some nights, before drifting off to sleep, Samantha would picture in her mind Sonny making love to her. She could almost feel his body on top of hers, and envisioned his swollen member buried deep within the furthermost regions of her loins, all-the-while pleasuring herself. It didn't ease the loneliness in her heart, but it did release the passion in her loins. Even still, Sonny was her consummate lover.

Could it be that Sonny was spending those nights sharing his passion, his body, his lovemaking, with others? Surely not, she wished. She wanted to ask him. She was afraid to. She wanted to ask him. Yet she didn't want to hear his answer. Indeed, she wanted to ask him, but then run away in fear of the truth. It was this paradox that hauntingly inhabited her thoughts.

Samantha had a plan though. Surely she could talk Sonny into leaving with her. After all, Sonny had always been supportive of her career. If he would just leave with her, just this one time, all his trespasses she would forgive. Surely he would accept such an offer. She couldn't bear to think of life without him. She felt certain that he could catch on with some government agency to do some type of security work, like maybe training police officers and such.

"Hey baby, what's up? I just ran into your father, said that you wanted to see me about somethin'. Also invited us up to the billiard room for a night' cap. Guess there's a pool game going on up there."

"Sit right here for a moment, Sonny. I've got something I want to talk with you about. Rick Jamison offered me a job with WYNG," she flatly stated.

"What kind of offer was it, Sam? Was it for an anchorwoman's position?"

"Well, yes and no. I should say, no and yes. At first, I will be a field correspondent. Then, I'll get the job in front of the camera."

"That sounds okay, Sam. What does your dad think about all of this, or did you tell him yet?"

"Oh, he knows about it. He's okay with it; how about you, Sonny?"

"Whatever you want, darlin', is okay with me."

"I want you with me when I go out into the field."

"Well, if I'm not on a case I guess I can hang with you some."

"I don't think you quite understand the job offer, Sonny. They want to send me to Iraq as a foreign correspondent until a job opens up for me in New York City at the CSN station."

"Whoa! Back that horse up a minute. I don't think you want to go to Iraq just now, or ever. People are getting killed over there everyday."

"I know, Sonny, but I want the job, and I need you with me. You said whatever I wanted."

"Yeah, but I wasn't expecting you to spring this on me."

"You must understand, baby, the benefits will outweigh the danger in all of this."

"I don't think so. Besides, you know how squeamish you are at the sight of blood."

"That's why I need you there with me, darling."

"What about the girls? What about our pets? Who's gonna' pay the bills and collect the rent?"

"Face it Sonny, the girls are all grown up. Mary can watch after the pets and Myra can handle the rest. Anyhow, we'll only be out of country for three to six months."

"Yeah, that's what they tell you now. I don't like the smell of this, Sam."

"But Sonny—"

"Hey, let's go upstairs and shoot some pool. We'll talk more on this later."

"But Sonny—"

"Come on. I can hear those balls breaking from down here. Let's have some fun before we close this place tonight," insisted Sonny.

"Havana's best" stung their eyes and pierced their nostrils as Sonny and Samantha entered the billiard parlor. The "one for the roadies" had gathered around the mini-bar, the only watering hole still open from the evening's bash. The boisterous Big John Taylor was serving up the drinks as his brown-haired paramour, Margo Solsta, clung to him unabashedly. They caught the big man's eye right away.

"Hey kids, come on in. I'll fix you both a drink. Sonny, grab yourself a cigar out of the humidor. Hell, take a couple. They're Castro's best," he boasted.

At the bar sat Gina Pirelli with her date, Lance Richards, along with Charlene Webb, who came with Troy.

"Hi, Sam," greeted Gina tipsily. "Introduce me to that good-lookin' man of yours."

Samantha smiled and presented Sonny to Gina and her friends, and Gina returned the same courtesy.

Sonny lit up the expensive stogie and watched the boys play their game while Samantha conversed with Gina and her friends.

"Congratulations, Sam. Your dad just told me that we're going to be working together for a bit."

"Well, it isn't exactly etched in stone yet, but it looks that way."

"I'll be glad to have you with me in D. C. again. We'll do the town up right, this time."

Samantha rolled her eyes at the thought.

"What does Sonny think about you leaving?"

"He doesn't like it at all as far as I can tell. I'm trying to get him to go to Iraq with me. He could get a job there in security, I should think."

"You better hope so, Sam. That place can drive a person stir-crazy."

"I'll have to manage, I guess."

"Don't fret, you'll do just fine, girlfriend. So, when you get back, it's New York, eh?"

"Yeah, that's the good part, I guess."

"You don't seem too enthused about it, Sam."

"Aw, I guess it hasn't sunk in yet."

"I have to excuse myself now, Samantha. There's a Frenchman downstairs that wants to draw me. I must not keep him waiting. You know those Frenchmen, ooh la, la. I like your husband, Sam. He's cute. Give me a call tomorrow. We have some planning to do, girl."

"Sure thing, Gina," Samantha replied.

"Lance, you coming with?" she asked.

"No, Gina. Charlie and I have to get back to the hotel soon, but I'll call you again sometime. Thanks for a lovely evening," he said, sending her off with a quick kiss.

"So, you're both part of Senator Charbonau's entourage?" asked Sonny.

"We *are* the senator's entourage," said Charlene.

"So, are you two CIA personnel?"

"Oh no, we're nothing like that," said Lance, "We push papers, mostly."

"We, more-or-less came along for the ride," added Charlene.

Lance checked his watch, "We have to leave now, nice meeting you both," he said with a quick handshake.

Sonny looked at Samantha, "I'll tell you one thing. They're not paper pushers."

"How can you tell?"

"By their hands, and their physique," said Sonny.

"Who do you suppose they are?"

"Probably CIA or FBI," he said.

"What would they be doing here?"

"They're probably here to watch over the senator, for one thing. But Charbonau doesn't seem that high profile to me. They could be here for alternative reasons, also."

"Boy, Sonny, your mind never stops churning, does it?"

"That's why I'm a P. I., my dear."

The sudden crack of a pool cue turned their attention to a game of eight-ball being played by Chance Taylor and Troy Charbonau.

Samantha's heart fluttered at seeing the handsome senator, in his shirtsleeves, shooting pool with her brother. She caught herself staring at him and looked away. Sonny took notice of her but sloughed it off, because Troy did have those Hollywood good looks about him. He was more interested in the woman in the cheesecloth tunic and thong that sat in the corner, partially hidden by her pool-playing husband. He could have sworn that he put her to bed two hours ago to sleep off a drunk. Other than looking a bit sleepy-eyed she seemed to be regenerated. As Sonny stared at Liz, she shot back a hard look that warned him not to mention to her husband about her little spree with Rico earlier that evening.

Chance caught sight of Sonny and relaxed his shot stance. "Hello, Sonny, long time, no see," he smirked.

"I don't know if that's good or bad, Chance," Sonny replied.

"It depends on whom you talk to, I guess," said Chance.

"So, you're Samantha's husband?" said the senator, offering his hand in friendship. "I'm Troy, Charbonau. I've been wanting to meet you. I met your wife a few years back in Washington D.C. She spoke highly of you then."

"Not too highly, I hope."

"Oh no, I guess she just missed you, that's all. She seemed a bit homesick, as I recall. We met at some dinner function that she and Gina came to. You have a beautiful wife there, Sonny."

"Thanks, Senator. I think so too."

Samantha was becoming a little uneasy. She felt like she was sitting on top of a powder keg. She knew that Troy was toying a bit with Sonny and with her too for rejecting him earlier in the summerhouse. Sonny was ignorant of it all. It was a most uncomfortable feeling for her, being that close in the same room with her once lover, and with her brother and husband who were throwing darts at each other.

"Come, join us, Sonny. You can play the winner," said Troy.

"Nah, I'll just watch. I'm on duty, you know."

"On duty, off duty, it's all the same with you, isn't it?" chided Chance.

Sonny didn't like Chance's smart mouth but kept quiet about his snide remark.

Chance began running the table. The more he worked the table, the more excited he got. The more excited he got, the more belligerent he became, towards Sonny that is. "You see, Troy, Sonny used to be a cop but he retired early. The stress was too much for him so he became a private dick. But he doesn't get much work; seems like every time he works a case someone gets hurt, or killed. So, Big John gives him odds and end jobs to hold him over until Samantha brings home the bacon."

"That's enough, son," said Big John from behind the bar. "I think Mr. Charbonau has heard enough about Sonny."

But Chance wasn't done yet. "Hell, he hasn't even carried a gun since his colored partner and a little girl got killed in a bungled motel raid, six years ago."

"That's not fair!" exclaimed Samantha, "That couldn't be helped."

"Let him go, Sam. Let's see just how much shit comes out of his mouth," said Sonny.

"Couldn't be helped? What about that kid you killed at the Devil's Bone Yard, Sonny. Tell us about that. Tell us how you shoved his nose into his brain."

"How do you know about the Bone Yard, Chance? Tell me, huh? We would all like to know," seethed Sonny.

"I said that's enough!" yelled Big John.

But Chance couldn't stop his tirade. "Why Sonny, you're the only one that doesn't know what happened because you got your fool head bashed in," he gloated. "You're lucky they didn't kill you, *Kill you, Kill you*, **Kill you!"**

"I said that's enough, Son!"

But it was too late. Chance's last words reverberated through Sonny's head as Sonny saw Chance's mysterious dark figure, along with Jamaica Red's, standing over him. Chance's arrogant bullying retrieved the last vestiges of Sonny's memory loss. Sonny suddenly lunged over the billiard table, clipping Chance with a right to the chin. But Chance, like the mongrel dog he was, busted his cue stick over Sonny's head and kicked the big guy as he struggled to keep his feet. Fists were thrown, with Chance going down and Sonny on top of him. Big John and Troy struggled to pull them apart with Liz screaming at Sonny while her contemptuous eyes stared daggers through his wife.

"You'll get yours, Sonny. Just wait and see," snarled Chance, wiping the blood from his mouth.

"We'll see," said Sonny. "We'll see."

Big John took over the conversation, "Liz, take Chance home and cool him down. Sam, you get your man out of here, now!"

"I'm staying to finish my job tonight," said Sonny. "That's what you're paying me for."

"Very well, but you two boys stay away from each other, hear."

Neither answered; they just nodded while sneering at each other with contempt.

"It's about time that I headed out too, Big John," said the senator.

"Sorry about this, Senator."

"Don't be. I come from a family of boys. I'm used to this. It's nice to infiltrate into the enemy's camp every now and then to shoot a game of pool with one's adversary. Chance beat me quite soundly this time. Maybe I'll fare better come November."

"We're going to give you a good run."

"I expect nothing less. Goodnight, sir."

With fire in her eyes, Samantha briskly led her brooding husband down the stairs and into the kitchen to attend to his head wound. Disappointment in Sonny's response to her new job offer, plus the embarrassment of his childish sparring with Chance in her father's house, and in front of the senator, caused a tempest to stir in the redhead. While slapping a bag of ice to Sonny's head her pot finally boiled over. "What the hell was that all about, Sonny?"

"What do you mean? You were in there. You saw what happened."

"Yeah, I was in there. I saw Chance getting a bit rambunctious and you losing your temper and starting a fight with him."

"What can I say? Things finally came to a head. I don't like his smart mouth, and I don't like the way he's treating Liz."

"Liz, what the hell is Liz to you? Are you banging her too?"

"I don't understand. What are you talking about?"

"Don't play coy with me, Sonny. I heard all about you and your women friends. Who's Jamaica Red, Sonny?"

"I don't know who's been talking to you, Sam, but it's not what you think."

"It never is, Sonny, is it? Just exactly where were you last weekend?"

"What? You don't trust me anymore?"

"Just tell me where you were."

"I was looking for Candy's killer."

"What happened this time down at Scoville, Sonny? What about the thirty grand that you gave Angie Garza?"

"That was just a loan. Most of it has been paid back, already."

"How did Angie pay you back, Sonny? Did she spread her legs for you?"

"You're being ridiculous now!"

"Am I?"

"Samantha, what's happening to you? You know you're the only one that understands me."

"Understand you, hell! That's the fucking problem, Sonny. Nobody understands you. I've tried but you've finally tuned me out. I've been trying to tell you that someone is out to kill you, and now I'm on their list too. And as usual, Daddy is stuck helping us."

"We don't need him. I'll protect you."

"Can't you get it through your thick skull that you can't do everything? You are not God!"

"You've got that right, Sam, because if I were, I'd sure as hell do a better job of it so we wouldn't be faced with a dilemma every time we turn around."

"Geezus, Sonny, you're the dilemma. Can't you see it? You think you're a comic book superhero or something. That's your problem!"

"How could you say that, darlin'? You don't really know my problems. You don't know me at all, do you, Sam?"

"I once knew a Sonny Rafferty," she cried, "But this person I'm looking at now is a stranger to me. I don't want him coming home tonight, sleeping in my bed. Do you hear me?"

"Is that the way you want it?"

"That's the way it has to be, Sonny, until you change." With tears of frustration sliding down her florid cheeks, Samantha turned her back to Sonny and walked out the kitchen door. Then out of the mansion . . . out of Sonny's life.

She saw him in the shadows just standing there, as if waiting for someone. Her mind said, "Don't go with him, no matter what." But her body disagreed, and her heart quivered in anticipation. She eased up next to him and slid her arm in his. He looked into her eyes, and she in his. Together they walked leisurely to his limo in waiting. When inside, she said not a word, just forlornly lay her soft red curls gingerly against the handsome senator's shoulder while he gave directions to his driver.

Samantha had never talked that harsh to him before. Sonny was

333

stunned and hurt, and was bitter about it all. His thinking was that he didn't deserve this. Maybe it was time for a change, for both of them.

He was making his rounds throughout the capacious mansion, ejecting any late-night stragglers that happened to be about, when he heard a disturbance near the botanical gardens. As soon as he stepped through the back door he recognized Lucrecia's voice spewing out unflattering remarks to the likes he had never before heard from her.

"God damn it! Old man, get your scrawny ass out of that pool!" she ordered. "You old drunken fool, leave that girl alone."

The old drunken fool was Jaques, frolicking bare-assed in the water with the saucy Gina Pirelli. It looked to be a sketching gone bad, for Gina was splashing around the pool in her expensive evening gown. Apparently, she must have fallen in, thought Sonny.

"Oh Sonny, Frenchie's had too much to drink. Will you help me get him out of the pool?" asked Lucrecia.

Sonny persuaded his drunken friend to climb out of the water and back into his clothes. It was a humorous sight, the both of them.

Lucrecia folded up Jaques' easel, thanked Sonny for his assistance, and then abruptly left with her little wet Frenchman right behind her.

Sonny walked over to help the dark-haired temptress from the pool. She offered her hand to him while clutching the bodice of her décolleté gown with the other, trying to keep it from sliding down.

"Nothing like a midnight swim, eh?"

"It's not bad. You ought to try it, Sonny."

"Can't; left my trunks at home."

"You can swim in the nude. I won't mind," she said with a snappy smile.

"But I moon burn easy."

"I'll just have to rub you down with lotion afterwards. I've got soft hands, you know."

Sonny smiled large as he watched Gina struggle with her soggy dress. "Do you want me to find something you can change into?"

"That would be nice."

"I'll see what I can come up with. Be right back. Don't go anywhere."

"Yeah, right, like I'm gonna go somewhere," said Gina.

Sonny hadn't noticed Kitty being around for awhile so he decided to check with Big John for some dry clothes for Samantha's Italian friend.

But he found the big guy passed out on the bar while Margo was spread out on the billiard table.

Sonny decided to check the linen closet at the end of the hallway. As he approached the closet he heard a woman's voice, along with a sound akin to a ruttin' buck. He followed the quaint sound to the guest bedroom, next to the linen closet. Curiosity got the best of him so he slowly opened the door and peeked inside. What Sonny saw next would forever leave an indelible impression on him. Mrs. T was having her own night-cap. There she was in all her splendor, her legs splayed high and wide with the good doctor in between, huffin' and puffin' and plowing Kitty's furrow deep and straight, causing her newborn globes to jiggle like twin Jello molds. Sonny stared at her, and she smiled sleepily back at him while Carl was delivering his goods. Sonny then thought it time to leave.

"All I could find is this bathrobe," he said to Gina.

"That'll do just fine," replied Gina.

Sonny handed her the robe and turned his back while she changed out of her wet things. "So, how are you getting home, tonight?" he asked.

"I don't know. My date left me."

"You mean, Lance?"

"Yeah, I think he dumped me for Charlie tonight, the bastard!"

"I can take you home. Where do you live?"

"I live by Gasoline Alley. That's a good ways from here."

"That's alright. I don't mind."

"Let's see what Sam says."

Sonny turned back around. "Sam has already left. I guess she took a cab home."

"Was she sick?"

"No. We had a fight. She doesn't want me coming home tonight so I'm staying at my office. It's not far from here."

"Why can't I just go with you tonight?"

"You mean, to my office?"

"Sure, why not?"

"Well, if you don't mind sleeping on a leather couch."

"Sounds good to me, where will you sleep?"

"I probably won't, but if I do I have a big office chair that suits me."

"You don't mind?"

"Of course not, I need some company anyway."

"We ain't left yet?"

Sonny smiled big.

Chapter Twenty-Three

Do Me Right Love Me Wrong

Troy watched with anticipation as Samantha unsnapped her garters and delicately slid her silk stockings down her long slender legs. He was enamored by her beauty. From the first time he laid eyes on her, at a dinner function back in D. C., he became infatuated with the red-haired journalist. She dazzled him with her wit and candor, along with her feminine pulchritude. He couldn't help that she belonged to another. She pulled on his heartstrings like none other. He waited six long years to confront her. He tried other women. He and Gina even had a brief fling, nothing serious, just sexual. Nothing could erase Samantha Rafferty from his mind. Though, hopelessly in love with her, Troy was a realist. If Samantha were to accept his offer and leave Sonny to be with him he would call off his dogs and go back to Washington with her by his side; to hell with the campaign trail. Chance was no threat to him. If he couldn't persuade Samantha that they were made for each other then he'd have no choice but to proceed with the real reason he came to Indianapolis.

With Troy's soft blue eyes upon her, Samantha slipped out of her blue-sequined evening gown; the one that she had meticulously picked out to capture Sonny's attention. She then stepped out of her wispy panties, showing herself to him as she made herself ready for bed.

Troy poured two Cognacs and walked up to where she lay, and offered her one. She accepted his offering, taking a sip and then, ravenously drank the rest straight down. "Would you like another?" he asked politely.

"Yes please. Bring the decanter back with you. I have a distinct liking for Brandy tonight," she said thickly. Those were the first words she spoke since she left the manor. Her dress, her under-things; even the redolence of Cinnabar from her body, were all for Sonny tonight. Yet now, Troy had it all. It was her father's concise report on her husband's infidelities that brought Samantha to this precipice; that, and his desperado tactics. Sonny Rafferty was freefalling from grace at a rapid pace.

At first they just cuddled in quietude. Then, her flaxen-haired lover touched her ever so lightly in all the right places. He knew all of her spots, all her erogenous zones. He remembered them well from when he was just 29 and she, a mature but vulnerable woman of 37. He finally broke through her icy dignity and gained unfettered access to her plush, rich, love canal, where he imbibed her mysterious musk.

Gina was more than happy to go with Sonny to his office and spend the night. She wanted to see what it was about Sonny that impressed Samantha so.

She studied his features on the ride over. His nicked and scarred face made him rugged looking, which, in itself, was enough to turn a city girl's juices loose. But he didn't possess the movie star looks of Troy Charbonau, and he also lacked the suavity and the polished mannerisms of the gentleman senator. He looked to be strong and masculine, and dangerous; a protector, someone to snuggle up to on a cold winter's night, and someone to keep the wolves from the door. She liked that. He didn't seem pompous and self-aggrandizing like most of her lovers in Washington, who massaged their own egos by bragging on their stock market earnings and business dealings. Sonny seemed like a man that might know about real love, in which there was a shortage of in D.C., where politicians were businessmen and businessmen were politicians, and where love and compassion were deemed a weakness and tossed aside in exchange for pure carnal pleasures, however bought and paid for.

"Are you comfortable in your bathrobe? I have some shirts in my closet, if you prefer," offered Sonny.

"I'm okay for now," said Gina.

"Let me at least hang your wet dress up."

"Sure, go ahead. I like your sofa," she said, testing it with a bounce. "Is it okay if I dry my undies on your window sill?"

"Sure, go right ahead. I'm just gonna' sit down and relax for a little while. This has been a long day for me, what with Samantha being pissed and all. So, what do you think of my pad?" he said, loosening his tie.

"It looks antiquated, like something out of a detective novel. You have it all, the big wooden desk, the ceiling fan, the steam heat registers. Hell, you even have the old style window blinds. It looks like a scene right out of a Robert Mitchum film."

"I'm not really up on the movie watching, but Samantha is."

"Are you trying to tell me that you're a private eye and you don't watch detective movies? How strange you are."

"No, I find them too contrived. Not real enough to suit my taste."

"You fascinate me, Sonny Rafferty."

"In what way?" he asked.

"I'm not sure yet. I'll let you know when I find out."

"I'm really not all that interesting. What about you, Gina? I know that you are one of Sam's good friends, but she's told me little about you. So what's your story?"

"Why, I declare. Is this an interrogation, Mr. Rafferty?"

"Of course, Miss Pirelli," he grinned.

"Okay. I was a bitch of a kid. My ol' man kicked me out of the house at 17, so I ran off to New York to be somebody. I got lucky and ran into a benevolent man that took me in as his ladylove. Then, when I tired of him, I moved on to another, and then another, until I worked my way up to some distinction."

"Boy, what kind of life was that for a young girl?"

"It was great! I became quite the Italian inamorata, and my lovers actually paid for my higher education. I became a news journalist and moved on to bigger and better things in Washington D.C. Now, sex with dignitaries, that's where it's at, it's a necessary expedient to my business."

"What business is that?"

"The business of me being financially mature by the time I retire."

"What, you retire? I don't see that in your future, Gina."

"Oh yes. I soon plan to run off to Maui and live as a hermit crab."

"You, alone?" asked Sonny.

"Maybe I'll take on a lover. You know, to fight boredom."

"Just one?" he asked.

"Oh yes, sex with one man. What a quaint idea. Sonny, tell me, how does that work?"

"You ought to ask Samantha that question. I might be a little biased. I know it works well when there is a marriage certificate involved."

"How does this marriage thing, work? I've noticed that Samantha seems quite attracted to the idea, also."

"Well, first of all, you need a soul mate. Sam is my soul mate. She is also my best friend. We have a strong allegiance to each other. Anyway, we've been together for 23years, so far."

"Any drawbacks?" asked Gina.

"Kids, they can be a problem if you don't like children."

"Is, liking children a prerequisite for marriage?"

"No, but it would help, because they usually do come along."

"I knew there was a catch to this wedded bliss thing. I'm okay with it until we get to the part where the woman has the baby."

"You don't think you would like birthing a baby?"

"No, I can't see myself walking around for nine months, looking like a pot-bellied pig and then stretching out my most delicate body part in such fashion. It hurts to think about it."

"Oh, don't worry, it snaps right back into shape. You women are resilient in that way."

"No thanks, not for me. You know, Sonny, you should let Sam go to D.C. with me. I'll teach her everything she needs to know to stay out of trouble. She wants that job real bad."

"It's not that, Gina. I don't mind her bettering her career. The trouble is, she wants me to come along, and I'm not going."

"I can understand that. It would be unprecedented if you did go. I'm not even sure if the network *or* the federal government would allow you to go. What's her big push?"

"The way Sam put it to me is that her ol' man is into it with a crime syndicate, and they're apparently making threats on her life and mine."

"I can see where that would be reason to run," said Gina, sitting down next to Sonny on the sofa arm.

"Huh-uh, not for me, I don't scare that easy," said Sonny.

"I thought Big John was legit," said Gina.

"So does everybody else. Big John plays it close to the vest. He doesn't act like a criminal. He just is."

"Let me speak with Sam for you, Sonny. Maybe I can talk some sense into her about you staying here while she goes it alone."

"I'm afraid that wouldn't do any good, Gina. We have other issues."

"Trouble with you, Sonny, is that you're too uptight. Let me massage your neck and get rid of some of your tension."

Sonny enjoyed the feeling of Gina's long, soft fingers probing and kneading the tight muscles of his neck and shoulders. He was more than a little concerned about Samantha not wanting him to come home tonight. Sonny knew that she was hardheaded, but she wouldn't even give him a chance to speak his peace. It wasn't her accusations of infidelity that bothered him so much, for he knew that jealousy is a woman's greatest vice. Jealousy can destroy the best of relationships. But he was tired of always competing with Big John for Samantha's heart. He had warned Samantha of her dad's false prophecies before, many times, but she falls for his lines, still. The more he thought about it, the more anger he felt, and the softer Gina's fingers became.

Gina slowly eased herself around the sofa arm and fell into Sonny's lap, pulling his face to hers, closing her mouth over his. Sonny liked the new taste of Gina's lips, and she his. Her taste was sweet, dangerously sweet. Sonny sensed that and forced himself to push her away.

"Hey, don't be doin' that girl," he said.

"Why, do I scare ya?"

"No, but I have enough trouble with the girl I'm married to. I don't need to add to the situation."

"Cool your jets, stud. A little taste don't mean nothin'. Besides, you're a big boy and I'm half-drunk. I think you can fight me off if I get too frisky." Gina kissed him again, hard, and let her robe fall open, revealing two bountiful breasts with their giant wafers staring up to Sonny, begging for his attention. They were hot to Sonny's touch but he treated them well by the sounds Gina emitted through her kisses. Sonny pulled away again.

"I can't, I've got to think about this, Gina. No matter what I think of Samantha right now, she has never cheated on me. What we're doing now feels strange, especially since you are her girlfriend."

"What if you found out that Samantha *has* cheated on you? Would that make a difference?"

"I don't know. I guess so. Why do you ask that?"

. . . "Oh, no reason, it was just a what-if. Hey, Sonny, I'm hungry. Is there anywhere we can get some food tonight?"

"Hungry, didn't you eat at the party?"

"Women don't eat on dates. You ought to know that."

"Most everything is closed at this late hour. Lucrecia's pub might still be open if you're not too particular in what you eat."

"I'll eat anything, Sonny. I'm famished."

"Make yourself at home. I'll be right back. We'll continue this later. Okay?"

"I'll be ready for you, detective."

"Am I any less a woman than I was six years ago?" whispered the husky voice.

"No, my darling, you are even more ravishing."

Troy caressed Samantha's yearning body with his lips to bring her to a fever pitch. She, in return, awakened the sleeping giant. He impaled her captivating flesh many times throughout the night. They made love to each other in many various forms. At first he was gentle with her, and several times during the night, begged for her to leave Sonny and accompany him back to Washington for a new life together. Tears were shared because she still cared, but in a different way. They were two lovers with high intentions but with negative results. Tonight she gave him her body for one last go-around. She figured she owed him that, but she denied him the rest. Rage wasn't in the senator's nature, but he came close to it when Samantha denied him for the last time. Troy felt himself drowning in futility.

By early morning they had lost their love but not their lust. To Samantha, it was akin to shaving her legs with a dull blade. They eventually fell asleep in each other arms.

Gina smiled euphorically as she closed the door behind Sonny. She gave Sonny an out for now. She didn't want him to rush into things, not just yet. She wanted to tease and entice him a bit more. She wanted it to be as great for him as she seemed for sure it would be for her. The tease and snatch game, that's what she was good at. Only this time it wasn't for money. It was for Sonny's heart. It was a bit devious but Gina thought him fair game and figured Samantha to be in the arms of another tonight. That was, if Troy brought the same allure with him that he captivated Samantha's heart with back in D.C.

Samantha was a strong woman for sure. That's what attracted Gina to her. But Troy had the kind of hold on her that wasn't easily discarded. It wasn't a made-up version of himself either. It was the real thing with Samantha.

Though she was sorely tempted, Gina suppressed her desire to tell Sonny of Samantha's infidelity. After all, Samantha was her good friend. If she was going to vie for Sonny it would be on her own merit. .

Gina scampered over to a street window and peered out as Sonny climbed into his V8-Ford and pulled away. She giddily slipped off her robe and capered about the room ecstatically, her unique breasts jiggling wildly about with each youthful squeal. She came to a halt in front of a vanity mirror next to the door. Gina then examined her formidable body closely and conversed with her counterpart, "Damn, girl, you still look fine. You sure could use a bikini wax though. What the hell, he's a man's man. He won't care about such an unruly bush."

She noticed Sonny's brown fedora hanging next to the mirror. She snatched it off the hook and placed it on her head, trying several different poses with it. "P.I., Private Eye, Private Investigator, Private Dick, I like the sound of that. Yes I do, very much," she said, experimenting with her hat placement. "I wonder what it feels like to be a private dick. Hell, I'd like to know what it feels like to have a dick! Oh, the things he must have seen, and the romances he must have had, and the capers he must have been on. A real Dick Tracy, I bet. Now I see what entices Samantha so. Let's see what he has in his closet."

Gina skittered over to his closet and picked out a dress-shirt and tie for herself, but decided to forego the sport coat due to the heat of the night. She also figured a pair of gabardine slacks to be too uncouth. Gina did manage to pull out a pair of boxer shorts from Sonny's dirty laundry bag. "This will do just fine," she said, giving them a good sniff. "Nothing like the smell of stale male musk, is what I say," she laughed. Gina slipped on Sonny's things and ambled over to the big oak desk and plumped down in the chair behind it.

While sitting there, she eyed the photographs on Sonny's desk. She studied them carefully. They were pictures of Sonny's family. Gina felt strangely sad, realizing that there was a lot more to Sonny then being a detective or a male object. It was an odd feeling for her since she herself had never experienced a real family life. "Come on, girl," she snapped, "let's check out some more Sonny."

She pulled out the middle drawer and found one of Sonny's Cuban cigars that Big John had given him. She lit it up, put her feet up on the desk and pretended that she was he. After several more relaxing moments of pretend, Gina declared, "Goddamn it, Sonny, where are you? I'm hot, I'm horny, and I'm hungry, and not necessarily in that order." She pulled open a drawer on the left side of the big oak desk and discovered an odd combination of Hershey bars and Hemingway. "So what have we here? A sweet tooth, big time I see, and a Hemingway addict," she said. "Good choice, Sonny. Now there was a man's man, that Hemingway. He was one tough motherfucker." She closed the drawer back, short two Hershey bars.

By the time Sonny reached Lucrecia's, it was officially closed. He did manage to confiscate a cold pizza where someone failed to pick up their order, and he happened to snag a bottle of Bordeaux Merlot. Sonny didn't do too much thinking while driving back from the pub. He figured Samantha would come to her senses by this time tomorrow night, and as of right now with Gina, he decided he would go with whatever developed, if anything. He was tired of thinking all the time, and tired of worrying about things. He just wanted to relax and go with the flow for awhile.

Sonny parked his car right in front of the flower shop at a spot he could rarely find unoccupied during daylight hours. He grabbed the pizza in one hand and the Merlot in the other and closed the door with his elbow.

As Gina finished the last morsel of sweet chocolate, the sound of Sonny's car could be heard from an opened window, directly behind her. "It's about time, baby. I hate filling up on your chocolate bars. Bad for my complexion, you know."

For some reason, the bottom drawer on the right side of the old desk caught Gina's eye. "I bet that's where you keep your booze, isn't it big guy? Every private eye has a booze drawer. Let's get it out and get this party going again, honey." She pulled on the drawer but it was stuck. Gina got out of her chair, and as she heard the sound of Sonny's car door closing, she pulled hard with both hands and . . .

He never heard the blast, just the ringing in his ears as he was knocked to the ground from the concussion, and the bricks, and chards of glass that spewed down on top of him from the second floor. In the same instant, but as if in slow motion, he saw Gina's body violently tossed out the window, landing with a sickening thud on the pavement just a few feet from him, while her right arm flew twenty feet further. For a second he thought he was in Nam, at An Loc, until he saw his brown fedora floating softly towards the ground. In shock, Sonny reached out and touched her hand and felt those long, soft fingers for the last time.

Samantha was awakened by the annoying sound of the clock radio alarm. The morning light stung her eyes as she peered from underneath the bed covers to see what time it was. She winced in pain from last night's love session, as her sensitive places ached from Troy's harsh possession. She managed to reach over and douse the blaring noise while glancing at the time. "Damn, 9:00 o'clock, two hours of sleep just isn't enough," she declared. She then realized that her lover from last night wasn't around.

Just as well, she thought. There are no easy goodbyes with someone like him. She then discovered a note on Troy's pillow. She picked it up and read it, "It could have been a good thing, you and I. It would have been really nice. I guess better luck for me next time, eh?" It was signed, "Your pal, Troy."

Not a very romantic ending to such an auspicious beginning, she thought. What the hell, it's over. Samantha actually felt liberated, for she now finally had closure with Troy and felt less guilt for cheating on Sonny because she was just paying him back for his infidelities.

With her head pounding from too much drink and her body tender from last night's sex, Samantha slunk back underneath the covers to sleep and heal. But her respite was short-lived as the alarm again bellowed out a wake-up call. This time, instead of hitting the snooze she reached out from underneath the covers and switched to the radio channel to catch the day's news, "*We have an update on the early morning explosion in South Broad Ripple. It has been determined that the majority of damage to the Wright's Flower Shop building is confined to the upstairs, which houses the Sonny Rafferty Detective Agency. We have one confirmed fatality. The name of the victim is being withheld pending notification of the family.*"

"Sonny!" screamed Samantha.

Treated and released from the hospital with just superficial wounds from the fallen debris, the shaken and distraught Sonny Rafferty sat slump-shouldered against a cement block wall, fielding questions as best he could from the precinct's captain. As soon as the captain finished his questioning he handed his clipboard over to the chief of homicide who had just entered the office.

Truman Burrell was large in stature, and a very disciplined, by the book type of cop, yet he was well aware of Sonny's accomplishments with the Metro police force.

Burrell sat on the edge of the desk next to Sonny and read through the report. "According to the report that I have been handed, you and the victim, Gina Pirelli, were spending the night together at your office. You say the affair was platonic, even though the victim was wearing your clothes, including a pair of your boxer shorts. You had just returned from Lucrecia's pub with a pizza and a bottle of French wine. Is that correct?"

"Yes, but fooling around was not my intention."

"That's what I told my last two wives, Rafferty. Hell, admit it, Sonny. We're just men, you and I. We're weak of flesh. Admit it. You were helping yourself to a piece of Italian pie and someone didn't approve. Does your wife know about this affair?"

"I told you, it wasn't an affair," said Sonny.

"Okay then, does your wife know about your and Pirelli's slumber party?"

"No. Of course not," said Sonny.

"We are trying to find Samantha now and bring her in for questioning."

"What for?" he asked.

"She's the prime suspect, at this moment. You know how it

works."

"Samantha should be at home. We had a disagreement while at the Governor's Ball and she left for the house, early."

"Did she leave with anyone?"

"No. Not that I know of." answered Sonny.

"Well, I've got news for you. Samantha's not at home and hasn't been there for quite some time. We haven't been able to locate her."

"You don't think something has happened to her, do you, Truman?"

"No. There are no other reports of any suspicious nature at this time. She might just be in hiding."

"For crissakes, Truman, Sam had nothing to do with this. Hell, she doesn't know anything about explosives."

"Maybe she knows someone who does."

"I doubt that, seriously."

"So, you're telling me that Samantha had no suspicion of you and Pirelli having this affair . . . I mean this little rendezvous?"

"No, our getting together was just by happenstance. It's in your report. Nothing was planned."

"Okay then. You're free to go of your own volition, my friend."

"What about Samantha?"

"Well, if and when we find your wife, we'll bring her in for questioning. If she doesn't have an iron-clad alibi I'll have to hold her on suspicion of murder."

"I'd like to stay, if I could."

"Sure, hang around as long as you please."

Samantha came through the door first, followed by Big John and Nick Parmalay. "Sonny, I thought you were dead!" she squealed, rushing to her husband. "The radio said that you were killed in the explosion. I thought I lost you, baby. I'm sorry for leaving you in such a huff last night."

"You ought to hold off on your celebrating for a minute, ma'am," said Burrell.

Samantha gave the chief a puzzled look.

"I need to know your whereabouts last night."

"What? I don't get it," she said, looking back at Sonny.

"What the radio said, ma'am, was that there was one fatality from the explosion. They weren't allowed to give the victim's name until her next of kin was notified."

"What's he talking about, honey?" she asked Sonny.

"It was Gina, Sam," said Sonny dolefully.

"Gina, not Gina, she wasn't with you last night. It can't be Gina," she begged.

"Yes, it was darlin'. She fell into the swimming pool and needed a change of clothing, so I took her with me to my place."

"Gina and you?" said Samantha

"It's not how it sounds, darlin'."

"Mother or Daddy would've given Gina a change of clothing."

"I looked for them, baby. Your dad was passed out by then, and your mother was . . . asleep," lied Sonny.

"I don't understand, Sonny. You were screwing Gina? You got Gina killed? I can't believe this. She was taking me to D.C. with her you son-of-a-bitch!" she screamed, beating his chest with her fists.

Sonny let her beat on him and said no more. He was shaken and his senses were numbed. He didn't know what else he could do or say at that moment. He felt like crawling back into himself, back to his mansion at Paradise Woods where his hurt and guilt would go away.

"Why do you need my daughter's whereabouts?" asked Big John. "You don't suspect her of—"

"I don't suspect much of anything right now," said Truman. "I just need her whereabouts of last night. This is just routine questioning, Big John—and yes, she could be a suspect. She had the motive."

"So what exactly was her motive, Truman?" asked Parmalay.

"Her husband's infidelity, and a woman's jealous rage," said Truman.

"This is bullshit!" exclaimed Big John.

"So, where were you last night, Mrs. Rafferty?" asked Burrell.

"I was home in bed."

"All night?" he asked.

"Yeah, all night," she replied.

"Any witnesses?" he asked.

"No."

"What would you say if I told you that my men were at your house at five o'clock this morning and you were nowhere about?"

"I was probably out jogging. I do that on Sunday mornings."

"You must be a long runner because those boys are still waiting at your house right now for your return, and it's nigh on ten o'clock. You weren't home at all last night, were you, Mrs. Rafferty?"

"That's enough! She'll answer no more questions without our lawyer being present," said Big John vehemently. "Come on, Nick, do something about this."

"I'm sorry, John. Truman is right. He can hold her overnight for questioning if need be. She doesn't have an alibi, John."

"I'm her alibi," answered the voice of Troy Charbonau, standing in the doorway. "I'll vouch for her whereabouts."

Samantha was startled; even more so than the others.

"Senator Charbonau, do you wish to shed some light on this conversation?" asked Truman.

"Samantha was with me last night, at my suite in the Adams Mark motel."

"What was the occasion?"

"She and I danced at the Governor's Ball last night. I liked her company so very much that I invited her to spend the night with me."

"Did that include . . . romance?"

"We became romantic. Yes."

"Is the senator speaking the truth, Mrs. Rafferty?"

"Yes, It's true," she said, staring away from Sonny.

"So you lied to me before then, didn't you, Mrs. Rafferty?"

"Yes, I did. I'm sorry."

"You could possibly get jail time for lying to an officer, you know, but in this case I can understand."

Samantha quickly turned to Sonny, but Sonny turned away in hurt and disgust.

"*Now* can I take my daughter home?" asked Big John.

"Wait just a minute, Mr. Taylor. Listen up people. I don't want anyone to leave this city for the next four days while we verify your stories. John, tomorrow I'm coming by your place to check out your guest list. We'll start our search there to find the perpetrators of this crime. Senator, I'll need your cooperation, also."

"Sure thing, Chief; Gina was a dear friend of mine too. I'll do anything I can to help."

"What will we do about the media?" asked Parmalay.

"I don't give a fuck about the media. I suggest if you don't want word of this getting out that you send me a P.R. man right away, Mr.

349

Commissioner. Everyone is now free to leave."

Samantha sorrowfully looked into Troy's eyes with tearful gratitude and walked quickly past the young senator.

It is said that when you get older, love hides its face and lust comes out of the closet. Sonny didn't know it but he was wrestling with some of the same demons that Samantha fell prey to. It is a trick of the ages, the only difference being that Samantha's lust for Troy wore a mask of love and promised his uniqueness with it, such as she experienced six years prior. It is these things that have tried and sometimes succeeded in the ruination of many great relationships. No one is privy on how this happens. It just does.

Chapter Twenty-Four

Confessions of the Wounded Heart

The two young sweethearts, Amy Harris and Jimmy Hansen, embraced comfortably against a big maple tree that shielded them from the September moon.

The tree was just one of many that lined this Brendonwood street that followed the winding Fox River along the outskirts of the affluent neighborhood. This particular spot had become their secret meeting place since they first came together at one of Jimmy's swim meets, in which he was the star swimmer and captain of the team.

Amy, the pixie-like cheerleader, already an expert in French kissing, was now in the process of teaching Jimmy the fine art of heavy petting. Jimmy, a little less advanced in that area, was learning at a rapid pace, as Amy allowed his roaming hands inside her cheerleading blouse but not under her tri-colored, pleated skirt.

Jimmy was just two years removed from the dastardly trick that Danielle Rafferty played on him in her backyard that caused him to fall out of his parent's big oak tree and break his leg. But even that incident didn't put a crimp in the boy's curiosity of the opposite sex.

Jimmy placed his mouth hard against Amy's, mashing her soft lips against the braces on her teeth. The harder he kissed, the farther her young tongue shot forth, reaching and probing, all the while accepting his awkward fondling of her pert little breasts.

It was the metal against metal sound that first distracted Jimmy and his young coquette. Then they heard the rev of the engines as the cars sped up. When the lights came into view, they broke their embrace and looked up the street to see what the racket was about. One car was slamming into the other, trying to force it off the road. As the cars approached, the teenagers became nervous with the action closing in on them. Just as the vehicles passed, the dark car on the outside forced the inside car off the road. Jimmy and Amy looked on helplessly as the bright red Chevy veered down the embankment into the Fox River.

"Oh my God! Oh my God! Oh my God!" cried Amy.

As the Chevy submerged, Jimmy ran down the embankment with Amy right on his heels. "That looks like Mrs. Rafferty's car," he yelled. "I'm going in after her."

"Jimmy, what can I do to help?"

"Run back up to the road and flag someone down, hurry!"

Jimmy felt lucky that the river was shallow at this point, plus, the streetlights shown down, giving him some vision underneath the water. Finding the vehicle was easy enough, but getting the door open became a problem. Jimmy struggled but eventually persevered and reached the unconscious driver. Sure enough, it was Mrs. Rafferty. As he floated to the top with the injured woman, Jimmy was met by two other motorists that Amy had flagged down. Once on the riverbank, Jimmy put his face to her mouth to see if she was breathing. He quickly maneuvered her arms back and forth over her head and pushed on her diaphragm to purge her lungs of the river water. She soon began breathing and the crowd rejoiced at her revival and congratulated the young man for his heroics. Relieved but exhausted, the neighborhood boy looked around at the smiling faces of the people, and saw tears of joy flowing down Amy's face. He thought to himself, how ironic, as a younger boy, I used to strain for a glimpse at Mrs. Rafferty's naked body, and here tonight, I save her life. Jimmy felt good. He felt real good.

When Samantha came to, things seemed blurry, out of focus to her. Her head was pounding and her memory banks shut down. But she did feel a warm hand holding hers. "Sonny, is that you Sonny?" she asked.

"No, dear, it's your mother. I'm with your father. Officer Truman Burrell is here also. You have been in a serious auto accident."

"How bad am I hurt?"

"You have a bump on your head, just a mild concussion, dear. The doctor says that you will be fine after some rest."

"What happened?"

"Someone ran you off the road. Can you remember any of it, dear?"

"No, Mother, things are a little fuzzy right now. Is Sonny here?"

"What do you want Sonny for, sweetheart?" answered Big John. He's nothing but trouble for you, my dear. Besides, I'll take care of you, baby. This won't happen again. I promise. You just rest now and get some sleep. We'll be near."

"Thanks, Daddy, for being here," she whispered while drifting off to sleep.

"I didn't really expect to receive any pertinent information from her today," said the homicide chief. "With a concussion like hers, it sometimes takes a day or two to regain full memory of what happened. I'll be back tomorrow. Till then stay vigil and let me know if she reveals anything about the accident. By the way, I have a guard posted right outside the room, just as you requested, Big John."

"Thanks, Truman, see you tomorrow."

The commotion outside the hospital room stirred Big John from his chair. It was Sonny, arguing with the young guard who was refusing him access to Samantha's room.

"You have no right to stop me from seeing my own wife," argued Sonny.

"I have orders from Chief Burrell not to allow anyone into this room unless he or she is authorized hospital personnel; Mrs. Rafferty's parents and children being the only exceptions."

"I'm going in, Junior, so don't try stopping me."

"I can't let you do that," said the young officer easing his hand down to his revolver.

"Don't pull that piece out, Junior, or I'll have to break your fuckin' arm!" Sonny voiced firmly.

"Hold it, officer. I'll take care of this," said Big John, intervening.

"Sonny, what the hell are you doing here, anyway? You know Sam doesn't want you around anymore. She has someone else in her life now. Besides, you're dangerous for her. You'll get her killed."

"You're doing a piss poor job of keeping her alive yourself, Big John."

"You know, Sonny, you've been a thorn in my side for too long now.

If you would have stayed out of my business, you and Samantha would still be together today, but no, the sleuth that you are, you've got to stir up trouble in my facilities."

"Your evil empire is so spread out I can't help but run into it somewhere. You ought to come clean with Samantha about your business dealings, Big John. I'm on to ya, but you have blinders on Samantha and she only sees the world the way you have it portrayed to her."

"I give my daughter what she wants."

"Except for me," snarled Sonny.

"She wants no part of you, Rafferty. Go back to your people. Go back to your whores, to the streets, where you belong. You're working the wrong side of the fence."

"That's funny. I was just thinking that about you."

"You won't win, Rafferty. Not against me."

"I'm not ready to give up on my wife, just yet."

"Let him see Samantha," answered Kitty's voice as she appeared from behind the door. "Please John, let him see his wife."

"Oh, all right then," grumbled Big John. "But if she turns you away this time, I don't want to see you again." With a hard glare, Big John turned and walked down the corridor.

"Go on in, Sonny. I'll keep this young officer company for awhile," said Kitty.

Sonny looked longingly into his wife's pain-filled eyes. "Hey, baby, how ya feelin'?" he softly greeted.

"Hi, Sonny, I feel like a Tennessee mule kicked me in the head," she murmured. "I guess you heard about me getting run off the road."

"Yes, I did."

"They say that Jimmy Hansen rescued me from drowning. I lost the Impala though."

"Don't worry about that, darlin'. I'll get you another. Did you get a good look at them, Sam? Can you tell me anything that might be helpful? 'Cause, I'll get 'em for you."

"Can't you stop thinking like a detective for one minute, Sonny? For once, can't you just think about me instead of getting' back at somebody?"

"I am thinking about you, darlin'. I just want to help you."

"You want to help me! When I asked you for your help in finding Loni Jacob's killer, you turned me down. Now, when I don't want your help, you want to volunteer it. No thanks, Sonny. I don't want your help. You have too many secrets you don't want to give up."

"You know, Sam, a man has a part of his life he doesn't want to expose. Women don't understand that. I know. But it's just things that he wants no one to know."

"You mean like a skeleton in the closet?"

"No. Not at all, darlin', it's not something that I'm necessarily ashamed of. It's just things better off kept quiet."

"You mean about your girlfriends, and like what happened down at Scoville?"

"I have no girlfriends, Sam. Not the way you think."

"Well, how about my girlfriend getting killed in the prime of her life because of your secret dealings that you don't want to talk about? How about that, huh?" she said tearfully.

"Don't cry darlin'. Whoever killed Gina was trying to kill you and me. It had to be someone that knew we were going to spend the night up in my office. Did you tell anyone?"

"No, of course not," said Samantha.

"It also had to be someone that was familiar with C-4 explosives. It must've been the same people that ran you off the road last night."

"I don't know, Sonny. It's all too confusing for me right now. All I know is that someone tried to kill me last night and my best friend was murdered in such a heinous way that they had to collect her body parts and put them in a body bag. I can't even see her face for the last time. Life was going along smoothly until you went down to Centralia again and came back home all busted up. Now, people we know are dropping like flies, and we're being hunted down like fish in a barrel, all because you stuck your nose where it shouldn't have been. Now, you have too much pride to deal with the situation properly. I'm tired of trying to figure out your complexities. You've become too much a burden for me. So go on, live your life, Sonny, but don't include me in it right now. I've got too many things to worry about as it is. It's time I took an inventory of my life."

"You're not talking sense, darlin'. I can't stand the thought of living without you."

"Sonny, you once told me that crazy things make the world go around, and no matter how messed up things get, it never stops turning. Face it Sonny, we're no good for each other anymore. Our time's run out."

"But, darlin', how about the pact we made with each other at Paradise Woods?"

"Geezus, Sonny, we're not living a fairy tale anymore. Grow up, will you?"

". . . Look, Samantha. That deal, with you spending the night with Troy Charbonau; don't worry about it. We can put that on the back burner. I'll get over it. Hell, I'm almost over it now. It was my fault anyway for not supporting you on your new job."

"Listen to me, Sonny. That wasn't the only night that I spent with Troy. He and I had an affair six years ago when I was in Washington on assignment. I've been sorry for that ever since, but now I guess it doesn't matter."

Tears formed in Sonny's eyes. "I have never been unfaithful to you, darlin'. I never cheated on your love for me." With that, Samantha's broken-hearted prince turned and walked out of her life.

Victorio Delveccio was not a patient man, but with Big John he had always bent his rules somewhat. Over the years he had become quite satisfied with his partnership and business dealings with Big John Taylor and his friend, Johnny Losch. His only qualm with Big John was that he was too slow in bringing down his fury on those that needed it. Plus, this time he let his personal family members interfere with business, which to any syndicate is a cardinal sin, and to the Italian mob, was unconscionable.

"Hello, my Irish friend. Dominic told me that you were going to call, but I wasn't expecting to hear from you this soon. He said that you treated them very well while they were there, and that you understood the dilemma that we are in. I hope they didn't act up during their stay. They are like two sons to me, you know. Sometimes I have to rein them in a bit."

"Look, Victorio. Losch and I want to cut ties with the Italian family. We are willing to part with our half of the gaming units and gambling halls, sports betting and all."

"I must say, that's a lot to give up, my friend. What do you wish in return?"

"Losch keeps Waverly and I keep everything within the city limits of Indianapolis."

"Who's going to pay for the Bone Yard loss?"

"Hell, our take on the gaming joints alone will pay for three Bone Yards to be built," said Big John.

"How am I going to find management replacements and such?"

"Keep the ones that are already there. I hired most of them. They're good people. I won't need them anymore. Also, we would like to keep Miramar as our parent corporation. John and I started Miramar and we'd like to keep it in our control. Besides, bogus companies are easy to come up with."

"Anything else?" asked Victorio.

"Yes. Call off your thugs."

"What are you talking about, my friend?"

"I'm talking about you running my daughter off the road into a river, and I'm talking about your goons blowing up her friend. That's what I'm talking about!"

"You must be mistaken, my friend. We have done no such crimes."

"Come on, level with me, Victorio. Constantine made his threats while he was here."

"Like I said, I do need to rein in my boys now and then, especially that one. As you may know, we keep up on such things. I am sorry about Miss Pirelli. We send our regrets in the form of flowers for the young lady's grave. We also regret your daughter's mishap. But I must add that my boys had nothing to do with it. Dominic did mention that your number one lieutenant, Parmalay, I think his name is, made him an offer of killing both your daughter and her husband in return for your part of Miramar. He was going to do it soon to prove his worth to us. So I suggest that you clean your own house before accusing us of harming your family. You Mics, you always lose your temper before making the proper investigation. You are so predictable."

"Are you sure about Parmalay?"

"Unlike your lieutenants, mine are most loyal, and very reliable. I haven't lied to you yet, my friend. Is the offer still on the table?"

"Yes. Yes it is." "You get your papers together, a meeting place, and a date set. Don't call me. Send a runner. The Feds are all around. They're probably listening to us right at this very moment. Don't make it a public place. Make it a warehouse or someplace clandestine. Also, bring

Losch with you. Maybe we can make him a good offer on Waverly. You know, one of those offers you can't refuse."

"So we agree then that we'll be rid of each other after the meeting."

"That's a rather rude way of putting it after all these years of friendship, but yes, you'll be rid of us, my Irish friend."

"You'll hear from me soon. My carrier will go by the name of Bullet. .Got it?"

"Till then, my friend," answered the Don.

"Till then," said John.

Chapter Twenty-Five

Paradise Lost

Gina's funeral was quite an event, as several Washington dignitaries showed up. Another dozen or so sent flowers. Many friends and co-workers from WYNG and CSN were present. Rick Jamison gave her eulogy.

Though still a little shaken from her head injury, Samantha was there, escorted by Troy Charbonau and several bodyguards that Big John had assigned to her. Three of the Fab-Four showed up to give support to Samantha in her loss. Only Merle was missing. She was in Gary, managing Chance's campaign.

Gina's burial site was a little cemetery that sat atop a hill near some rolling woods on the outskirts of the city. Though the weather was inclement, it was quite a picturesque setting.

It was an ironic ending for the ebullient news journalist, for she was the quintessential rolling stone, starting with Baltimore, her birthplace, the wild New York City lifestyle, and then on to D.C., with several stays in Europe and the Middle East, until finally coming to rest amidst the Indiana countryside. Gina's friends and cohorts were puzzled as to why she chose such a quiescent spot as her final resting place. She had such a zest for life. She so enjoyed living in the fast lane. One only wondered what gave her the preconceived notion to buy a burial plot in the first place. Could she have had a premonition? Whatever it was, her friends and peers gathered to mourn their loss.

The graveside ceremony was cut short as the ominous cloud that hung overhead burst forth a barrage of tears of its own and chased the people back into their vehicles, thus back into their everyday lives.

Through the gray wall of water appeared a man sporting a glistening rain slicker and battered brown fedora. Sonny Rafferty had been watching from afar. He shunned the crowd, for he had been cast aside by his pretty wife and castigated by her father and his kind.

Sonny made his way up to where Gina lay peacefully in the ground. The grave diggers had also abandoned her for now. Sonny grabbed a hand full of dirt and tossed it onto her casket. He then said a silent prayer for his short-time friend. And why shouldn't he? He was her final remembrance, the last lips that kissed her mouth. It was his hands that caressed her tender flesh, and it was her long, soft fingers that last soothed him. He was the last person she saw before she passed over into the abyss. But Sonny had a deeper bond with her than that. Whatever God's intentions, she took his and Samantha's place at death's door. To him, she became his angel, his guardian angel.

The whole scenario was filled with a lot of what ifs. Sonny yearned for the answers. Not only to Gina's demise, but to why his life was unraveling so. It hurt him deep when Samantha denied him her love. Without her he was just another lost soul. All the women he once cared for were vanishing right before his own eyes, Candy, Angie, Gina, and Samantha's love for him. He wondered why everything he touched got torn asunder. As Sonny pled his case with God, loneliness slowly crept up his spine.

He barely heard the crack of a fired Lugar through the pouring rain, but when he saw the jostling of the flowers next to him, Sonny knew that something was amiss.

Sonny dove and went into a roll, and then jumped back up, vigorously searching the gray wall behind him. He saw a dark figure raise his sights again. Once more Sonny dove and rolled, hearing the zip of the bullet pass ever-so-close to his head. Sonny got up, and without looking back, rushed to the woods for cover, for he knew the strange gunman was in hot pursuit to take his life.

Sonny sped through the brush and bramble, making quick turns in zigzag fashion to avoid giving his pursuer a clear shot at him. Despite his 48 years, he moved through the woods like a hunted cougar, and glanced back now and again to keep track of his aggressor. Sonny longed for his old police revolver that he had, locked away in his desk drawer, back at the house. He now wondered how smart it was, retiring his weapon in search of the more peaceful existence. But that thinking soon dissipated. Sonny knew that he had to use his cunning to survive. He soon came upon a glen and maneuvered his way through the narrow pass. At the end of the little valley Sonny quickly tossed his coat and placed his hat on a bramble bush, making it just visible enough for someone to get a clean shot at, if they had killing on their mind. Sonny then climbed up the eight-foot embankment adjacent to the hat and hid behind a wild elderberry bush, waiting to see if the stranger was who he thought he was.

It wasn't long before a shot rang out and blew the brown fedora off the bush. Sonny watched anxiously as the rain-soaked gunman walked into his trap. Upon his arrival he found nobody and realized that he had been duped. Before he could react, Sonny jumped down and quickly wrested the Lugar from his hand.

"Lujack! You son-of-a-bitch!" yelled Sonny.

With fear in his eyes, Lujack reacted, "It's not what you think, Sonny!"

Sonny backhanded the detective, driving him to the ground. "Give me a reason not to kill you, Frank!"

"Bernice, and my boys," he said in desperation.

"Okay, Frank. You tell me, what makes one friend try to kill another friend? I don't get it. Explain it to me."

"I, I wanted a piece of the good life for Bernice and myself. After all those years working the streets and raising the boys, we deserve it," he said with nervous eyes.

"You still haven't told me why you tried to kill me just now."

"Well, I, I got to gambling in Big John's gambling parlors around town. You know the ones. I won big at first, but then I couldn't stop. I don't know what it was that came over me, Sonny. I just kept on betting and losing. I got myself in a hole, Sonny, a big hole. So, Nick Parmalay told me that if I worked for him on the side that he would help me pay off my debts. You see, Sonny, I was desperate. I had nowhere to turn. At first it was just little jobs, and soon they became bigger and rougher. Things were out of control. I tried to get out but Parmalay said that he would expose me, make me the fall guy. He said I would go to jail. So I couldn't quit. I had an obligation to Bernice and the boys."

Sonny grabbed Frank by the lapels of his coat and stared intently into his rain-spanked face. "You listen to me, Frank. Listen to me good.

I'm going to give you names. I want answers. Loni Jacobs!"

"That was me and Parmalay. He did it for Big John. I didn't kill her though. I just set her up. He ran her off the road. I was with him though. I planted the whiskey bottle. We passed ourselves off as reporters. We took her to a bar to get her drunk. She didn't buy it, so we took her out back and forced it down her, and then let her run. We followed her and forced her off the road, into the quarry. After we pulled that caper I wanted out, but I was in too deep to the sharks."

"Gina Pirelli. Was that Big John?"

"No, that was all Nick's idea. He wanted to take over Big John's empire. Parmalay told me at the ball that all I had to do was to take care of you and Samantha for him, and all my debts would be paid."

Through clinched teeth Sonny asked, "Tell me, Frank, how much was Samantha's and my life worth to you, huh? Tell me!"

"Fifty thousand," strained Frank.

"How could you? How could you forget all that we've been through? You killed an innocent person three nights ago, Frank. She didn't have anything to do with your fucking gambling debts! Don't that bother you any?"

"I, I, I, I, can't hardly live with myself, Sonny."

Sonny backhanded him again. "You're a goddamned disgrace, Frank! You're a disgrace to me and Sam, you're a disgrace to Bernice, and most of all you're a disgrace to your boys! Now tell me, did you try and kill Samantha Monday night?"

"No, I didn't."

Sonny hit him again. "You lying sack of shit!"

"No, honest, Sonny, you can kill me if you want, but I swear on my mother's grave that we had nothing to do with that."

Sonny felt him telling the truth, but his answer puzzled him. Who was it then if not he or Parmalay? "What does Bernice know about all this, Frank?" said Sonny.

"Nothin', Sonny, she can't know nothin'! It would kill her to find out what I've done."

Sonny hesitated in thought while holding on to his captive friend. The frightened detective nervously stared back hoping for leniency, and some form of forgiveness. "So, what are you gonna do, Sonny . . . kill me?"

"No. I'm not going to kill you, Frank. I believe in Bernice, and she believes in you. I don't figure that you will let her or me down again. I'm gonna let you go free, but you have to straighten your life up, right now."

"What do you mean, Sonny?"

"I mean that for once in your life, Frank, do the right thing. If not for yourself then do it for Bernice. She loves you, Frank, and you love her. I know you do. Don't let her down, Frank. Leave her a legacy— Hell, leave your boys a legacy. You're their roll model, Frank. They look up to you. So does Bernice. Whatever you choose to do from here on in, don't let Bernice down. You owe her that."

Sonny released Frank, then, grabbed his fedora and slicker. The two friends walked together silently out of the rain-drenched woods.

They called it Jimtown. It was 16 square blocks of Irish life amongst the very bowels of the city. There wasn't much noise coming from this sector of the city, for they kept to themselves a lot. They called Big John the mayor of Jimtown.

Flannery's Tap was an Irish pub in Jimtown that he frequented often. Kip and Butch Flannery were the owner-operators of the bar. Butch ran the bar and Kip ran the bookie joint in back. The Flannery boys also collected monthly dues from dozens of other establishments for Big John. The Irish connection also provided their renowned mayor with the thugs he needed to remind the area merchants to keep his cash flowing. Big John was always free with his time and his money. He always took care of his kind. It was something he learned, growing up in New York City's bowery.

His empire was not on his mind today. It was Nick Parmalay's birthday, and what a better way to celebrate a good friend's birthday than shooting pool with him at Flannery's Tap, especially when John brought along a spicy five-foot-five inch redheaded present for them to share the evening with.

Scarlet Flaherty was tough and cold on the outside, but when between the sheets, she became soft and warm as mother's milk. Her bright red curls were matched only by a wealth of red ferns between her thighs that she refused to trim. John himself had many times been where the red ferns grow, and loved every minute of it. For the last three years Scarlet had been Big John's bookkeeper plus. He set her up in a nice brownstone apartment near the city college and was paying for her to become a C.P.A., an investment that he deemed would reap many benefits for him down the line.

She had big girl looks and a tomboyish attitude, and she loved playing pool and smoking big cigars with the best of them. Some said she even pissed standing up. But tonight she was game to shoot pool with Nick, smoke John's Cubans, and share her bed with either or both of them.

As Nick carefully eyed up his shot, he couldn't help but notice Scarlet, staring intently at the table. Nick didn't mind losing to Big John because John always beat his ass at pool, but losing to the crimson-haired beauty could be a bit embarrassing.

That wasn't all that was on Nick's mind though. He left his wife at home waiting anxiously for his return to celebrate his 45th birthday with her. She had a special present for him this year. She had lost 48 pounds in the last six months and wanted to reveal her new svelte body in her pink chiffon lingerie that she purchased special, just for this occasion. She was prepared to make love with the lights on tonight, something they hadn't done in quite sometime.

"Come on, Nick, shoot the damn ball. Don't stare it to death," badgered Big John.

"Hey, this is a big shot for me. This is for my manhood," he countered back. Nick, of course, missed his shot, and Scarlet finished by running the table to end the game.

"You pussy, you lost to a girl," Big John guffawed.

"I guess I stole your manhood, huh?" kidded the redhead. "How about we all go over to my place and see if I can restore it back for ya?"

"Nah, I best be going," said Nick.

"Come on, Nick, the night is still young, and Scarlet hasn't given you her present yet, have you darlin'?"

Scarlet smiled, "No I haven't, and it's all packaged, all pretty-n-pink."

As the three amigos headed out, Cathy Parmalay lay in bed in her pretty, pink lingerie, waiting patiently for her husband's return.

At Scarlet's apartment everyone had a couple of drinks and got comfortable. Scarlet shed her clothes, and shared her warm body and mouth with each until she finally pulled Nick out of his chair and into her bedroom for a raunchy, raucous round of lovemaking. As she closed her bedroom door she promised Big John that she would do them both while smoking one of his Cubans. He just laughed and told her that there was a bonus in it for her if she did.

John loved listening to Scarlet when she made love. She was so loud and forceful with every movement. She always sounded as if she were with Columbus, and they had just discovered the new world together. As the bed springs squeaked, and with Scarlet giving out her wild utterances, John pulled Parmalay's snub-nose 38 from his holster that hung on the back of the chair. He reached into his coat pocket and pulled out a pair of gloves and snapped them on firmly. He then took out his handkerchief and meticulously polished the black revolver. He smiled at the sound of Scarlet reaching her zenith, while flipping out the cylinder to check the ammo. Feeling satisfied, he snapped it closed and spun the cylinder.

As the grunts and squeaking bedsprings came to a halt, John stealthily walked in on the two lovers as they gasped to retrieve their spent air. Scarlet looked clownish, but oh so sexy, with her red lips puffing on the big stogie while rivulets of sweat made her pale veined breasts glisten. Nick was just resting his eyes while recovering from the redheaded vixen's ravishing.

Big John drew closer to the bed. Scarlet noticed the revolver in his hand. Her humorous face suddenly changed into a look of first, surprise, then terror, as she froze in time. John raised the gun and fired point-blank into the middle of her forehead. Scarlet never blinked, just slowly fell over.

Nick's eyes popped open at the ear piercing sound. "What the hell, John. What'd ya shoot her for?" asked Nick nervously.

"I didn't. You did," was his bone-chilling reply. "Besides, I can always get another bookkeeper, Nick . . . I trusted you as my friend, Nick, but you tried to kill my daughter."

"I don't know who told you that, but I would never harm your daughter, Big John, never!"

Big John raised his arm.

"I wouldn't do that, John, if I were you," said Nick in desperation.

"I guess you wouldn't, but I've got the gun," he said coldly. The bullet went into Nick's temple and ricocheted out the front, blowing his left eye out. With Nick still breathing, John placed the gun in his quivering right hand and folded his fingers around it.

"Come on, Nick, hold on to it, just for a bit longer." John put his mouth to Nick's ear, "You're dying, Nick, and I killed you. In the paper tomorrow it will read homicide-suicide. You'll be a disgrace to your wife and your family, Nick. They'll receive no insurance, no nothin', just a few scraps from the government. They'll hate you for that, Nick. They'll see you as I see you, as a traitor in disgrace. I'm gonna take care of your pretty wife for you, Nick, real good." The gun fell to the floor.

Cathy Parmalay's anticipation of her husband's return gave way to peaceful slumber as her smiling eyes surrendered to sleep. She dreamed of strong hands upon her slim, svelte body. And she looked oh so pretty, lying there in her new pink chiffon nightie; the one that she bought special for the occasion.

Sonny never disrespected the Christian faith of any kind, on purpose anyway. He always believed in some version of the holy-scriptures. He even held the Catholic Church in high esteem.

"Forgive me Father, for I have sinned."

His voice was washed out and wavered somewhat, but Father Harrington recognized his friend, right off. "Sonny, is that you?"

Again, the confessional walls hear the lachrymose plea of the worn-out soldier of society. "Forgive me Father, for I have sinned."

"But, Sonny, I cannot listen to your confession, and I cannot grant you absolution, for you are not of the Catholic faith."

"That's okay, Father. God's left me anyway."

"No. No, God has not left you, my son."

"You must hear me out, Father. I need help. I'm at the end of my rope. I have nowhere else to go. God has left me, and so has my wife," cried Sonny. "I seek answers but they are nowhere to be found. I feel my life spiraling out of control. I can't figure right from wrong, anymore. I've fallen into darkness. Why has God forsaken me?"

The sagacious priest fought back his emotions while searching in thought for words to soothe his sobbing friend. "Nonsense, my friend, God has not forsaken you, nor has he given up on you. You're an unhorsed rider, that's all. You've been thrown off. You just need to brush off and climb back on for the ride again."

"I know too much about certain people, Papa. I mean bad things, real bad. I've also held things back from Samantha for fear of hurting her, and by doing so, I've lost her. I've turned into the enemy, Papa. I'm not her protector anymore. Her father and his goons are. I'm so scared for her."

"No one can hide their loved ones from the harsh realities of life for long. Not even you, my boy. Ever since we've known each other, you never did want anyone taking care of you because you were always hell-bent on being the responsible one for the others. That's what makes you such a great cop."

"Centralia took care of that," said Sonny somberly.

"You've taken a bad rap, Sonny. I can relate to that. We, in the priesthood feel the same way about ourselves, some of it being true, most of it not. We must carry this burden, you and I; you for different reasons. For whatever the reason, you're the chosen one, Sonny. You recognize evil where others can't."

"Tell me, Papa, why am I the way I am?" begged Sonny.

"That answer, I do not have, my son. Look, if the memory of Centralia still haunts you, go back and face the demons. Chances are that they are but no more than a dark, haunting memory. Sometimes memories are like ghosts from the past. You can't shake them until you confront them. You never forgave yourself for Centralia. Until you do, the ghosts of Centralia will haunt you forever. You must find out to retrieve your happiness again. You were right, Sonny. The road through life is crooked. I know things seem very bleak right now, but having known you and Samantha for such a long time, I believe that she will be waiting for you at journey's end. But who am I but an old, broken down chaplain priest anyway?" joked the Padre.

"Thanks for your advice, Papa. It's good to know that I have such a friend to come to."

As they both left the confessional, Sonny reached to shake the Father's hand, but the priest hugged him as if he were his son. "I will pray for you."

"Please do, Papa."

The laughter of little children was everywhere. As Sonny walked onto the playground he saw Danielle keeping a watchful eye over the youngsters. His daughter had now made her final step from childhood into womanhood. She wasn't his little girl anymore. Not like she used to be.

Danielle smiled as she watched her father draw closer. But it was a worried smile, for she knew that her parents were in conflict with each other. "Hello, Daddy," she said softly.

"Two weeks into school and you've got them tamed already," smiled Sonny.

"I got lucky. They gave me the second grade."

"Those are the easiest?"

"Let's put it this way. They're at a stage in their lives where they still like school, yet they don't think they know everything. So yeah, I guess you're right. What brings you out today, Pop?"

Sonny stared at his feet nervously. "I just wanted to see how my favorite girl was doing at her first real job. That's all."

"You're checking up on me like you always did, aren't you?"

"Well, I guess you're all grown up now. You don't need me anymore, do you?"

"You can check up on me anytime you want, Daddy," she said.

Danielle placed his hands in hers and looked him in the eye. "You didn't come here for the sole purpose of checking up on your little girl, did you, Daddy?"

"No. I came to tell you that I'm going away for a while. Your mother and I haven't seen eye to eye lately. She doesn't want me around anymore."

"No! You can't leave, Daddy. I won't have it."

"Listen to me, Danny. It's best for right now. I got into a skirmish a little while back and upset some people, real bad; the wrong kind of people. These people are trying to harm your mother. I always felt that I could protect Samantha. I have in the past, but somehow this is different. Your mother and Big John think that she's in great danger with me around."

"But, where will you go?" she asked tearfully.

"I'm just going to go somewhere, who knows where, to find myself. Don't cry, baby. I tried. I really did."

"But, I need you, Daddy."

"These kids need you. That's why I made you so strong and independent."

"I still don't want you to leave," she said, wiping away her tears.

"I love your mother too much to stay."

"It's not fair to you though."

"Sometimes, life just isn't fair, Danny. I wouldn't hurt you for anything in the world, baby, but I have to do this. I will keep in touch with you. I promise."

As the alarm sounded to end the recess, the children swarmed around their new young teacher, pulling her with them back to their classroom. "Daddy, I need to talk to you some more about this," said Danielle hastily.

"Looks like you have your hands full, Danny. I'm proud of you," he yelled while leaving the yard.

Danielle cried out one last time, "But Daddy!"

"Look after your little sister," was his last words to her as she disappeared inside the school.

Chapter Twenty-Six

Redemption Draweth Nigh

Driving down U.S.31 had a different appeal to it this time then during his two previous treks. Sonny's mind was running on empty, looking for a refill station. He was at odds with himself. He hated leaving Samantha with her life in danger but she wanted it that way. He tried to win her back but she would have none of it. She hurt him deeply. He tried to re-evaluate their relationship and came to the conclusion that he was hopelessly in love with the tall redhead. His feelings for her were very special. She was more than anything he had ever bargained for in life. He never tired of her, never. Sonny reasoned with himself that he was of the wild kind and she had her own aspirations, separate from his. Samantha's infidelity with Troy Charbonau stuck in his craw, no doubt. It would leave an everlasting scar on his heart, but Sonny was willing to forgive Samantha of her transgressions if she would only forgive him of his.

Sonny was enough of a realist to know that life was a rough battle at times. Maybe some people were to stay in their holes and bury their heads from the onslaught, but Sonny's credo was to stand tall and fight. He learned that from Maggie Mae. He practiced it in Vietnam. Losing his life for doing the right thing wasn't what bothered Sonny. He could accept that. But losing his wife had a much harder bite to it. Sonny was determined to pick up the pace with his life and wait for Samantha to come around.

The lights of Centralia, once again, loomed ahead for the washed-out detective. He wasn't about to try and figure out his outrageous journey from Centralia to the Bone Yard. Whatever the reason, it wouldn't make any difference now, anyhow.

Sonny felt awkward, walking into the small hotel office to rent a room for the night. He wondered how Junior must have felt on the night of his death, talking with the manager, not knowing that one of the manager's sons would take his life that evening.

The nameplate on the desk read, "Shirley Rucker, Motel Manager." After ringing the bell several times, the motel clerk finally showed. She was a stout looking woman with stringy hair, and seemed about Sonny's age, and probably would look decent with a new makeover.

"Sorry 'bout that, got caught up watching Seinfeld in the back room. Do you watch Seinfeld?"

"Yeah, he's a hoot," said Sonny disinterested.

"So, I take it you want a room?"

"Yes, I'm looking to rent a room for the night," said Sonny.

"That'll be thirty-two ninety-five, mister. I'll assign you to room number two."

"I prefer room number four, if it's not being used, ma'am."

"But they're all the same."

"Still, I would like to have room number four, if at all possible."

"Suit yourself, mister. Let me guess, that's the room you spent your honeymoon night in, twenty years ago, with your ex-wife. Either that or it's where you first popped her cherry."

"No, that's not it, ma'am. I just left some old memories in that room that I must deal with. That's all."

"You're not gonna' get drunk and go crazy tonight, shoot'n out windows and stuff, are you?"

"I got some weird shit going on in my head, lady, but it ain't that bad."

They both shared a smile, he more than she.

Shirley strangely eyed Sonny as he signed his name. She turned the registry to her to get a proper read, "Rafferty, Sonny Rafferty, the name sounds familiar. Have we met before?"

"No. I don't believe so."

"Well, let me run your credit card through. Then I'll give you your receipt and a room key," said Shirley. Suddenly, a thought came to her, "Wait a minute. I remember now. You're the cop in that raid about six years ago that killed the Cassian brothers."

"Yeah, that was me," said Sonny reluctantly. "I only killed one of them though. Frank, the oldest, shot his own brother to death."

Shirley gave Sonny the evil eye. "That may be, but the way I heard it is that it was a botched job, and none of those people would have died, if not for you."

Sonny was starting to feel a little chilled by the lady, and didn't feel like arguing his case anymore. "People can say what they want, but that was a long time ago," he said.

"Well, if you didn't feel guilty about somethin' then you wouldn't have come back to the scene, mister."

"You're probably right, Shirley. May I have my room key now, please?"

"Sure, hope things work out for you, mister."

Sonny was glad to get away from that busybody. She was starting to give him the creeps.

Room number four didn't look the same as when he broke down the door in that raid so long ago. The bullet holes had been spackled over and the walls repainted. The room also had new windows and new furniture, and the infamous door to the other room was still there. Sonny checked it to make sure it was locked. The big bed sat in the same place, across from the door that Frank Cassian burst through firing that hellish Mac 10.

Sonny was glad he came. He felt that it would do his psyche some good. Papa Harrington was right. Tonight he could say good-bye to Junior, once and for all. The Wright girl weighed heavily on his mind, as well.

After he put his meager belongings away, Sonny walked over to Peggy Sue's Diner, hoping to share some pie and coffee, and conversation with Peggy, and to rekindle their unique but brief friendship. She wasn't there but he met Kristin, her oldest daughter, waiting on tables. Apparently Peggy was out on a date with some farm boy. He also found that Kristin wasn't very talkative to men, so he cut his visit short.

Hoping to flood out his thoughts of Samantha and the strange turn of events from the past few days, Sonny stretched out on his bed and clicked on the television. He didn't really watch it, just stared at its glow. Memories abounded as his mind floated back in time.

He thought of Junior and Shauna, how much they looked alike, especially when they smiled. He pictured a sad image of Mindy, getting out of the cab with the cigarette hanging from her painted mouth, struggling with her backpack, just moments before her life ended. The ugliness of that night tried to emerge from hiding, but Sonny put it out of his mind. He only wanted to think of them alive. Sonny didn't remember when he fell off to sleep. One rarely does.

His mind journeyed back to lesser times when he and Samantha were both young, audacious creatures, roaming this earth. She was a spirited filly, and he a wild stallion. Paradise Woods, what a place. It was his home, his shelter from the world outside. It was where he deflowered this rare species of a woman that had not yet felt the warmth of a man's body lying next to hers. The copper-haired beauty took his breath away and smothered his senses. It was a most rapturous time, she becoming his princess, and he her knight in shining armor.

Suddenly, Sonny's thoughts went dark to the sound of crashing thunder. He reverted back to that stormy summer's eve as the happenings of that night emerged again from the dark recesses of his mind. Their death faces faded in and out as he wrestled to push them away. He so wanted them resurrected. With eyes wide shut, Sonny could smell the stench of death, and the harsh, sulfurous odor of gunpowder. It was mayhem again, as the deafening Mac 10 fired repetitiously through anything in its way. He could hear the screams from the naked little pixie cowering in the corner, and he saw the pallid death mask of Mindy Wright, posing as a rag doll sitting against the wall. It was a horrendous night, almost too much to bear the second time around.

Sonny desperately struggled to open his eyes to rid himself of this nightmare when a sudden streak of light from the electric storm outside shot across the room to the silvery blade of the long butcher's knife coming toward him. Sonny's quick instincts and great reflexes allowed him to deflect the stainless steel spear from his throat to a superficial slice of his left shoulder. One quick jab from Sonny's right fist sent the dark shadow flying across the room, leaving the knife imbedded in the mattress.

Sonny quickly jumped to his feet and turned on the room light. What he soon discovered made him realize that there was one more demon to exorcise from the Starlight Motel. Sonny's attacker was no other than Shirley, the motel manager. She had come through the side door as Frank Cassian had done long ago. But why Shirley, he thought. Sonny was determined to find out. He checked on the woman that he had just cold-cocked. She was out like a light, but breathing normally. Sonny decided to head on over to Peggy's house and bring her back to witness the scene. He planned on doing some investigating of that motel office.

Peggy awakened easily, for she could barely sleep, knowing that Sonny had called upon her earlier that evening. "Sonny, is it really you?" she gushed, while opening the screen door.

She looked different to him than before. She lacked her heavy make-up, plus she had fleshed out some. Sonny still thought her to be very pretty, but his concern for Peggy wasn't what was on his mind, right now. "Good to see you again, Peg. Did Kristin tell you that I was looking for you at the diner earlier?"

"Yes, she did, Cowboy. Sorry I missed ya. I was at a church social with a friend."

"Peggy, I need you to come with me. I just punched out the motel clerk," said Sonny.

"Do you mean, Shirley?" she said confused.

"Yeah, she tried to kill me. Grab a coat. I'll explain it all on the way over to the motel."

Peggy had no idea that Shirley Rucker was the type to try and kill someone. Shirley would come over to the diner every morning to have coffee with her. She liked to gab, and at times seemed a bit peculiar to Peg, but she never showed signs of violence.

Sonny and Peggy carried Shirley back to the motel's office. They took her to her bedroom and laid her on the bed. Peggy watched after her while Sonny searched the place for some clues.

"You should really call the police," said Peggy.

"No. We're not gonna' do that, not just yet."

"But she tried to kill you."

"I'm well aware of that. I'm just trying to find out why. How long was it after Ray Jenkins's death that Shirley appeared?"

"Oh, it was about a month; a month and a half, maybe. Why, do you think she has some connection with Ray and his boys?"

"Could be," said Sonny.

"I don't see how."

Sonny gave her a slanted glance while rummaging through Shirley's dresser drawers.

"Do you think you ought to be looking in her personal things like that? Isn't it illegal?"

"She tried to kill me, Peg. Do you think that was legal?"

"No, I guess it wasn't."

Sonny discovered a large brown envelope buried under some lingerie. He opened it up and pulled out several photographs. Most of the pictures showed a man with a young woman, or teenager maybe. It must be his daughter, thought Sonny. The more pictures he looked at, the more intimate they became. No, can't be, must be a young wife, or girlfriend. The woman looked a lot like a young Shirley Rucker.

Sonny handed the pictures to Peggy, "Here, take a look at these and tell me what you think."

"Why, that's Ray Jenkins, and the girl looks like . . . Shirley. They seem to be much younger in these photos."

"Looks like they were an item at one time," said Sonny. "I'm gonna' check her closet. She's bound to have some skeletons in there."

"Sonny, she's starting to wake up!"

"That's alright. Just keep that ice bag on her cheek and talk to her. You both know each other."

"But, what should I say to her?"

"Hell, I don't know. Talk women talk with her. Just draw her attention from me until I check through her things."

Shirley woke up, dazed and confused. Meanwhile, Peggy rattled on as if they were sitting down over a morning cup of coffee.

Sonny soon discovered a large hatbox with a picture of two cherubs on the top. As soon as he opened the box he knew he had struck gold, for it was filled with letters, documents, certificates, and such. In the very bottom he found an old family Bible. Sonny thumbed through the book and noticed that the insides of the pages had been carefully cut out, allowing a secret hiding place. Inside the cut-out Bible was a hand-held tape recorder. Sonny was so overwhelmed with his discovery that he did not hear the commotion going on outside the closet.

"Hey, Peg, I found the mother-load," he said, bringing the box out of hiding.

"Hold it right there, mister. Drop that box and hold your hands where I can see them."

The startled detective did as he was told. "Who might you be?" he asked.

"I might be this woman's daughter," she said curtly. "And you, sir, are caught breaking and entering."

Sonny turned to Peggy, "Why didn't you warn me?" he asked.

"I didn't see her in time," said Peggy.

"Look, darlin', that's not a joystick you have in your hand there. That thing shoots real bullets," said Sonny.

"Don't be a wise-ass, mister. I know how to use this."

She was pretty enough, a tassel-headed blonde with puffy lips, smeared red as if coming in late from a successful night out. But she was no killer. Sonny could see that in her eyes. He also recognized her as the girl from the yellow truck.

Sonny eased towards her as he spoke, "First of all, things aren't what they seem. Your mother tried to kill me tonight with a butcher's knife while I was asleep on my bed. That's why she has a swollen right cheek."

"And that's why you're rummaging through her closet, right?—Hold it right there, before I drill a hole right through ya!" she ordered.

"You're not going to shoot me darlin'. What would you tell the cops?"

"That's easy," she smiled, "Self-defense."

"But I have a witness. Are you going to kill Peggy too, your own neighbor?"

"Hey Jeri, listen to Sonny. He's right. Shirley did try to kill him. Check in room four and you'll find the knife buried in the mattress where she near-missed. Better yet, look at the blood running down his arm where she sliced his shoulder open."

"Don't listen to them, baby," interrupted Shirley, coming into consciousness. "This man is Sonny Rafferty. He's the cop that killed my brothers. He's the man that your grandpa swore me to kill!"

"What are you talkin' about, Ma?"

As Jeri glanced at her mother Sonny grabbed the gun from her.

"You son-of-a-bitch!" screamed Jeri.

"You can't do this. We have our rights!" squawked Shirley.

"As far as I'm concerned, you lost your rights when you came down on me with that butcher's knife," replied Sonny.

"You killed Frank and Harold—you deserve to die!" exploded Shirley.

"Is what my mother says about you true? Did you kill my two uncles?" queried Jeri.

"Yes, I'm Rafferty, but as far as your uncles go, they brought on their own demise. They were running a child pornography ring out of this motel. We came to make an arrest but they resisted."

"So, what brings you back, tough guy?"

"Actually, you did darlin'. One evening, about three months ago, I tailed you and a man by the name of Jim Weiler, from Speedway to the Starlight motel. You were helping him cheat on his wife. I got it all on film."

"You didn't!"

"Oh yeah, in color too." said Sonny.

"You bastard, Jim really liked me. He was going to marry me and you fucked it up."

"Don't be so quick to give me the credit, darlin'. His wife paid me well to track the both of you down. She wasn't about to give him up to some cheap floozy without a fight."

"Hey! Who you callin' a floozy?" snapped Jeri.

"Oh, did I say floozy? I meant, mistress."

"Hey, a gal has to make a living some way."

"Prostituting yourself is a hell of a way to make a living."

"Don't kid yourself, fella. We all prostitute ourselves in some way or another."

"You're probably right, there, darlin'. Besides, the way you earn your living is none of my business."

"I still don't understand why my mother is so bitter towards you."

"She still blames me for the deaths of her brothers. That's why."

"Yeah, I guess maybe she does, but enough to want to kill you? I never even knew my uncles, or my grandpa. I only know of them by pictures that Ma has of 'em. Hell, we were living down in Paintsville 6 years ago."

"It doesn't make since to me either. That's why I'm looking through her things, hoping to find some clues."

"I'll sue you for everything you own Rafferty. You broke my jaw, you bastard!" screeched Shirley.

"That was just a love tap, dear. You'll be just fine in no time."

"Stop him, Jeri. Please, I beg of you," she frantically pleaded.

"I can't, he's got the gun, Ma. Shouldn't you have a warrant to enter our home like this?" she asked Sonny.

"Look, darlin', it's either me or the cops. I don't plan on pressing charges, but the cops will. I'm just trying to find some answers."

"Don't listen to him!" cried Shirley, rising up in bed.

"Lay back down, Ma, let's hear him out."

"After following you and Weiler here to the motel, I left you both to your sexcapades and went over to Peggy Sue's for some coffee. After conversing with Peggy for awhile I soon found out that she knew Ray Jenkins. Apparently he took Peggy and her kids in when they first arrived here. Isn't that right, Peggy?"

"Yes, Sonny, I was at Ray's bedside the night he died. He told me about that dreadful night, 6 years ago, how he was involved, and everything. I'll never forget the last thing that he said. It was the way he said it that made it stick in my mind so. His last words were, "Rafferty, I will drag you down to hell with me for killing my sons. It chilled me to the bone. I'm sorry to speak of your dad that way, Shirley, but it's the truth. I'm so surprised that you even knew him. All those morning chats, and you spoke not a word of him."

"No, you're lying, Peggy. Daddy had nothin' to do with that porno stuff. Daddy was a good man," defended Shirley.

"Shirley, tell me, why did your dad take on an alias?" questioned Sonny.

Shirley didn't answer. Her mind suddenly went into a fog.

"Shirley?"

". . . What?"

"Why did your dad change his name?"

"What? I don't understand."

"What was your dad's last name? It was Cassian wasn't it?"

". . . Yes."

"Your maiden name, it was Cassian too, right?"

"Yes, of course."

"What was your mother's name?"

"What? I had no mother."

"Sure you did. Was your mother's name, Thelma Jenkins?"

"I . . . don't remember."

"You better leave her be, Sonny. She's not looking right," said Peggy, holding Shirley's hand in comfort.

"Sometimes she gets like this when she gets upset," said Jeri, "especially when talking about Grandpa Cassian. Mama, you okay? Mama, speak to me," she said while lightly spanking her hand.

"I'll leave her alone, kid. I'm just gonna look through this box, and then we'll leave," said Sonny.

As Shirley's mind faltered, Sonny began putting things together. But he needed proof, not just for his sake, but for Jeri's. He started feeling sorry for her, for he felt that there were some deep dark secrets hidden in that round box with the angels on top. As he began opening the old envelopes, the answers began to emerge.

"Let's see here. We have Jeri Rucker's birth certificate, born June 6th, 1978. Father, Augustine Woodrow Rucker. Mother, Shirley Ann Cassian. Where's your father now, Jeri?"

"He died when I was eleven. We lived in Paintsville, Kentucky at the time. Daddy was a farmer. One day he was pulling a wagon of tobacco up a steep hill, when the tractor reared up on him and tossed him off. The wagon rolled over his head and crushed it," said Jeri sadly.

"Did you live in Paintsville your whole life?"

"Yeah, until we moved here about a year ago," she answered.

"Sorry about your dad, kid."

"Don't fuss over that. It was a long time ago. Besides, that red dirt slickens up real bad when it rains. It'll cause that tractor to do that to ya."

"Let's see what else we have in here. We have Shirley and Augie's marriage certificate. They were married May 9th, 1978, just a month before Jeri was born; interesting."

"Why? That happens to a lot of people," defended Jeri.

"I know. All I said was, interesting," said Sonny, deep in thought. "Here's a letter from Roy Waterman, Attorney at Law, addressed to Shirley Ann Rucker of Paintsville, Kentucky. It's about Ray's will. It states that Ray Jenkins leaves his estate, which includes the Starlight Motel and all bank accounts, to Shirley Ann Rucker of Paintsville, Kentucky. Along with the letter is a copy of Shirley's birth certificate. This is quite interesting. Her father is listed as Johnny Ray Cassian, and the mother as Thelma Louise Jenkins. That tells a lot right there. Shirley, listen to me. Do you know where your mother is?"

"No."

"Was your mother, Thelma Jenkins?"

"No, she left us when we were kids. Daddy went to jail and Mama left us."

Jeri and Peggy shed tears to the sadness now in the room.

"So, Shirley, who took care of you kids until Daddy got out of prison?" asked Sonny.

"People, all kinds of people, some not very nice," she answered. "But Daddy came and got me, but not the boys, not then."

"You loved your daddy, didn't you?"

"Yes I did, very much."

"Sonny, this is too torturous to all of us. Are you about through?" asked Peggy.

"Just one more thing, Peg, then, I'll end my questioning."

Sonny pulled out the family Bible and opened it, revealing the hand-held tape recorder.

The room went quiet as Sonny turned on the recorder. Click!

Shirley rolled her eyes like a nervous caged animal when she heard the gravelly voice of her Daddy: *"Dearest Shirley, If you are listening to this tape, I am already dead. I have apologies to make, and I have a favor to ask of you. We were some couple, you and I. I'm sorry that I ran off and left you in Paintsville. That was wrong of me, with you being pregnant and all. But you see, baby, if people found out that you were pregnant with my child, they wouldn't understand. They would throw me back into jail. That's why I also changed my name. I just couldn't take that chance, baby. I'm glad you married Augie. I always thought he was a retard, but he helped you raise Jeri. For that, I'll give him credit. Too bad he got his head crushed. Thank you for sending me Jeri's pictures over the years. After all these years you're probably still pissed at me, but I took good care of you, baby. That cash Christmas present that you received from Santa each year was really from me. I guess you figured that out by now. I'm leaving you a small motel in Centralia Indiana, and what little cash I have left. The woman next door is real nice. Her name is Peggy Sue. If you need any help, just ask her, and she will be your friend, I'm sure. She's always been good to me, kinda like you used to be towards me. I suppose Jeri is grown up now and probably married off. She made as pretty a daughter as you did. I also owe a debt to my sons, Frank and Harold, your own flesh. They were killed by a no good bastard cop by the name of Sonny Rafferty. I have left a message on the end of this tape for Rafferty. I have also written down his phone number. Every so often, I want you to go to a pay phone and call that number, and play this message to him . . . Is this Rafferty? Hey Rafferty, you're going down! Do you hear me? If I'm going to hell, you're going with me.' Pause . . . And if you ever see him and are able, kill that son-of-a-bitch for me,*

380

will you darlin'? I would be forever grateful. It is very important that you do this, darlin'. I need revenge for what he did to Frank and Harold. Do your Daddy right, baby. Goodbye my lovely".

Shirley had slipped over the edge alright, but it wasn't her fault. It started long ago when Johnny Cassian bedded down his young daughter as a woman, and then abandoned her. Then again, in the throes of death, he manipulated her into becoming his killing machine. He could do it, for he owned her misplaced love. She was Johnny's weapon for killing Sonny from the grave. Everyone in that motel office was stunned by the revelation of Shirley's sordid past with her father.

Sonny and Peggy sadly retreated back to her bungalow where she put on a pot of coffee to take the chill off the morning. Peggy soon left Sonny at the table to ponder his own predicament while she went back to help Jeri make arrangements for psychiatric care for her mother.

Sonny awkwardly became acquainted with Peggy's daughters as they arose for breakfast, finding a male stranger sitting at their breakfast table instead of their mother. Sonny helped Peggy and the girls at the diner that afternoon. He wasn't much of a grill-master, but he cleaned tables off with the best of them. Karen took to him, but Kristin kept her distance. Kristin was edgy, very protective of her vulnerable mother. She had followed Peggy down too many one-way streets when it came to the men in her life. She didn't like seeing her mother hurt.

As the evening waned, Peggy and Sonny grabbed an iced tea and took refuge on the front porch of Peggy's bungalow. Peggy adoringly studied Sonny's profile while he stared out coldly into the dark, ominous night. She traced his strong face with her soft eyes, as she once did with her fingers.

"I feel a storm brewing tonight. I heard on the weather report that a cold front would be movin' in by midnight," said Peggy.

Peggy's nearness felt good to Sonny, but he wasn't up to small talk, not just yet.

"What's bothering you, Cowboy?"

"You know, Peg, I met Shirley's mother twice. I can't even explain to you the circumstances."

"Give me a try, baby. I'm a good listener."

"I met Thelma Jenkins the night that I left you. When I left here that evening I just wondered aimlessly throughout the isolated countryside. I don't know what I was looking for. There was a time where I couldn't even remember that night. But I now realize that I was running, running from my past at Centralia. I couldn't cope with the fact that my reckless actions on that night cost innocent lives, and then finding out that I even failed at getting the fucking leader. Running into Thelma Jenkins is almost too strange a tale to tell. I met her at an obscure roadhouse out in the middle of Nowheresville. She had mysticism about her that I can't explain. But I do know this. She knew about the Centralia raid, and she knew that I had been involved in the deaths of her sons."

"But, Sonny, Thelma left her children when they were quite young. She never kept in contact with them. So how could she know so much about your involvement?"

"That has me puzzled, too, but what's really bazaar is that she claimed that Ray talked to her from the grave, and told her of me."

"You know, that's really spooky," said the wide-eyed waitress.

Sonny put his arm around Peggy to ease her fears. "Say, Peggy, would it be okay if I stayed with you for a while? I don't think I want to room in the motel anymore."

"Why sure, Sonny, may I ask why?"

"My wife just kicked me out of her life."

"You're kidding, for how long?"

"I don't know. It's really up to her."

"Hell, you've been married forever. How'd this come about? Or am I being too nosey?"

"Nah, you're not being too nosey. She wanted me to make some changes with her, and I guess I let my pride get in the way of my decisions. She then found another, and I got tossed."

"All I can say, baby, is that she must be crazy to let go of you."

"Thanks, Peg. She did throw me for a loop. I'll have to say that."

"Don't worry, Cowboy, you can sleep in my bed tonight."

"If it's alright with you I'll just sleep out here on the porch."

"Oh, I'm sorry. I didn't intend for it to sound that way. What I meant was that you can sleep in my room while I sleep with the girls."

"Nonsense, I'll sleep just fine out here on the porch. It'll only be for a while, until I get my wits about me again. I'll help you out in the diner some if you want."

"Do you work for tips?" teased Peggy.

"I just need a place to lay my head, darlin', that's all I need right now."

Peggy shared a smile with Sonny before going inside to get some blankets for his bed on the porch.

A peal of thunder woke Peggy from her sleep as a ferocious wind blew the rain wildly against the house. Peggy crawled out of bed to go relieve herself, but the lights in the hallway flickered, and then went out. She grabbed a flashlight off the nightstand next to her bed to light her way to the john. She sleepily sat down and released a rigid yellow stream when a sudden crash of thunder caused her to tighten up. She suddenly realized that she'd left Sonny outside! She quickly pulled up her panties and rushed through the front door to find him. The porch was empty, but she noticed that his car was still parked in the driveway. The storm didn't bother her now, and the rain felt good against her face. She was just happy that Sonny hadn't left her again. She sprinted to the car and found him lying in the front seat rolled up in the wet blankets.

"What's wrong with you? You'll catch your death of pneumonia out here," she scolded.

"Aw, I'll be alright. This car's my second home, you know," answered Sonny.

"Come on inside, Cowboy. Let's get you out of those wet clothes."

Peggy led Sonny to her cozy bedroom, stopping by the bathroom along the way to fetch a couple of towels. "Go ahead and get out of your clothes and dry off with this towel. I'm going to light us a candle so we don't stumble all over each other. The batteries are getting low in the flashlight."

"But, I don't have anything to change into," said Sonny.

"No time to be modest now, Cowboy. Get nekid and jump in that bed under those covers where it's warm."

As Peggy lit the candle, Sonny noticed that she was as wet as he was. Her negligee clung to her like a second skin. The wet silk hid very little of Peggy's well-defined body. Instead, the diaphanous fabric enhanced the roundness of her curves, and crept into forbidden slits and crevices. Sonny imbibed her beauty while drying himself off with the towel. He couldn't keep his eyes from her gumdrop nipples that poked from her swollen mounds.

Peggy also glanced at him, accidental-like, sneaking a peek at his dangling manhood that wasn't dangling anymore, but instead, was reaching out toward her at an enormous growth rate. Sonny caught her eye and blushed shamelessly as he jumped in bed, covering up to hide his thrill. The warmth and smell of Peggy Sue's body still permeated the bedcovers, arousing Sonny even more.

Peggy slithered out of her wet, silky garment by pulling it over her head, presenting to him her milk-white breasts with a matching belly that rounded down nicely into her panty top. She had fleshed out some since their first meeting, yet it seemed only to enhance her sexuality that much more.

Her shyness from her weight gain took over and she quickly blew out the candle and climbed in bed alongside Sonny. She rolled over to face him and sensed his smile. She moved in closer until she could feel his warm breath and hardened chest against her breasts. Sonny covered her mouth with his, his tongue probing deep into her throat, tasting, searching. He ran his fingers through her long curls while savoring her mouth juices. Peggy reached under the covering and wrapped her hand around his huge protuberance. The tumescence of Sonny's unsheathed sword whet Peggy Sue's sexual appetite, bringing forth a gasp, and an extreme sexual urge from within her furry love pouch. Peggy lifted her pelvis up while Sonny ripped the white silk from her loins, laying bare her womanly assets. Her legs fell open and his fingers quickly delved into her wet desire, causing her to purr softly like a kitten.

Her voluptuous white body invited more of Sonny's curiosity, so he plunged his fiery rod into Peggy's moist love glen, taking her breath away. Then, while sucking for air, she began moving with a rhythmic, rocking motion of making love. Sonny plowed her fertile valley with long, deliberate thrusts, banging hard against her pronounced womanhood, setting off a firestorm that he stoked furiously.

Peggy stifled her moans as best she could so as not to wake up the girls. At first she cried tears of pain, then tears of pleasure. As his pace quickened so did Peggy's love grunts. She hid her screams in loud hisses, and buried her head in a pillow during her final climax.

Sonny and Peggy lay silently next to each other. Sonny had never traveled down this road since his marriage to Samantha. He didn't feel guilty, but he felt kind of sad. He still yearned for Samantha, but also loved the washed-out blonde. He couldn't figure it out. He adored Samantha. She was his queen. On the other hand, Peggy Sue was more like he was; a brawler in life. She was tough but needed loving, and he was the same. Sonny now had little choice for pleasure, for his life had unraveled into nothingness.

"So, what about that fella' you've been dating?" he asked Peggy.

The question sounded quite humorous, but it broke their silence and sent a broad smile across Peggy's face. "What fella' are you talking about?"

"That farm boy you've been dating."

"Oh, him?" she said. "He's a nice boy, goes to church and all of that, but he's too young for me. Hell, Cowboy, he loses his seed every time he cops a feel. I don't get much from these rubes around here. I guess I was just meant to be a giver. So, if you're gonna be around a while, forget about that farm boy."

Peggy Sue didn't delve into life as deeply as Sonny. She appreciated the small gifts of life. She considered Sonny to be just that, but hoped for more. "What about you, Cowboy. Do you have any plans?" Peggy felt Sonny tense up and realized that it was way too soon to be asking that question.

"Listen Peg, I can't commit right now. I don't know what my future holds. I love you, kid, and that's all I'm gonna say. I can't promise you anything."

"That was stupid of me to ask you that question, Sonny, and I apologize. I try not to make too much out of rejection anyway."

"Don't apologize, Peg. I'm not rejecting you. Hell, I think you're great. I'm just having trouble with rejection in my own life right now. How do you handle it?"

"I draw strength from my daughters, and faith in the 'Almighty'. Look, Sonny, fate brought you here and fate will take you away, if anything does. I hold no strings attached to you, darling. Just hold me tight tonight, lover. Hold me real tight."

The unmarked police cruiser was a lonely sight as it sat off the side of the road in Eagle Park. Even under the florescence of the heavens, the car looked abandoned and uninteresting. But, ever so often the moonlight would reflect silvery off a whiskey flask from inside.

Being a lieutenant on the vice squad was a tough job, but Frank was a tough cop. Tonight, he had to be especially tough. He had some bills to pay and the price was high. Frank knew that his luck had run out. Sonny as much told him that. But on this evening, Frank was at peace with himself.

He was supposed to be in Speedway, canvassing house to house to find the whereabouts of a habitual criminal. Instead, he came to the park where it was quiet, where it was serene, and where he could gaze at the night sky. Sonny once told him that peering into God's universe was where he gained his inner strength. It was where he knew God was listening to him. At most every backyard barbeque where Sonny and Samantha were invited, he and Sonny would ultimately end up the evening sitting in the backyard, drinking their beers, while staring at the firmament in amazement, like two young boys trying to paint the sky with stars.

Frank took another swig of sour mash whiskey from his flask and turned up the sound to hear the mellifluous voice of Enya, another sweet discovery that Sonny shared with his friend. **Paint the sky with stars**. If only life on earth were that beautiful, thought Frank.

Frank smiled to himself while thinking of the little beauty in life that he did possess, at home resting peacefully in bed with his warmth inside her.

Sonny was right, and Frank knew it. Sonny could have killed him, but he didn't. Did that make Sonny weak? Not to Frank. It made him brave. It made him strong, and in this instance it made him right. Frank had sold his soul to the devil but Sonny got it back. But the price was high, and Frank would pay that price tonight.

Frank took his last drink and threw the flask out the window. He took a deep breath while starting the engine. He pulled out onto the road and picked up the transmitter. "Metro 1 this is Victor Mike 2."

"Metro 1, over."

"I have a possible 10-55 driving erratically at a high rate of speed, heading south on Raceway road. It's a blue, late model sedan, license plate: # 49N3700. Request a 10-28, check."

"Roger that . . . Victor Mike 2; be advised that we have a stolen vehicle here."

"Roger that. I am turning east onto 56th Street, possible heading, the 465 expressway. Request a black and white at the expressway entrance."

"Metro 1 this Metro 6, I'm in the vicinity, E. T. A., eight minutes. Victor Mike 2, you copy?"

"Copy that Metro 6, meet you at the expressway. Victor Mike 2 out."

Frank turned on his lights and siren just prior to crashing his car through the guardrail. The car hurled through the air toward the sky before hitting the water in the reservoir. Frank was a good swimmer, but not tonight.

There was an ironic twist to Frank's death. It was discovered the next day that the spot where Frank jumped the guardrail and went into the reservoir was the exact spot where Loni Jacobs lost her life. They also discovered the stolen vehicle that same morning, parked comfortably in front of the flower shop which once housed Sonny Rafferty's Detective Agency above it.

Bernice was devastated beyond belief, but Frank left her a $250,000 life insurance policy, payable upon his death. He had purchased it the day before he died. He was buried with full honors for dying in the line of duty.

Frank Lujack, like Sonny, once was a warrior. He just lost his way, that's all.

Only one question now remained. **Who will paint the midnight stars?**

Chapter Twenty-Seven

The Fall of Babylon

Big John arose early, expecting "the Bullet" Jake Mueller to arrive with Victorio Delveccio's confirmation to the meeting that John had set up for tonight. The crisp, October air felt refreshing to the big man as he exuberantly jumped into the heated pool for his morning swim.

Samantha and Kitty soon joined him poolside while having their morning breakfast of grapefruit, toast, and coffee.

"My, my, a prettier sight I have never seen," blandished John, while looking up from the pool's edge.

"You're just flirting with us because you're looking up our robes," said Kitty.

"Morning, Daddy," added Samantha.

John pulled himself up from the pool. "No, dear, I'm flirting with you two because you both happen to be the most beautiful women that I know."

"Now I know you're up to no good, John. What is it that you want?" asked Kitty.

"Some of that hot coffee will do for a start, just to stop my teeth from chattering."

"That's what you get for swimming this time of day."

"But it's so refreshing, darling. You should try it with me."

"I might just do that, after I eat."

"Uh, let's take a rain check on that, Kitty," said John, his attention diverted to the house's rear entrance where Jake Mueller stood waiting. "I have some business to take care of. I'll get with you girls later."

"Well, Mother, it's you and me. Do you want to go for a swim?" said Samantha.

"No, I've changed my mind, Sam. I'm going inside to try and find out what your dad is up to. I don't much care for that Jake Mueller character. You go ahead without me Sam. Take a swim, it'll refresh you. Do you want one of my swimsuits to wear?"

"Nah, it wouldn't fit me now that you've gotten new breasts. My little tiddies would be lost in one of your suits. I'll just swim in what I slept in."

When Kitty left, Samantha dove into the warm water, wishing she could wash away the last month and a half of her life.

"Do you smoke, Jake?" asked John, opening his humidor to "The Bullet."

"No thanks, Big John."

"You ought to try it. It's a bad habit but a good vice. Not as good as a young, wanton woman, but regardless of what the experts say, it's not as harmful either."

Jake forced a smile as John lit one up. "Pardon me a minute, Jake, while I turn on some music in case the Feds have us bugged . . . Okay, Jake, give it to me straight. What did Delveccio say?"

"He wants to meet tonight, just as you planned. At first, Victorio was kinda cool to the idea of the meeting place being in Jimtown."

"That's too fuckin' bad," said John with an edginess in his voice. "This Irishman has made Victorio a lot of money over the years, and I'm cuttin' him a sweet deal tonight."

"One of his boys knows the area, and assured him that it would be safe."

"Who all is he bringing with him?"

"From the take I got on it, his whole entourage, just about."

"That's not a good sign, Jake. Either he really doesn't trust us or he has something else up his sleeve."

"He told me to have you make sure that Losch shows up with his paperwork."

"Just as I thought, he wants Waverly, and he wants to take over Miramar, that Wop bastard! Okay now, listen to me good. My right-hand man blew his fuckin' brains out last week. I'm putting my trust in you, Jake, how about it?"

"You've got it, Big John. Just tell me what you want me to do."

"Get a couple of men and haul two of our banquet tables to the Westgate warehouse on Haliburton. Do you think you can find it?"

"Yeah, I know where it's at. They house beer cans or something to that nature."

"Actually they warehouse soda-pop cans; King Cola mostly. They come on pallets, each about 10-foot tall, stacked four high. When you first walk in there you feel like you're in a can maze, but don't let that bother you. Tell the manager that Big John is using his building for tonight. Tell him to shut the warehouse down at 9:00 pm, and don't come back until six in the morning. That means that nobody's in there but you. If anyone gives you a hard time, call me. Have him cancel all shipments for the night. We don't want anybody coming in or out except for the Italians. If King Cola complains to the manager tell him to call me. King Cola and I are real tight. I'm the one that negotiated the sweet-ass deal they have with the can company in Chicago."

"How's that, boss?"

"Hell, it was easy. Those can companies will suck a dick to get a beverage contract. Actually, they sucked mine. They paid me a cool hundred thou to negotiate a three year deal for them. Hell, them bastards will make it up on the slave labor of the Mexicans and Blacks. Those can companies have such piss-poor unions anymore that it's easy to take advantage of their labor force; Chicago, the city that works. Amen to that."

"Set the tables up between the cans and the loading dock. Check any empty trailers. I know Delveccio will have a scouting party there early. That's okay. Just feel 'em out. The meeting is at 1:00 o'clock. I'll be there between 12:30 and 1:00. While you're doing all that, I'll touch base with Losch, and get with the Flannery brothers to supply us with the needed firepower."

"Do you think it's going to come to that, Big John?"

"Meetings like this rarely ever do, but you've got to show your strength, as I'm sure they will. It's a power show, Jake. It's like big countries with nuclear weapons. We don't really plan on using them on each other. It's just a way of showing our teeth. Anyway, Delveccio has a couple of trigger-happy thugs that I don't trust."

"Is Rico Constantine one of them?"

"You got it."

"I thought so. He kind of gave me the willies when I was delivering your message to Delveccio."

"Yeah, he's a troublemaker, so keep an eye out for him. If we take precautions, I think the meeting will go just fine."

"Anything else, boss?" asked Jake.

"No, Jake. I appreciate you coming on board like this. You're a good man. If I make any changes, I'll call you on your cell. Other than that, let's keep a tight lip on it. I'll see you tonight, Jake."

"Okay, sir."

Samantha slid eloquently through the water with long, smooth strokes as her wet, crimson locks glistened from the morning sun. With the speed of a Yankee Clipper she swam effortlessly lap after lap until fatigued. When she pulled her exhausted body from the water she found herself standing directly in front of Troy Charbonau. Startled, Samantha gasped and quickly covered herself with her hands and arms, knowing well the transparency of her beige camisole. Just as quickly, Troy's charming smile released her of those inhibitions, as he did not glare at her rosebud teats, or her burning bush, but instead, into her emerald green eyes.

"I'm sorry. I didn't mean to startle you so," said Troy.

"Oh, it's not that," said Samantha, "It's the chill in the air that took my breath away."

"Here, let me help you on with your robe," said Troy, snuggling the terrycloth around her shoulders. "I, myself was captured by your beauty and the gracefulness of your swim."

"I guess I take after my mother. She's the real swimmer in the family. So, how did you get in?"

"I rang the doorbell and nobody answered. So I guess I let myself in. I just had to see you once again."

"Oh, Troy, you are persistent. You don't give up easily do you?"

"Look, Samantha, I just wanted to tell you that I'll be leaving for Washington pretty soon and—"

"Let's go upstairs to my room and talk while I change from these wet clothes."

As "The Bullet" left the house, Kitty slid open the door to the parlor, finding her husband sitting in his favorite chair, deep in thought. "What's wrong dear?" she asked in earnest.

"Oh nothing, baby, everything's just fine," he said quietly.

"Well, I don't care much for that Jake Mueller fellow. He looks like a street thug to me," she opined.

"On the contrary, my dear, he is very intelligent. He's going to take over our books until I find a replacement for Scarlet, God rest her soul. He's a good man, Kitty. Give him a chance."

"Well, if you say so, darling. I always go by what you say, John."

"That's what I like about you, Kitty. You're always by my side no matter how bad I fuck up."

"What can I say, big guy, I'm just hopelessly in love with you."

"Come here, honey, and sit in my lap a moment."

"John, it's been so long since you've held me in your arms," said Kitty, resting her head against his chest.

"Too long, I'm afraid. I know that I've neglected you lately, Kitty. It's just that I've been so busy trying to help our daughter."

"Don't worry, dear. I understand. I worry for her safety, also."

"I had hoped that Samantha would have been safely out of country by now, but circumstances prevented it. I have a plan that will soon solve our dilemma for good."

"What is your plan, John?"

"I can't tell you now, Kitty. You'll just have to trust me on this. I've got to run, dear. I have a thousand things to do today. That newspaper won't run itself."

"Okay, big guy," said Kitty, straightening herself up.

"Listen, Kitty, I'd like for us to spend some time together tonight, just the two of us."

"Why, sure, John, do you want to go out to dinner? I'll make the reservations."

"I have a better idea. Why don't I bring us something home to eat? Then we can have that swim tonight."

"Like we used too?" she asked.

"Yeah, like we used to."

"But John, it's supposed to get awfully chilly tonight."

"But the water is warm, dear, and so are you."

As Samantha unblushingly slipped off her wet undergarment, Troy envisioned another bedroom escapade with the alluring redhead. Samantha instead slipped from view to shower off. The senator reminisced of the past, and then thought ahead to what could have been. If he could have bagged this trophy he would've had the grandest of prizes.

The hissing of the shower soon stopped. Shortly thereafter, Samantha appeared, wearing sweat pants and a halter top while patting her hair with a towel. "So what's the purpose of your visit, Troy?"

"Like I said earlier, I'll be leaving soon, so I wanted to stop by and see how you're feeling."

"I'm feeling better. I do get monster headaches now and then."

"Well, I talked to your dad, and we both agree that's it's time for you to start making plans for New York, a new job, a new life, darling."

"Actually, Troy, I'm feeling better, yeah, but I'm still not ready to leave just yet. I have some family issues that need to be cleared up before I leave."

"Gina and I were pretty tight, you know. I think that she would have wanted you to be her replacement. I know the media, Sam. I can hook you up with all of Gina's people."

"You never quit trying, do you?" said Samantha in a sad smile.

"Don't be too hard on me, darling, for thinking you worthy of another try."

"I know I hurt you bad, Troy, and I'm sorry for that. I'm sorry for leading you on when we were back in D.C. I was infatuated by you, honey. Hell, a lot of women are. You have traits that most men don't possess, good traits. In truth, you are a great lover, the best I've known, but I'm in love with Sonny. That's all there is to it. I can't help it. Sonny has my heart."

Troy's own heart sank for the last time.

At that moment, Danielle walked through the bedroom door. She was unpleasantly surprised to see the senator in her mother's chambers. She gave him a cold stare. Samantha noticed, and went to her daughter and gave her a soft hug.

"Danielle, this is Senator Charbonau. He was a close friend of Gina's. He's here to talk to me about Washington D.C., and Gina's job."

"Mother, I know who Troy Charbonau is. I need to talk to you alone." she said flatly.

"Sam, that's alright. I was just leaving," said Troy, trying to ease their awkwardness. "I only stopped by to see if you needed any help preparing for D. C. When you finally do arrive, call me, and I'll get you set up with Gina's boss. You have my number. Goodbye, Samantha. Nice meeting you Danielle."

With the senator leaving, Samantha turned to Danielle. "That was very rude of you, Danny. What's wrong?"

"Mother, have you forgotten about Dad, or have you already moved on to someone else?"

"Danielle, don't be ridiculous. Your dad and I are having some problems, but it's our business. Not yours."

"How can you say that? Dad came to my school a while back, stating that he was leaving because of you. I thought you would call, but of course you didn't. And today I find you here with the man that escorted you to Gina's funeral. Is that why Daddy had to leave, because you've found somebody else? Sonja has been calling me because she can't get an answer at the house, except for Mary or Myra, and they don't know what's going on either. If you cared, you would live back home so Daddy could come back to all of us."

"Young lady, I'm your mother, and I deserve some respect. Have you forgotten that I, myself was almost killed, and recuperating, still?"

Suddenly, Kitty seemed to appear from nowhere and took Danielle by the hand. "Why are my girls bickering so? You two sound like a couple of hens arguing over who laid the egg." That garnered a smile from the girls. "I think you both could use a time out. Danielle, darling, is Sonja coming home soon?"

"Yes, Grandma, she plans on coming home next week to help me straighten our parents out," she said, giving her mom a harsh glance.

"Yeah, like you're going to do any good," said Samantha.

"Mother, you're starting to turn into a real smart-ass."

"I learned how from my oldest daughter."

"Come now, girls, you mustn't badger each other so. I have some tea boiling downstairs, and have made us some crumpets. Let's drink some tea and relax some. Shall we?"

While walking down the stairs Danielle turned to her mother, "What's a crumpet?"

"Aw, it's some concoction that your grandma puts together to have with tea."

"Crumpets, doesn't even sound good. I'm gonna have to pass on the crumpets, Grandma. I've been feeling really sick the past few mornings; been pukin' my guts out."

Kitty and Samantha glanced at each other with a quick smile of surprise.

The tall shadow hovered over the aqua velvet water that lapped up gently around Kitty's shoulders. "Hello, handsome. I've been expecting you," said Kitty.

"Are you hungry, doll?"

"I could eat, but you know what they say. Wait an hour after eating before you go swimming."

"It isn't swimming that I have in mind."

"Well then, break out the grub."

Big John smiled in anticipation of Kitty's reaction to the cheeseburgers, pop, and peanuts, as he pulled them out of the sack. "What does this remind you of, baby?"

"How could I forget? This is reminiscent of our first real date together, back in West Virginia. As I recollect, we went skinny dipping that night in a little tributary leading into the New River Gorge. I also lost my virginity in that river, to that big, tall boy from New York City. I was but 15 years old, as I recall. "

"Yeah, but you were big for your age."

"No, you've got that wrong, John. You were the big one. Believe me, you were big, or at least it seemed so to me. Up till then I had never seen one of those things in full salute before."

"Any regrets, Kitty?"

"No, darling, none, as a matter-of-fact, I think we ought to reenact that night."

"But the burgers will get cold."

"As I recall, we ate cold burgers on that night too. Take your clothes off, Johnny, and come on in. It's a lot warmer where I am than where you're standing."

While Big John slipped out of his clothes, Kitty slithered out of her swimsuit. John dove into the water and Kitty went down after him. They both emerged on top in a wild embrace. Anymore, this was a rare occasion for Kitty and John, and she planned on taking advantage of the situation. An excellent swimmer and underwater sex-pert, Kitty could do things to a man under water that some women wouldn't do above it. When she had him primed, they made love vigorously until he quenched her sexual thirst, and she his.

"I've wanted this for so long, darling. How was I? Did I satisfy you, my big hunk?" she asked in earnest.

"You needn't ask, Kitty."

While they ate their dinner from the edge of the pool, John and Kitty reminisced about the old days of their relationship.

"You know, Kitty, I never did understand about the peanuts in the pop."

"Oh, it was just a cool thing to do back then. A big Double Cola with a package of peanuts in it was often my main meal for the day. You remember? That's how we met, darling, down at Sewell Robert's garage, in Cunard."

"Certainly I remember. I remember a bunch of pester-some little school girls laughing and carrying on all the time, poking fun at me while I was working on cars."

"As I remember, you seemed to like it."

"I guess I did. I just had trouble figuring out what you all were carryin' on about all the time."

"Well, we were at that curious stage in our lives, about boys, that is. You intrigued us, John. Here we were, a bunch of young girls still stuffing our bras, hanging out with a big tall lad that spoke with a funny New York accent. You even ran moonshine for ol' Sewell. That excited me. We used to joke about what size hammer you carried in those dirty cover-alls that you always wore."

"Oh yeah, as my memory serves me, you were the little girl with the pigtails and freckles," smiled John. "Then there was Linda Haines, and a girl named Misty. I popped all your cherries that summer. That Linda Haines, she must've siphoned a lot of gas when she was younger. Misty got knocked up the first time we did it. She tried to get me to marry her, but I said, No-way! She got that Dabler boy to marry her though."

"What I would like to know is how you ended up with me?" said Kitty.

"Well, Kitty, you were the only one that had enough guts to go on a moonshine run with me. If it wasn't for your appendicitis attack that night, I would've gone to jail for sure."

"Yeah, I remember that excruciating pain that I had in my side, and you rushing me to the hospital at Oak Hill with that cop on your ass."

"You proved to me on that night how tough you were, Kitty, and I liked that. You and I were a lot alike. We had goals, real goals. You didn't want to grow up being a coal miner's daughter and I didn't want to run shine for a living either. We both had much higher aspirations. Besides, darling, you were the best lay of the bunch."

Kitty smiled and playfully pulled Big John back into the water for another lovemaking session.

When physically depleted from their love bouts, the two lovers opted for Big John's bedroom where he showered off the chlorine from his body while Kitty laid his clothes out to wear to the big meeting..

Kitty soon joined her husband in the shower just to be near him. Maybe it was the hot swim, the night air, or maybe it was the remembrances, but the evening had become quite special for the king and queen of Taylor manor.

Kitty saw the sadness in Big John's smile, and she felt it when he held her in his arms. Big John was tough, and for a long time, the toughest of his kind. But he was now getting old, sentimental, and getting chinks in his armor. The walls of his Babylon were starting to crumble. He knew it himself, tonight. It came to him almost as a premonition.

Big John made Kitty happy tonight. That was his intent. If only he could talk with his little girl once more before he left. There was so much that he wanted to say to her. If only he could take her to the dance, one more time.

As Kitty helped Big John get dressed she noticed a cloud of disappointment hovering around her big lover. "What is it, dear? Is there something wrong?"

"I was hoping to see Samantha before I left."

"I told her today about our little soiree tonight, and she thought it proper not to be here. She wanted us to spend time alone. That's just like our daughter, thinking of us first."

"Where did she go?" asked John.

"She went back to her house this afternoon. She wanted to visit Impala and the rest of the hole-in-the-wall gang. She also wanted to visit with Mary, Myra, and Shauna. I guess Myra's been beside herself since

Sonny left. She misses Sonny real bad, and so does Samantha."

"Well, if you ask me, they're all better off without him," grumbled Big John.

"But Samantha's scared, John. With Sonny she felt safe."

"But he's gonna get her killed."

"Maybe, but shouldn't that be her decision?"

"No, because she hasn't been thinking straight lately; she'd be better off with Chance's arch rival, Troy Charbonau. At least she would be out of harms way."

"You ought to listen to what you're saying, John. You want to send Samantha away with someone she doesn't love?"

"But we almost lost her, Kitty. I couldn't stand living without my little girl."

"You never liked Sonny from the beginning, John. I didn't either until he showed me something. He showed me that he was a lot like you. You told me once that you would wrestle the world for me, and that's what Sonny did for Sam. You two are so much alike, and that scares you. Maybe I'm wrong, but that's why she's so miserable. She needs Sonny, and she needs you."

"Don't talk like that. Why are you turning against me?"

"I'm not against you, honey. I'm just trying to get you to look at the truth. The truth is that Samantha could have left the Times, ten . . . twelve years ago, but she didn't. Why? Not because you talked her out of it. No, because she likes her job here working with her father and being with her husband. The trouble is you wanted her to walk that thin gray line between right and wrong, like you have your whole life, but she couldn't. She's too honest. For that, she loses the job she loves, and the husband she loves."

"What about his affairs with other women, Kitty?"

"None of us are who we used to be, darling. Should that stop us from loving each other?"

"I guess you're right, Kitty. I've been going about this all wrong, it seems. I'm going to put a change to all of that, tonight. I promise. I just wish Samantha was here now so I could tell her that." Big John looked at his watch, "I've got to be going."

Sudden desperation flooded Kitty's mind. She grabbed onto the big man's arm in a futile attempt to keep him by her. John bent down and warmly kissed her quivering mouth.

"I don't want you to go. Please stay here and hold me in your arms. I don't want to sleep alone tonight," begged Kitty.

"I can't, baby. I've got to do this thing."

"At least tell me where you're going."

John smiled softly at his worried wife. "You know that I usually don't give out that information, dear, but tonight, I'll make an exception, just for you. You have to promise not to say anything about this to Samantha."

"I promise, darling."

"John Losch and I are going to meet with the Italian family at a can warehouse in Jimtown. We're breaking away from the Italians, completely. Now, does that satisfy you?"

"The only thing that will satisfy me is your safe return."

"Don't worry, baby. I'll be sleeping right next to you at mornings light."

It was getting late and Samantha never showed. John scoffed at Kitty's suggestion of calling her, for he didn't wish to interfere anymore into Samantha's life than he already had. Kitty had finally convinced him that maybe he had overstepped his boundaries as a parent in trying to protect his daughter. But to Big John, she was still that little girl, crying on the school steps at the prom. Kitty didn't tell him about her and Samantha's discovery of Danielle's soon-to-be motherhood. She wanted his daughter to inform him of that.

John tucked Kitty snuggly into his bed and kissed her soulfully, as if for the last time; then got up to leave.

"You will come back to me, won't you, honey?"

John sensed her intense fear of his leaving. "If I don't come back, stick with the plastic surgeon. Even if you don't love him, he'll keep you pretty," said John, smiling as he left.

On his way out he stopped in the den to grab a handful of his favorite cigars. He then took down the big painting of J. F. K., exposing a wall safe. Once opened, he carefully took out his old 9mm with a shoulder holster, and an old Colt 45 from Sonny's Viet Nam years that Sonny had given to him as a present. Big John re-hung the portrait and slowly walked out of his home to meet with Johnny Losch at Flannery's Tap in Jimtown.

Samantha leaned over to kiss her mother softly on her forehead. She found it satisfying to find her mom sleeping in Big John's bed. Samantha was well aware of the eccentricities in her parent's marriage. She was less than happy when she saw them with other partners. She detested Margo Solsta, and was, to say the least, surprised at her mother crossing over the line with Dr. Carl Frances. But tonight it looked as if they both had consummated their love once again.

Kitty opened her eyes at Samantha's touch.

"Mother, where is Daddy?"

"He has left us, my dear. He has left us for good, I fear."

"What do you mean, Mother? What are you talking about?" exclaimed Samantha with fear in her eyes.

"Your dad once shook hands with the devil. For that, he paid a dear price; the fear of losing his daughter. That's why he always disliked Sonny. He feared that Sonny would take his daughter from him. He loved me as a wife, but he loves you more than life. You're his little princess, and to keep your life happy, he is willing to sacrifice his if need be."

Kitty's doleful reply brought Samantha to near hysterics. "Mother, you must tell me where Daddy went! I want to talk to my father!"

"He went to try to right his wrongs, to make it up to you. He's in Jimtown at a warehouse on Haliburton Street. He's meeting with the heads of the Italian mob. He wants to break with them. I saw it in his eyes, Samantha. For the first time in my life I saw fear in Big John's eyes. He tried to hide it but he couldn't."

"I'm going after him," cried Samantha. "I'm going after my dad."

"You won't have time, darling. They meet at 1:00 o'clock, and it's a quarter till, now."

"I'm going after my dad! Bye, Mother."

"Good luck, baby," whispered Kitty at the closing of the door.

Losch was handed a 38 special and John had his two pistols while Butch and Kip Flannery had their Uzi submachine guns. Hiding their weapons under their long trench coats, Big John and his boys seemed reminiscent of the Earp brothers and Doc Holiday, back in time at the OK Corral.

It was an ominous feeling, walking up to the Westgate warehouse, expecting to be greeted by the "Bullet" but instead, finding two of Delveccio's button men waiting for them. One guy looked quite dangerous while the other looked wet behind the ears.

"Hold it right there, Big John," ordered the young hoodlums while pulling their weapons.

John and his men stopped in their tracks.

"Mr. Delveccio wants you to turn in any firearms to me. He promises their return after the meeting."

"Where the hell is Jake Mueller?" fumed Big John.

"He's inside waiting for you, along with his two buddies," smiled the dangerous looking one. "Now, hand over your weapons," he demanded.

"Fuck you!" came a reply from John's left as a burst of bullets flew from under Butch Flannery's gray slicker, ripping through the hoodlum's face.

The younger thug had already dropped his gun in submission. Kip grabbed the man, turned him around, and pushed him forward with the barrel of his Uzi jammed in his back. "You're takin' us in to see Delveccio, you son-of-a-bitch. One wrong move and you'll be whistling 'Dixie' through your ass. Do you hear me?"

"Yes, sir," said the boy.

The warehouse seemed larger on the inside then from the outside. Millions of decorated cans were stacked all around from ceiling to floor in an orderly fashion. Kip Flannery was point man, and led the way through the can maze with the barrel of his automatic weapon embedded in the back of his nervous young prisoner. Big John followed with Losch close behind, while the trigger-happy Butch Flannery secured the rear.

John had been there before, several times in the past, doing family business. He couldn't remember the warehouse being this full. Business must be slow, he thought.

When they reached the rear of the warehouse they turned and walked down, what seemed to be a long corridor, with a wall of red and white beverage cans stacked to the left, and the loading docks to the right. Big John saw his estranged business associates waiting for him at the banquet table near the end of the corridor. Delveccio's men were standing all around, some half hidden, some in the open. Kip and Butch scoured the area and kept a mental picture on where each of his men were standing, just in case.

Big John didn't like the setup. He didn't like it at all. This was his place of choosing, and his people were the ones that came here and set it up, yet Bullet and his men were nowhere to be found. Big John didn't want a confrontation. He and Losch both did business by negotiating, not by intimidation. John didn't like violence, per se. Oh, he ordered the execution of Candy Adams and Loni Jacobs, but they left him no other choice. They crossed that thin gray line. Nick Parmalay was a traitor, and Scarlet, well, Scarlet happened to be in the wrong place at the wrong time.

The closer Big John got to Delveccio and his bunch, the hotter his blood boiled.

Victorio Delveccio didn't resemble what most people pictured as a Godfather. He was a small man with oily skin and a thin mustache. He looked more like a California migrant worker, all polished and packaged in an expensive pinstripe suit. Dattilo looked more the part, and someday would probably take over as the Godfather. Sitting by Dattilo was their attorney, and standing next to him was Rico Constantine. The tall Italian seemed larger than the man that Big John pinned against his billiard room wall on the eve of the Governor's Bail. John assumed that it had to do with the hidden cache of weapons that Rico hoarded under the trench coat that he had on.

As they got closer, Rico and Butch sneered at each other like two mongrel dogs. After all, they both were cut from the same cloth.

"What did you do with my man, Jake Mueller?" snarled John.

"John. John, is that a way to greet an old friend?" said Victorio.

"I didn't come here to play games, Victorio. I'm here to make you an offer, a damn good offer."

"I take it that it's the same proposal you made to us over the phone. Is it not?"

"That's correct," said Big John.

"My colleagues and I mulled it over and decided that we want Waverly and Miramar in the mix, and that includes their assets."

"That's preposterous!" snapped Big John. "Losch and I started Miramar and Waverly years ago. You were just an added partner."

"Waverly is all I have," pleaded Losch, "You wouldn't take that from me would you, Victorio?"

"Don't worry about it. Big John can stake you in another business," said Dattilo. "Besides, you're both partnered up in Indianapolis anyway."

"We'll even swap your man back to you for ours," added Rico with an uneven smile. "It seems that we're missing a man though. Where's Johnny B? You know; the guy that greeted you boys out in the parking lot."

"I'm afraid he's dead," Big John said bluntly.

"Yeah, he insisted on taking our guns and we didn't like that," added Butch with a death gleam in his eye.

Delveccio gestured to a couple of his men that were guarding the dock entrance to open up the doors. They each pushed a button, raising the overhead doors to where the empty semi-trailers were backed up to the dock. As the doors slowly opened, they revealed a sight that sent shock waves through Big John and his men. Each unit had one of Mueller's men hanging naked from the trailer's ceiling with a chain around his neck. Both men had been disemboweled. Big John winced at the sight. Delveccio had gone too far this time, but John was at too great of a disadvantage to do anything about it.

Butch Flannery couldn't deal with it though. The sight of the butchered men caused him to freak. He grabbed the young hostage from Kip and put his gun to the frightened boy's head, causing a stir.

The metallic sound of guns being cocked echoed throughout the building, as everyone got set for battle.

"Maybe I ought to put a bullet through your man's head to even the score!" screamed the crazed bar owner.

"Hold on, Butch," said Big John. "We didn't come here to start a war. Let him go."

Butch leered at his boss with disapproval as he let go of the captive. The kid nervously walked to the other side of the table to stand next to Constantine.

"So, you want to even the score. Is that what you want? Huh, is it?" Rico taunted. "Here, I'll even the score for you." The kid looked up at the crazed Italian in disbelief. Rico shot him, point blank in the head. As the young mobster lay on the floor going through pre-death spasms, Rico turned and smiled wickedly at Big John. "Hell, he was just one of our lackeys, anyway."

Rico's barbarous act even unnerved Delevicco, but he kept his composure. "So, how about it Big John, let's close this deal before anyone else gets hurt," said Victorio.

"First, tell me Victorio, did you kill Mueller too?"

"The Bullet's not dead, John, least not yet. Just look up to your left, all the way up to the top pallet of cans near the ceiling. My boys didn't like his wise-guy attitude so they had a little fun with him. They banded him to a pallet and nailed his hands to the top frame."

"Yeah, we played a little game with him," added Rico. "You may have heard of it, Big John. It's called, how many soda cans can a Kraut shove into his mouth at one time."

Big John glared at Rico in disgust.

"The answer is 18, if they're smashed in with a rifle butt. Of course we had to remove some teeth and cut his lips off to make room," mocked Rico. Rico Constantine emitted a chill that wafted through the corridor like a black plague.

With fear set deep in his eyes, Losch looked over to his friend, "Let's make the deal, John, I can get into something else. Let's just take their offer and get out of here."

Big John was reluctant to give in, but he had no choice and agreed with his old friend.

"Okay, now everybody relax and put your weapons away," ordered Delveccio. "John, you and Losch bring your papers up to the table and our lawyer will take care of things, nice and proper."

It was a huge blow for Big John to turn his Miramar holdings over to the Italian mob. Only out of respect for his good friend, Johnny Losch, and the love for his daughter could the big guy crack through his large ego and give up Miramar and Waverly. That wasn't all that was bothering John, and Delveccio sensed it.

"It was never our intentions to harm your daughter, John. That was your own people's doings. You just keep your business in Indianapolis, and you won't see us again."

John didn't respond to Delveccio, but was relieved to hear that his daughter would be safe.

As tensions remained high the warehouse became quiet again, as only the rustling of papers and murmurs from the table could be heard. The Flannerys were wild-eyed, but held steady, as the nefarious Rico stared them down with a slanted, evil grin on his face. Suddenly, the silence was broken by the sound of footsteps running up the long corridor. Everyone turned their attention to the unknown figure that was headed toward them. One of Delveccio's thugs intercepted the runner and brought her forward. Noting the girl's bouncy red mane, Big John knew right away that it was his daughter. His heart sank at the thought of Samantha being there at the mercy of the Italians, in spite of what Delveccio assured him.

Struggling to break loose from her captors, Samantha cringed when she saw the grisly scene on the loading docks.

John stood up from the table. "Let her go!" he demanded.

"Go ahead and release the girl!" commanded the Godfather.

Samantha broke away and rushed to her father. "Daddy, Daddy, I'm so glad you're okay," she cried out, embracing him tightly.

"Yes, I'm alright dear, but how did you find me here?"

"Mother told me."

"That Kitty, she lied to me," said John.

"Don't blame Mother. I made her tell me," said Samantha.

"Young lady, does anyone else know that you are here?" questioned Victorio.

"No, I didn't tell a soul, honest I didn't."

"Did you happen to notice if anyone followed you here?"

"If I was being followed, I didn't notice it, sir."

"Don't listen to her. She's lying!" said Rico, reaching inside his coat.

"Put your gun away. I'm still in charge here!" snapped Delveccio. The mob boss directed two of his men to go outside and check on things.

In the meantime, John conversed with his daughter, "So what are you doing here, Sam? This is no place for a woman," he lightly scolded.

"But Mother told me that you might be in some trouble. I was afraid that you weren't coming back home. I don't want to lose you, Daddy."

"Don't worry, baby, I'm negotiating a deal here that will make everything okay again."

"I just want to tell you that I'll do whatever it takes to help you, Daddy. I'll go to D.C. and take Gina's job if you want. Troy visited me yesterday. He said that he would help me get established there."

"I think Troy wants it to be more personal then that, sweetheart."

"That's alright. I'm okay with that, now."

"But what about Sonny?" he asked.

Samantha stiffened and stared coldly out into space. "Sonny's my problem, Daddy. I'll deal with it. I'll try to work him out of my life."

"Are you sure, Baby?"

. . . "I'm sure."

"Come on, John! Sit down and finish signing the papers so we can all go home and be with our families," said Delveccio in a rush.

Big John found Delveccio's callousness very unsettling, talking about going home to families while in the midst of the dead and dying. He sensed that something just wasn't right. The fiendish Rico was glaring viciously at Samantha, and becoming skittish like a caged animal.

John stood firm, holding tightly to his daughter's hand. Suddenly, a barrage of gunfire erupted from outside the building. Then, just as suddenly, came a voice from a loudspeaker, "Everyone inside drop your weapons. This is the F.B.I.! You're surrounded. Drop your weapons!"

"Goddamn it! She brought the Feds!" screamed Rico, pulling his Uzi from under his coat.

"Douse the lights!" yelled Dattilo.

Big John quickly stepped in front of his daughter to shield her from Rico's onslaught. He reached inside his coat for his own weapon but it was too late. Rico fired off a zipper of bullets into Big John's body with the impact causing him to fall into Samantha, taking them both to the floor. Then the lights went out. It became total chaos as men were screaming and bullets flying.

Samantha became so frightened at the noise and mayhem that she lost her senses about her. She didn't even realize the 260 pound weight that lay on top of her, rising to do battle once more. With several wounds already, Big John struggled to his knees and pulled out Sonny's Colt 45 from under his belt to compliment his other firearm. He began blasting away at the muzzle flashes coming from Rico's position. The air became a sheet of steel with lead flying from all directions. The noise was thunderous, and the warehouse choked on gunpowder. Big John was hit by another burst of gunfire, sending him to the cold concrete. Samantha saw her father fall and covered his body with hers, trying to shield him from any further damage. She prayed desperately for the nightmare to stop, but it didn't. Feeling the warmth of her father's blood, Samantha didn't fear for her life anymore, but tried shaking him for some kind of sign that he was alive. She begged him mournfully to speak to her.

With bullets still flying, out of nowhere lunged a dark figure that tackled Samantha and rolled with her over and over several times before coming to a halt behind a pallet of cans. Samantha was stunned at being tossed and grappled in that way, yet she was now cognizant enough to know what was going on.

"Samantha, stay here and keep your head down! This pallet of cans only gives the illusion of cover. Bullets will pierce right through it."

The voice was strong, but familiar to the frantic redhead. "I need to go to my dad," pleaded Samantha.

"No, you can't. It's too dangerous. He's already down. He's not a target anymore."

"Who are you?"

"I'm agent Webb. We met at the Governor's Ball. Remember?"

"Yeah, I remember. They call you Charlie."

"That's right. I'm a federal agent."

"I don't get it. You were Troy's date at the ball, weren't you?"

"I haven't got time to explain now, Sam. They've got too much firepower going, and I've got to neutralize it."

"What are you going to do?"

"I don't know yet," answered Charlie while scoping the area. She looked down to the far end of the isle from where she and Samantha lay, and spotted a fork-truck in the dim light of an emergency exit sign. She then looked up at the pallets of cans stacked four high and thought; domino effect! "Samantha, I've got an idea. You stay here, don't move. I'm going to stop those bastards!"

Samantha watched intently as Charlie sprinted down the isle to the fork-truck. Charlie holstered her pistol and quickly climbed onto the truck. She started it up and gauged what rows that Delveccio and his men were in. She lowered the forks into the bottom full pallet and raised all four pallets off the floor. She then backed the truck up, tilted the cans forward, and rammed the next stand of cans which toppled into the next stack, and then into the next, until the domino effect ended with an avalanche of cans burying the enemy at the far end of the row. She repeated the same process with the next four rows of cans until finally, the gunfire quieted. It was a success. She had buried Delveccio and his men with thousands of aluminum cans. Charlie rushed back to check the results. Soon the lights came on and the F.B.I., with their guns drawn, scoured the area for survivors.

Suddenly, a crazed Rico Constantine emerged from the deep pile of cans, firing randomly with fight still left in him, until a well-placed bullet from Agent Lance Richard's 44-magnum put the Italian mobster down for good.

Samantha rushed to be at her wounded father's side while awkwardly stumbling over the dead bodies of the Flannery brothers in her haste. With the redhead tearfully begging her father to wake from his slumber, Charlie checked the big man's vitals. They were weak, very weak. She pulled open his suit coat and ripped open his shirt to check his wounds. It was just as she expected. He had been shot too many times, lost too much blood. She and Samantha both were kneeling in a pool of his red life force as it was. With rivers of tears flowing down her cheeks, Samantha held her father's cold hands to her face, kissing them softly; hoping the warmth of her lips would convince him to open his eyes, to see his little girl once again. Samantha looked to Charlie for help. Charlie sadly shook her head, "He's lost too much blood, Sam."

"Don't die, Daddy, don't die. Please!" she pleaded.

Even though she was trained to keep her own emotions in check, Charlie was having a hard time doing so. Feeling helpless, she lifted Big John's head and placed it into her lap. The jostling caused him to moan and open his eyes slightly.

"Daddy, Daddy, do you know who I am?" Samantha asked anxiously.

"Of course, you're my little red-haired girl," he said weakly.

"You're gonna be alright, Daddy. You're gonna be all right!"

"No baby. I'm afraid not."

"You're wrong, Daddy. You're wrong," she sobbed.

"Listen to me, Sam. I've not much time left. I was wrong. I thought I was doing right by you, but I was all wrong. I didn't really want you to leave. I knew no other way, darling. Kiss your mother for me. Goodbye my little red rose," he whispered while softly closing his eyes.

"Daddy, Daddy, you can't leave me. Please! You can't leave your little girl," she sobbed, "Who will take me to the dance?"

John opened his eyes once more and tried to speak as Samantha put her ear to his face. Barely audible, she heard him whisper, "*Sonny.*"

Troy had just finished packing when he heard a knock on the door.

What he saw when he opened the door startled him somewhat. "Why, Samantha, what are you doing here? I was just getting ready to leave."

Samantha barged in, forcing her onetime lover back into the room, "Is it true? Tell me Troy, is it true? Are you working with the F.B.I.?"

"Where did you get that notion, honey?"

"Don't play games with me, goddamn it! I was at the warehouse last night. And so were Charlene Webb and Lance Richards."

"It's amazing how a woman loses her dignity when she gets a little blood on her," Troy retorted.

Samantha looked down at the blood on her shirt and pants, the same blood that once ebbed and flowed through her daddy's veins just a few hours earlier. "You haven't answered me, Troy." I want a goddamn answer!"

"Yes, Samantha, I participated with the Federal Bureau on this particular assignment."

"But why?" she asked.

"Because I could use my influence with you to get on the inside, and I did."

"You used me? I don't get it. We once were in love with each other."

"You're right, baby. You *don't* get it. Love hurts, Sam. You left me dangling. You broke my heart back in Washington. You didn't even have the common courtesy of telling me goodbye. You led me on, Sam. I really fell for you. I would have done anything for you. I even wrote my mother about you. The girl of my dreams, I said. She wrote back, wanting to meet you so. Then you stepped on my heart, crushed it like a bug. You could have asked Gina about that. She would have told you. But you can't now. She's dead too, thanks to you. Congratulations, Sam. You came into our lives and managed to kill us all off in some form or other."

"You hurtful bastard!" she cried.

"You see, when you left me six years ago, I got to checking into your life. I found a lot of discrepancies in your family's wealth and earning power. That interested me, so I pursued your family's interests, and guess what I found? I found greed and corruption, which led me directly to Victorio Delveccio who the government has been trying to take down for years. Big John was good. He kept hidden for all these years. Who would have thought that a chance encounter with a naïve, country bumpkin reporter, in the nation's capital would lead to the demise of the most powerful crime figure in the Midwest?"

Samantha's mind was becoming muddled with Troy's revelations. She shook her red curls back and forth as if trying to toss her burdens away. "But why did you use me that way?" she asked, begging for an answer.

"Better to scorn the woman you love then to be scorned by the woman you never had. You were once a great love of mine, Sam. Now you're just another trophy for the mantle above my fireplace. You were my sacrificial lamb, tied to the stake to draw in the wolves. And we got 'em, Sam. We got 'em all, Delveccio, Big John, and Losch."

"I hate you!"

"Hate is a pretty strong word, darling. It wasn't hate that caused you to make love to me the other night, was it? I don't believe it was hate that allowed me to defile your body all night long, was it? No, Sam. You're just daddy's little whore. Face it, you're the cause of your own father's death," he taunted.

"I should have brought a gun and killed you, you son-of-a-bitch!" cried Samantha.

"Come on, Sam, you're not a killer," mocked Troy.

"I wish Sonny were here. He wouldn't hesitate," she fired back.

"Aw yes, Sonny boy. I heard about Sonny Rafferty. Gina told me some, and then this Miramar case. Sonny's influence seems to pop up everywhere in this case. We can't pin anything on him because he's too slick. He's becoming the Dirty Harry of the Midwest. We'll save him for another day, Sam. Besides, I stole his wife from him; not just once, but on two different occasions. I know your body like he knows it, inside and out. He has nothing on me. He may have plucked your cherry, but I got the juice, honey. He can have his tainted woman back now. Let's face it. You're spoiled goods."

With his insults of Sonny, Samantha's rage turned into shame and hurt, for he reminded her of her own betrayal. At a loss for words, Samantha's lips quivered and her eyes turned down as she lowered her head, straining to hold back a floodgate of tears.

Troy reached in the closet and took out his carry-all and briefcase before heading out the door. "I'm all wrapped up here, Sam. I'm going back to D.C. I'm to talk to the President. I hear they have an award waiting for me there. By the way, Chance can have my senatorial seat.

I've just been named the new head of the CIA. They like my work, I guess. I get results, Sam, at all costs," he said coldly while stiffly walking past her to the door.

Suddenly, a rustling from inside the room drew the attention of the both of them.

Samantha couldn't believe her eyes as she looked up and saw a bedraggled Jessie Coltraine emerging from the suite's bedroom, with only a sheet around her body. The strain lines on her face showed a night of merrymaking for the disheveled blonde. It was clear to see that Jessie wasn't too thrilled at being dislodged from her slumber by the clamor that she was hearing from the suite's foyer. But when she saw her boss staring at her, Jessie was aghast. "Samantha! What are you doing here?" she exclaimed while pulling the sheet up around her breasts.

"Aren't you supposed to be at work today?" asked Samantha.

"I took off to be with Troy," Jessie replied.

"I don't believe this, Jessie. How could you do this to Jack? What about Cassie?"

"Don't be preaching to me, sister. I have as good of attributes as you do to please the senator with," Jessie retorted. "Besides, he answers all my needs. I know what you saw in him, Sam. He's a great lover. If you don't mind, I've got to shower. Troy, honey, are you coming back?"

"No, this is my last day. I'll catch you and Jack the next time I'm back this way, baby."

"Oh, I was so looking forward to spending the day with you. You know, Jack won't be back from his trip until tomorrow."

"I'm sorry, baby, maybe next time."

With a pout, Jessie disappeared into the bathroom.

"How could you, Troy?" said Samantha.

"Hey, I gave you your last chance yesterday, Sam, and you turned me down."

"But why Jessie?" she asked.

"Oh, I met Jack and Jessie at the Governor's Ball. They seemed to be such a delightful couple. Heck, Jack and I shot a round of golf yesterday at the country club. He had to leave on business today, so Jessie decided to entertain me while Jack was gone. Jack should be proud of her. He has a dynamite woman there."

Troy walked out the door with Samantha following, not knowing why. Troy turned and addressed Samantha one last time. "Would you be a dear and turn over the 'do not disturb' sign for me, please? Jessie and I kinda mussed up the room last night. There's one thing about you married women that I find so fascinating. You are all so insatiable," he said with a pretentious smirk. "That Jessie, she sure has all the right equipment. What a hell-cat," he said, shaking his head.

Samantha could not get the lump out of her throat or the ache from inside as she watched the gentleman senator saunter down the hallway, whistling a tune. Rivers of sorrow flowed from her eyes as she turned over the sign, just as she was told. Evil had cast its cold, ugly shadow upon the forlorn redhead.

> They once were warriors, big and strong
> As they fought a good fight but their time had come
> The trumpets blew a death knell sound
> And the walls came tumbling down

Chapter Twenty-Eight

Gathering of the Pieces

"Come on, Peggy, let's stop when we get to the top this time," begged Jeri while gasping for air. "My legs are killing me."

Peggy turned and smiled at the sound of her newfound friend's stress call, yet kept trudging along. When they finally reached the top, Jeri collapsed to the ground while sucking in as much crisp October air as her lungs would hold. Sweat drenched herself, Peggy rested while bent over with her hands on her knees.

"Peggy, you are evil. You're trying to kill me aren't you?" said Jeri humorously.

"Heck, you're the young girl, and skinny to boot. I'm the 36 year-old overweight hash-slinger, trying to get in shape for her man. I'm the one that ought to be complaining."

Jeri responded by flipping Peggy the old "Indiana howdy".

"Come on, girl, we'll cool down by walking back to the car," said Peggy, offering a hand to her fallen companion.

"I don't get it. Going through all this pain just to make a man happy," said Jeri.

"You have a lot to learn about love, girl."

"I do alright in that department."

"You mean, swindling old men out of their hard earned money for a piece of your young tail?"

"It's a moneymaker. What can I tell you, Peggy? Besides, fleecing old men out of their money ain't a bad way to make a living."

"Who told you that?"

"Ma did. Hell, she was the one that helped me get started. She said that I was a real looker. She taught me how to flirt with guys and get my way with them. I remember what she first told me. She said, 'Jeri, if you love a man right and give him what he wants then he'll love you back and treat you nice.' She was always hoping that someday I would marry a rich gentleman. Ma wouldn't let me date boys my age. She said that they were too immature and brought nothin' to the table. It took me a while to figure out what she meant."

"Geez, how old were you when you started dating men?"

"I was old enough, but younger than what you would approve of, I suspect."

"But, Jeri, that type of love isn't what I'm talking about. I'm talking about something special. I'm talking about the kind of love that you feel deep inside ya; the kind that takes your breath away when you first look into his eyes."

"Yeah, yeah, I get what you mean. I kinda felt that way with Jim Weiler. Then, *your man* came along and put a kibosh to that."

"I'm not sure that Jim was your ultimate love, dear. He was somewhat older than you, and had a loving wife and family at home. I think he might have been infatuated with having a sexual liaison with a younger, pretty girl such as yourself."

"Are you saying that we didn't love each other, Peggy?"

Peggy carefully pondered her young friend's question before answering. "Tell me, Jeri, do you think of him often?"

"Not really, not anymore."

"That's what I'm talking about, dear. Real love stays with you."

"What about you and Sonny? He's older than you, and has a wife and family doesn't he?"

"Well yeah, but this is different. I just know it is. No man has ever made me feel the way that Sonny Rafferty has."

"Tell me, Peggy, just what does real love feel like, I'm curious. What's it like between you and Sonny?"

Peggy's eyes turned up and sparkled at the sound of Sonny's name. She slowed their pace and turned to her sandy-haired jogging partner, and with a large smile, tilted her head in a euphoric search for the right words to express her feelings. "So you want to know what real love feels like."

"Yes, I'm serious. What's it like to really love someone, Peg?"

"Every time you see him, you get a tingling from the base of your neck all the way down your spine. When he touches you, you tend to want to giggle like a little girl, but you don't. And when you are in his arms, you become drunk with passion. You become his to do with what he wants, but you trust him, and he respects you for that. Add to that a breath of fresh air and a ray of sunshine, and there you have it, real love"

"That sounds dreamy."

"It is, dear. Believe me. It is."

"Say, Peg, why didn't Sonny want to press charges against Ma for trying to kill him?"

"Sonny's just not that way. He realized that Shirley was a victim of Ray Jenkins. Let's face it, Jeri, we are all victims of Ray Jenkins."

"You also?" she asked. "What did my grandpa have to do with you?"

"It's a long story; Jeri. Let's just leave it at that. Anyway, Sonny didn't want to hurt your mom or you any more than what you've been hurt already.'

"It's too late for Ma and me. She's put away and I have to take therapy every week for being a bastard kid in an incestuous relationship. I'm damaged goods, Peg."

"Don't say that. It's not true. You're just as sane and normal as anyone I know. Except that you are a bit too loose with men for my satisfaction. Heck, Sonny and I were just talking the other day about you, and how we thought you ought to sell the motel and use the money to better your education."

"What, and leave Ma?"

"You can still visit your ma and go to school too."

"Nah, I'm too dumb for that sort of thing."

"You finished high school, didn't you?"

"Well, yeah."

"Sonny told me that you worked as a secretary for Weiler Construction, right?"

"Yeah right, I worked on my back most of the time."

"Never the less, I think you ought to give it some thought, going back to school, that is."

"You're probably right, Peg. I'll give it some thought. Tell me some more about Sonny."

"Well, Sonny is a religious man. In what way I don't know yet. He doesn't like going to church. He as much told me that, but he knows the Bible, and he talks of God as a person, almost. In that way he may be a bit strange, or maybe he has an inside track. Hell, I don't know. He's a Godsend to my life. I know that, and the girls like him."

"Tell me, Peg, how is he . . . you know, in the sack?"

Peggy burst out in laughter, putting a smile on the otherwise serious face of her friend. "Lord knows, you and I both are experts on that subject. Of course he's good in the sack. What did you think I would say? Hell, I love the guy." She then slid her eyes to the side to reflect for a moment. "Being under the sheets with Sonny Rafferty is like entering an enchanted forest, with new, delightful surprises springing up all of the time. He magically turns two lives into one, two bodies into one. He connects with your soul in a way that I can't describe. That's how intimate he is, Jeri. Sonny is a mystery to behold. That's for sure."

"Aren't you afraid of him running back home to his wife?"

"Sure, a little; the way I see it, 'tis better to have loved and lost than never to have loved at all. Look, Jeri, I have only one shot at life, so I'm going to make the best of it. That's the reason I keep running up and down this damn hill. I'm trying to be the best for Sonny. So if he ever does leave my life it won't be on my account."

"So, you think shedding a few pounds will influence his thinking?"

"Maybe it will and maybe it won't, but it's gotta help not to look like Miss Piggy."

"You're far from that look, Peg."

"I want to stay that way too. You know, today is our one month anniversary of being together."

"No shit!"

"That's right. It's been a month of paradise, and we are going to celebrate it tonight," she said gleefully.

"Are you two going out tonight?"

"Nah, it's nothing like that. Sonny prefers the peace and quiet of home life, and working at the diner with me. But I did have Good's Bakery make us an anniversary cake for the occasion. It's chocolate, Sonny's favorite."

"Well, that's nice, I guess."

"Hold on, girl. I'm not stopping there. After I pick up the cake, I'm going to Trudy's Hair Tailor to get my hair colored and styled, plus I'm going to treat myself to a manicure and pedicure," exclaimed Peggy.

"Yeah, I like Trudy's. She has a girl there that gives really good manicures. She's foreign, I think."

"Then, after I get spiffed up, I'm going to Lucy's Dress Shop on Main Street and buy that French silk nightgown that she has hanging in the store window. You know, it's the one that the church ladies all stare at when they walk by."

"Yeah boy, you're going all out now, Peg. That gown's gotta cost a pretty penny."

"I know, but I'm using my mad money that I've saved up. Now you know why they call it mad money. Besides, I want to surprise Sonny tonight. Both my girls are spending the evening with school friends just so I can spend some time alone with Sonny."

"That's nice of the girls."

"Yeah, they really understand me. You know, Sonny has never seen me completely naked yet, not in the light anyway."

"You're kidding, why the hell not?"

"I guess I've been too self conscious of my weight and all."

"And the therapist said that I have a problem," chortled Jeri.

"It's not just the weight that I gained that bothers me, but I have those woman scars. You know; a caesarean scar, an appendix scar, and some stretch marks from having the kids."

"Give the man some credit, Peggy. If he cares for you at all, I don't think he expects a Rolls Royce of a woman. Besides, what does he look like naked? I counted three scars on his face myself, and I only saw the man one time, close up. Being a cop and all, I bet he has some battle scars on his body."

"Yeah, he does. He's been shot twice, and has several scars from knife wounds. He's told me about some of them. But it's different on a man's body. It makes him tough, like a warrior."

"Well, I always say if a man still has his pecker and a small ass, he's okay in my book," said Jeri with a mischievous smile. "You go on and treat yourself nice today, Peg, and for chrissake, show off that pretty French gown in the light tonight. I guarantee you won't be wearing it long," she said with a silly grin. "So what's Sonny doing today?"

"He's doing some plumbing work for me at the diner, and at the house. You know, repairing leaky faucets and such. Say, why don't you come along with me today and keep me company?"

"You mean you want to hang with me?"

"Of course, and I'll buy you lunch, how about it?"

"Yeah, why not, that motel can run itself for awhile. Besides, my cleaning lady can keep an eye on it for me. Yeah, I'd like to hang with you, Peg. I'd like that a lot."

Luminaries and dignitaries from all around the country arrived in long limos and large numbers to see Big John Taylor laid to rest. There was no antipathy for the big fellow, for he had done so much good for the community at large. Big John coveted, and then conquered that ever familiar thin gray line in life. He then tried to manipulate his way around it, but he couldn't stay the course. He crossed over that line one too many times, and he paid the price, the ultimate price. Unlike other crime figures in the past that were taken down, John's ego was not his enemy, but was what fed him, kept him alive. No, Big John's downfall was the love of his family, particularly a cute little carrot-topped girl who grew into a woman that was independent and strong-willed like her old man. For that, he was proud. For that, he was now gone from life, as we know it.

They were all dressed in black, even Sonny's girls. Samantha saw to that. Samantha herself hid her sorrow behind a long black veil, but was calm during the ceremony, for she had already spent her time in hell, and was still in recovery.

Kitty took it hardest. She stood stoic at the church but collapsed at the graveside, even with Dr. Carl Francis waiting in the shadows to comfort her. After all, Kitty and John had come a long ways together since they first met; he, a dirty faced pump jockey, and she a gum popping schoolgirl with a crush on the big guy. They were always there for each other, but now, one was gone.

Chance cried like a baby at the church. He and his father had had their differences, and he felt that he could never live up to Big John's expectations, but never-the-less he loved his old man deeply. Everyone had noticed a change in Chance's demeanor since his return from the road with Merle. One thing for sure, Liz was glad to have the new Chance back, even if only for a short while. The Feds left Chance alone. They had nothing on him substantial enough to waste the taxpayer's money on. Besides, they got what they came for, in spades.

Myra, Mary, and Shauna were there to show their respect, and in hopes of Sonny showing up. Toward the funeral's end, little Shauna with her high expectations quickly diminishing, searched desperately through the crowd at the gravesite for her beloved Sonny, but left brokenhearted and cried herself to sleep in Mary's arms.

A grand buffet was set up at the banquet hall of Taylor manor, hosted by the Greater Indianapolis Chapter of the women's auxiliary in which Kitty belonged to. It was quite a show of support for the departed Irish crime boss, as the people refused to believe what they had heard. The people were the city, and the city was like a mother to Big John. And to a mother, her son could do no wrong.

It was quite a feast, enjoyed by many. But in the middle of the festivities, the Taylor family, along with certain members of the Times, one by one slowly slipped away into Big John's billiard parlor to take care of business. Kitty called the meeting together, but Samantha was put in charge of things.

"I know it seems early but we have to take care of Daddy's business, his legit business," said Samantha. "Mother is now sole owner of the Times, but she doesn't want any part of being editor-in-chief, so we need to pick Daddy's replacement."

"John always wanted you to have that job, dear, after he retired. Why don't you take it?" suggested Kitty.

"No, Mother, I'm not going to work at the Times anymore. It just wouldn't feel right without Daddy."

"Are you sure, Sam?"

"I'm sure, Mother."

Kitty turned to Chance, "Well, how about you, Son. Do you want to tackle the job?"

"No, Mother, I'm not cut out for that kind of work. I'm a good salesman though. At least Daddy thought so. Hell, that's what I'm doing now, trying to sell myself to the voters. With the elections drawing near Merle thinks that we have a chance on winning in spite of the scandal surrounding our family."

"It's true, Mrs. Taylor. Charbonau has dropped out of the race and will be replaced by another republican," said Merle.

"Oh yeah, who do think they will run against Chance?"

"We're speculating that it will probably be Ralph Ames from Porter

County. He is one of the stronger republicans in the state, and is very popular with the people. But he will only have three weeks to take over where Charbonau left off. We don't think that will give him enough time to get the exposure he needs. Anyway, we feel that our campaigning has really paid off for Chance."

"Well, Sam, I'm leaving it up to you to choose who you want to take your dad's job."

"I think I have it pretty well figured out, Mother, if everyone is in agreement with my decision. Merle Bullock will become editor-in-chief of the Times after she first helps get Chance elected senator. I feel that she is capable of the job. Is that alright with you, Merle?"

Merle stood in awe, while nodding her head, yes.

"But what about me?" argued Margo, "I know Big John's job inside and out. Hell, we were—"

"Lovers?" said Samantha.

"Well, yes, we were," she answered while shying away from Kitty.

"Look, you aren't the only skirt that Big John's been under, so don't count yourself so privileged. As a matter-of-fact, your editing job goes to Jessie Coltraine."

"What! You can't do that to me. Big John wouldn't allow that!"

"I'm not Big John," said Samantha firmly.

"But, but we were good for each other. He loved me. He told me so."

"I want your desk cleaned out by tomorrow morning. Do you hear?"

"But, I've got a contract," Margo spouted back.

"I've already checked. Your contract has two more months to run, and you will be paid in full."

Margo looked around the room for sympathy but there was none. In a huff, she turned and walked out the door with the billiard room giving way to applause from the Fab Four.

Samantha continued, "Larry, you take my old job."

"But Sam, I don't know if I'm qualified enough to do your job."

"Nonsense, you're a damn good reporter, Larry. That's why you're getting my job. You have some mighty big shoes to fill, buster," she added with a smile.

Samantha then turned and faced Lisa Dawson, "So that leaves you, Jitterbug. You're the only member of the Fab Four that's left. Do you think you can do the job of four people?"

"Yes, I guess so," answered the timid reporter.

"Don't worry, my dear. We'll recruit you some help."

"I'd like to work as a news reporter, Mother," interjected, Sonja.

"You, a news reporter?" said Samantha a bit surprised. "What makes you think that you are qualified, young lady?"

"What were your qualifications when you first became a cub reporter, Mother?"

"I didn't have any. I was a junior in college at the time. What I had was the desire to become a news journalist, and my dad saw that in me so he hired me."

"I also am a junior in college and have the desire to become as good a news journalist as my Mother."

Samantha smiled proudly at her veracious young daughter. She saw herself standing there right before her eyes.

"I can transfer from Ball State to Butler. That way I will be close to work."

"No, Sonja, you have your friends at Ball State. You don't want to leave your friends. For having good friends is very important, believe me. You can do as I did. Go to school and work part-time at the newspaper. It'll be a good experience for you. It was for me."

The meeting of the minds ended with lots of hugs, tears, and condolences for one another.

Jessie sought out Samantha before she left. "Sam, I'm so sorry for the way I behaved towards you the other morning. I didn't know that Big John had been killed. I had a terrible hangover from the night before. I wouldn't blame you if you fired me."

"No need for that, Jessie. Let's just leave our personal lives to ourselves. Hell, I'm no saint anymore either. Troy saw to that."

"Let's always stay friends, Sam. Okay?"

"Okay," agreed Samantha..

Big John's women left the billiard room hand in hand. They felt a little better about themselves and a whole lot wiser as they walked down the open stairwell with Chance and Liz.

"Mother, shall I go home and stay with you? I would really like that," said Sonja.

"Why don't you be a dear and stay with your grandmother tonight. She needs someone to keep her company in this big house. I myself need to be alone for awhile. I have a lot to think about, honey."

"Okay, Mother."

Danielle started to speak but Samantha interrupted, "Danny, you go home with Matt and take care of each other. That's your responsibilities now, until the little one comes along."

Danielle tearfully hugged her mother before leaving.

"Sam, what are your plans for the future?" asked Chance.

"Oh, I'm just gonna go home and be with my pets for awhile. Impala misses me so, and I miss her. I guess we've spoiled each other," she smiled. "After a rest, I don't know, maybe New York."

"Don't worry about Ma. Chance and I are going to move in with her for a while until we see about Big John's finances," said Liz.

"We may have to sell the manor, but Ma can move in with us if that happens," assured Chance.

"That's great. Thanks a lot, both of you."

As they reached the main floor Big John's family uncoupled and went their separate ways.

Samantha stopped to talk to Myra and Mary before departing. "I'm sorry that Sonny didn't show up today. I know you all were hoping he would. I was too. After what I've done to Sonny, I doubt he'll ever come back."

"Don't blame yourself, dear. Part of that was your daddy's doings," said Myra.

"Not really, Myra. Daddy was just looking out for me. I've got to move on, away from here, away from my troubles."

"And away from your friends and family," added Mary. "You can't run away from your troubles, honey. You've got to face 'em. That's what Sonny would've done."

"Sonny, that's all I hear anymore, is what Sonny would have done. Sonny would have done this. Sonny would have done that. It's always about fuckin' Sonny! And you know what, Mary? You're right. Sonny would've done things a lot different. I wish to God he was here right now. I wish I would have never gone to Washington in the first place. I wish I wasn't so goddamn weak when it comes to men. I can wish all I want, but it's not going to bring Sonny back," cried Samantha. "I'm sorry, Myra, I've made my mistakes and now I'm going to have to live with them."

"Now dear, don't cry no more. Sonny will be back soon. I just know he will," said Myra in a calming way that only a mother could. "You just go home and rest, dear, and tomorrow will be a brighter day. You'll see."

Samantha raised her tear-stained face to Myra. "Thank you so much, Mama, for your support, and you too, Mary . . . and you too, Shauna," she added while bending over to kiss the little pixie that clung to her leg.

"Are you sure you don't want one of us to go home with you tonight?"

"I'm sure, Mama. I just need to be alone for a while. I'll be alright."

"Earle's supposed to be watching your place tonight, Ms Samantha, so if you have no need for him, send him on home to me," said Mary.

"Why, Mary, you and Earle really *have* become an item, haven't you?"

The one-eyed housekeeper beamed a big white smile at Samantha's discovery.

"Oh yeah, Mary and Earle were married two weeks ago," informed Myra.

"Yeah, we may as well have gotten married. He kept hangin' 'round all the time. Besides, he got religion, my religion. I told him that if he didn't stop drinkin' that I would have nothin' more to do with him. So he don't drink no more, 'least around me. Even I take a little nip once in a while to thin my blood, you know," said Mary with a wink from her good eye.

Samantha broke away from her friends and left in good standing. She was glad for that, for Sonny's leaving had hurt them badly. He was part of their family, and so was she.

But Samantha was a realist. She knew that Sonny wasn't coming back. He had been gone too long now. He was never gone this long before, even when he went out of the state on a case. The little glimmer of hope that Myra had given her soon vanished when she left Taylor Manor.

Just as when she had left the pernicious Van Rochelle, many years ago in that failed interview, Samantha just wanted to go home to familiar surroundings and to stay there. Not to come out for a long, long time. Samantha now realized that Sonny had it right on that first day together when they frolicked in his Paradise Woods. Everyone needs a

Paradise Woods to come back to.

Peggy quietly slipped in the back door to the kitchen while carrying the surprise anniversary cake that she had bought for her lover. She heard the sound of the television playing and figured Sonny to be in the living room watching it. He was probably asleep from doing all that plumbing work today, she thought. Peggy felt somewhat relieved, for it gave her time to set up for their special occasion.

The cake was a sheet cake. It had to be to have room for all the wording that she had put on it. It read, "Sonny, Thanks Cowboy for one month of heavenly bliss. Love you, Peg." Peggy smiled while reading the words again. She also put a bottle of champagne on ice. She wasn't really a wine drinker, but thought it appropriate for the occasion. There was one thing left to do, and that was to change into her new French nightgown. The voluptuous newborn blonde hurriedly slipped out of her clothes and into the desirous red silk. If only I had a mirror to see myself, she thought.

Peggy liked her new body, and she loved the satiny feel of her new gown, the way it accented her well-rounded curves. Peggy was in love, all around. Everything seemed perfect. It was time to surprise Sonny.

As she got close to the living room door a chill came over her. The smile of her eyes soon diminished. The time had come. She could feel it, even before walking into the room. She knew it would happen, sooner or later. She had dreaded it for so long, and now that time was upon them. With hope tugging at her heart she lifted her head high and proudly walked into the room, but Sonny paid no attention to her as he was entranced with what was on the television screen, a close-up of a beautiful woman in mourning. It didn't take Peggy long to realize that Sonny was staring at his wife. Even behind the long black veil, Peggy could tell that it was her, for the sadness within her eyes matched the sadness in Sonny's.

The newsperson was spouting something about the burial of an Irish Mafia Don from Indianapolis. They kept talking about a Big John Taylor, and they spoke of his daughter, Samantha Rafferty. It all sounded jumbled to Peggy, but it didn't matter. Her mind was spinning and her heart ached, for she knew the obvious.

"Is that your wife, Sonny?" she asked softly.

"Yes it is," he answered back.

"She's pretty, very pretty."

No reply.

"Samantha is such a pretty name for her."

No reply.

"So, that was her father that was killed?"

Again, Sonny said nothing.

"Come on, you can talk to me, darling."

"I'm afraid so, Peg. He was her protector. Now she's all alone . . . all alone." Sonny became teary-eyed but constantly stared at the screen.

"I understand, Sonny. She hurts, thus you hurt. I see the sadness in your eyes, my darling. If you must, go to her. Go to the one that you really love."

Sonny pulled his eyes from the television and turned to Peggy. "But Peg, I love—"

"Don't say it, Sonny, if you don't mean it. Look, you've treated me swell, and I appreciate that, Cowboy. I love you so very much Sonny, but you have no life on earth with me."

Sonny looked confused, as if he wanted to say something to her but didn't know how. So Peggy helped him along. "Take your old brown fedora with you. You're lucky I haven't thrown it out by now."

Sonny reached for her, but Peggy backed away.

"Go on. Get out of here, Cowboy. You don't owe me anything. Go home to your wife. She needs you." Peggy quickly turned away from her lover so he wouldn't see her cry.

With a wounded look on his face, Sonny turned and bolted out the front door, and out of Peggy's life, forever.

Chapter Twenty-Nine

End of the Rainbow

Some people say that it is wrong for a woman to love two men at once. Some say that it can't happen. It was one of those simple dilemmas in life that turned tragic for Samantha.

Others say that a woman like that is lucky, for real love is so hard to find, and even harder to keep, and she found it twice in one lifetime. In the back of her mind there was always that gnawing fear that her dilemma would never set her free.

A strong cold front was moving into the Hoosier metropolis, pushing out the last vestiges of Indian summer.

"Where to, ma'am?" asked the driver while reaching back and opening the door.

"Anywhere, nowhere . . . just drive," she said.

With a shrug of his shoulder the cabbie turned around, set the meter, and pulled away from Taylor Manor.

In spite of her mother's objections, Samantha chose a Metro Cab to take her home. She was exhausted. She was suffering from the obscenities of life that she had witnessed over the past several months. It had taken its toll on her mentally, and physically.

The cabbie kept glancing in his rearview mirror and became concerned for the green-eyed woman who stared forlornly out the window. "You know, the radio said that there's a storm fast approaching the city. I can get you where you want pretty fast, ma'am, if you just give me an address to take you to."

"Why? Are you scared of storms?"

"No, I just thought that you might be. I find that most women are, you know."

"I've been through enough storms in my life, mister. One more isn't going to make any difference now."

"Yes, ma'am" said the cabdriver.

"Do you have a smoke?"

"Sure." The cabbie pulled out a pack, shook one out and offered it to the lady with the shadow around her eyes. He then lit her cigarette and turned back around.

"M-m-m-m, it's been a long time. I've forgotten how good these things taste," she said while breathing out a plume of blue smoke.

"You sound like a lady that's seen some trouble."

"Oh, yeah, what makes you such an expert on things?"

"I've been driving a taxi for a long time, ma'am, and I've seen lots of things, and heard a lot of stories from the back seat of this cab. Most have to do with trouble. You've had your share. I can see that."

The redhead took another long drag off her cigarette. "Well, I've gotten rid of all my troubles, mister . . . all of them," she said distantly. "Drive out to Brendonwood. Drive me by the high school, and the big Catholic Church."

"Yes, ma' am."

Shortly thereafter the cab, with its mysterious rider, arrived in front of the schoolhouse steps. The driver stopped the car and stared straight ahead. He didn't have to see her hands and face pressed against the window to know that this place was special to her. He didn't have to see her eyes to know that she was crying, for he knew that doleful sound anywhere. This was the one part of his job that he didn't like. It made him sad. The cabbie pulled the pack of smokes from his shirt, shook one out and lit it up.

"This place is very special to you, isn't it?"

"Yes, this was the night of the dance," she said through sniffles.

"A high school prom?" asked the cabbie.

"Yeah, something like that, only better." As her memory of her father began to fade, Samantha ordered the cab driver to take her away.

A few minutes later they pulled up in front of the big church. "This is where I was married," she boasted with a smile. "Boy, Daddy wasn't happy that day. He didn't want me to marry Sonny."

"Are you and Sonny still together?"

"No. He's gone," she said, her smile turning down.

"He turned out bad, huh?"

"Hell, no, Sonny was a good man, too damn good for the likes of me."

"Don't be so hard on yourself, lady."

"Drive on, mister," she said curtly. The Cabbie drove on a ways, waiting for another command from the lady behind the blue smoke. "Stop, Stop here!" she said eagerly. Pull up to the curb. "This is the house where I grew up as a kid."

"Nice place."

"My little brother and I used to see who could climb up that big maple tree the fastest. He was a skinny little runt, but I beat him to the top every time."

"All the way to the top?" asked the cabbie.

"Hell, yeah, I was a good tree climber. We felt that we could see the world from up there. Boy, were we wrong. Then one day, my brother fell out of that tree and broke his arm."

"So what happened then?"

"Mother and Daddy sent me out east to a fancy, all girls' school to get some refinement. That ended my tree climbing and pretty much ended my childhood," she said reflectively.

"Where do you want me to take you to next, ma'am?"

"Take me home, please, 863 Laurel Drive."

The autumn sky turned dark and ominous as the approaching storm changed day into night. With the black clouds churning, hard pelts of rain lashed out at the disconsolate redhead while paying the cab driver for his time and effort.

Fighting the harsh wind, Samantha made her way to the front door of her house. "Home at last," she said under her breath. She unlocked the door and walked into the familiar surroundings. The lights were on but Impala was nowhere to be seen. Samantha called out to her several times, but Impala never showed. She thought it quite odd, for her canine friend was always there at the door to greet her, unless maybe Earle took her to the park to run, which Mary said he did from time to time. With the weather being as bad as it was outside, she discounted that thought. Impala was probably gathered with Rufus and Napolean in her doghouse out in the kennel, protecting them from the storm. She was motherly that way, and Rufus and Napolean were both cowards when it came to storms. Earle's truck wasn't parked in the driveway either, so he must have lit out with the storm coming and all. That was alright with Samantha. She just wanted to be alone with her canine friends and get some well sought-after rest.

The rain-soaked redhead pulled off her coat and kicked off her heels and headed toward the kitchen to find some brandy to warm up with. Along the way a frightened Captain Midnight skittered down the stairs from Samantha's bedroom to greet his trusted owner. Samantha reached down and picked up her furry friend and cuddled him in her arms like a baby.

"What's wrong, Midnight? Frightened by the storm? Don't be scared, Mommy's home to take care of you. What's this on your paw? Looks like blood. Has Rufus and Napolean been mean to you again? I'll have to have a talk with them, dear."

Samantha took the wide-eyed feline into the kitchen to have a better look at his paw. After further inspection, she deemed Midnight to be a fit cat and surmised that either Rufus or Napoleon got the worst of the battle.

She then set Captain Midnight down on the kitchen counter and took out a decanter of brandy and a glass from the liquor cabinet. She filled the glass, three fingers high, and sipped on the cherry wine while leaning back, taking in the feel of her kitchen once again. She drank the rest down and poured herself another, three fingers high. Sam took a sip and swished it around in her mouth to feed her taste buds before swallowing the distilled wine. She then downed the rest of the savory beverage, causing a slow burn in her throat and a warm glow to her body.

Samantha checked her answering machine for messages as Captain Midnight affectionately rubbed up against her. What she found was call after call from the print media and the T.V. news people for interviews, wanting her take on the demise of Big John and his Irish empire. "I don't need this shit, Midnight. Let's you and I go out and find Impala, how about it?" The cat meowed nervously as Samantha picked him up. Just then, the phone rang.

"Hello."

"Ms. Samantha."

"Oh, hi, Mary, you're looking for Earle, I suppose?"

"Yes Ma'am, that too, but Myra wanted me to call you to see if you made it home all right. She frets about you somethin' terrible, girl, being there alone and all."

"Well, you tell her not to worry herself over me. I'm a big girl and I can take care of myself. As far as Earle goes, I assume that he's on his way home because he wasn't here when I arrived."

"You just now gettin' home, girl?" asked Mary.

"Yeah, I kinda took the long way home."

"I guess you did. Well, I told that old man to wait until you got there before he left. When he shows up I'm gonna kick his black ass all the way back to Georgia."

Samantha suppressed a laugh from her comical housekeeper's rantings. "Oh, Mary, don't be so hard on Earle. He's real shy, you know, especially around me."

"Shy, hell, he's probably at a booze-joint right now, gettin' all liquored up."

"I'm sure he's not, Mary. He probably left on account of the storm coming. That old truck of his probably doesn't run all that well either. So, take it easy on Earle. Okay?"

"Okay then, but you gonna be alright in this storm? It's a bad 'un, especially for this time of year."

"I'll be okay, Mary. You just make sure you tell Myra not to worry about me so."

"I'll tell her, Ms. Samantha. I surely will. Maybe she'll quit whinin' then."

"Okay then."

"Goodbye, darlin'."

"Goodbye, Mary."

Samantha looked out the window at the storm raging outside and felt glad she was in the friendly confines of her house. Suddenly, the phone rang again.

"Hello."

"Is this Rafferty? I'm gonna' get you Rafferty, I'm gonna' take you down! Tonight you die!"

Samantha slammed the phone down and backed away nervously, as a lump rose up in her throat. It was that raspy voice again, but why now? Who could it be? Fear pranced through Samantha's head as she tried to calm herself down. "Come on, Sam, get your shit together, just another prank call like all the others." Then she thought, after all of the things that have happened, Gina's gruesome death, Daddy, Loni, and then Sonny's problems. Were they prank calls, or are they real? She shuddered at the thought.

Then suddenly, the lights went out, must be the wind. It's really howling outside. "This is bullshit!" she said aloud. "Who could be out there after me now? I have no more to give. They're all dead," she cried. "Come on, Sam, quit pitying yourself. You're stronger than that," she said while gathering her senses. "You're starting over, remember? You stand alone, must be strong. You can do it."

Samantha wiped her eyes with the palms of her hands, a little girl habit that she never rid herself of. She knew that tonight, even without the storm, would be a testament to her survival without Sonny. But tonight she missed him more than ever. She longed for his touch, and to hear his voice. If only she could see his face one more time. She used to love it when Sonny would come home late at night and slide into bed beside her and put his hands on her hips, pulling her to him to match her naked body with his in a spooning fashion. Oh, the ecstasy. And oh how she missed the little things that he did, the way he accidentally touched her. The way he looked at her when he thought she was unsuspecting. The way they played with the dogs in the park, and earlier, the way they played with the children in the park. But that's all gone now. Samantha wondered if maybe she didn't over-react to her father's claim of Sonny's infidelities. After all, in his dying breath he as much admitted that Sonny was the one for her, that she and Sonny should be at the last dance together.

With her fear now under control the emotionally drained redhead found a candle to light the way up to her bedroom to change out of her wet clothes. Her reunion with the Hole-in-the-wall gang would have to wait.

Samantha let out a sigh of relief when she entered her bedroom. A month is a long time to be away from something so familiar, so personal.

It was her haven away from the rest of the world. Sonny saw to it. He completely renovated the upstairs bedroom to Samantha's taste. The golden oak furniture, the mansion bed where they shared many a splendid night, the oak flooring, and the antique porcelain tub from New Orleans, were all gifts to her from Sonny. He saw to it that she would always have her own little Paradise Woods, a place to come home to, a place that was distinctly her own. He even expanded her closet so she could fill it with all her designer wardrobe. Samantha loved nice clothes and Sonny enjoyed seeing her in them. And to top it off was Frenchie's nude painting of her that hung above the bed. That painting was priceless to Sonny.

While stripping off her black mourning apparel, Samantha became distracted by the long, dark shadows that were cast upon the walls by the candle's light. It made her feel uneasy. There was certain sadness in the room. It felt as though the walls were crying. It was as if they were trying to tell her something. Entranced by the deep shadows along the wall Samantha carefully reached behind her back and unhooked her bra, allowing her meek little mounds to fall out to their freedom. The once pert little breasts had now become soft crescents hanging from her chest, expressing the physical toll from the upheaval in her life. She unsnapped her garters and slid the silky black stockings down her long legs with chill bumps following close behind. This time, when she slipped off her thin, French briefs she didn't feel the freedom of fresh air rushing up through her loins as before, but instead she felt shameful of her nakedness, wanting to hide herself from the prying eyes hidden within the shadows on the walls. She quickly slipped into her favorite azure pantaloons and matching top, which was her favorite lounge clothes along with her blue Japanese komono which she had hanging in her closet.

Samantha's closet; that was what the big wooden sign said hanging on the door. The sign put a smile on Samantha's otherwise solemn face. Sonny had made it for her. He said that any woman that had a closet that big deserved her nametag on the door.

The closet door was ajar as Captain Midnight attested to by walking in and out of it, constantly meowing. Samantha hadn't noticed Midnight's incessant crying due to her mind pain. She also didn't notice Midnight's little red paw prints all over the oak flooring. "Hush up, Midnight. Let me get my komono, then I'll take you downstairs and feed ya if that's what you're bitching about," said Samantha.

Samantha opened the strangely heavy door. Suddenly she fell back, stifling a scream. Utter terror shot through her veins at the gruesome sight of her trusted companion hanging from the door, bloodied and beaten . . . and dead! Impala's once pretty red fur was matted with the darker red of her own blood. Her beautiful dark eyes were open and seemed fixed upon her master while her long pinkish tongue hung dry and lifeless from the side of her mouth.

It was more than Samantha could take. She fell to the floor from the shock of it all and back peddled desperately to get away from Impala's death stare. She cringed in the dark corner of the room and shuddered convulsively as warm bodily fluids seeped into her azure blue pantaloons. She wanted to cry out, but couldn't. She tried to speak but only uttered little stuttered whimpers. She struggled to breath, but air seemed hard to come by. Samantha breathed in short spurts and then listened. She breathed and listened. She could almost hear their whispers. It was as if the walls were casting aspersions on her. The shadows seemed to be closing in around her. Samantha stayed huddled in the corner as seconds seemed liked minutes, and minutes seemed like hours.

Finally, she calmed down enough to regain some of her senses. What kind of fiend would do this? She questioned herself. It can't be Sonny, but who's left? Nobody! It just can't be Sonny. It can't be. He wouldn't come back and do this. I know I did him wrong but Sonny's not evil. Chance! I must call Chance! He will help me!

Samantha crawled slowly toward the mansion bed and reached up to the nightstand and picked up the telephone. She put it to her ear but didn't get a dial tone. In disbelief, she dialed Chance's number anyway. No answer. It's dead! She pulled desperately on the cord and found that it had been cut. Samantha's eyes widened as terror put its grip around her neck once again, for she knew that someone else was in the house, someone that wanted to see her dead!

She slowly edged back up to the closet, hoping that what she saw in front of her was an apparition of some kind, hoping that this would just all go away. But she knew better.

Samantha just couldn't stand it anymore seeing her faithful companion hanging on the door like that, like a piece of raw meat. She grabbed Impala around her middle and lifted the Irish-Setter off the hook, and then laid her gently on the floor. She tearfully kissed her warm nose and talked to her softly while rubbing her ears. But her eyes didn't sparkle and her ears didn't perk up as in the past. And she didn't bark happily at her lady friend's jokes, for there were no more jokes. There was no friendly bantering between the two ladies of the house. There was no more joy to be shared between them, just death.

Samantha's fright soon mixed with anger, a raw combination that tends to carry the mind past no return. With rage in her eyes, Samantha took the lighted candle into the room where the bludgeoning took place. What she witnessed next made her stomach churn. She saw her blood-splattered clothes hanging on the racks, and felt the sticky red wetness under the bottoms of her bare feet, and noticed in a puddle of Impala's blood the weapon that was used. Danielle's softball bat!

Samantha vomited profusely until she had nothing left to give. She then picked up the bat, doused the candle, and slowly opened her bedroom door to escape from the dark shadows, to escape from the craziness, and hoping to escape from her own house!

Step by step, Samantha walked lightly down the stairwell, wishing herself invisible. All seemed quiet except for the pounding of her heart. It was deafening. With the exception of some sheet lightening appearing through the drapes, the downstairs was icy dark. While sneaking through the living room in a low crouch, with only Danielle's metal bat for protection, Samantha's destination came into view; the front door. Her plan was to make it out the door and to the neighbor's to call for help.

When she reached for the handle, the doorbell rang. Samantha quickly jerked back as the sound of the doorbell pierced her body like a thrown lance. Her heart rose to her throat and her knees weakened, but she recovered and cautiously opened the door. She strained a peek through the windowed storm door but saw nothing but the rainy darkness. Then flashes of the storm showed a dark image standing on her sidewalk with his arms folded looking straight at her! Samantha slammed the door shut and quickly locked it.

Gotta get to the pantry door, she thought. She hastily stumbled through the darkness, several times tripping over things before reaching the pantry door. She secured the door and limped back into the kitchen and sat down to rub the pain from her banged up legs. But her respite was short-lived as she heard a loud, crashing sound from within the garage. Where's my bat, she thought. Where's the goddamn bat! No good anyway. I can't fight that monster off with just a bat. He's too big!

Approaching near hysterics Samantha remembered *the gun!* What did Danny do with Sonny's gun? She must've placed it in a kitchen cabinet, but which one? I haven't time to search through all of them, not in the dark! Wait a minute. Let's see, what were we doing? . . . Drinking tea, that's it, we were drinking tea!" Samantha rummaged through the cabinet containing the tea until she came across the feel of cold hard metal. She pulled out the revolver and massaged it to make sure it was real. It was Sonny's 38 special all right, and it felt like gold in Samantha's hand. Now she had a chance, to live.

Samantha suddenly heard a dog's injured cry. "Sounds like Rufus," she whispered to herself. She then heard Rufus's cry for help end in one final yelp. "Leave my dogs alone you son-of-a-bitch, they've done nothing to you!" she screamed.

The sound of heavy footsteps approached the pantry door. Samantha broke out in a cold sweat. She leaned against the corner of the refrigerator to steady her quivering body. She raised the weapon with both hands and trained the barrel towards the center of the pantry door, just like Sonny had shown her many a time. Hyperventilation took over her lungs, keeping pace with a pounding heart that seemed ready to burst through her chest. Again, that cold, malevolent voice resonated in her head, **"Is this Rafferty? I'm gonna get you, Rafferty, I'm gonna take you down! Tonight you die!"**

The footsteps were now at the door, and Samantha expected him to try and break through at any moment, but instead she watched in awe as the doorknob slowly turned.

Her trembling hand released the safety and she pulled back the hammer, but she felt so … dizzy … so faint … so … weak.

With the thunder fading and the rain subsiding, the wipers on the big Crown Vic came to a rest as forgiving blue eyes stared warmly through the windshield at the rain-slickened pavement. It felt refreshing driving down the familiar streets of Brendonwood again. Even through the darkness and drizzle Sonny could see that the colors of the landscape were now cast in an autumn hue. A most beautiful time of year, he thought. A most beautiful time to reunite with his lovely wife to rekindle the fire they once had. Sonny had good reason for his optimism, for he had just gotten off the phone with Danielle. She was ecstatic to hear from him. He tried to explain his absence from Big John's funeral and his absence from his cell phone the last few days, but Danielle would have none of it. Her daddy was coming home! That was all she cared about. She instructed him on Samantha's whereabouts, and how much

Mom needed him. Before Danielle would let her father hang up she had him promise a family get-together the next day. Danielle also mentioned to him that she had a little surprise of her own to tell him about.

The creaky pantry door opened ever-so-slowly. An eerie dark image appeared from behind the door and leered at the lady in waiting. The shadowy figure held its arms open as it stepped heavily toward Samantha. In her weakened state, the pallid skinned redhead vacillated from left to right and right to left with the 38 special, trying to squeeze the trigger which seemed to have become a monumental task. She finally fired the weapon and missed high right. The odious looking creature lurched forward and swatted the revolver out of her hand. He then backhanded the panic-stricken girl, which sent her flying into the kitchen table, and then again, sending her crashing onto the terrazzo floor.

Dazed, Samantha tried crawling towards the den, but two large hands grasped her ankles. She kicked furiously, scraping her knees against the hardened marble and concrete flooring.

Through her wild kicking, Samantha managed to free herself, leaving her soiled silk pantaloons behind in the hands of the dreaded intruder. As she got up to run she was pounced upon again. This time the malicious viper pummeled her ribcage, and then flipped her onto her back. He clasped his hands around her slender neck and squeezed tightly.

That was when she saw his face, inside the black hood, just a few inches from hers. Even from the dark dank floor of the kitchen she could see those red eyes. It was a hideous face, evil, satanic!

Samantha's life was ebbing away with every second. She wanted desperately to live but she was outmatched by the evil one. She finally gave up trying to hold off her attacker as her arms helplessly fell away. She frantically searched the floor with her hands, for something, anything, to pry loose the death grip of the dark intruder. While sensing Samantha at death's door, the stranger smiled . . . ***that Lucifer smile!***

Samantha felt something familiar along the floor, something that might help, an old friend of sorts. She brought up the crystal decanter, smashing it into the temple of the intruder's head, knocking him away.

Samantha still lay on the cold floor, gasping for life as her throat strained to open again and fill her lungs with new air. Once renewed, she made it to her feet and used the walls and cabinets for support while making her way out the pantry door. She winced in pain with every breath she took as her cracked ribs tore at her flesh. She knew that her only real hope to survive was to crawl through the hole-in-the-wall and join what was left of her canine friends.

She figured that she was small enough to fit through the opening, though her busted ribs could hinder her some. She had to get away from this monster anyway she could. Samantha cried out to near collapse as she raised her arms above her head and wriggled her slender body through the tiny opening.

She stopped halfway through as the pain became too intense. She needed to rest a moment. She was met with lots of wet kisses from a frightened Napolean, glad to see his master once again. Rufus lay on the other side of the wall, dead from his neck being twisted into. Revived from Napolean's attentiveness, Samantha made a renewed effort to pull her hips through the narrow opening, when all of a sudden something grabbed at her legs trying to yank her back through the hole.

She tried to hold on but the pain was just too much for the dispirited redhead. She began losing her grip as her strength and her hope began to wane. Things were looking hopeless, but then a familiar sound pulled into the driveway. Samantha listened intently. Her eyes turned up in a smile. She became ecstatic. Sonny's home! she thought. I would know the sound of that big old Crown Vic anywhere. She wanted to scream it out, but her damaged body wouldn't allow her, so she cried tears of joy instead.

The lights were out in the house but Sonny figured Samantha to be in bed. It must have been a long, grueling day for her he thought, dealing with her father's funeral and all.

Sonny felt that the transition of going from Peggy Sue back to Samantha to be an easy one, for Samantha was his longtime soul mate, and Peggy, well; she had to be an angel of some sort, at least in his mind. Sonny realized that he and Samantha had some hurts to heal, but he was confident that they could do it. His plan was to slowly win back her heart. He would be gentle, not rush things, for he knew how much her father meant to her. Right now he just wanted to be by her side, to hold her hand, and to bury his face in her luscious red curls.

Sonny flipped on the light switch when he came through the front door, but the house stayed dark. Could be from the storm, he thought, but the streets lights were on. I'll go down in the basement and check. It might just be the breakers.

As he made his way through the house, Sonny yelled out to Samantha so as not to frighten her. He received no answer in return, but that was okay with him because it meant that she was probably asleep. He felt his way down the basement stairs and then groped his way to the electric box. He took out a book of matches from his pocket and lit one to see. As he opened the breaker box, an icy chill ran down his back. There are no breakers! They've all been pulled out! "Samantha!" he cried. Sonny turned to run up the stairs, but in haste bumped into a strange hanging object. He quickly struck another match and held it up in front of him. A dead, glassy-eyed Earle Rose was staring straight at him! Sonny jumped back with fear cascading down his Spartan-like face. The demons were back! He could feel them all around! But he couldn't think the worse. Not right now. He just couldn't lose her now. Not after all they had been through. Sonny whispered a plea, "Please God, don't let her be dead, don't take her from me. Please. I've tried my best. What more do you want from me? I did things the only way I knew how."

Angry with rage and angry with God, Sonny rushed back up the basement stairs. He sought this evil entity that lurked in his house. He knew that he would face him soon. He just didn't know who he was.

Sonny had to be extra cautious in the darkness. His eyes were becoming adjusted to the night but the eyes of the enemy could see even better because they had been in the house much longer. He wished he had brought his flashlight with him, but in his haste to see his wife, Sonny left all of his belongings back in Centralia with Peggy Sue.

Sonny found his way up the winding stairwell to their bedroom. He was hesitant of opening the door for fear of what he might find. He cautiously entered the room. His heart palpitated, as he could see her, resting under the covers in the big mansion bed. Even in the darkness he could see those red locks of hair. But the room wasn't right. There was no redolence of spice in the air, no female fragrances that he was accustomed to. While carefully walking toward the big mansion bed, he felt a stickiness to the soles of his shoes. He remembered that stickiness from before. Where was that at? he pondered . . . It was at Candy Garza's beheading!

Sonny quickly yanked back the covers, exposing the bloody remains of the redhead! But it was the red head of Impala that he saw instead of Samantha's. Sonny's heart jumped to his throat and he quickly turned from the hideous sight, into the path of an aluminum club smashing into his face with a resounding thud. With his busted nose spewing blood, Sonny fell back onto the bed with Samantha's favorite pet.

Stunned, but still cognizant, he brought his arms up to deflect several more blows to his head and face. He then rolled off the bed and onto the floor where he was repeatedly struck in the back by the bat-wielding maniac. Sonny played possum, hoping to lure his attacker into some false sense of victory, or at least get a short respite while he sized up his enemy, for he had not yet the chance to even see his assailant's face. His idea worked somewhat as his attacker let up with the bat but kicked him several times in his ribs with the pointed–toed cowboy boots that he was wearing. Sonny didn't flinch, just held his breath. When the boot made its way toward his face, Sonny grabbed it with both hands and twisted, getting a yelp from his opponent before pulling his feet out from under him.

Sonny climbed on top of his silent foe, giving him three jack-hammered shots to the face before being tossed with a knee to the groin. The dark intruder made for the bedroom door with Sonny on his heels. He caught the intruder at the top of the stairs and began a fierce slug-fest with him. Sonny was the better of the two in the fisticuffs, but the evil one was wearing some kind of a leather mask that helped buffer some of Sonny's hard blows. Just when it looked as if Sonny was getting the best of the match, the dark intruder lunged forward, shoving Sonny down the winding stairwell with him. They landed hard at the bottom of the stairs with Sonny being pinned beneath. But he again slugged his way out with his opponent breaking away and retreating towards the kitchen. Sonny tried to follow but the hard landing put a bad twist on his ankle. The man in black was tough, maybe too tough, thought Sonny. He was every bit as big and strong as Sonny was, and looked to be younger and very resilient. Sonny needed a greater weapon if he was going to defeat the hooded stranger and save Samantha. That is, if she was at all alive.

Barely able to stand, Sonny painfully hobbled his way to the den to retrieve his ultimate weapon, his Smith and Wesson 38 special. He rummaged through the drawer of Samantha's secretary until he found the key to his desk. He then unlocked his desk and felt around desperately for the revolver. He could hear the man in black coming back for him. "Where's my gun, goddamn it! Where's my fuckin' gun!" he cried while searching frantically.

"Is this what you're looking for?" came the strange voice from the dark shadow lurking in the doorway.

Sonny raised his head and found himself looking down the barrel of his own revolver. "What did you do with my wife, you despicable, sick bastard!"

Sonny was stunned by the two bullets that pierced his body. He felt as though he had been stabbed with two hot pokers. His knees buckled and his head felt light. The last thing he remembered was looking past the barrel of the 38 special into the smiling face of the intruder in black.

The third shot at Sonny went astray as a lunging Samantha Rafferty knocked the weapon from the attacker's hand. In her weakened and painful state Samantha was no match to vie for the pistol lying on the floor. She just wanted to be with Sonny so they could die together. She crawled to where he lay, kissed him gently on his cheek, and tearfully whispered, "Wake up darlin', it's me, Sam, your wife. You know; Highpockets. Please wake up, dear."

But Sonny didn't respond. He just faded to black.

Chapter Thirty

Mansion on a Hill

Dreams are figments of the mind, phantasms so to speak, something merely imagined. How your mind becomes detached so from life, nobody really knows, as people dream of places they've never been and of people they've never seen, people with no faces. Trauma causes a mind to see a lot of things not normally seen by the human eye. Severe trauma can lead to nightmares beyond belief. But the phantasmagoria that one experiences while in the midst of dying is of real images of one's own life. And they move through one's mind at an unprecedented pace.

Samantha sensed the dark intruder standing over her with the gun pointed directly at the back of her head. She turned and looked up into his evil eyes and then screamed, "What do you want with us? What did we ever do to you?"

"I told you to keep your man out of my backyard," came back the stern reply.

"What?" asked the bewildered redhead.

Samantha received no reply, just a hated glare. She turned back to Sonny and softly kissed his blood-warmed lips and readied herself for the death blow. She heard the metallic click of the hammer being brought back and then the loud burst! . . . But she felt nothing.

Samantha looked up at a harsh light that shone brightly upon the back of the stunned intruder. The evil menace turned around in disbelief while pulling off the leather mask, letting her blonde curls spring forth while looking hurtfully past the light at the uniformed officer that shot her.

She stumbled forward, holding out her arms, asking why, when Angelina Garza coldly fired another round into the broken heart of her lady-love, Eva Swenson, thus ending her life, while saving Samantha's.

"My husband is dead. Sonny is dead. Eva killed him!" sobbed Samantha as she hovered over Sonny.

Angie rushed to where Sonny lay and shoved the frail redhead aside. "I should have let her killed you," she snapped with an icy stare. "Here, hold my flashlight."

While responding to her demand, Samantha couldn't help but stare at Angie's mutilated face. With her eyelid sewn shut and multiple scars on the side of her sunken left jaw, the once beautiful Hispanic woman was now hideously disfigured.

Angie listened to Sonny's chest and found his entrance wounds, then looked up into Samantha's eyes, but this time with little anger. "He's still alive! Put your hand here on the wound in his chest and apply pressure to slow the bleeding. I'm going to call an ambulance."

With tears streaming down her face, Samantha did as she was told. Before leaving, Angie leaned down and looked straight into Samantha's crying eyes. "I loved him too," she said. Samantha nodded her head, for she now felt a common bond between her and Angie, as they now shared the same hurt, the same feelings, for the same man, Sonny Rafferty.

"Don't sit on Sonny. Don't sit on the baby," was the next sound the confused Sonny Rafferty heard.

"Who belongs to that voice? I've heard it before. Where am I? All I can see is a grooved wood ceiling staring down at me from above. I can hear the crackling sound of a fire in a hearth, and the familiar smell of burning oak. It feels so cozy, yet I feel so sad."

Suddenly, another voice entered the room. *"Mother,"* came the sorrowful sound of a most familiar voice.

"I already know, dear daughter, I'm dying. You needn't to bring Doc Gaines here to tell me that."

"But, Mother, you can't leave me. I can't bear to let you go."

"Nonsense, Fannie, it's my time and I'm ready. Sonny has taken my place on this earth. You look after him, dear. He is very special. He will do you proud, you'll see," said the tired sweet voice . . . "You'll see."

The Metro police dispatcher sat up and took notice as the frantic call from Officer Angie Garza screamed for her attention.

"Officer down! Officer down! Need an ambulance at 863 Laurel Drive, Brendonwood. Metro one, get me some goddamn help!"

Sonny suddenly found himself standing in a drab, opaque house of bones. He couldn't see his body but he knew that he was there. It was dark and dank in the building of bones.

Sonny felt the soft touch of Samantha's warm lips on his but didn't see her anymore. In the back of his mind he heard her crying. He heard her arguing for their lives but he didn't quite understand, for he couldn't see her anymore.

But he did feel something flittering about the room. The best he could make out was that it was an evanescent female entity of some type. She was sylph-like in structure with beautiful, bare, pinkish skin and golden hair as her only defining features, and she revealed them somewhat sparingly as she faded in and out while darting about all around him. "Maggie!"

"Uh huh, it's me, little brother," she answered sprightly.

"But you don't look like—"

"Of course not, I have no freckles, no red hair. I left my coverings back on Dunes Highway, remember?"

"You can't be Maggie Mae. You must be an angel. That's right, you're my guardian angel!"

"Sonny, you have had many guardian angels in your life. I was but one of many. Most are with us now but some are with you still . . . Hush! Mama's here!"

Sonny listened intently and heard a continuous metallic sound of scissors slicing through newsprint. Soon, from nowhere it seemed, newspaper articles started falling all around him, hundreds of them. Sonny was startled as he read the headlines of some of the articles: PEACE NOT WAR, 15 DEAD 23 WOUNDED IN AMBUSH, VIETNAM WAR CASULITIES RISING AT ALARMING RATE, B52's BOMB HO CHI MINH TRAIL, MORE

443

G.I.'S DEAD, AMERICAN EMBASSY IN SAIGON FALLS, 600,000 TROOPS IN COUNTRY, B52's BOMB HANOI, CAMBODIA, MORE G.I.'S DIE, 58,000 AMERICAN BOYS KIA, KIA, KIA! And finally, LOCAL WAR HERO, SERGEANT SONNY RAFFERTY RETURNS HOME FROM VIETNAM FOR MOTHER'S FUNERAL.

"Stop It, Mama! Stop it! Sonny's come home! Yes, Mama, it's true. I've talked with him. The war is over. You'll see him soon."

"It's true, Mother. It's true. I'm sorry for leaving you, Mother. I'm sorry for fighting in that crazy Asian war. They said it was the domino effect, Mother. We had to fight because of the domino effect."

Suddenly, Sonny saw a maze of dominoes falling everywhere, one against another, over 58,000 of them, and he seemed to have counted them all. But horror filled his eyes as the black tiles turned into young, disillusioned soldiers, lying on the battlefields and in the jungles!

"Don't let us down, Sonny. I promised Mother you would come. Don't let us down."

In an instant, the sylph-like creature of Maggie's soul disappeared.

"But Maggie Mae, take me with you, for I have no wings. I have no wings!"

He saw her not again but heard her voice, "Wait for the angel of death, for he is near. Don't be afraid, brother, but ride the death angel's wings and he will free you from your purgatory. Wait patiently, my brother, and don't be deceived," she said, her voice fading into oblivion.

"How's Sonny holding up?" asked Angie upon her hurried return.

"Angie, he, he's not breathing. Sonny's not breathing anymore," sobbed the despondent redhead.

"What! That can't be. We can't lose Sonny!"

"I did as you told me. I pressed on the wound."

Angie rushed to Sonny's side and felt his neck for a pulse, at the same time putting her head to his chest. "We're losing him!" She quickly ripped open his bloodied shirt and then reached into his mouth to clear his air passage. She formed his lips to fit hers and blew her air into his lungs. She released his lips and then placed the palms of her hands on Sonny's chest and pumped, hoping to revive his lungs and his heart. She then breathed into him again and then pumped again, a process that she would continue until all hope was gone. "Come on, Sonny, don't die on me! Breath goddamn it!"

"Angie, what can I do to help," cried Samantha in desperation.

"Just pray, darling. Hold his hand and pray."

He was a soldier of fortune in life's crazy game
He believed in real justice, he called on God's name
The sirens wailed through the streets for their champion to hear
They sang their sad songs as his death drew near
But two women who loved him, two women that cried
They struggled to save him, to bring back his life
It's trials like this that bends one's mind
And tonight, all three were of the desperate kind
Tonight, all three were of the desperate kind

He first showed himself as a white dove, and then flew away at Sonny's touch. Sonny next saw him as little more than a baby boy with cherub-like features and golden hair.

As the little angel grew closer, Sonny noticed him crying. His hands were cupped together as if hiding something. "Are you here to fly me to heaven?" he asked.

The little angel looked up to Sonny with sorrow in his eyes.

"What is it? What's wrong?" he asked softly to the little cherub.

He opened his hands and his revelation fell out in accordion-like fashion.

*Sonny was stunned, as the angel cried, "**I have only paper wings!**"*

About the Author

William Vickers was born in Sparta Tennessee to a struggling tobacco farmer. When he was a child his family moved to northwest Indiana for a better life. He served in the military in Vietnam as radio operator. A lot of his ideas for "Paper Wings" came from his own life experiences which include an affiliation with the Indiana Prison System, and the state's extended care facilities. He has recently returned from Key West where he spent a year writing a sequel to "Paper Wings."

Printed in the United States
51539LVS00006B/67-111